JUSTICE DELAYED

Center Point
Large Print

Also by Patricia Bradley and available from
Center Point Large Print:

Logan Point series:
 Gone without a Trace
 Silence in the Dark

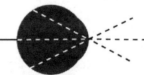

JUSTICE DELAYED

Patricia Bradley

CENTER POINT LARGE PRINT
THORNDIKE, MAINE

This Center Point Large Print edition is published in the year 2017 by arrangement with Revell, a division of Baker Publishing Group.

The text of this Large Print edition is unabridged. In other aspects, this book may vary from the original edition. Printed in the United States of America on permanent paper. Set in 16-point Times New Roman type.

ISBN: 978-1-68324-273-4

Library of Congress Cataloging-in-Publication Data

Names: Bradley, Patricia (Educator), author.
Title: Justice delayed / Patricia Bradley.
Description: Center Point Large Print edition. | Thorndike, Maine : Center Point Large Print, 2017.
Identifiers: LCCN 2016048286 | ISBN 9781683242734
    (hardcover : alk. paper)
Subjects: LCSH: Murder—Investigation—Fiction. | Large type books. | GSAFD: Mystery fiction.
Classification: LCC PS3602.R34275 J87 2017 | DDC 813/.6—dc23
LC record available at https://lccn.loc.gov/2016048286

In memory of Mary Sue Seymour,
who exemplified the fruit of the Spirit.
"But the fruit of the Spirit is love, joy, peace,
forbearance, kindness, goodness, faithfulness,
gentleness and self-control. Against such
things there is no law." (Galatians 5:22–23)

Prologue

New Year's Eve

Paris, France. She should be ecstatic to be here on the cusp of a new year. Stephanie Hollister pushed aside the hotel's heavy brocade curtains and looked out over the city. The setting sun provided a beautiful backdrop for the Eiffel Tower. She didn't have to ask how her ex-boyfriend afforded such a room.

Stephanie turned from the window, and her mouth dried as she stared at the diamonds on the crimson duvet. Briefly, she closed her eyes, but the image of the stones remained, and she opened her eyes again.

"Beautiful, aren't they? Not a one under three carats." JD's voice was as slick as snake oil.

Stephanie clenched her jaw. She had promised herself after the last shipment that there wouldn't be another. She drew her gaze away from the bed.

"I told you last time was it." She hated the fluttering in her voice. She hated, too, the way her heart pounded just from being this close to him. *Get a grip. He used you.*

"It'll be ten thousand cash, like before."

Ten thousand dollars could not buy peace of mind or wash away the shame of breaking the law. "I only came here to tell you to leave me alone. If you don't, I'll . . . turn you in to the authorities."

"That would not be a wise thing to do." He ran his thumb down her cheek.

The suggestion in his eyes sent shivers through her body. *He only wants what you'll do for him.* She scooped the diamonds into the velvet pouch beside them and slapped the bag into his hands. "Get Jillian to do it—what's a few more diamonds for her to smuggle? And don't ever ask me to smuggle diamonds for you again. I'm not doing it."

He grabbed her wrist. "Don't get any bright ideas about going to the authorities. I'd hate for anything to happen to that pretty little sister of yours."

"You touch my sister and I'll kill you."

He laughed softly, the menace in his face vanishing as he released her arm. "You know I wouldn't hurt her. So, when's your flight leave?"

His personality changed like a chameleon. She wanted to step away and escape the seductive scent of his aftershave, but his gaze kept her feet from moving. "Two hours. You're not on it?"

"No. I'm not going back until the weekend. So I have a couple of days to see the sights of Gay Paree." He fingered the top button of her blouse, sliding it open. "Too bad you can't hang around."

"Yeah, too bad." Stephanie jerked away from him and turned again toward the view of the Eiffel

Tower. Not in a million years. She fastened her button, then gathered her purse and jacket. She would not come under his spell again.

"See you in the States." His voice held a promise.

Not if she saw him first. She shut the door firmly behind her.

On board the 747, Stephanie's fingers shook as she adjusted a passenger's carry-on and closed the overhead bin. As hard as saying no had been, she'd done it. Then why didn't she feel . . . free?

Because he'd crooked his little finger, and she'd gone running to him. Had she really believed JD wanted to see *her?* It was never about her, always about him. *He* didn't take the risk. No, he had his network of flight attendants to do the dirty work for him.

Stephanie shivered. That first, and only, time she'd been standing in line to go through customs, she realized if they caught her smuggling the diamonds into the States, she would face jail time. The thought scared her so much that she almost fainted. She'd seen JD for who he really was that day, and she didn't like what she'd become because of him.

But that hadn't been the only reason she refused to smuggle again. She hadn't known a lot about conflict diamonds because she chose not to, but one day while she was flipping through the TV channels, she stopped on a story about the diamond mines in Sierra Leone.

When she saw the emaciated children mining for the rough stones, the horror of what she'd done hit her. It was because of people like her who looked the other way that children were forced into slave labor, working twelve hours a day or more to pan for the stones. And it didn't end there. The documentary went on to show thirteen-year-old boys bent over a table for hours, squinting through an eyeglass as they cut and polished the gems. She couldn't be a part of that again.

"You want to give me a hand here?" Her co-attendant stood on tiptoes, pushing against a bulging duffel bag.

"Sure, Lacey." She frowned at the weight of the bag, wondering how the passenger got the bag up there in the first place.

"Thanks." Lacey Wilson dusted her hands. "Did you see JD?"

Stephanie jerked her head around. She'd told no one she was meeting him and shot her friend a warning frown, then ignored Lacey until they'd secured the cabin.

Once they were in the air and in the relative privacy of the galley, Lacey asked the question again.

"What are you talking about?" Stephanie said.

Lacey shrugged. "I saw the note with the Hôtel Plaza Athénée on it. I figured you were meeting him, since we don't know anyone else who could afford to stay there. You're smuggling again, aren't you? Does Jillian know you went to see JD?"

"No." The disapproval in Lacey's voice about her seeing JD again sent a dart straight to Stephanie's heart. How had she let herself get taken in by JD's charm, knowing that her best friend Jillian was in love with him? Shame filled her again.

A call light flashed, and Stephanie said, "I'll take care of that."

"I don't believe you." Lacey grabbed her arm. "He's not worth it, Steph. Don't do it. He'll discard you like yesterday's news when he gets tired of you. Look how he treated Jillian."

"I don't know what you're talking about." Stephanie shook her hand off.

She turned, and several passengers in first class averted their gaze. Heat crawled up her neck. Hopefully, they'd only heard the tail end of the conversation. She lifted her chin and flipped a switch in her brain. Everything except her duties faded for the next ten hours as they winged toward Memphis International Airport.

Once they were off the plane, Stephanie hurried to the parking garage.

"Can I catch a ride?" Lacey asked.

She was tempted to say no, but that was silly. If Lacey wanted to get on her case, she could do it at her parents' old house they shared with three other women. A house her parents would be returning to as soon as they found a buyer for her mom's dream home. "Sure."

Lacey got in the car, and Stephanie drove her small Miata toward I-240. In the passenger seat, Lacey sighed.

"When do we have to be out of the house?" she asked. "I know Jillian has found an apartment near Memphis State so she can finish her degree in her off hours, but I just wondered how much time we had."

"By the end of the month." Maybe she should have taken the diamonds. Ten thousand dollars would go a long way to help her parents until her dad could get another job, and then maybe they wouldn't have to move.

No. It was wrong, and besides, her dad wouldn't take money from her without knowing where it came from. To escape her thoughts, Stephanie turned on the radio and cranked up the volume. Strains of "Where Have All the Cowboys Gone?" filled the car.

Lacey switched the music off and faced her. "When do you deliver the diamonds?"

Stephanie had hoped that Lacey would decide to drop that subject. "It's not really any of your business, but I'm not."

"I don't believe you."

"Well, I can't help that." Stephanie was too tired to argue with her.

"Look, I know you want to help your parents,

but you were out of this business. God knows I wish I were. JD would give you money if he cared about you."

"I don't want *anything* from him." It would do no good to argue with Lacey about whether she was smuggling diamonds or not. When her friend got something into her head, there was no changing it. "And please, never mention anything about JD and me around Jillian. It would crush her to know what happened."

"Don't worry. I don't want her hurt, either," Lacey said. "But you should have thought about that before you got involved with him."

"They weren't seeing each other when I dated him, and I thought their relationship was over." It had almost killed her when JD and Jillian got back together, but her pain wasn't Jillian's fault. Stephanie slowed to exit the interstate. No, she owned that mistake. And Lacey was right. She and Jillian not only worked together but also lived in the same house. Stephanie should have known it would get sticky.

Her friend shook her head. "I've never seen what you two see in him. Jillian says it's because he's exciting and she's never bored, but how about you?"

"No one else ever made me feel the way he did," she said. That was hardly an explanation, but she didn't know how else to explain her attraction to JD. It wasn't so much his good looks, which he had plenty of, but the way he carried himself, the confidence he exuded. He was the kind of man mothers warned their daughters to stay clear of. Her friends didn't understand why she seemed to be drawn to men with bad-boy attitudes.

She understood. These men, who could have anyone they wanted, chose her. And she believed she would be the one who would reform them.

Except it hadn't worked. Especially not with JD. Stephanie doubted anyone could tame him. He'd caught her in a vulnerable moment and then used that mistake to continue a relationship in secret once he and Jillian reconnected.

She turned into the drive and pulled to the back of the house to her pottery studio. "Be careful you don't make the same mistake with Adam Matthews."

"Adam is not like JD."

Stephanie snorted. "He's a man, isn't he?" She opened her car door.

Lacey put her hand on Stephanie's arm. "Wait. I'm your friend, and I hate to see you get back in this mess. You stopped once, don't get involved again. If I had your courage, I would stop too. So would Jillian."

She sighed. "I don't know how to be any clearer. I. Am. Not. Smuggling. Diamonds."

Lacey's eyes narrowed. "If that's true, then you better watch your back. JD can be very vindictive." She bit her bottom lip. "And I don't think you should talk to the cops. They might not believe you once they know you smuggled a package of diamonds through customs."

"It's the only reason I've kept quiet. My dad would be so disappointed in me if he ever found out. But I'm not doing it again."

"Good." Lacey opened the passenger door. "I'm going upstairs to take a nap."

"And I have work to do in the pottery shop," Stephanie said as she climbed out of the small car. Although as tired as she was, resting a bit tempted her, but she'd been commissioned to make a horse sculpture, and it waited.

At the shop door, Stephanie rummaged for the brass skeleton key in her purse, and it slipped from her hands. She tried to catch it but only succeeded in turning the purse upside down. With a huff, she knelt to gather the scattered items. Her fingers hovered over a soft velvet pouch.

Where had that come from? It wasn't hers. Gingerly, she picked it up and peered inside at three dirty-looking pieces of glass. Stephanie closed her eyes and tamped down the nausea that rolled up from her stomach.

How had JD gotten the uncut diamonds in her purse? *The window.* When she'd gazed out the window at the Eiffel Tower. She ground her molars until pain shot to her ears. What if customs had gone through her purse?

She once more bent down and retrieved the key to the studio. Inside the darkened room, she sat at her worktable.

The police. Yes. That's what she'd do. She'd go to them and explain everything, and she would take the journal where she'd documented every step of the smuggling process. But first she'd have to get it from her bedroom. She glanced toward the fireplace, where she'd hidden sheets torn from the middle of the journal. No, that was her ace in the hole. She rose to go get the journal, then sat back down.

JD had said he had friends in high places. He would deny everything and point out she was the one with the diamonds. What if they didn't believe her?

She buried her face in her hands. She needed time to think. *Wait.* JD wouldn't be home for a day or two. If she could just get some sleep, she could think more clearly. But she needed to hide the diamonds. She lifted her head, and the first thing she saw was the wrapped sculpture.

Stephanie dumped the three diamonds on her worktable and then unwrapped the half-finished horse sculpture. With deft hands, she pressed two of the diamonds between the wires supporting the belly and slid the third one between the withers, then smoothed clay over them. When she finished, she examined her work.

Perfect.

— 1 —

18 Years Later

Andi Hollister flipped her wipers on high. It was a lousy night to be on I-240. The early April thunderstorms that swept across Arkansas earlier in the day were now taking dead aim on Memphis. A cloud had swallowed the setting sun, making it seem much later than six o'clock.

She took the airport exit and gripped the steering wheel as her Corolla hydroplaned, sending the car sliding toward the outside of the curve. A second later, the tires regained traction, and she blew out a breath. At least she'd lost all the traffic heading in to the FedEx Forum for the first game of the Final Four.

This was the first time in years that the University of Memphis Tigers had made it to the finals of March Madness. The town was crazy, traffic was crazy, and now the weather was crazy. Her cell phone played "Rainy Days and Mondays." Treece. If Andi didn't answer, Treece would call out the National Guard. She pressed the answer button on the steering wheel. "Hello, Ms. Rogers."

"Where are you?" The drumming rain practically drowned out Treece's voice.

"Almost to the airport." The two of them had

worked together since after college, when they both went to work for WLTZ as reporters, Andi reporting the weather and Treece the traffic.

Andi slowed as she approached the terminal, searching for the entry to the short-term parking garage. Lacey had said to wait for her at the Delta check-in area, that she would find her.

"I don't feel good about this," Treece said. "You don't even know this woman or if she's actually Lacey Wilson. It could be someone pretending to be your sister's old roommate."

Andi lowered her window, rain dripping off her car onto her arm as she punched the button for a parking ticket. She took the ticket the meter spit out. A dark SUV appeared in Andi's mirror, almost on her bumper.

"Are you still there?" Treece asked.

"I'm trying to get into the short-term garage," Andi said as the arm lifted and she pulled forward inside the garage. She followed the arrows to the fourth level, looking for a parking spot. "And I'm not in any danger—what could go wrong with a hundred TSA agents around?"

She spotted an empty space and wheeled into it.

"You have to ask that after the trouble you get into?"

"That was three months ago." Treece was referring to when she ruptured a disc in her back while climbing a fence to video a pit bull chained outside in the cold weather with no shelter.

"I am not talking about three months ago, I'm talking about two weeks ago when I taped you interviewing that gang leader, and he lost his temper. If Reggie hadn't insisted on coming with us—"

"Interviewing him seemed like a good idea at the time." Until Treece's cop boyfriend had to twist the gang leader's arm behind his back after he blew his top and threatened her. The Memphis police lieutenant hadn't liked Treece videoing Andi's segments after that. "Even you thought it'd be a good story."

"After that episode, my perspective is a little different. You have to be more careful."

"I'm trying to change, but investigative reporting comes with risk. I hope you're not thinking about changing fields," Andi said.

"No, at least not yet."

"Good." Treece had been her friend since grade school, and while she was a good reporter, she was also the best videographer the station had. Andi tossed the parking stub on the dash before unhooking her seat belt. The SUV inched by her car, and she tried to see the driver. *Isn't it against the law for windows to be tinted that dark?*

"What's going on? You're not meeting this woman inside the garage, are you?"

"No. We're meeting at the Delta check-in, and don't be such a worrywart. I need to do this. She promised answers about my sister. How could I say no?" Andi had so many unanswered questions about Steph and her life just before she was killed, and it wasn't a topic anyone in her family talked about.

"I hope she tells you more than she did the last time you two met."

"Yeah, me too." Andi had met Lacey for lunch once before, thinking the woman might share information about Steph, but she'd talked around every question Andi asked.

"Call me as soon as your meeting is over," Treece said, "and don't let your overconfidence get you into trouble. Got it?"

"You're not old enough to be giving me orders."

"Somebody needs to," Treece said dryly.

"I'm going in now."

Andi climbed out of her car, gritting her teeth at the pain in her back. She reached into the car and grabbed a water bottle, then took out a small prescription bottle and shook a pill into her hand. After gulping the pill down, she scanned the cavernous building and shivered.

Underground tombs. That's what these garages were. Using her phone, she snapped a photo of her parking spot with the Level 4 and Row 7 signs in the background. A few rows over, a woman her age rolled her luggage smartly toward the elevator, and since Andi did not want to be locked in that elevator alone, she hurried after her. At least the woman looked athletic enough to help her climb out in case the elevator stalled between floors. Of course, she could take the stairs.

Uh, no. She'd seen too many suspense movies. And it had only been a month ago that she'd reported on a mugging in the stairwell at the airport. No telling who or what she'd encounter in the two flights of stairs down to the walkover. Wails from a child caught her attention, and she looked to her right, where a young mother balanced a baby in one arm while another child tugged at her skirt as she tried to unlock her car door.

She shifted her gaze back to the woman approaching the elevator. If Andi hurried, she could catch her. The thump of keys hitting concrete pulled her back to the mother, and their eyes connected. Fatigue was etched in the mother's face and the slump of her shoulders.

The elevator dinged open, and the woman with the suitcase called out, "Would you like me to hold the door?"

"Uh . . ." *Get on the elevator.* Her feet itched to go, and then she sighed. "No. Appreciate it, though."

Andi turned to the mother. "I'll get those keys and unlock the door for you."

"Thank you so much," the mother said, shifting the baby to the other arm and smoothing her toddler's hair.

"No problem." Andi smiled at the small girl, who wrapped her arms around her mother's leg. Andi scooped the keys up and minutes later had the family on their way home.

When the elevator ride to the walkover was uneventful, she laughed at her fear. She could face a gang leader but let an enclosed box get to her. She really did need to work on that.

Inside the terminal, the check-in queues were practically empty. Evidently not many people were flying out of Memphis on a rainy Tuesday night. She found a seat where she could watch the doors and waited.

Thirty minutes later she checked her watch. Where was Lacey? She'd been adamant about meeting *tonight* and that her flight boarded at seven twenty. Andi called her for the second time and left a message, asking where she was.

Forty minutes later, she grabbed her bag and walked out of the airport and back to her car. Lacey was a no-show. It wasn't like Andi had never been stood up, but she hadn't expected it from Lacey. Not after the way she'd pressed her to come tonight.

The ringtone for Treece sounded again, and Andi answered. "I haven't called because she never showed."

"I bet you're hungry, then. There's pizza left. Then we can work on the outline for the cold case documentary."

"Be home in fifteen." The documentary on cold case murders and the one on runaways were their tickets to cinching anchor spots at the TV station or even to bigger markets, like Dallas or Atlanta. Then, maybe they'd attract the attention of one of the Big Three. They wouldn't turn down a cable news network, either.

She glanced in her side mirror as she exited the airport. Halos circled the car lights coming alongside her, and in the foggy mist she saw she was in the wrong lane and almost missed the exit for I-240. She glanced sharply over her shoulder, and when the lane was empty, she shot over. Her breath caught as a dark SUV with tinted windows swept past her under the lights. It looked like the one she'd seen earlier. Was it following her? Or was her vivid imagination kicking in again? No. If she hadn't abruptly changed lanes, she would have never known the car was behind her.

She kept an eye out for the SUV as she drove to Midtown and was prepared to drive past the older two-story home where she lived if she spotted the vehicle again. Andi checked her rearview mirror and saw that the street was empty. She turned into the drive and pulled behind the 1940s house that had been turned into three apartments.

Mrs. Casey, the older woman who owned the house, occupied the first floor, and Andi and Treece lived in the two upstairs apartments. Instead of taking the outside stairs, Andi went through the back door on the main floor to pick up her mail that Mrs. Casey always placed on the hallway table.

Bill, bill, advertisement. She looked up as Treece peered over the bannister, a grin pasted on her face. "Don't say 'I told you so,' " Andi said.

Treece descended the steps, holding a pitcher in one hand. "I was thinking more along the lines that you must have been speeding to get here so quickly. You're going to get caught one of these days."

"Nah." Andi shook her head and climbed the stairs. "But if I do, I'll get Brad to fix it. Or Will."

This time Treece laughed out loud, her dark eyes dancing. "You know that's not happening. They might hover over you like mother hens, but neither of them has *ever* fixed one of your tickets."

Andi gave her a sour look. They were mother hens, all right. Had been ever since she was diagnosed with a bad heart valve as a child. Her protectors, they called themselves. Guards, she'd called them, and their attitude hadn't changed after her surgery, and had lasted even to this day. "What are you doing with the pitcher?"

"Mrs. Casey called from Nashville. She forgot to water her plants and asked if we would do it," Treece said as she unlocked their landlord's door. "If you'll help me, it'll be quicker."

"Sure." Andi followed her friend inside the apartment that was directly under Treece's, where they found another pitcher and filled it with water. Fifteen minutes later the plants were watered, and she and Treece were climbing the stairs.

"I have the makings for a salad if you'd like it to go with your pizza," Treece said.

"That sounds good," Andi said as they topped the stairs and she walked to her door. "I think I'm going to change into something more comfortable. Do I need to bring over anything for the salad?"

"I don't think so." Her friend tilted her head. "Why do you think Lacey didn't show?"

She hesitated with her hand on the door. Maybe she'd eat first, then come home and take a hot shower and go to bed. "I don't know, but it sure wasn't any fun driving to the airport."

"Did you ever figure out who the person was that she mentioned on the phone?"

Lacey had rambled about someone. Andi tried to recall the name. "Do you remember who I said it was?"

Treece shook her head. "No. Only that you said she mentioned a name."

"It was someone with initials . . ." She shrugged and trailed Treece into her apartment. Whenever they got together, whether it was for work or for social reasons, they always gravitated to Treece's apartment. Maybe it was because she cooked, or because her apartment was more inviting.

She glanced around Treece's living room. Their apartment layouts mirrored each other, but that's where the similarity ended. Other than a couple of paintings, Andi's walls were bare, and she certainly didn't have knickknacks sitting around waiting to be dusted. The only pottery she owned was a sculpture her sister had been working on when she was murdered.

Treece, on the other hand, was a decorating maven. Bright paint covered the walls and bold fabric hung on the windows. African pottery, along with pieces from local artists, graced tables and bookcases. Andi really did need to make an effort to spruce things up over on her side.

She set her bag on the counter. "Where's that pizza? I'm starving."

Treece pointed to the top of the stove. "Microwave or oven?"

"Not the microwave," Andi said, turning on the oven.

"While we wait for it to reheat, tell me more about this friend of your sister. You wouldn't discuss her this morning, but I think you need to. Was she there the night Stephanie . . . ?"

Andi's stomach curdled. She'd managed all day to push that night out of her mind. She'd been barely thirteen, and two days after the funeral, she'd had surgery to replace a heart valve.

Steph had been eight years older than Andi, and Andi idolized her big sister. Finding out who Steph was as an adult had been the reason for agreeing to meet Lacey at the airport. Not to discuss Stephanie's death—the man who killed her sat on death row.

Andi turned around and slid the pizza into the oven. "I don't remember. And I still don't want to talk about it. Let it go. Okay?"

When she turned back around, her heart sank. Treece had that reporter gleam in her eyes that said she was not dropping the subject. Andi broke off a stalk of celery for her salad. Why did people always think they knew what was best for her? She sliced the celery in the wooden bowl with a rounded Ulu blade. She did not want to discuss Stephanie's death.

"That celery isn't your enemy," Treece said. "What I can't understand is why you won't discuss your sister. You never back away from anything, except Stephanie's death."

"There's nothing to discuss. My sister's ex-boyfriend shot and killed her. My mom and I found Jimmy Shelton sitting by her body with the gun. He confessed, and Sunday night it will finally be over. What else is there to talk about?"

"For one thing, from what I read about the case on the internet, he recanted the confession. Said it was coerced."

Andi stared at her friend. She'd been researching Jimmy's trial?

Before she could say anything, Treece continued. "And another thing, he's Will Kincade's cousin. How do you handle it with him?"

Will was her brother's best friend, and lately her heart had been reacting strangely when she was around him. She placed a carrot in the wooden bowl and attacked it with the blade. "We don't talk about it."

"Here, let me make your salad before you turn everything into mush." Treece took the knife away from her. "How do you feel when you think about your sister's death?"

Andi pinched her mouth together as her friend raked the carrot into a bowl of lettuce and dropped a handful of grape tomatoes on top. "Horrible, Dr. Phil. That's how I feel. And angry that Jimmy is alive and Stephanie isn't. Anything else?"

"You haven't forgiven him."

Andi narrowed her eyes, ignoring the dart of guilt pricking her conscience. "Forgive him? How do you expect me to forgive him for taking Stephanie's life? I was ten when she left home for college, thirteen when she died, and I never got the chance to really know her. Satisfied?"

Treece palmed her hands up. "Sorry, didn't mean to rile you. So how's it going with Will? And don't tell me you're not attracted to him."

"Give me a break. I haven't had time for a

boyfriend. Besides, I know better than to fall for him—he only sees me like a sister. No way would it ever work out. And how about you?"

"We're not talking about me."

Andi wasn't going to let it go that easily, not if it would shift the conversation to Treece's boyfriend problems. "Have you called Reggie? Or answered any of his texts?" She raised her eyebrows, waiting. "See, I'm not the only one who doesn't like to get up close and personal."

Before Treece could say anything, Andi grabbed her apartment key. "And now I'm going to go across the hall and get my bottle of raspberry vinaigrette."

Andi fled the apartment, leaving Treece with her mouth gaping. Sometimes she pushed their friendship too far. *She worries.* Andi pushed the thought away. Living next door to Treece at times was like living at home with her parents.

Andi unlocked her door and frowned. She didn't remember leaving the living room light on. Had to do better than that if she was going to cut her electric bill.

She was halfway to the refrigerator when the unmistakable click of the door shutting stopped her. The apartment plunged into darkness. Andi froze, her heart pummeling her chest. She turned to run, but rough hands yanked her back in a chokehold. Cold steel pressed against her temple.

"Yell, and your friend dies along with you."

The raspy whisper raked her senses. Andi's mind whirled, seeking an escape. As if he read her thoughts, he tightened his grip around her neck, cutting off her air.

"Where are they?"

Black dots swam in her vision. She tried to answer him. "What—"

His arm relaxed slightly, but the gun barrel pressed harder against her head. "I won't hesitate to kill you," he said. "Now where are they?"

"What? I don't know . . ." Her lungs cried for air.

"The diamonds. You have them. They belong to me."

"I . . . can't . . . breathe . . ."

— 2 —

All day the cold April rain had fallen from clouds that belonged more to winter than spring. The dampness seeped through the window into Jimmy's bones, but he couldn't pry himself away from the window where halos ringed the overhead lights. Night 5,935 here at Riverbend. His birthday. And it would be his last. Tennessee's ban on executions had been lifted.

"Shelton, you got mail."

Reluctantly, Jimmy turned and nodded at the corrections officer who had been here almost as long as he had. Except Walter Simmons went home every morning. "Is it from my lawyer?"

That was meant as a joke—he hadn't heard from his public defender in years.

Walter grinned. "Looks like a woman's handwriting, and not your mama's."

Jimmy blinked. His mama was dying a slow death from heartache, but she wrote him every week. He'd gotten her birthday card yesterday—one of the few times he'd actually received mail early.

What other woman would be writing to him at Riverbend? Curiosity moved him from the window to the small opening in the door to accept the letter.

"Don't know why you're just now getting it. It was sent weeks ago," the officer said.

He stared at the envelope. Like Walter said, the writing on the envelope bearing his name did indeed appear to be a woman's handwriting, and the flowery script was nothing like his mother's.

He slid his finger under the flap and removed the single linen sheet with the name Lacey Wilson embossed at the top. Below it, a March 17th date. Nineteen days ago.

Dear Jimmy,

You may not remember me. I was one of the flight attendants who roomed with Stephanie Hollister.

He remembered Lacey. Petite blonde with brown eyes. She'd been kind to him at a time when he wasn't the nicest person to be around because of alcohol. He continued reading.

First, I want to apologize for not coming forward sooner. I have no excuse except I was afraid to. Even after I became a Christian three months ago, I couldn't make myself take responsibility for what I did, really for what I didn't do. But I want you to know there hasn't been a night that I haven't thought about you and your circumstances. When I saw in the paper your date had been set, I knew I had to do something.

I have decided to leave Memphis and go where no one can find me. That's why I'm writing to ask if I can visit you before I leave. I'll explain everything when I come, if you'll allow it. Most of all, I need your forgiveness for not telling you sooner that I have proof you didn't kill Stephanie.

The rest of the words blurred as his knees buckled, and he stumbled to his bed.

He didn't kill Stephanie?

Suddenly the dreams that had returned flashed through his mind. Steph on the floor, him with a gun in his hand, blood everywhere, and something else . . . or someone hovering in the shadows. No matter how hard he'd tried, he'd never been able to decipher what was in the shadows.

He stared at the letter, pain ripping him apart. The court-appointed lawyer had entered a plea of not guilty for him even though Jimmy had confessed, stating the unsigned confession was coerced. He'd then fought the conviction, but Jimmy's heart hadn't been in it. He had accepted the death sentence because he believed what the police said—that he'd killed the only woman he ever loved.

And now Lacey was saying he hadn't killed her?

— 3 —

Will Kincade stepped around a fingerprint tech in Lacey Wilson's living room and noted the suitcase by the back door and absence of clutter in the room, except an empty bottle of wine. Why would someone who was obviously leaving town suddenly decide to drink enough wine to get totally drunk and then sit in her running car with the garage door closed until carbon monoxide killed her?

The case wasn't his—it was his friend Brad's—but after four years as a beat cop and seven as an investigator, Will couldn't keep from doing what he was trained to do. And his gut said Lacey didn't kill herself.

His friend rounded the corner from the hall and walked toward him. Like Will, he wore a Tigers sweatshirt and jeans. They'd stopped by Corky's BBQ on their way to the FedEx Forum for tonight's game when the call came in, ruining what was supposed to be a celebration over Will's almost-certain promotion to the Cold Case Unit. His stomach growled at the memory of the pulled pork sandwich sitting in a to-go box in Brad's car.

"Sorry our celebration got interrupted. You want me to drop you off at the arena before I start chasing leads?" Brad said.

Tonight's game would determine whether the Memphis Tigers advanced in the NCAA Tournament. "Nah," Will said. "I'll catch the highlights tomorrow. We'll go to the play-offs when the Tigers win."

He and Brad bumped fists. They'd been friends ever since Will could remember—Will had lived with his aunt and uncle, but he'd spent every minute he could next door at the Hollisters'. One of the saddest days of Will's life was after Brad's sister was murdered and his cousin was accused of it. His aunt couldn't bear to live next door to where the murder happened, and they'd moved two counties over.

Will nodded toward the garage. "This case intrigues me. You think it's a suicide?"

"Maybe, maybe not. If not, someone tried to make it seem that way. I don't like that there's no note, and the next-door neighbor who found her said she was leaving on a trip to Hawaii. But she did say Lacey Wilson suffered with bouts of depression."

"Is that who called it in?"

"Yeah. Wilson had an 8:00 p.m. flight," Brad said, "and when the neighbor arrived to drive her to the airport around 5:30, she found her in the garage."

Will winced. Death was never easy, but to find someone you know unexpectedly like that . . . it'd be hard to get over. "Why was she going to the airport so early?"

"The neighbor talked to Wilson around nine this morning and indicated she was meeting someone before she flew. The ME's preliminary report puts her death around noon." Brad turned as a uniformed officer called his name from the front entryway.

The officer thumbed toward the door. "Got a guy here who says the deceased is his ex-wife."

Will had seen nothing in the house that indicated Lacey Wilson was married. He followed Brad to the front door, where the officer stood with a man in an airline uniform. Judging from the four gold stripes on his sleeve, the man was a pilot.

"Mr. Wilson?" Brad said.

"No, Adam Matthews. When Lacey and I

legally separated years ago, she took back her maiden name. The divorce became final five years ago."

Matthews stood a couple of inches taller than Will's six feet, and the pilot's shoulders filled out his uniform jacket. "What airline do you fly for?" Will asked.

"ConwayAir. Can you tell me what happened?"

"Your ex-wife was found behind the wheel of her Lexus with the motor running and the garage door closed," Brad replied. "How did you find out she was dead?"

Matthews nodded toward the street. "Neighbor called, said the place was crawling with cops. So it was a suicide?"

Brad tapped his pen on the notebook. "Didn't say that. Do you know anyone who would want to see your wife dead?"

"Other than me, you mean?"

"Why you, Mr. Matthews?" Will asked. The man was too calm and collected to suit him. And with his size, he could have easily put his ex-wife behind the steering wheel.

Matthews shifted his gaze to Will. "Isn't the husband, or in this case, ex-husband, always the first suspect? I can lay your case out for you . . . if it is a murder, which I doubt. Bitter divorce, ex paying through the nose, and said ex doesn't have an alibi if the death occurred today, since I spent the day alone. Did I cover everything?"

"Would you like to come in and sit down so we can discuss this further?" Brad asked.

Matthews removed his cap, revealing thick blond hair. He crossed the living room with the assurance of a person who was usually in command.

Once he sat on the black sofa, Brad and Will took the wingback chairs across from him, and then Brad took out a notebook. "If there were bad feelings between the two of you, why are you here?"

"I write an alimony check on the fifth of every month for three thousand dollars. Tomorrow's the fifth."

Either the man was cold or brutally honest . . . or trying to throw them off. He wouldn't be the first murderer to revisit the scene of the crime. Will cocked his head. "And now you won't have to write one."

"Bingo." He glanced toward the kitchen. "Is her . . . uh, body—"

"Already been transported to the morgue." Brad flipped his notepad over to a fresh page. "Do you know if she had been acting unusual lately?"

"I haven't talked to her for a couple of months, but as for your question—do you mean more strange than usual?"

"What do you mean by that?" Brad said.

"Lacey was bipolar. When she was in a manic period, she was really high, and the same was true of her lows. I can see her killing herself in either state, especially if she realized she was coming down." He palmed his hand out. "She decorated this room in one of her depressive states."

Will glanced around the room. The walls were bare except for a grouping of paintings over the black sofa. If Lacey was in a low state of mind, that would explain all the dark furniture.

"One time I came home," Matthews said, "and everything in our house was white. Sofa, walls, bedrooms, carpet—she was in a manic period that time."

"Was your ex-wife on medication?" Brad asked.

Matthews shook his head. "When we were married, amitriptyline was prescribed, but she refused to take it and preferred self-medication."

Will was familiar with the antidepressant as well. "You remember what antidepressant your ex-wife used?"

The pilot shrugged. "After the divorce, I became depressed and that's what my doctor prescribed too. Unlike Lacey, I took it until the depression cleared."

"Did she use alcohol?" Brad asked.

The pilot nodded. "It was her medication of choice then. The alcohol and her uncontrolled mood swings were the primary cause of the divorce. Add her sharp tongue and I couldn't stand to be around her." He ran his finger across the brim of his airline cap. "I heard later she started taking the prescribed medicine and had gotten better. So, I am a little surprised she took her life."

"That's still up for debate," Brad said. "Did your wife have any enemies?"

Matthews snorted. "Only everyone who spent extended time with her. Lacey could have an acerbic tongue."

"What type of job did she have?" Brad asked.

"She didn't work."

Will frowned. Lacey Wilson drove a fairly late model Lexus and had high-end furniture, and the art he'd noticed were Grant Wood lithographs. These were not items purchased on a three-thousand-a-month budget. "How did she afford this expensive neighborhood?"

"Her parents left her a decent inheritance, but . . ." Matthews shrugged. "I wondered myself how she bought that car six years ago, and from what the neighbor told me, she planned to buy another because she was having trouble with it."

Brad made notes in his book. "Any ideas on that? Maybe a boyfriend?"

A hollow laugh came from Matthews's lips. "Definitely no boyfriend."

He seemed so certain about that. Will said, "And you know this how?"

A sour expression crossed the ex-husband's face. "I have a friend who's a private investigator, and he gives me a cut rate to follow her a couple of times a year—just in case she's living with someone. If she does, the alimony stops. Every year I paid him to sit in front of her house because she rarely went anywhere. Except this last time." He shook his head. "Would you believe he followed her to church and to a children's shelter where she volunteered? And that was it."

Sounded like Lacey Wilson had made a change for the better. Will cocked his head. "Did you know she was flying to Hawaii tonight, or that she didn't have a return ticket?"

"What?" Matthews's eyes widened. "Are you sure?"

Brad nodded toward the kitchen. "She printed out her ticket this morning, and her suitcases are packed and by the back door."

"That doesn't sound like Lacey."

Will leaned forward. "How did you meet your wife?"

Matthews shifted toward Will. "She was a flight attendant back in the late nineties, and we occasionally worked together. It went from there."

Brad looked up from his notebook. "Did you know Stephanie Hollister?"

"Who?"

Will observed Matthews as Brad repeated the question. It had unsettled the pilot. But Brad mentioning his sister unsettled Will too.

"Not that I know of. But there've been a lot of flight attendants over the years."

"He didn't say she was a flight attendant," Will said.

"I guess I assumed based on the previous question." Matthews checked his watch and stood. "Gentlemen, unless you plan to arrest me, I have a plane to fly."

"Are you flying internationally?"

"Not tonight. Just shuttling to Charlotte, North Carolina."

"One last question. Did she have any new friends or hobbies?"

"Don't know the answer to that one, but you might check with that church she went to. Covenant something-or-other." Matthews pressed his lips together. "You might want to look at her old friends. The crowd she ran around with when we first got married."

"Can you give me a list?" Brad said.

Matthews checked his watch again. "There were several people we used to have dinner with, but I'll have to think about it."

"Can you remember any of them offhand?"

He glanced toward the ceiling. "Laura and Spencer Delaney. Madeline . . . something-or-other." He shrugged.

"Laura Delaney, the district attorney?"

"They'd been friends a long time. Look, I always have time to kill once I get to the airport.

Can I text you any other names I remember from there? I really need to leave."

"Just don't skip the country."

Matthews's eyes narrowed. "I didn't kill her. If I had, it would have been years and thousands of dollars ago."

He stopped at the door. "Oh, you might want to check the mechanic at Taylor's Garage. That neighbor who told me she was buying a new car—Lacey claimed it was because the mechanic there who worked on her car did something to her transmission. She'd threatened to ruin his business, and he didn't take too kindly to her accusations."

Will turned to Brad when Matthews drove away. "Why did you ask him if he knew Stephanie?"

"She was working with the airlines during the time he said he met his wife. When Steph was murdered, she was sharing the house where my parents live now with four other women, and three of them were flight attendants."

"I remember that. Don't remember any of their names, though. Do you?" Will asked.

"The only one I remember is one called Maggie," Brad said.

"I remember her—helped crank that old mower more than once." He and Brad had been about fifteen then. "What do you think about Matthews?"

"He's either telling the truth or he's a really good liar. Not sure which yet. But at least we have a few leads to check out if the medical examiner rules it a homicide."

"You think he will?"

"I could go either way on this one. If she was bipolar, she could have slipped over the edge."

It would surprise Will if she committed suicide. Why would she have gone to the trouble of packing for Hawaii? He turned Lacey Wilson's name over in his mind. "Does the victim's name ring a bell?"

Brad rubbed his chin. "You too? Ever since I heard it, I've tried to place how I could know her. In fact, this whole case has a déjà vu feeling."

"Hey, Brad." A tech approached them, holding the victim's purse and cell phone. "Found something I think you'll find interesting. Looks like the victim had your sister's phone number in her phone."

He took the phone, and Will looked over his shoulder at the screen. "What's Andi's phone number doing in Lacey Wilson's list of recent calls?"

Brad shook his head. "I don't know, but I'm going to find out."

— 4 —

"Andi, what happened? Talk to me."

Treece's voice filtered through the darkness holding Andi prisoner. *Go away, Treece—don't come in* . . . A cold cloth touched her face, and she groaned. "Is he gone?"

"Who? What are you talking about? You fainted. I've told you not to skip meals!"

"Didn't . . . faint . . ." Andi struggled to sit up, but the room wouldn't stop spinning. She covered her eyes with her hand.

"Lay still," Treece commanded. "Have you eaten today? And why did you leave your kitchen window open? It's cold in here."

No, gotta get up . . . Why couldn't she get the words out? She peeked through her fingers, and slowly the room stilled. Treece came into focus. *The man.* Andi tried to push her friend away. "Go. He'll hurt—"

"What is wrong with you?"

Andi squinted against the light shining from the ceiling. "Is he gone?"

"Is who gone? Are you telling me someone was in here?" Treece's voice cracked. "I thought you fainted. I'm calling your brother."

Andi didn't stop her. She tried to pull out

what happened, but pounding on the front door scrambled her thoughts even more.

"Brad and Will are here."

Already?

"They were on their way when I called. You sit tight while I let them in."

Treece didn't have to worry about her moving. She didn't think she could stand if her life depended on it. And why was Brad coming to see her? Her brother hardly ever came, and Will never. She raked her fingers through her hair. "Ouch!"

Andi jerked her hand away from a lump on the back of her head and stared at the blood on her fingers. No wonder she couldn't get her thoughts together—he'd knocked her out.

"I found her on the floor," Treece said as she came back into the apartment. "I thought she fainted."

"Why is it so cold in here?" Brad asked.

Andi closed one eye and looked up at her brother, then to the opened back window next to the door that led to the deck and stairs. "Maybe that?" She pointed toward the window.

"Can't be too much wrong," Will said, "if she can put you down."

Andi shifted her focus to her brother's best friend and tried to ignore the flutter-dance in her heart when Will smiled at her. Or maybe it was the blow to her head.

"Did you leave the window open?" Brad asked.

"Of course not. May not have locked it, though. Must be how he got in."

"Are you saying someone broke in and attacked you?"

"That's what I was trying to tell you," Treece said.

Her brother's attitude changed instantly. He unholstered his gun and moved cautiously toward her bedroom.

"I'll take her next door," Will said.

"Let me get my door unlocked," Treece said.

The spinning started again, and Andi squeezed her eyes shut, then opened them. Better, except her head still throbbed. "I'm sure he's long gone," Andi said as Will helped her to stand. The room tilted, and she swayed against him.

Will scooped her up in his arms, his biceps taut as he carried her across the hall. Andi sank into his chest, momentarily forgetting her aversion to anyone helping her. In Treece's apartment, he gently set her on the sofa.

A few minutes later, Brad towered above her. "Your apartment is clear, and I've called for a crime scene unit."

It was a little more than Andi could process. Why would anyone break into her apartment? She tried to focus on what her brother was saying. "What did you say?"

"I need you to start at the top and tell me what happened."

"I was warming my pizza." She caught her breath. "My pizza—did it burn?"

"No," Treece said. "I took it out before I came to see why you didn't come back to my apartment."

"Save it." Maybe she could eat it later. "I went to get a bottle of salad dressing from my refrigerator, and he was there. He flipped off the light and came up behind me and wrapped me in a choke hold."

"So you couldn't see who it was?" Will asked.

She shook her head. "But I felt his hands. He wore gloves."

"What did he want?"

The memory of the man's raspy voice sent shivers down her spine. She wrapped her arms across her stomach as the shaking spread to the rest of her body and tears threatened. "I—I . . ." Her teeth chattered. Why couldn't she remember what he said? "He wanted something."

"What?" Brad knelt beside her. "Think. What did he want?"

"I don't know!" Tears streamed down her face. She swiped the back of her hand across her cheeks. She hated it when she cried. "Stop pushing me."

"Here," Will said, his voice soft.

She looked up and took the box of tissues he

47

held out. "Thanks. My head is killing me where he hit me."

"What!" Three voices raised at the same time.

"Andi! Why didn't you tell me? We need to get you to the ER," Treece said. "You probably have a concussion."

"Why didn't you say he knocked you out?" Concern filled Brad's voice.

"I don't want to go to the hospital. Treece has an ice pack. Just let me have that."

"You don't have any choice, little sister."

"I'm not your little sister anymore. I'm thirty-two years old. And you're not the boss of me." She lifted her chin. "Besides, I'm not dizzy anymore. All I have is a little headache."

"Andi," Brad said with a groan. "People die from internal bleeding after a bump on the head sometimes. You can go in an ambulance or you can let one of us take you."

She did not want to spend hours at the ER.

"Or I could call Mom." Brad held up his phone. "Which is it?"

"Don't call Mom!" Sure, her brother was worried about her, but did he have to be so bossy? She tried to think of a way out of going to the hospital. Her heart stilled when Will lifted her chin and examined her eyes.

"Your pupils *are* slightly dilated," he said. "I think you ought to listen to your brother and get checked out."

Staring into his cobalt-blue eyes was what made her pupils dilate. This was her brother's friend—why did his nearness suddenly make her heart rev up like an Indy 500 car? *Get ahold of yourself.* "Please, I don't want to spend five hours waiting to see a doctor. Would you settle for a walk-in clinic? There's one two blocks away, and Treece can take me."

The corner of Brad's mouth twitched as he hooked his phone back on his belt, then his eyes softened and he turned to Will. "Would you take her while I wait for the crime scene techs?"

"Sure," Will said. "Do you want me to ask her about . . ."

"About what?" Andi asked. She looked from Will to her brother. For the first time it dawned on her they were wearing jeans and U of M hoodies. Somewhere in the back of her mind, she remembered it was March Madness and the Tigers had made it to the Final Four. "Wait a minute. You're supposed to be at the game cele-brating Will's promotion to the Cold Case Unit."

"Yeah," Treece said, "but you were almost here when I called. What's going on?"

Will frowned. "How did you hear about the promotion? I haven't told anyone except him." He jerked his thumb at Brad.

Her brother winced. "I told Mom, and she called, right?"

"This afternoon. Congratulations." She glanced

at the clock. "But it's eight thirty, and the game started an hour ago. What's going on?"

"A possible suicide, maybe murder case," Brad said. "We were coming to find out why your cell phone number is on the victim's phone."

"What?" Andi combed her mind, trying to imagine which of her contacts could have ended up dead, and more than one popped into her mind. "Who's your victim?"

"That conversation can wait," Will said, and Brad nodded agreement. "Let's get you checked out first."

"No, I want—"

"Don't argue with the man. My case isn't going anywhere, and I'll be here when you get back." Brad crossed his arms. "And the sooner you go, the sooner you get answers."

She narrowed her eyes at the two men. Sometimes she got her way with them, but the looks on their faces said that wasn't going to happen tonight. "Okay," she grumbled. "But don't be surprised if my blood pressure blows the machine."

Now that JD knew where she lived, he should have waited for a better time, but in this neighborhood, there wouldn't ever be a *good* time. Too many prying eyes when it was daylight, and who knew how long he'd have to wait for Andi to be away at night.

Eighteen years he'd wondered what Stephanie

50

did with the diamonds. And after he read Lacey's letter to Andi with a reference to her having the diamonds, he hadn't wanted to wait any longer.

Andi had been easy to tail from the TV station to the airport, but he'd almost run over her at the exit. If he hadn't caught up with her on I-240 just before she'd exited on Union, tracking her down would have been difficult. While Andi Hollister's phone number was listed in Lacey's phone, her address wasn't.

JD almost missed her again when he dropped back on the residential street, but he hit pay dirt when he saw her taillights turn into the drive. After parking and walking to the house, he'd walked around to the back where her car was parked. One apartment was lit up, the other dark. JD risked climbing the back stairs and discovered the silly girl had left her window unlocked.

He'd been inside Andi's apartment when he heard the two women climb the stairs, and was about to leave when Andi accepted the other woman's invitation to eat pizza. How was he to know she'd pop over in only fifteen minutes? It hadn't been enough time to find the diamonds or even a likely place to hide them.

"Stephanie, why couldn't you just give me the diamonds?" He spoke the words aloud in the darkness of his vehicle. They were the same words he had used eighteen years ago after he'd discovered what she'd done . . .

JD took a threatening step toward her.

Her eyes narrowed as she pulled a .38 from her pocket. "Don't come any closer."

"Give me the diamonds, or I'll take the gun away and use it on you."

"I don't think you can." Stephanie waved the gun.

"Be reasonable," he said. "Hand over those diamonds I put in your purse, and we can all walk away from this."

"How many times do I have to say this? They are going to stay where they are until I need them."

He took another step closer to Stephanie, and she raised the gun level with his chest. "Stop right there."

Just what he needed. A crazy woman with a gun. "Come on, honey. You're not going to shoot me. Not after all we've meant to each other."

The gun didn't waver. Stephanie jutted her chin. "You're wrong about that, just like I was wrong about you. You never loved me. You used me, just like you did Jillian. I just hate it took me two months to figure it out."

He moistened his dry lips as he took a step back. "I don't know what you're talking about. Come on, give me the gun and then tell me where the diamonds are . . ."

Except she hadn't told him, and the money he had to pay the supplier had wiped him out. He'd bounced back, but the loss was like a burr in his shoe. He wanted *those* diamonds. He couldn't believe they had been under his nose all these years. Tomorrow he'd search the apartment.

As he started his car, something one of the women said came back to him.

"It was someone with initials . . ."

Cold chills raced over his body. Evidently, Lacey had mentioned his name to Andi. He'd been so focused on the diamonds that the words hadn't registered until now. If she remembered his name and repeated that to the wrong person . . .

He should have killed Andi Hollister instead of knocking her out.

— 5 —

Will waited in the reception area while Treece accompanied Andi to the examining room. Waiting gave him plenty of time to worry about what Andi had possibly gotten herself into this time. As a girl, she hadn't known how to stay out of trouble, and nothing had changed now that she was a woman. A beautiful woman at that. He quickly squelched that thought.

"I told you I was all right," Andi said as she and Treece came through the clinic doors. "We just wasted an hour and a half."

"She does only have a mild concussion, but the cut on her head required five stitches," Treece said.

"Yeah, big waste of time." He winked at Treece. "I could've sewn that up."

Andi made a face at him and made a beeline for the door.

He hurried ahead of her. "Stay here and I'll get the car."

A few minutes later, Treece was in the backseat, and he had Andi buckled in before he walked around to the driver's side. His heart sank when he slid behind the wheel and saw her reading the *Commercial Appeal* he'd left on the console.

Jimmy Shelton to Be Executed Sunday.

She looked up from the newspaper, her eyes wide. "Seeing this in black and white . . ." She ducked her head. "The DA notified Mom and Dad, but they told her they wouldn't be there."

Will blew out a breath. "It's all I can think of— that he'll die, and I can't stop it."

Andi leaned against the seat. "He confessed, Will."

"A confession his attorney tried to have suppressed because it was coerced." But it wasn't the right time to discuss her sister's murder, and he kept quiet for the rest of the drive home.

Two cars other than Brad's sat out front. "Crime scene guys," he said when Andi questioned him. After he parked behind the house, he helped her out of the car while Treece got out of the backseat.

His heart dipped at the dark half circles under her eyes, and even though her grip was firm, frailty radiated from her slender frame. If he had his way, he'd scoop her up in his arms again and carry her inside, but she insisted on walking. At least she clung to his arm as they climbed the stairs.

"Where's Mrs. Casey?" he asked once she was settled on the sofa in Treece's apartment.

"Went to see her daughter in Nashville this afternoon, thank goodness." Andi leaned her head back and then quickly moved it. "Ouch. The feeling is back. Where's Brad? I want answers, since you won't give me any."

"Look, try to go easy on him," Will said. "He worries about you."

Resignation settled on her face. "I know, but I'm not some orchid that's going to wilt every time I bump my knee."

"It wasn't your knee you bumped," Brad said as he came into Treece's apartment. "It was your head because some burglar broke into your place. You could have been killed."

She swallowed hard and seemed to be on the verge of tears.

"Did the crime scene techs find anything?" Will asked.

"No. Andi must have surprised the intruder

early. The only evidence he was even in her apartment was the open window. And the attack." Brad sat in the chair across from Andi. "Are you really okay?"

His best friend's voice was gruff, but Will knew Brad cared deeply about his sister. It was just that Andi Hollister could get into more trouble than any woman he knew, and her brother often operated out of fear for her.

When Brad saw her number on Lacey Wilson's cell phone, his face had reflected the worry that latched on to Will. While Brad might think it was a suicide, he knew, just like Will, it was too early to rule out murder.

"Yeah." She touched the back of her head and winced. "Hate to admit you were right about getting checked out. Now tell me who was murdered."

"Or committed suicide. They're finished with your apartment. Why don't we go next door and talk?" Brad said.

"No," Andi said and nodded toward a salad on Treece's bar. "I missed supper, and I'm hungry. Besides, I'll end up telling Treece whatever we discuss as soon as you leave anyway." She raised her eyebrows. "I bet you two haven't eaten either. You can have some of my pizza."

"Not me." Will shook his head. His stomach burned from the barbecue they'd wolfed down on the way over.

"Me either," Brad said. "We'll talk while you eat. Have you recalled what the intruder said to you?"

Andi allowed Will to help her from the sofa.

"Thanks," she murmured. "No. The doc said I might and I might not. All I remember is how insistent the man was that I had something that belonged to him. Either I didn't hear what it was or I just don't remember. Now, who is the murder victim?"

Will exchanged a look with Brad. "A woman named Lacey Wilson," he said. "And we're not sure it's a murder."

Treece gasped, and Andi sat down hard at the kitchen table. What little color she had drained from her face. "She was supposed to meet me tonight before she left town. How was she killed?"

"We're not sure yet," Brad said. "How did you know her? And why does her name sound familiar to me?"

"Because you should remember her. She lived at the house with Stephanie, and they were friends," Andi said. "They worked together."

Brad snapped his finger just as the image of a younger version of the victim popped into Will's mind. The Lacey Wilson he saw tonight didn't look anything like the cute little blonde he remembered coming and going from the house next door.

"Oh yeah," Brad said. "Blonde hair. Not big as a minute. She worked with Steph as a flight attendant and came to the funeral. That's why I had this odd feeling about this case."

Something about Brad's voice caught Will's attention. He always felt a barrier between them when the subject of Stephanie came up. They hadn't discussed Stephanie's death since it happened. Partly because Will hadn't known how to talk to Brad about it after his cousin confessed to killing her. Then Will moved away the next month. When he returned to Memphis five years later, the murder was something they simply didn't discuss.

"Have you released the information about Lacey's death to the media?" Treece asked.

"Yeah." Andi looked first at Will, then at Brad.

"Not yet, and when we do, you don't need to cover it," her brother said.

"Why not? I bet she was going to tell me something tonight, and someone murdered her before she could."

Will's stomach clenched. That was exactly why she didn't need to cover it. "Hey—you've just been attacked. The last thing you need is to get involved in this case," he said.

She shifted her gaze back to him. "I'm not helpless. Tomorrow I'll be as fit as ever. Since someone is going to cover it, it might as well be me."

"But it hasn't been released, so you don't need to do anything tonight," Treece said.

"We don't even know if it is a crime," Will said.

Andi smelled a story, and if it turned out to be murder like Will figured, it was possible the break-in to her apartment was related. He'd lost more than a little sleep since Andi left her position at the weather desk. It looked as though he might lose more.

Then her shoulders slumped, and she shook her head as if to clear it. "I can't believe I'm worrying about covering this story. Someone I know just died," she said, a pained expression in her eyes.

Will's relief was short-lived as she swayed.

"Andi!" Treece cried.

Brad and Will jumped to catch her, but Will reached her first. He steadied her in the chair.

Treece wet a cloth and placed it on her fore-head.

Will wanted to reach out to her as quiet filled the kitchen, but Brad acted first, patting her arm.

"Squirt, you know you don't have anything to prove here."

She moved the cloth and stared at him. "But I do. Ever since I was a kid, everyone always treated me with kid gloves because I was sick. I have to show I'm okay, that I can handle things."

"But you don't have to risk your life like you

do," Will said. "Everyone knows you're a great reporter."

"But don't you understand? That's why I'm good. I go after the hard stories." She pressed the cloth to her face again. "I need to tell Maggie about Lacey."

"Who's Maggie?" Brad said.

"Madeline Starr. She was one of the other women who lived in the house with Steph."

"The defense attorney?" Will said. He didn't realize the Maggie who had mowed the yard next door was the Madeline Starr who mowed down weak cases against her clients.

Andi nodded. "We have lunch together sometimes."

"Good," Brad said. "This is the stuff I need to know."

Treece set the salad and pizza in front of Andi and looked at the two men. "Andi needs to eat. Your questions can wait until she's finished."

While Andi ate the pizza, Brad motioned to Will that he was stepping out into the hallway to get a report from the crime scene unit. It was also a silent request to get information from Andi. After wandering around Treece's living room for a few minutes, Will sat at the table with the two women. "How does your head feel?"

"Hurts like I had a jackhammer inside it. Not that my brother cares." She stabbed a piece of lettuce in the bowl and brought it to her mouth.

"Cut him some slack. He's worried about you. It scared us both when we saw your name and phone number in the dead woman's phone."

Andi glanced toward the door. "What happened to her?"

"I'll trade information."

"Deal. You go first."

"Oh no you don't. First you tell me how you knew her other than from the past." He didn't understand how Andi got involved with so many of the wrong people. Not that the Wilson woman was necessarily the wrong sort. She lived in an exclusive neighborhood, and the furnishings in the house were costly . . . but still, she was dead.

"You two don't fool me. Text Brad to come back in. I feel better, but I don't feel like going over it twice."

He texted Brad while Andi ate another slice of pizza and nibbled at her salad.

"Tell me how Lacey died," she said when Brad rejoined them. "Then I'll explain why she had my number."

Brad stared at her briefly. "It's still up in the air, but I think it's carbon monoxide poisoning— she sat in her running car with the garage door closed. When I saw the empty bottle of wine, I thought she might have alcohol poisoning, but preliminary reports indicate she only had a blood alcohol level of .15, which is not lethal by itself. I'm waiting to hear from the medical examiner on a more detailed tox screen. Now, your turn."

"Wait—it wasn't a homicide?"

"I told you that we don't know yet," Brad said. "Now, talk."

"Okay. Lacey Wilson has called me several times over the years."

"What did you talk about?" Brad took out a notepad.

"Mostly about Lacey and how she missed Steph. She didn't call that often." Andi placed her fork on the empty plate, and Treece whisked it away.

"When was the last time you talked with her?" Brad asked.

"This morning. She wanted me to meet her at the airport tonight at six, and I drove there in a blinding rain, but she never showed."

Will leaned forward. "You're the one she was meeting? Why? And why wait until tonight? Why not earlier?"

"She planned to go to Riverbend."

"Riverbend Maximum Security Prison?" Will asked. That's where his cousin was incarcerated. Why would Lacey be going there?

"I don't know. She wouldn't discuss it over the phone, said something about her phone being tapped. Said she'd tell me everything when we met." Andi's eyes widened, and she put her hand to her mouth. "The SUV at the airport."

"What are you talking about?" Brad demanded.

"A dark SUV followed me into the airport. And

if I hadn't suddenly changed lanes and it passed me, I never would have seen it when I left. Do you think it was the man who attacked me? What if the break-in at my apartment is connected with Lacey's death?" Andi asked. "If her phone was bugged, maybe he knew I was meeting her, and then he followed me home." She halted. "But why?"

"Did you get a tag number?" Will asked as his phone rang. He pressed ignore when he didn't recognize the number.

"No."

His phone rang again, same number. He almost ignored it, and then thought better of it. "Excuse me," he said and walked away from the table. "Kincade," he said into the phone.

"Will, it's Jimmy. I need your help. I have proof I didn't kill Stephanie, and we don't have much time."

Will's heart pounded as he recognized his cousin's voice. "What do you mean, you didn't kill her? You confessed." He pressed a hand to his forehead. With five days until he was set to die, was Jimmy pulling some kind of stunt?

"Please, just listen to me. I—"

"How did you get a phone?" Prisoners on death row did not have access to cell phones.

"One of the guards. He could lose his job because of it, but he's trying to help me." Jimmy's voice cracked. "I got this letter from a friend of Stephanie's asking to come see me, only it wasn't delivered for three weeks. But right now that's not important. In the letter she said I didn't kill Stephanie and she had proof. Can you come to Riverbend tomorrow?"

The hair on the back of Will's neck raised. "Did she tell you what the proof was?"

"No. She's coming to see me. Says she'll tell me what it is then."

If only it was true. He'd never wanted to believe his cousin had murdered Brad and Andi's sister. "Who is this woman?"

"Lacey. Lacey Wilson."

Will's throat tightened. "What? Are you sure?"

"Of course I'm sure. I'm looking at the return address and her signature now."

"Let me talk to the corrections officer." Will waited while Jimmy handed the phone off.

"Hello?"

"Who is this?" Will asked.

"Walter Simmons. I'm one of the COs here at Riverbend where Jimmy is incarcerated. He's telling the truth."

"You've seen the letter he's talking about?"

"Yes, sir. It looks like the real deal."

"Can you take a photo of it and send it to me?"

"I'll take a picture, but I don't have one of those smartphones. I'll have to get my granddaughter to help me tomorrow."

Will bit his bottom lip. "Tell Jimmy I'll be at

Riverbend first thing in the morning," he said and disconnected. He'd take his own photo. But if it was true and Jimmy didn't kill Stephanie, then who did?

Lacey Wilson hadn't shown for her meeting with Andi, and now she was dead. If she'd written Jimmy a letter saying he didn't kill Stephanie, was she going to tell Andi the same thing? And maybe divulge who did?

People had been killed for much less.

Andi kept her gaze on Will as she pushed her salad bowl away. He had turned as pale as Treece's plate.

"You okay?" she asked when he stuffed his phone in his pocket and returned to the table. He looked like he'd been punched in the gut.

"I don't know." He sat in the chair he'd vacated and stared into space.

Goose bumps raised on her arms. "What's wrong?"

He turned to Brad. "I may know why Lacey Wilson was murdered—if she was. She wrote my cousin Jimmy a letter stating he didn't kill your sister. And from what you said earlier, she was going to see him before she left town."

Silence rocked the room. Andi clenched her fists, and the pizza settled in her stomach like concrete. "That's not possible. He confessed."

"I know, but I've always had a problem with

that confession . . . with Jimmy being Steph's murderer," he said.

"But he did it!" Her heartbeat pounded in her ears. "Your cousin still had the gun in his hands when Mom and I walked into the studio. He had blood on him—Steph's blood—and she had a restraining order against him. He's a violent person." She held Will's gaze. "Just what part are you having trouble with?"

"Look," he said, "I didn't mean to stir up trouble."

Brad leaned forward. "Well, you have." He turned to Andi. "But like Treece said, sit down and let's hear Will out."

"No!" Her brother's calm voice threw gas on the fire raging in Andi. How could he sit there so calmly and want to hear anything that contradicted the evidence that Jimmy Shelton killed their sister?

It couldn't be true. She'd focused for so long on Jimmy as Stephanie's killer, her mind couldn't accept that he might not be. A thought wormed its way past her anger. Why did Lacey suddenly want to see her after all these years? She'd wanted to tell her something about Steph. And if Lacey had been murdered, was it because she knew something? "I want to see this letter."

"So do I," Will said. "I plan to drive to Nashville tomorrow right after my meeting with David Raines in the Cold Case Unit."

She crossed her arms. "I'm going with you."

Will mimicked her action. "No, you're not. I'm not sure I'll go until I clear it with the lieutenant."

She tried to stare him down, but Will wasn't easily intimidated. "Will you let me know if you go?"

He hesitated and then finally nodded.

"Thank you." If Will Kincade drove to Nashville in the morning, she'd be in that car.

"Okay, back to our case," Brad said. "Have you remembered what the intruder said?"

"Diamonds." The word popped out of her mouth.

"Diamonds?" Will repeated.

It all came rushing back to her. "He said I had diamonds that belonged to him. I tried to tell him he had the wrong person, that I didn't know what he was talking about, but I couldn't breathe, much less talk."

Brad scratched his head. "Why would he think you have his diamonds?"

"I don't know. If he'd looked around the apartment, he should have realized I didn't have them." To say her apartment was sparse was an understatement. "Could he have made a mistake and broken into the wrong place?" she asked.

"I don't know," Brad said, "but tomorrow we get you two set up with a security system. Mrs. Casey too. When is she back in town?"

"She's planning to stay with her daughter a couple of weeks," Treece said. "I'll call her."

"You think you can get one installed that fast?" Andi asked.

"I hope so, because I'm spending the night here until you have one." Her brother gave her a look that dared her to contradict him.

Unexpectedly, Andi's heart warmed at his offer. "You'll give up your comfortable bed for my couch?"

"Ouch. I hadn't thought about that . . ." A grin spread all the way to his eyes. "I'm not leaving you and Treece unprotected."

"If you have an air mattress, I'll keep Brad company," Will said.

She blinked back tears. It was hard to believe these were the same two who years ago had locked her in what later became Stephanie's studio so she couldn't tag along to their ball game. She cleared her throat. "Sorry, no air mattress."

Will's shoulders drooped.

"I have one," Treece said. "I'll get it, then we'll go across the hall and set up everything."

Andi didn't argue, and ten minutes later she was settled in her recliner while they worked on getting everything set up. The headache had ebbed after she'd eaten, but it was now back with a vengeance. She took a tablet from the pill bottle she carried, then hesitated. The prescription said one or two as needed for pain, and one wasn't doing the job. After swallowing two pills, she leaned back and waited for the pain to ease.

Once the air mattress was inflated and sheets put on it, Treece dusted her hands. "Done. I'm going to bed."

"I'll go with you and secure your doors and windows," Will said. "Then we'll leave the doors to both apartments open."

Andi glanced at the clock. "Wait, the news is on. Our segment on runaways airs tonight. Let's watch it together."

"And sit where?" Treece said.

Andi really did need to do something with her apartment. Other than the recliner and sofa that now had sheets on it, she had one stool at the bar where she normally ate and a chair at the table where she usually worked at her computer.

"Drag the chair from the table over here by me, and they can sit on the floor," Andi said, nodding toward the men. Treece rolled her eyes but did what Andi said, and she clicked on the TV just as the ten o'clock anchor welcomed the viewers.

A twinge of jealousy pierced Andi's heart. Snagging an anchor spot was her goal, Treece's too, but she didn't see one opening up anytime soon at the station. The investigative pieces they did together were going to get them noticed and into bigger markets.

Fifteen minutes into the news, their segment with Andi interviewing a girl of sixteen aired. She was in silhouette with her voice disguised, and under Andi's questioning, she told how she started doing drugs at thirteen and ran away from home when she was barely fourteen. At the end of the segment, she thanked Andi and Treece for rescuing her from the streets.

"Wow," Will said. "Powerful stuff."

The admiration in Will's eyes tightened her chest, making it hard to breathe. "Thanks. Treece is a genius at editing. She knows just how to frame the segments."

Andi high-fived her friend even as she tried to figure out why Will was having such an effect on her. Must be from getting knocked in the head.

"It's good reporting," Brad said. "You do good sometimes, Squirt."

She made a face at him. He'd called her Squirt since she was old enough to tag along after him.

"Would you two consider coming down to the street mission where I volunteer and talking to the girls?" Will asked.

She'd forgotten he volunteered at the mission. "Sure."

"Set it up and give us a call," Treece said.

Andi nodded in agreement as her friend stood, and Will walked her to the door.

"See you in the morning," Treece said.

It was time for her to hit the sack too, and she climbed out of the recliner. On impulse, she hugged her brother. "Thanks for being here for me."

"I hope you know I've always got your back," he said.

Were those tears in his eyes? "I know, and sometimes I make that hard. I'll try to do better."

Her cell phone rang. Andi glanced at the ID. The station manager? "I'll take this in my bedroom."

Once in her room, she answered. "Hollister."

"Andi, there's a girl on another line saying she needs to talk to you. Won't say what it's about other than mumbling something about the runaway segment that just aired. Can I give her your cell number?"

"Of course." It wasn't uncommon to get calls after one of their segments aired. A minute later, her cell phone rang again, and she answered. "This is Andi Hollister. How can I help you?"

"Uh . . ." Silence stretched over the airways. "C-can you h-help me? I saw your program and how you helped that other girl."

"Are you a runaway?"

"No . . . yes . . . but . . . he promised me a modeling job. Two days later, he had me stripping and . . ."

Andi pressed her fingers to her temple, trying to ease the throbbing in her head. She didn't want to deal with this right now.

"I'm scared."

Fear in the girl's voice raised goose bumps on Andi's arm. "What's your name?"

"Chloe."

"Would you like me to help you get back home, Chloe?"

"No!"

Nothing was ever simple. "What do you want then?"

"I . . . want off the streets."

The pounding in Andi's head intensified. "Are you downtown?"

"Most of the time."

"Go to the mission—it's close to the Greyhound bus station."

"He'll find me and kill me if I do. I gotta get out of Memphis, and you helped that other girl to get away. Will you help me?"

Andi pinched the bridge of her nose. "Why did you call *me?*"

"Because . . ." Chloe took a jerky breath. "On the news, when you talked to that girl, you cared. It showed in your eyes. I don't trust anyone else. If you'll help me, I'll do an interview for you warning girls not to run away—but only if you can disguise my voice."

Another interview would be great, but that was not why she would help her. She did care. Too much, maybe. Which meant she had to do it. "When?"

"I'm working on Beale tomorrow night near the clubs on the east end. And if you bring any cops, you won't see me. He'll find out and kill me."

"Why not tonight?"

"Can't leave where I am. Tomorrow night. Nine o'clock at the corner of Beale and Third—there's a park." She caught her breath. "Gotta go. This guy's waking up."

The line went dead. Andi couldn't tell the girl's age from her husky voice. *She wants out.* And somehow, Andi would help her.

— 6 —

At eight o'clock Wednesday morning, David Raines picked up Will Kincade's folder and perused it one last time, satisfied with the choice he'd made.

"You wanted to see me, sir?"

He looked up. "Yes. Have a seat."

David placed the folder on the stack on the corner of his desk. He studied Will as the lanky detective sat in the straight-back chair and clasped his hands together. The sergeant's only sign of nervousness came from the way he pressed one thumb against the other. Time to put the man out of his misery. "As I'm sure you already know, you've been chosen to join the Cold Case Unit. This just makes it official."

A grin the size of Texas spread across Will's face. "Thank you, sir! And nothing is certain until it's official."

"You earned it."

Will was the first addition to the unit, and David hoped there would be more, but it depended on funding. He had several officers in mind who shared his passion for seeing that families received closure and justice for their murdered relatives. And Will did that. "Do you have any cases that need to be wrapped up?"

"Only one from last night I was assisting Brad Hollister with."

David nodded. Eventually, he hoped Brad Hollister would be one of the officers he added to his unit. "Good. Can you turn it over to him? Administration okayed you starting today. Take an hour and move your stuff to the desk in the next room, and then we'll meet in the conference room."

A slow grin crossed Will's face. "It won't take an hour."

David chuckled. "Then get a cup of coffee when you get your desk cleared. Harper retired, and I need to pick up his cases."

"Uh, sir. I'd like to talk to you about a case I'd like to work on—"

"Hold it until our meeting in an hour."

Will stood and extended his hand. "Thank you, sir."

"We're going to be spending a lot of time together. I may be your superior, but 'sir' and 'lieutenant' will get old quick," he said and accepted Will's hand.

"Yes, sir—uh . . . that may take some getting used to."

"Fine, just make it quick. And you can leave the door open on your way out."

After Will left, David opened the file cabinet to pull a folder he needed to drop off when he picked up the retired detective's cases. The Cold Case Unit received cases only after a detective either died on the job or retired. Otherwise, a detective's cases stayed with him until they were solved.

A throat cleared behind him, and he turned around. A mere slip of a woman stood in the doorway, loose gray curls framing her face. "May I help you?"

"I hope so. My name is Mae Shelton. Will Kincade is my nephew."

Her voice held the genteel Southern accent of the older generation, and he nodded. "Will isn't here. You just missed him."

"I know. I saw him when I got off the elevator, but I wasn't up to talking to him." She pinned him with eyes the color of steel. "I understand that he's likely to join your cold case team."

"Yes. We just made it official." David waited, uncertain where this was going.

"My son is Jimmy Shelton. He was convicted seventeen years ago for a murder he didn't commit."

Her reason for coming became clearer. He

motioned for her to sit in the chair Will had vacated. Unfortunately, the only thing he could offer her was a sympathetic ear.

"Thank you, Lieutenant." The soft-spoken woman leaned forward. "I know this isn't exactly a cold case, but I thought . . ." She took a deep breath. "My boy was framed and wrongly convicted of Stephanie Hollister's murder."

Stephanie Hollister . . . Jimmy Shelton. Hollister? Brad Hollister's sister? Details of the case flooded his mind . . .

David had been the first officer to arrive on the scene eighteen years ago. He'd been a rookie patrolman, and his main duty had been to take charge of the gun that Jimmy Shelton still held in his hand. Then he'd moved the woman and her daughter out of the small house where they had discovered the body. Once the homicide detective arrived and David had given his report, he left the scene.

He sighed. "It's really not a cold case since your son confessed to the murder."

She shook her head, the gray curls bouncing. "My boy was too intoxicated to know whether he killed Stephanie Hollister or not. Will went with me to see Jimmy in jail that night—he never remembered us being there. So I know somebody put words in his mouth. And he never signed the confession."

He wished she wouldn't look at him with such

hope in her face. "I don't know how I can help you—unless new evidence surfaces."

"Will is really good at detective work—you made a good choice adding him to your team. I thought with him working with you, maybe he could investigate the files, find out what really happened that night. I know my boy didn't kill anyone."

He leaned back in his chair. "There's not much anyone can do in a case like this." Jimmy Shelton would have been executed years ago, except for the automatic appeal process.

"But he didn't do it."

"The victim had a restraining order—your son wasn't even supposed to be at her house."

Her body sagged like an inflatable toy that had lost its air. Then, she took a breath and straightened her shoulders. "That girl was doing something she shouldn't have been. Drugs . . . something, and she was afraid Jimmy would find out."

Mrs. Shelton was grasping at the wind. Trouble was, he knew how she felt. He'd grasped at the wind often enough trying to discover who killed his wife. "It wasn't drugs. None were found in her body, and the home was clean. Not even marijuana."

He held the gaze she pinned him with, then with a sigh, she stood. "I won't take any more of your time, Lieutenant."

His heart broke for her. He'd heard the ban on executions had been lifted, and no mother ever got ready for a child's death. He scrambled to his feet and walked around his desk.

"I wish I could help you," he said, taking her papery, dry hand. Though the woman was probably only in her late sixties, she appeared as old and frail as his ninety-two-year-old grandmother. "I promise you, if *any* new evidence surfaces that points to your son's innocence, I'll reopen the case."

She squeezed his hand. "Thank you, but you better hurry."

After Mrs. Shelton left, he picked up the folder he'd laid down. He wished he could help her, but . . . maybe he'd discuss it with Will.

It didn't take Will half an hour to clear out his desk and set up the one in the room next to David. He grabbed a cup of coffee and hurried to the briefing room in case his boss had returned.

Even though the room was empty, Will took a seat at the table. Judging by all the folders spread on the table, David had been here. If it weren't for this thing with Jimmy, he'd be pinching himself to make sure he wasn't dreaming. He'd slept little all night, and what should have been an exciting day now took second place. *"I didn't kill Stephanie."*

Jimmy's words echoed even now through his mind. If Walter Simmons hadn't confirmed the letter, Will didn't know if he would have believed his cousin. His whole body itched to get to Riverbend to talk to Jimmy. He hoped David would be receptive to looking into the case.

The door opened, and Reggie Lane said, "Brad said I'd find you here. He told me about the break-in at his sister's. He said Treece was okay. Do you think she'll be safe there?"

"Brad's contacting someone today about a security system, so she should be. Why don't you call her?"

A dark blush crawled up Reggie's face as he stepped into the room and closed the door. "She won't take my calls."

"Sorry, man." A month ago, Treece and Reggie had been on track to get married, and Will didn't know what had happened to derail everything. "What happened with you two, anyway?"

He ducked his head. "I gave her an ultimatum. Quit her job when we get married."

Will sucked air through his teeth. "I thought you knew better than to ever give a woman that kind of ultimatum."

"I do." Reggie scrubbed his jaw. "It just came out of my mouth right after Andi got herself roughed up interviewing that dope dealer. Treece was in full mother-hen mode. Those two are tight. Treece thinks she has to watch over Andi."

Will knew the feeling. "I hope you two work this out."

"Me too. I'm sending her flowers again this afternoon with another apology. But as long as she thinks she has to look after Andi, we'll have trouble. If only there was someone else watching Andi's back, Treece might listen to me." Reggie's eyes narrowed. "You're sweet on her—why don't you do it?"

Will held up his hand. "No way. That would be a full-time job." Heat burned his neck. "And I'm not sweet on her."

"You're lying, man. I've seen the way you look when she stops by to see Brad. And now—your face is beet red."

Will laughed out loud. "Whatever, man. Brad's my best friend, and you know my history with women. Dating his sister would be a disaster, especially when we broke up—it always happens. Besides, it'd take someone a whole lot stronger than I am to convince her to quit sticking her neck out."

The door opened again, and David stepped inside. "Oh good, you're here. Morning, Reggie."

"Morning, sir. I'm just leaving," Reggie said. He stopped at the door. "Think about what I said."

"Don't you have work to do?" Will called after Reggie and then turned his attention to the lieutenant as he sat at the table and snapped open his briefcase. Time to focus.

"We won't meet here regularly," David said, "only when we need more room to work on a case, and you can choose your first one from the stacks of folders in the storage room. Unfortunately, you have plenty to choose from."

"Which ones are top priority?"

"All of them. Families want answers, and so do we. It's one reason I chose you. That and because of your extraordinary ability to sort out facts and get answers."

Will's face grew hot under the praise. "Thank you," he mumbled.

"That's why I'm not going to tell you *how* to investigate your case. Once you choose a case, I do suggest that you take a look at the original investigating officer." David leaned back in his chair. "We've all known investigators who don't follow up on clues like they should."

"Lazy ones," Will said. He'd known a few of the detectives the lieutenant referred to.

"That's about it for orientation. Any questions?" David looked expectantly at him.

"Sir, what if a case isn't officially a cold case?"

"Sir? I thought we covered that."

"Sorry—it'll take awhile."

David nodded. "Now, what were you asking?"

Will explained about Lacey Wilson's death and the call from Jimmy and how she was going to visit his cousin at Riverbend. "Like I said earlier, the Wilson case isn't really mine, and my cousin's case isn't officially a cold case, but if it's true he didn't kill Stephanie Hollister, there's not much time to find the person who did. His execution date is in four days."

David rubbed his jaw. "Actually, that's the case I wanted to discuss with you. Your aunt came to see me right after you left earlier. She—"

"Excuse me for interrupting, but did you say my aunt came to see you?" Aunt Mae never mentioned stopping in to see David when she called while he was getting coffee. Maybe because she'd been so busy telling him his mother was back in town and wanted to see him. That wasn't happening. "What did she want?"

"To tell me I made a smart choice picking you," he said.

Will felt his face grow hot again. "I'm sorry."

"Nothing to be sorry for. Your aunt seems like a fine Southern lady. She asked if you could investigate the case. She believes her son was framed."

"I agree with her, especially after the letter Jimmy received. I'd like to look into the matter."

"I told her if anything turned up, I'd investigate." David braced his hand on the table and stood. "So, let's check it out."

"Thank you." He caught himself before he said sir. "Since you've okayed it, I'm going to the prison to take a look at the letter and see what Jimmy knows about Lacey Wilson. Would you be interested in going with me?"

David shook his head. "Wish I could, but I have a meeting with the police director. But keep me in the loop."

Will assured him he would. Once he stepped out into the hallway, he called the prison to let them know he was coming to see Jimmy around one, and would they please let him know.

Then he dialed Brad. "Raines said I could investigate the letter Jimmy received," he said when Brad answered. "Want to ride along?"

"I wish I could, but I'm on my way to court to testify in a murder case."

Court cases were the bane of a policeman's life. Will didn't look forward to the drive to Nashville with nothing but his thoughts . . . that were sure to include his mother.

"Don't you think you're wasting your time?"

It was plain that was what his friend thought. They needed to talk about this case in depth, but not over the phone. "All I want is justice. And to make sure that no one gets away with murder," he said. "Besides, Jimmy is my cousin, and if there's any possibility he's innocent . . . well, if he is innocent, don't you want to know?"

Seconds ticked off. "Yeah. That's what I want too. Text me as soon as you see that letter."

"I will." He and Brad were like brothers, and Will hoped reopening his sister's case wouldn't put a strain on their friendship.

— 7 —

On the elevator ride to the first floor of the Criminal Justice Center, Will's heart skipped a beat. He'd promised he'd let Andi know what David said about reopening the case. But that could wait until he returned.

If she knew he was definitely going to Nashville, it would be next to impossible to keep her from accompanying him. And a three-hour trip alone with Andi Hollister was the last thing he needed. He didn't know when or how it had happened, but his feelings for his best friend's sister had changed. And he didn't know what to do about it.

If he acted on his feelings and she didn't reciprocate . . . or what if she did? Will's history with women was legendary among the cops he worked with—two dates and the relationship was over, usually because the chemistry just wasn't there. Brad knew all this, and he wouldn't want Andi's heart broken.

Will wasn't about to add that strain to his friendship with Brad. The elevator opened on the first floor, and he strode to the front door. But who said Andi would even date him?

Just as he walked out of the brick building into the cold bright morning, a microphone appeared out of nowhere. "Sergeant Kincade, what can you tell us about the death of Lacey Wilson? Is it true she had information pertaining to a case from eighteen years ago?"

He blinked in the sunlight and stepped back. Andi, dressed in a soft pink sweater that belied her aggressive questions, waited for an answer. And even though her ambush irritated him, he couldn't keep his heart from flopping around in his chest at the sight of her.

"No comment," he said and tried to walk away, but Andi and her cameraman kept up with him. He wheeled around. "Turn that off," he said, pointing to the camera. After this, no way was he taking her to the prison where Jimmy was housed.

Andi nodded to the guy behind the camera. "That's okay, Chris. Let me wrap the segment, then you can pack up your equipment and head back to the station."

She looked into the camera. "As you can see, Sergeant Kincade prefers not to discuss the case. But we'll be here when he does. This is Andi Hollister reporting from the Criminal Justice Center for WLTZ News."

When Chris lowered his camera, she said, "At least we got a 'no comment' this time."

Will had kept walking, but he stopped and turned around. "Brad wouldn't even give you a 'no comment'?"

She narrowed her eyes at him. "Have you talked to him?"

"Not about you. I just know him. If you attacked him like you did me . . ." He shrugged, then turned and walked toward the crosswalk to the parking garage where he'd left his car. It was impossible to ignore her as she ran to catch him.

"Are you going to the prison to see your cousin?"

He kept walking, and she caught up with him at the light. For a second, he thought about jay-walking. "I am."

"I want to go with you."

"Nope. Don't need a reporter tagging along."

"Come on, Will. I don't believe there's any letter, and if there is, it's probably a fake. But I want to see for myself."

"Don't you have a newscast to do?"

"Nope. I'm not the anchor, and until Lacey's death is ruled a homicide, I don't have anything to report."

Part of him wanted to relent. The drive to Nashville on I-40 was boring, something Andi was not. He wavered, remembering the thirteen-year-old Andi the night her sister was murdered. Pale with a blue tinge to her lips and fingernails, tears spilling from her huge brown eyes.

"All right," he said, huffing the words out. "But anything we talk about has to be off the record."

"No problem. I promise."

86

She held his gaze with those incredible eyes as a puff of April wind brought the fragrance of her jasmine perfume. He swallowed hard. "My car is in the garage. Yours?"

Her lip twitched. "I rode with my cameraman."

He turned without answering and strode inside the garage to his Ford Escape.

Andi glanced in the side mirror, checking for a dark SUV with tinted windows. None that she could see. She turned to Will, who was drumming the steering wheel. "Any leads on the man who broke in to my apartment?"

His fingers stilled. "No. None of your neighbors saw anything. You and Treece really need to leave your outside lights on."

"Believe me, we will," she said. The skin on her neck tingled, and she pulled the sun visor down, checking the traffic in the mirror again. "Can you tell if anyone is following us?"

"Haven't seen anyone suspicious, and I've been watching."

"Do you think it was a mistake? That he broke into the wrong house?"

He glanced over at her. "What do you think?"

"It's what I want to believe." Andi glanced in the side mirror again. "But he was so insistent that I had his diamonds."

Anxiety squeezed her chest, and she sucked in a deep breath. She had to refocus. Fear would only freeze her mind, and she didn't have time for that. Right now, she was safe with Will.

Refocus. Relax.

An incoming text dinged, and she read it. So much for getting her mind off the break-in. "Brad says the security system is in place, and that it's hooked in to the police station."

"Good. That relieves my mind."

"Mine too." Gingerly, she smoothed her hair over the stitches in her head, remembering the wave of fear that had washed over her when she woke this morning. Maybe she needed to talk about her feelings a little. "I didn't know what a number someone breaking in to your house could do to you."

"Violated is how I've heard victims describe their feelings."

"Yes! That's exactly it." It'd been the same when Stephanie was killed, only worse, and in two hours she would be confronting the man convicted of killing her sister. Her thoughts jumped on another merry-go-round.

What if Jimmy didn't kill Steph? She shook that question off. He killed her. Why else would he confess?

But what if he hadn't? It would mean Steph's murderer was running around free while an innocent man faced death. Her heart raced at the questions that wouldn't go away. It was why she was in a car with Will Kincade driving down

I-40 to Nashville. "Do you think the letter is legitimate?"

Her words sounded loud in the car, and Will jumped. "Sorry," she said. "Didn't mean to startle you."

"You didn't. I was thinking about something else, that's all, and you jumped subjects. You have a habit of doing that, you know. But to answer your question, I don't know."

What could he have been thinking about? Maybe his last girlfriend? Brad had mentioned at dinner a couple of weeks ago that Will was seeing some secretary. "Having trouble with your latest conquest?"

"What?" He shot a quick look at her.

Heat flushed her face. What a dumb thing to say. "Never mind."

"If you must know, my mother is back in town."

"Oh. Are you going to see her?" Andi didn't know why she was glad he wasn't thinking about a girlfriend.

"No. Cass won't be here long. Never is. Unless her last husband dumped her, then she might stay a month." His jaw tightened. "If you don't mind, let's talk about something else."

"Sure." She didn't know the whole story behind Will living with his aunt and uncle instead of his mother when he was growing up. But it must be bad for him to always call her Cass, never Mother or Mom.

89

She searched for something to say, but her mind blanked. Jimmy. They could talk about him. "Let's suppose this letter your cousin received is real—not that I think it is, but just suppose. Why do you think he confessed to a crime he didn't commit?"

This time Will laughed out loud. "That's the third time you've switched subjects in five minutes."

"Well, at least I got a laugh out of you."

"Yeah. Jimmy," he said. "Are we still on that subject?"

"Yes."

"Why did he confess?" Will sucked in a deep breath. "Eighteen years ago, Jimmy had a bad alcohol problem. So bad that even though he was crazy-drunk when they arrested him, he was still on his feet—his body had built up a tolerance to high levels of alcohol. I went with my aunt to see him in jail after they arrested him, and he never remembered us being there. I don't think there's anything he actually remembers about that night."

She wished she didn't. "Mom and I had gone to tell Stephanie that the doctor had agreed to waive his fee for my surgery."

Her sister had been so worried that without insurance, Andi might not get the heart operation she needed. She turned and stared out the window at the newly leafed trees whizzing by. A warm

March had given them an early start on spring. The dogwoods and wild plum trees were in full bloom against a backdrop of every shade of green from chartreuse to deep green. She chewed on her bottom lip. A freeze was predicted for tonight. Tomorrow all the blooms would be dirty brown.

JD flipped through the small black notebook once more and placed it on the padded yellow envelope he'd taken it from. He'd coaxed Lacey into telling him that she'd found the journal after Stephanie died. She was packing up her stuff to move out of the house, found the journal, and kept it. But there were at least five pages of Stephanie's journal missing. Where could Lacey have hidden them? What if she'd mailed them to someone?

He'd found the letter addressed to Andi Hollister and burned it.

"Alfie" played from the music station on his TV, and with his feet on the desk and his eyes closed, he released his mind to search for the answer that didn't come. The music soothed his anxiety, and he hummed along to the melody.

At dinner the other night, Lacey had been close to losing it, but he never dreamed she'd spill her guts to Andi in letters he'd found crumpled in the wastebasket. How Lacey had written Jimmy, but he hadn't responded, and before she left the country, she wanted to tell Andi that Jimmy hadn't killed her sister. At least she hadn't said who had.

Her last words wouldn't make sense to anyone but him. *You have diamonds in your possession.* Lacey hadn't finished the sentence, and in his mind, he could see her scribbling lines through the words and crumpling the letter into a ball. He figured she'd decided to tell Andi in person.

He'd wasted valuable time searching for the missing journal pages. Lacey claimed she didn't know their whereabouts, but he didn't believe her. They hadn't been anywhere in the house.

He should have killed her earlier this year when she got religion.

A cell phone in his desk rang, and he opened the drawer and took out the burner phone, recognizing the number. "Hello."

"You told me if Jimmy Shelton ever got any unusual mail to call you."

"Yes?" Over the past seventeen years, he'd paid different guards a hundred dollars a month to keep tabs on Shelton, and this was the fifth time he'd heard from one of them. The other four times had been inconsequential. With four days to go, he hoped that was the case now.

"Shelton received a letter from a Lacey Wilson, and she told him he didn't kill somebody named Stephanie."

The bottom dropped out of his stomach. He gripped the phone. "Where is the letter now?"

"I'm looking at it."

His hand relaxed. "I want it."

"I figured you would." The caller cleared his throat. "It's going to cost a little more than a hundred dollars, though."

"I see." He swiveled in his chair to turn down the music. "How much?"

"I figure twenty grand ought to cover it."

"That sounds fair." He smiled as silence filled the airwaves. The guard was probably kicking himself for not asking for more. "Can you bring it to Memphis?"

"Sure. I'll fake a stomach problem and get off work. Take me probably three hours to get there."

"No need to take off work—I can't meet you right now. Bring it after your shift ends. I'll meet you part of the way—there's a truck stop at exit 126 that will only take you two hours to reach. What will you be driving?"

"A white Silverado."

"Until nine, then."

He disconnected and tapped the phone as the music from *Alfie* segued into the theme from *The Godfather.*

— 8 —

"Looks like road construction ahead," Andi said as they passed a billboard proclaiming sizzling bacon and hearty biscuits, reminding her she hadn't eaten breakfast.

"I've never driven I-40 when there wasn't work going on," Will said. "Tell me something."

"Depends on what it is."

He laughed. "How did you get into news journalism?"

She sat back in the seat, memories of Stephanie warming her.

"In one of our last 'sister' talks, I told Steph I wanted to be a flight attendant like her, and she flipped out." Andi smiled at the memory. "Said she'd wring my neck if I didn't go to college and get my degree in broadcast journalism." She glanced toward Will. "She's the reason I'm a television reporter."

"I didn't know that."

"Yeah. This movie came out about an ambitious reporter about a year before she . . ." Andi bit her lip. It was so hard to say that she died. "Anyway, Steph said if she could go back a few years, that's what she'd go to college for."

Will frowned. "It wasn't too late then."

"She thought it was—said by the time she

graduated, she'd be too old to break into the business. Steph would have wanted to go all the way to the top, and since she couldn't . . ."

He shook his head. "You can't live someone else's life."

"I'm not." His skeptical glance sent a wave of protest through her. "Being a newscaster is what I want to do. And keep your eyes on the road."

"You scare me sometimes the way you go after a story," Will said. "Like when you interviewed that gang leader."

"He offered, said he wanted to let people know he wasn't all bad, that a gang was like a family. Then he blew up on camera." Adrenaline had been what got her through the interview. Her knees had knocked so hard, she'd been afraid the guy she was interviewing would hear them. "Treece was my cameraman then, but I'm going to get someone else for the edgy interviews. It's causing trouble between her and Reggie."

"Yeah, I know." He tapped his fingers on the steering wheel again. "Why do you take such risks, anyway?"

"To get a story that's unique. No pain, no gain." That wasn't totally true. Sometimes she took risks because she wanted to help someone, like the girl she helped get off the streets, and like tonight when she would meet Chloe. Even though Andi knew it would be dangerous, the girl wanted out, and she had to help her.

"I thought 'no pain, no gain' applied to exercise," he said.

Will's dry humor was one of the things she'd always liked about him. She flicked her gaze toward him, and an unexpected tingle shot through her as she studied his profile.

He wasn't pretty-boy handsome, but there was something about his face that drew her. He had a rugged appeal with his square jaw and high cheekbones and longer-than-usual hair that curled over his ears.

"When did you bleach your hair?"

"Subject jumping again."

"Sorry. But when?"

"A couple of months ago when I worked vice." He finger-combed his hair. "Haven't had time to get it cut, either." Will flicked on the left turn signal and went around a smoke-belching pickup.

She let a few miles pass by in silence as he navigated through roadwork, but at least it broke the monotony of the interstate that made the trip seem to take forever. "How much farther?"

"Probably another hour."

She settled back. "Do you remember that Easter egg hunt when you stole my eggs?"

"I didn't steal your eggs. Brad did."

She thought that would get a rise out of him. "But you didn't stop him."

"I can't believe you're holding that against me!"

"Oh yeah. That time ranks right up there with the time you and Brad locked me in Stephanie's studio so I wouldn't follow you to your ball game." Andi almost laughed at seeing red crawl up his neck into his face.

"I don't think I want to travel memory lane."

"Okay, but just so you know, you two are the reason I don't like places I can't get out of."

He flashed a quick look her way. "I am sorry about that." Then he tilted his head toward her while he kept his eyes on the road. "Why do you want to leave Memphis?"

"I don't, but it's the only way I can get ahead in this business. Anchor spots are hard to come by in Memphis and take more years than I want to invest. That's one of the reasons Treece and I are making documentaries—to get noticed by the news networks."

A billboard advertised a Subway shop at the next exit, and she said, "How about stopping for a sandwich? There's a food court five miles down the road."

"Sounds good."

Pain radiated from her back to her hip, and Andi rummaged through her bag for her pain medication. When she found the bottle, she shook two tablets into her hand. The one tablet she'd taken just before she left for work hadn't eased the pain. She really needed to get that disc fixed.

"What are you taking?" Will asked.

Andi lifted her water bottle to her lips and washed down the pills. "Something for my back."

"Ibuprofen?"

"Something a little bit stronger." She hoped he didn't ask *how* much stronger.

"Has this been going on for a while?"

"A few months. Ever since I climbed over a fence to get a story on a dog chained out in the cold weather."

He shook his head. "Well, you need to get it fixed—and stop taking so many risks."

"You sound like my mother and Treece. I plan to get a nerve block as soon as I can get an appointment. Would you hurry up? I'm hungry."

By the time they'd finished lunch, Andi was ready to tackle anything, even confessing to Will that the pills were prescription. Almost. She hated lying, even by omission, and she knew when she didn't say it was a prescription pain reliever, he automatically thought of something like Advil. But neither did she want another lecture. Besides, the doctor prescribed them and she knew what she was doing. She wasn't about to get addicted to the pills. They helped her anxiety too, and she certainly needed something for that right now.

The closer they came to Riverbend, the sweatier her hands became. She wiped them on legs that wouldn't stop jiggling and focused on the letter.

If it was real . . . No, she wouldn't go there

yet. "Will we have trouble seeing your cousin on such short notice?"

"No," Will said. "I called ahead and requested an interview, citing Jimmy's connection to a murder investigation."

"Will we be in the same room with him?"

"I have been in the past when I visited, but I'm not sure, since you're with me. It'll either be a small conference room or one with glass between us. Jimmy has a Level A classification."

"What does that mean?"

"He's not violent and can move about without restraints."

"On death row?"

"Every prison is different, but if a prisoner proves he's trustworthy, he gets benefits. Even on death row."

Her stomach rebelled at that news. She didn't want to be that close to the man who'd murdered her sister. *What if he didn't?* But he did. She kept swinging back and forth on that. And at this moment in time, she didn't think anything he said, or even showed her, would change her mind. "How does a murderer get labeled non-violent?"

"He's never given any trouble. Jimmy never was a violent person, but he would defend himself when he had to. Unfortunately, not too long before Stephanie's murder, he was in a barroom fight, and the other person hit his head on the corner of a table and ended up in a coma. The prosecutor didn't buy his defense plea and neither did the judge he went before. He should have asked for a jury trial."

"So that was why he was charged with capital murder in Stephanie's case?"

"Yeah." Will gripped the steering wheel. "If it hadn't been for the felony conviction, he couldn't have been charged with capital murder. But the DA was young and newly elected. Out to prove himself."

Andi had never considered that Jimmy could have been charged with something other than capital murder. "Did you know that the current DA, Laura Delaney, was one of the women who lived in the house with Stephanie?"

"You're kidding."

"No. I don't know her well at all, and we've never discussed Stephanie. I've thought about asking her questions, but . . ." Andi shrugged. "She seems kind of distant."

It wasn't long before they exited off the interstate and arrived at the prison. When they finally were escorted to a room, Jimmy Shelton was already there, waiting. In her mind all these years, he'd been the good-looking former athlete who rode a Harley, and his appearance now shocked her. His once-shaggy hair was now close-cropped and mostly gray, washing out his pasty skin. When he looked her way, his faded gray eyes had the look of someone whose dog had just died.

"You wasted your time," Jimmy said, his voice flat, unemotional. "The letter is gone."

"What do you mean, the letter is gone?" Will said. How could it have disappeared? Unless it never existed."

"Someone took it."

Will balled his hands. "How could anyone do that?"

Jimmy rolled his eyes and scanned the room. "You have to ask? This is a prison, not Sunday school."

Andi stepped forward. "Where is the corrections officer Will talked to on the phone? Can we talk to him?"

Jimmy turned and stared at her. Recognition lit his eyes. "Andi?" He gave a slight shake of his head. "You're all grown up."

"Can we talk to the CO who called last night?" Will repeated Andi's words.

"Walter Simmons?" Jimmy's shoulders slumped. "He won't be on until tonight at seven, and it could be his night off."

"Did anyone else see the letter?" Will asked.

"Of course. All mail is scanned for contraband to make sure no one is trying to break out."

"Maybe we could talk to whoever takes care of that," Andi said.

Will shook his head. "I doubt the letter would be remembered. There are eight hundred inmates who receive daily mail. Our time will be better spent talking to the CO who called."

Jimmy frowned. "Why is seeing the letter so important? Why don't you just ask Lacey?"

Silence descended into the room.

"What are you not telling me?"

"Lacey Wilson is dead," Andi said. "Murdered last night."

"Or she committed suicide," Will added.

What little color had been in his cousin's face drained away as he closed his eyes. "And without the letter, you don't believe me," he said.

"It doesn't matter whether we believe you or not—without it, there's nothing to work with."

"It matters to me. Do you or don't you believe me?"

Will held his cousin's blunt stare. "Before I tell you, why did you confess?"

Jimmy put his hands on the table. "That detective . . . he kept saying over and over again that I did it. I didn't remember anything . . . I just wanted him to shut up. To get off my back. My attorney had it suppressed, but until the letter from Lacey came, I believed I must have killed Stephanie."

"And now?" Andi asked. She sat in the chair beside Will and leaned toward Jimmy. "Did you kill my sister?"

He ran his tongue over his lips. "I thought I did. It's why I never really fought the conviction, other than to go through the automatic legal process and a couple of appeals my public defender insisted on. But now, I just don't know anymore.

"When I read Lacey's letter, something clicked inside me. For years I've had this dream, a nightmare, really. Stephanie and I are in her studio, and I hear her yelling." He squeezed his eyes shut. "But lately, I don't think I'm the one yelling back."

"Was someone else there?"

"I don't know. In the dream, there's someone in the shadows." He dropped his head.

Jimmy didn't kill Stephanie. The thought took root in Will's heart and settled there. "You asked if I believed you."

Jimmy lifted his head, hope stamped in the lines of his face.

"I do."

Jimmy sagged back against the chair. "Thank you. At least there's that, but without the letter . . ."

"We'll just have to work harder and quicker." Will turned to Andi. "Are you in?"

She gazed at Jimmy like she was searching for something.

"I can't believe I'm saying this, but I'm in. The coincidences of Lacey's death and the letter have raised enough doubt to make me question what I believed." She turned to Jimmy. "I'm not saying I believe you're innocent. I just want to know the truth. So, let's go find the officer who saw the letter."

"Let's finish here first." Will took out a notebook. "Do you remember what the letter said?"

Jimmy closed his eyes. "Not word for word. It was on blue paper, and she had pretty handwriting. At first she talked about being Stephanie's roommate and that I might not remember her. But I did. She was always nice to me, even when I was drunk." He pressed his fingertips against his eyes. "If only I'd quit drinking."

"What else did it say?" Andi asked.

"She apologized for not coming forward sooner and then said she'd become a Christian." He inhaled deeply and blew the breath out.

"Anything else?" Will asked.

"She asked for my forgiveness, then she said I didn't kill Stephanie."

"If only we had that letter," Andi muttered.

Defeat etched Jimmy's face as he slumped in the chair. "So, other than Walter Simmons, there's no proof of anything I've said." Suddenly he jerked upright. "Wait! After you hung up, Walter took a picture of the letter with his phone. It was blurry, and he took another one, but it wasn't any better. He said maybe his granddaughter would help him get the picture to you. That maybe you could fix it."

Will checked his phone. "He didn't send it." He stood. "We'll find him and get the photo he took. Can you write down a list of people Stephanie hung around with eighteen years ago?"

"You think someone close to her killed her?"

"That's usually the case. Do you remember who any of her friends were?"

"Yeah. Do you have a pen?"

Will handed him his pen and notebook. A minute later, Jimmy looked up.

"This last person—Jared Donovan—was pretty serious about Steph. Told me to leave her alone, that he was going to marry her." He handed Will the notebook back.

"This is a start," Will said. "Keep thinking and write down anything you remember. I'll be back, maybe Friday, but I'll be in touch."

"Wait. There's something else I want you to do."

Will sat back down.

"One of Stephanie's roommates is a lawyer." Jimmy shifted his gaze to Andi. "You might remember her—Madeline Starr?"

"Maggie?" Andi asked.

Jimmy nodded vigorously. "Yes, that's her."

Will looked from Andi to his cousin. "Do you think she'll remember you?"

"I hope so," Jimmy said. "She's the one who got another prisoner freed from death row. I want you to contact her, see if she will take my case."

"Let me go with you," Andi said. "I know a softer side of Maggie Starr."

"Deal." Will leaned back. He'd gotten to know Maggie when he helped Brad mow the yard at the Hollisters' east Memphis house. He couldn't believe this Maggie, the quiet, easygoing college girl five years his senior, was the bulldog attorney.

But if anyone could get Jimmy off of death row, it would be Madeline Starr. He nodded at Andi. "Ready to go?"

"Not quite," Andi said. "I have something to ask Jimmy."

— 9 —

Andi was good at reading people, and she'd been studying Jimmy's body language. So far everything he'd said indicated he wasn't hiding anything. Like now as he sat in front of her, his arms on the table, his gray eyes unguarded.

He was nothing like she had expected. And she certainly hadn't expected him to knock holes in her belief he was guilty.

"What do you want to know?" he asked.

"I want to hear you say you didn't kill my sister."

He tented his hands and rested his chin on his thumbs. Then he shook his head. "I can't. I don't remember." He sighed. "I don't think I killed her, but if I did, I'm willing to pay for it."

Andi stood. At least he was honest, and that made her want to believe that he hadn't murdered her sister. "We'll find the truth."

"And if you didn't kill her," Will said, "someone else did, and they need to pay."

At the door, Andi took one last look at Jimmy. She'd come here believing he'd fabricated the letter; now she wasn't so sure. But what if he was conning them both? And the guard was helping him.

What if he isn't? That would mean there was a strong possibility he didn't kill Steph. Which meant someone had gotten away with her sister's murder. Either way, she wanted the truth, and if the truth was that Jimmy was innocent, they only had a few days to prove it.

Outside the room, she turned to Will. "Can you get the CO's address from the front desk?"

"Someone stole that letter, and it had to be someone from here. I know a better way."

He took out his cell phone and dialed. "Emily, can you get an address for me? Walter Simmons. He's a corrections officer at Riverbend and should live in the Nashville area." He held the phone away. "Emily works in the Department of Motor Vehicles and can find anyone."

After a minute, a grin spread across his face. "Text it to me, and thanks! You're the best."

Five minutes later they were back in Will's Ford Escape, and he was programing the address into his GPS.

"Where does he live?"

"According to this, fifteen minutes away."

The GPS took them to a middle-class neighborhood and to a ranch-style brick home. She followed Will to the door, and they waited for someone to answer the bell.

"Yes?" The African-American woman who answered the door stood as tall as Will's six feet.

"I'm Will Kincade, and this is Andi Hollister." He showed her his badge. "Is Mr. Simmons available?"

"Is something wrong?"

"Oh no, ma'am. Just need to ask him a few questions about a prisoner at Riverbend."

She hesitated. "He's asleep. Didn't get home until nine this morning."

Andi checked her watch. A little after four. Seven hours, but he probably didn't get to sleep right away.

"We wouldn't ask you to disturb him if it wasn't really important that we see him," she said. She gave the woman her most winsome smile, the one she used when she was trying to snag an interview.

"Please, it's very important," Will added.

The dark brown eyes studied them both.

Finally, she nodded. "Would you like to come in while I get him?"

"Thank you," Will said.

Andi followed him inside to the living room, and the aroma of chocolate mingled with something tomatoey. Mrs. Simmons was making supper. How could anyone sleep through that rich smell? A worn Bible lay open on the coffee table, like she'd been reading it before they interrupted her.

On one wall was a mural of a tree with photos hanging from the branches like painted Christmas ornaments. Family members, Andi assumed. She looked closer and widened her eyes. Not just photos of family members but pictures capturing their baptisms.

It had occurred to Andi that maybe Jimmy and this Walter Simmons had concocted the story to buy Jimmy more time, but this house reflected people with integrity. She turned as footsteps approached from the hallway.

"He'll be here as soon as he dresses," his wife said.

Mrs. Simmons's calm demeanor puzzled Andi. Strangers, especially one who was a police officer, wanting to talk to their husbands would annoy most wives or at least make them nervous.

"I'm sorry we have to disturb him," Will said.

"He's off tonight, so he can catch up then," she replied.

"How long has Mr. Simmons worked at Riverbend?" Andi asked.

She lifted her brown eyes toward the ceiling. "Hmm. Junior was ten, and he's thirty-eight now." Her eyes widened. "I can't believe it's been twenty-eight years. My, how time flies."

Andi stared at her. The woman didn't look a day over forty herself. "You have a thirty-eight-year-old son, Mrs. Simmons?"

"And a forty-year-old daughter, but don't ever mention that to her. And call me Rose. Most people who call me Mrs. Simmons are prescribing medicine for me." She turned as a man filled the doorway. "Walter, these are the people who want to talk to you."

Walter Simmons came toward them with an outstretched hand. "What can I do for you?"

"I talked to you last night." Will shook the bear paw of a hand. "Jimmy Shelton is my cousin."

A wide grin spread across Walter's dark face. "Jimmy is a good man. He never killed anyone. I hope that letter will set him free."

Will exchanged glances with Andi. "Unfortunately, the letter is gone, and the woman who sent it is dead."

"What!" Disbelief spread across the older man's face and then hardened into narrow eyes.

"Do you know who might be responsible for stealing the letter?" Will asked.

"I have an idea, but I'd rather not say until I

know for sure. If the person I'm thinking of didn't do it, his reputation would be ruined."

"Jimmy said you snapped a picture of the letter," Andi said.

Walter slipped his cell phone from his back pocket. "It's not much good. Pretty blurry. My fingers are so big, it's hard to hit those little bitty buttons."

Andi looked over Will's shoulder, and her heart sank. Blurry was an understatement. But the letter did appear to be on blue paper like Jimmy said. "Can you do anything with that?" she asked Will.

He bit his lip. "I don't know. Mr. Simmons, may I send this to my phone?"

"Sure. I was going to get my granddaughter to do it tonight."

While Will transferred the photo, Andi turned to the couple. "Mr. Simmons, do you have any vacation time?"

"A couple of weeks."

If whoever murdered Lacey had someone steal the letter, there was no telling what else they might do if they found out Walter had seen it. She eyed them grimly. "This might be a good time to take it."

Andi turned to Will when he pulled in beside her car at the TV station. "Thanks for letting me tag along today."

He put the car in park and opened his door.

"You don't have to get out." Andi checked her watch. Seven fifty-eight. She'd been afraid Mrs. Simmons's insistence that they stay and have a bowl of homemade soup would make her late for the meeting with Chloe, but she had a good hour to get ready for it. The park on Beale Street was only a few blocks away.

"I'm going to check out your car, then follow you home."

That was why she hadn't told Will about the meeting with Chloe. He was like her brother—too protective. She'd thought about it a time or two, but she knew him too well. He'd find a way to keep her from the meeting or would want to go with her, and Chloe had insisted she not bring any cops. No, it was up to Andi to help the girl.

"I'm not going home," she said. "I have work to do here at the station." She pointed to a white Prius next to the building. "And Treece is here. We'll follow each other. And you don't have to worry about someone breaking into the house, since we have the security system. We're safe now."

"At least let me walk you to the door," Will said and climbed out of the car.

"You don't have to do this," she protested when he opened her car door and held out his arm.

"Don't be so stubborn. It's dark out here," he said. "You take too many risks."

"Risks are the price you pay to make a difference," she retorted but allowed him to loop his arm in hers. Sometimes, it was nice to have a knight in shining armor. Especially one with Will's rugged appeal.

At the station door, she turned to him, hoping he didn't want to come inside and hang around. "What time are you going to Lacey's house tomorrow? I'd like to meet you."

"I'm going right now if I can find your brother and get a key. She may have kept a copy of the letter she mailed Jimmy."

"Well, if you go back tomorrow, I'd like to tag along."

"Brad won't like it."

"I have a meeting with the police director in the morning. What if he okays it?"

"Then I won't have a choice, and neither will your brother."

She bumped him with her shoulder. "That's why I made the appointment."

He bumped her back. "Why does that not surprise me?"

Andi keyed in the code for the door, and when she turned back around to thank him, her heart stilled. Even though the overhead light cast his face in shadows, she caught yearning in his eyes. She bit her bottom lip, and for a couple of heartbeats, neither of them spoke.

Lights swung into the parking lot, breaking the spell. Will stepped back. "Well, see you tomorrow. I'll text you the time."

Andi collected herself. "Yeah. Tomorrow."

Inside the station, she walked to her desk, replaying what just happened. Was it possible that Will was interested in her? It seemed like he'd wanted to kiss her just then. Suddenly her steps became lighter.

"You look mighty happy," Treece said when Andi passed her desk.

"What?"

"Nothing. I'll be finished in about fifteen minutes if you want to wait. We can talk about what you learned in Nashville when we get home."

She'd texted Treece on the way to Nashville, but nothing since. "Ah . . . I have a meeting at nine."

"Who with?"

If she told Treece, she might call her brother or Will. "A source."

Treece eyed her. "Why are you being evasive?"

She never kept secrets from Treece. Not when she'd gone to interview the gang lord or when she'd gone to get the video of the dog, or any of the other times most people would've told her she was crazy. Treece understood her.

"A girl called last night after our segment aired. She's a runaway, and like the others we interviewed, she's working the streets. But she wants out. I'm going to meet her near Handy Park and go from there."

Treece's brown eyes didn't waver. "I see. And you plan to go by yourself?"

Andi nodded. "She said not to bring cops. That her pimp would find out and kill her."

"So you're not telling Brad or Will?"

"No. I'm just going to meet her, and if she'll come with me, I'll take her to the apartment. Then I'll tell them." She looked away from her friend's scrutiny. "Look, I know it's dangerous, but Chloe is expecting me. She wants off the streets, and I can't ignore it."

"Chloe, huh? I had a cousin with that name." Treece rubbed her thumb along her jaw. "What time?"

"She'll be there at nine. I planned to be there early." If Treece offered to go with her, she wouldn't turn her down. It was true that Beale Street was a tourist area, but a lone woman wasn't safe anywhere at night anymore. No one would probably bother two women, though.

Her friend heaved an audible sigh. "You know I'm not going to let you go alone."

"Kind of hoped you wouldn't." She rummaged in her purse for the Lortabs she'd put in an ibuprofen bottle. It might be a long night. Once she found it, she shook out two of the pills.

Treece eyed the bottle. "Glad to see you're changing meds. Those Lortabs you were taking were pretty strong."

"They're not that strong—besides, the doctor

gave them to me." She brushed away the guilt that pinged her conscience. "And I'd never get addicted anyway—don't have the addictive personality."

Heat rose in her chest as her friend pinned her with a frown.

"Stronger people than you have become addicted to pain pills. You start out taking only one and then you're taking two and pretty soon two doesn't do it . . . It happens before you realize it."

At nine forty-five, there was still no sign of Chloe—if that was even her name. In fact, there was little activity on Beale Street, probably normal for a Wednesday night. Andi pulled her jacket tighter against the April night and swallowed hard when the full moon disappeared behind a cloud.

She bunched her muscles tight, then released them to fight the anxiety surging through her. Her mouth was dry, but she curbed the impulse to pop another pill. That would only bring another sermon from Treece.

Treece shivered and rubbed her arms. "What was I thinking? Handy Park at night? So help me, Andi Hollister, if you get me killed, I'll never forgive you."

"Come on. She'll walk by, and we'll hustle her in my car. What can go wrong?" If only her insides would quit shaking.

"Are you kidding? A, she's a no-show. B, two women on the wrong end of Beale Street after dark is not smart. How did I let you talk me into this?"

"First of all, you offered. And she wants out, and if I can help her, I will."

The tapping of high heels came from up the street.

"Shh. She's coming."

"Somebody's coming," Treece muttered.

"Andi, are you here?" The disembodied voice sounded like a teenager's.

"Over here." Andi stepped out of the shadows so Chloe could see her and caught her breath. She'd expected a teenager, but not this kid.

Her jaw tightened. She would nail the lowlife who prostituted this young girl no taller than Andi's five-four and who couldn't be over fifteen, if that. She grabbed the girl's hand. "Let's get in my car where we can talk."

"Wait! No! Who's that with you?"

"My friend. Now come on."

"I told you, don't bring anybody. Is she a cop?"

Treece stepped forward. "No, and you're coming with us."

She turned wild eyes toward Treece, then looked over her shoulder. "I gotta go. He'll kill me."

"I'll get you protection," Andi said. She under-stood the girl was afraid, but she'd gotten the courage to call her earlier and ask for help, and Andi wasn't going to let her change her mind now.

Tires squealed, and a dark SUV roared down the street. The girl broke away from them, kicking off her heels as she ran.

"Call 911!" Andi yelled.

She tackled the teenager, and they both hit the ground as bullets sprayed the wall. Treece fell, her phone clattering to the sidewalk. Hot fire seared the top of Andi's arm. The teenager rolled on top of Andi as the car sped away.

Dead silence fell in the wake. Andi shifted under the weight of the girl, wincing at the burning pain in her arm. But at least she was alive. She wasn't so sure about anyone else. "Treece, are you okay?"

No answer. Andi tamped down the bile rising in her throat and slipped out from under Chloe. She turned the girl over and felt for a pulse, her fingers slippery from the girl's blood. Barely there, but she was alive.

Andi turned to Treece, who was struggling to sit up, her skin ashen. "Treece!"

"How's the girl?"

"She's alive. Are you hurt?"

Her friend pressed her arm to her body. "I think I broke my arm when I dove for the pavement."

"I'm so sorry about this."

"You should be."

Andi's heart plummeted until a thin smile curled her friend's lips.

"I offered, remember?"

The teenager groaned. Andi shifted and cradled the girl in her arms. "It's going to be okay, Chloe. Help is almost here. What's your last name?"

"It doesn't matter," she whispered, closing her eyes. Suddenly, her eyes popped open, fear clouding them. "Don't let him find me."

"Who is he?" Andi asked.

The girl's head rolled back, and she slumped in Andi's arms.

— 10 —

Will stepped out of his car and grabbed a light jacket as a cold wind blew down Beale Street. He scanned the area for Andi. He'd barely had time to brief Brad about the trip to Nashville when she called and asked him to come to Handy Park. He certainly hadn't expected to find a crime scene with a half dozen policemen milling around. A uniformed cop double-timed it toward him.

"Andi Hollister is right over here," the officer said. "She wouldn't let me call her brother."

"What happened?"

"Drive-by shooting. Teenage girl took a bullet to the chest. A bullet grazed Andi's arm. And her

119

friend Treece Rogers has a possible broken arm."

"Andi was shot?" His heart nearly stopped. How could all this possibly have happened when he left her only two hours ago? How did anyone get into this much trouble that fast? And what were Andi and Treece doing on East Beale? He'd left her at the TV station.

"She's fine. Bullet barely grazed her arm, and she refused to go to the hospital in an ambulance. Treece is already being treated at the Med. I heard the paramedic say she would be okay. The teenager, though . . . It took a little longer to get her stabilized to transport." Shaking his head, the patrolman turned.

Will followed his gaze to where paramedics loaded a gurney into one of the waiting ambulances.

"It doesn't look good for her."

Will took out his cell and dialed Brad, wasting no time when he answered. "You need to get over to Handy Park. Andi's been shot."

Brad groaned. "Is she okay?"

"I don't know, but I'm about to find out." A hundred yards away, a paramedic bandaged Andi's wound. "I see her now, and she's upright. Treece is at the Med with a possible broken arm. Would you let her family know?" He hesitated. "I'll call Reggie."

"Yeah. See you as soon as I can get there."

Will pocketed his phone and trudged toward

Andi, still trying to wrap his mind around how all this could happen. And why she made his heart do crazy things. He'd almost kissed her earlier.

He masked a grin at the face she made when she saw him coming.

"Thanks for coming. I guess by now you've called Brad."

"You know the answer to that. He'll call Treece's family, and now that I know you're okay, excuse me a minute while I call Reggie." He nodded to the paramedic, one he'd often seen at crime scenes, then dialed Treece's boyfriend and told him what had happened. "She's in the ER at the Med."

"I sure wish you'd marry that girl before she gets Treece killed," Reggie said.

"Yeah, right." Will cut his eyes toward Andi.

"Tell him I'm sorry," she called out. "And to get himself over to the hospital ASAP."

"Did you hear that?" Will asked.

"Yeah. Do you think Treece would kick me out?"

"I think she'll be glad to see you." He ended the call and turned back to Andi, who was rolling her shoulder.

"Did you find anything at Lacey's house?" she asked.

"Didn't have time to do anything but brief Brad before you called. Does it hurt much?"

"What do you think?"

Gunshot wounds hurt, even when it was just a graze.

"I was just trying to help someone." Her gaze followed the ambulance as it pulled away with the siren going full blast. "That girl is not going to die. She can't."

So much power in such a tiny package. He ordered his heart to slow down. "You can't dictate life and death. What were you doing here, anyway?"

"The girl, Chloe . . ." Andi glanced toward the paramedic putting away his equipment. "Did you get her last name?" she asked him.

"Afraid not. She never came to," the paramedic said. "The ambulance is waiting to take you to the ER. You'll need IV antibiotics."

"I'll drive myself—I'm not riding in that wagon. Last time I did, it nearly killed my back."

The paramedic flashed a plea to Will. "Can you do something with her?"

"Sergeant Hollister will be here in a minute. He'll take care of his sister."

She punched his arm. "I really wish you hadn't called him."

This time he allowed the grin to surface. "I'd like to live to reach retirement."

"Cops," she muttered. "You stick together, no matter what."

"You got it. Now, do you want to tell me what happened, or should I guess?"

He almost missed her slight shrug.

"I got a call from this runaway last night, and I thought she'd be around eighteen, nineteen. Had no idea she was just a girl. Do you know her pimp was putting her out on the street? A child! If I get my hands on that—"

"Let us handle it—it's our job." Sometimes following Andi's train of thought was like watching a pinball bounce from one obstacle to another. "What did she say when she called?"

"She wanted to get away from him, except she was afraid. She would only tell me her first name, Chloe, and that she was a runaway. He promised her all sorts of things—she thought he would get her a modeling job. Instead, he put her on the street after two days. That was a month ago. Last night, she caught my news segment on runaways and called the station, and they gave her my cell number."

Pain shot through Will's clenched jaw. He'd seen this over and over again at the street mission. Last month, he'd discovered three girls under fourteen working as prostitutes, and now this one. At least those three were off the streets and two of them were back home with their parents. "Go on," he said.

"She agreed to meet with me, but it had to be near the clubs where her pimp has her working. I was going to call you as soon as I got her to the apartment." Her face darkened. "Treece wouldn't let me come alone. That's why she was hurt. I never should have let her—"

"You shouldn't have been here at all," Brad said as he walked out of the shadows. "And don't tell me it was totally altruistic and that it didn't cross your mind that her story might be your ticket to Atlanta or Dallas."

Will waited for the explosion as his best friend planted his feet and crossed his arms. He didn't have to wait long.

"That's not fair! Reporting the news is what I do. I was here because I wanted to help that girl." Andi fisted her good hand on her hip. "It's no wonder that I want out of this town. You expect the worst of me, and you're always telling me what I can and can't do."

"If you'd quit pulling these too-stupid-to-live stunts, I might get off your back. First last night and now this."

Will cringed. Brad shouldn't bait Andi. It was like taunting a bull in a pasture.

"Last night was not my fault, and you know it."

"Maybe so," he said, taking out his cell phone, "but one of these days you're going to get yourself in a situation you can't get out of. I'll feel better if I know where you are."

A cricket chirped on Andi's phone.

"That's a request to allow me to follow your location. Accept it." Brad's tone indicated he would not accept no for an answer.

"No."

His eyes narrowed, and his jaw shot out. "Then I'll put a tracking device on your car."

They stared at each other like two boxers in the ring, and Will waited to see who would back down first. He was surprised when it was Andi.

"Oh, all right." She tapped on her phone, and a second later, Brad's phone dinged.

"Thank you," he said and hooked his phone on his belt.

"I can always unfollow."

"And I'll know when you do."

Will wouldn't be surprised if Brad put the tracking device on her car anyway. He nudged his friend. "The paramedic wants Andi to go to the hospital for an antibiotic drip. I thought I'd take her. You want to get someone to take her car home? Then after she's finished with the treatment, I'll drop her off at her apartment."

Brad shook his head. "You ought to make her ride in the ambulance."

"It's not a problem," Will said.

A flush rushed through him at the look of gratitude Andi shot his way. He steeled his heart —he had to quit reacting to every little crumb Andi tossed him. Nothing could ever come of it. He would always only be her brother's friend and the peacemaker between the two siblings.

"Thank you," Andi said, looping her good arm through Will's.

Once again he'd smoothed things over. It was the way it had always been. Since they were kids, Andi had been like a cocklebur they couldn't get rid of, tagging along after them, and Will was always the one who defused the bomb before it exploded between the two siblings.

As soon as they were out of Brad's hearing, Will said, "Please be more careful. I never want to knock on your parents' door some night and tell them you got yourself killed."

She blew out a sigh. "It's just that she sounded so scared. I thought I could save her from a horrible situation." Andi ducked her head. "Instead I almost got us all killed."

"Your heart is in the right place," he said, "but you're not Captain Marvel. If you had just called me—"

"I can see that now." Impatience crept into her voice. "Can I check on Treece and Chloe before they hook me up to the drip?"

"No. And I bet you haven't had a tetanus shot in years, either."

"Wrong. Had one last year when I did the story on drugs and cut my leg getting into that warehouse." She moved her arm and winced.

He'd rather she didn't remind him of another of her escapades. "Arm feeling any better?" he asked as he opened the passenger door.

"Not as bad as when the paramedic cleaned it out. Come on, let me check on them first."

"No! Treatment first."

She rolled her eyes at him. "You're worse than Brad."

"I'll take that as a compliment. Get in." Two nights in a row of taking Andi to get treated. He hoped there wasn't a third.

The white Silverado pulled into the truck stop, circled around, and parked two cars down from JD. He couldn't believe his luck. Johnson had raised the suspension on the pickup to put over-sized tires on it—his job just got easier. He fingered the hammer in his hand as the guard climbed out and scanned the parking lot.

With the dark tint on his windows and his black clothes, JD didn't worry that Larry Ray Johnson might see him. As soon as the guard was inside, JD pulled on a black cap and slipped out of his car, walking behind the other parked cars to the passenger side of the Silverado.

Less than a minute later, he was beside the wheel and feeling his way around the undercarriage of the truck. He couldn't risk a light, but this was something he could do in his sleep. He loosened the nut that held the tie rod to the steering knuckle, and once he had it down to the last threads, he used the hammer to break the tie rod away from the steering knuckle. With the potholes on I-40, the nut should come off about five miles down the road, and Johnson would be history.

Finished, he returned the tools to his SUV, then removed the cap and brushed his clothes. He sauntered across the parking lot, observing the row of darkened cars bathed only by the pump lights and the neon sign advertising the Blue Cafe. After entering the cafe from the convenience store side, he walked to Larry Ray Johnson's table and slid into the booth.

Johnson jumped. "Man, where'd you come from?"

JD jerked his head toward the store. "Side door." He took an envelope from his jacket. "The letter?"

The other man pulled an envelope from his back pocket and hesitated. "I want to see the money."

He couldn't believe how untrusting Johnson was. Did the guard actually believe he would cheat him . . . or snatch the letter and run? He opened the envelope and thumbed through the bills. "Satisfied?"

He nodded.

"Then how about on the count of three, we both lay our packages on the table."

"Sounds good."

JD counted and on three laid the money down. Johnson did the same and then snatched the envelope up. JD examined the letter, recognizing Lacey's flowery script. The woman should have known better than to mess with him.

The corrections officer cocked his head to one side. "How do you do it? Look different every time?"

JD shrugged. "I have resources. And why are you trying to figure out who I am? You do, and I'll have to kill you."

Johnson laughed, but when JD didn't laugh with him, he scrambled out of the booth. "I don't want to know what you look like. I'm outta here."

"Have a safe trip," JD called softly. Then he looked up and smiled at the waitress who walked toward the table. "I think I'll have a steak sandwich to go," he said when she asked him what he wanted to order.

Andi surveyed the mess. So much for making Treece breakfast this morning. Charred tops on the biscuits. Brown scrambled eggs because she let the butter get too hot. She picked up a piece of the brittle bacon, and it broke off, falling back on the plate. All because she had so much running through her mind. Treece would be off the rest of the week with her arm in a sling, Chloe was clinging to life, Andi's arm burned like fire, and Jimmy Shelton would die if she didn't find evidence of his innocence.

Chloe and Jimmy were her biggest worries. If the girl died, Andi would never forgive herself. And if Jimmy died, and they discovered later he was innocent . . . well, she wouldn't get over that, either.

Andi had spent eighteen years hating him. Now she had major doubts that he killed Stephanie. But was there enough evidence to stop the execution? She made a mental note to stop by and see Maggie Starr later today . . . after her meeting with the station producer, and the police director, and . . .

She checked her phone for the time. Eight o'clock? She didn't have time to stand and cry over burned biscuits. Andi grabbed her purse and phone, dialing as she bolted out the door. She should have gone to Sally's Bakery and picked up muffins in the first place. "Don't eat breakfast until I get back," she said when Treece answered.

"Too late. I'm done."

Par for the morning. Andi turned around on the stairs and trudged back to Treece's apartment. The *Commercial Appeal* still lay where she'd dropped it in front of her door earlier, and she picked it up and rang the doorbell.

"Hold on while I turn off the alarm."

Andi bit her lip. She'd forgotten to set the alarm when she raced out of her apartment. And earlier when she went to the grocery.

Her friend wrinkled her nose when she opened the door. "What did you burn?"

"Your biscuits and bacon. And eggs. I thought

it was the least I could do. Cook your breakfast, I mean."

"How do you burn eggs?" Treece moved so Andi could enter the apartment. "Never mind. I don't want to know. Good thing you *don't* have a husband to cook for. How about an English muffin with honey?"

The aroma of fresh-ground coffee beans made her mouth water. "How about just coffee? I haven't had any yet." Andi had forgotten to grab a bag when she bought the bacon and eggs.

"Just ground some."

"I know, I smell it. And, as far as husbands go, if cooking is part of the deal, it won't happen—I don't have time to learn."

The memory of thinking Will was going to kiss her last night brought heat to her face. For him, she might be willing to take cooking lessons. Sometimes Andi thought she'd been waiting all her life for him to notice her.

She placed the newspaper on top of three unopened editions. Treece was as busy as Andi was. A wooden angel and a bottle of mineral oil sat on the island. "Is this new?"

"Relatively. I bought it last week at the flea market, and I was polishing it with the oil to bring out the grain. You should go with me sometime."

"Maybe." Andi took the mug of Italian roast Treece handed her. "How's your shoulder?"

"So-so." Treece winced as she picked up the

mahogany angel. "It hasn't stopped me from working on this."

"It's beautiful," Andi said. "How did it go with Reggie last night?"

"Okay." Then Treece shrugged. "At least he didn't say I told you so, but he thought it. How's your arm?"

"Barely a scratch." She wouldn't admit to Treece how sore it was, not when Treece had been hurt much worse. Even though her arm wasn't broken, she'd jammed her elbow and pulled muscles in her shoulder. Evidently, Treece had a high tolerance for pain or she wouldn't be working on anything. "Look, I'm sorry—"

"Like I said last night, I offered to go with you—I wasn't about to let you go alone."

She should never have told her where she was going. "Brad said I only did it to get the attention of a bigger market." He was partially right about that. She cupped the mug in her hands, letting the heat soothe her frazzled nerves.

Still, her mind whirled with the day's activity. With Treece out, Andi was left to meet alone with their producer later this morning. If he noticed the bandage on her arm, he'd probably send her home as well. She shifted her gaze and stared out the kitchen window. Heavy clouds hung in the sky, matching her mood.

"Your brother shouldn't have said that."

Treece's soft voice brought Andi back to earth.

Heat flushed her cheeks. "I have to admit that the possibility of producers in Atlanta or Dallas seeing the story crossed my mind."

She shifted her gaze to her friend, who was still in her housecoat. The right sleeve hung limp, and Andi fixated on the white sling. "Nothing like this will ever happen again."

Treece laughed. "Don't make promises you can't keep. You wanted a story. You just need to temper that with common sense and learn to accept help from others."

She couldn't remember the last time she'd needed help with anything. "You may be right about the common sense part, but if I know how to do something, I like to do it my way."

"Andi, that's your problem. You're too capable. You leave everyone else out of the equation, including God." Treece poured mineral oil on a soft cloth. "Do you ever even pray about your decisions?"

"Sure." Usually after she got into trouble.

"But do you ever listen to what God tells you? Or are your prayers more like, 'God, I'm climbing over this fence to video this poor dog. You want to come with me?' "

"Look, God is busy with people who *need* help." She stopped short of saying he was too busy to bother with her. That would set her friend off for sure.

"I can read your mind. You think you don't

need help." Treece concentrated on rubbing the oil into the wood. "One of these days you're going to learn that you're not God."

"I don't think I'm God." Her face grew hot when Treece rolled her eyes. "Okay, maybe sometimes I get a little impatient waiting for him to act."

"A *little?*" Her friend laughed and set the wooden angel down.

Pain pinched Andi's shoulder and she flexed it. "I have an appointment with the producer this morning to talk to him about a couple of things."

"Have you decided what story we're going to work on for our cold case documentary?"

"I'm rolling one around in my head. Do you have any preference?" She wasn't quite ready to tell anyone, not even Treece, that she wanted to do a story on Stephanie's murder.

"No, you're good at coming up with the ideas." Her friend handed her a ponytail band. "Would you . . ." She gestured to her long hair. "I can't do anything with my left hand."

Andi jumped up. "Sure."

She smoothed her friend's curly black hair with her hand. "Do you want it all in the band? Or maybe a strand or two framing—"

"All of it. I'm too old to be in a beauty contest."

"You're only thirty-two," Andi retorted.

"Which is ten years too old. Besides, been there, done that."

134

With her classic looks and creamy brown skin, Treece could still give those young contestants a run for their money.

"Will seems quiet lately," Treece said.

"Yeah." Andi twisted the band around her friend's hair, then picked up Tuesday's edition of the newspaper and slipped it out of the sleeve. "He's stressed about Jimmy's execution."

She turned to the second page and pointed to the story she'd read in Will's car Tuesday night. "It's set for Sunday night at eleven fifty-nine."

"How do you feel about that? We never got a chance to talk about what you learned at the prison."

Andi stared at the newspaper. "I don't think Jimmy killed Stephanie."

Will looked away from his computer screen and shrugged his shoulders to work out the kinks. He'd arrived at his desk at seven and spent the last hour and a half running down phone numbers for the list of people Jimmy had given him.

The last hour he'd concentrated on Jillian Bennett, but now that he'd obtained her married name from the alumni office at the university, he was searching Facebook for Jillian Knight. If he didn't find something this time, he'd give up the search and move on.

A list of accounts popped up, and he scanned the page for a mention of Dickson, Tennessee.

That was the last address the alumni office had for her. They'd given him a phone number, but it had been disconnected.

None of the names on the page fit the profile. He clicked See More and other Jillian Knights appeared. Halfway down the page, Dickson popped up, and he clicked on the name. No photo, and no posts in three years. He checked for any photos she'd posted. No personal ones, but on the About tab, a list of her past jobs included flight attendant. Maybe he'd hit pay dirt.

Leaning back in his chair, he took a deep breath and released it. Dickson was fifty miles from Nashville. It wouldn't take long to run up there. Might even ask Andi to go with him.

Andi. His heart warmed at the possibility of spending another whole day with her.

A text dinged on his phone. His aunt. *Call me.*

He started to ignore it. He did not want to talk to his mother, and that's what his aunt wanted. But he knew she would keep texting him until he responded, so he dialed her number. "Good morning, Aunt Mae."

"Have you talked to your mother?"

His shoulders drooped. "Not yet. I'm busy with Jimmy's case." Maybe that would divert her.

"But she only wants five minutes of your time."

"You should know better than anyone I don't have five minutes. After today, there's only three days—"

"I know how long it is, but your mother is important too. And five minutes won't make any difference with the case."

"Did her last husband boot her out?"

"Will, that's unkind. You need to forgive her, and not just for her sake, but your own."

For as long as he could remember, the only time his mom came around was when she had nowhere else to go. Forgiving her wasn't on his to-do list for today. Or tomorrow. But he needed to get his aunt off his back. "I'll try to call her when I get home tonight."

"Good. Any new evidence on the case?"

"Not yet. I'll let you know if there is."

After he disconnected, he stared at the phone a minute. *How much does she want this time?* Then he shook his head. He didn't have time to waste thinking about Cass. He had a case to work on. He walked down the hall and around the corner to Brad's office.

"Can I get an update on the Lacey Wilson case? And have you pulled the files from eighteen years ago?" He just couldn't make himself ask if Brad had his sister's murder case files.

Tight-lipped, Brad paused writing and nodded to the box on his desk. "Nothing new on the Wilson case. And there's no connection between these two cases, other than Lacey and Stephanie's friendship eighteen years ago."

When he'd told Brad about Lacey's letter to

Jimmy, Will danced around the rift these two cases had brought to their friendship. But no more. Will planted his feet wide. "Let's talk about the five-hundred-pound gorilla in the room."

"I don't know what you're talking about."

"Your sister's murder and my cousin's involvement. And the fact that if this involved any case other than Stephanie's, you would have already made the connection."

"I'm telling you there is no connection. We don't know that Lacey Wilson didn't commit suicide."

Will braced his hands on the desk. "I think you should turn the case over to someone else."

"Why should I do that?"

"You can't look at it objectively. You're reshaping the puzzle pieces to make them fit."

"And that's not what you're doing?"

"No." Will rubbed his forehead. "I'd think that you of all people would want to make sure the right person pays for your sister's death."

"I believe Jimmy did it."

"I don't. I looked up the newspaper articles written about the case. He wouldn't even be on death row if it hadn't been the new DA's first case, and if he hadn't been trying to make a name for himself. He pursued the death penalty because it made him look good."

"That doesn't change the fact that your cousin confessed," Brad said through tight lips. Suddenly he rolled his chair back and lifted his hand. "I'm sorry. None of this is your fault. You can't help it if Jimmy is your cousin."

"His attorney said the confession was coerced." Will took a step back. He didn't have time for this argument. "It's irrelevant that Jimmy is my cousin. I believe an innocent man was convicted, and I'm doing everything in my power to make sure an innocent man doesn't die Sunday night." He crossed his arms. "And the two cases *are* connected."

"You've made that plain," Brad said. "What about the trial and evidence that backed up Jimmy's confession that he killed Steph? He was convicted and given the maximum penalty."

"You don't have *any* doubts?"

"No. He never recanted the confession."

"He didn't take the stand because he didn't remember what happened."

"So he says now." Brad leaned forward. "It wasn't your sister who was killed. If the case gets reopened, I have to rip the skin off my scar, and not just mine, but the whole family's. I haven't even told Mom and Dad about any of this. I'm not sure they can go through it again."

"You're not giving your parents enough credit. They wouldn't want the wrong person to be punished for their daughter's death."

"I know, and I don't either," Brad said. "But I haven't seen enough evidence to change my mind. There's no hard proof there ever was a letter."

"So, you're saying if I find a letter, you'll come on board?"

His friend's shoulders lowered. "Depends. Wilson was bipolar and depressed. She could have written anything. Now, if evidence surfaces that she was murdered . . . I might change my mind. But given what we know at this point, she most likely committed suicide."

"Has the medical examiner given his ruling?"

"Not yet, but I expect it today."

Will didn't believe it was a suicide, but he wasn't sure there was enough evidence to prove it was murder, either. He picked up the box with Stephanie's case in it. "Did you look at the files in here?"

"Scanned them." He pressed his lips together. "I talked to Andi this morning. We're going to tell our folks tomorrow night at dinner that the case might be reopened."

Might? Will almost bit his tongue to keep from saying something he'd regret. Brad paper clipped the papers he'd been working on and slid them in a folder, then turned and opened another folder.

Will took the hint. "If I find anything I think you might want to see, I'll let you know."

— 11 —

Andi entered another name into her laptop. She had time to check out one more guard before she had to dress for her eleven o'clock appointment with the producer. Treece's knock drew her away from the computer screen.

"It's open," she called, and Treece opened the door and came in. Andi's conscience pinched again when she saw the sling.

"How about a cup of your own coffee?" she asked, nodding toward the coffeemaker. She'd borrowed enough coffee from her friend until she could get to the store.

Treece wrinkled her nose. "No, thank you—looks like it can float a spoon and smells even stronger." She raised her eyebrows. "Are you going to work today?"

"What, you don't think grunge will look good on camera?" She hopped up and dragged the barstool over to the table for Treece to sit on.

"Hardly. What are you doing? I thought you had an appointment."

"It's at eleven," Andi said and checked her watch. It couldn't be after nine. She'd have to hurry if she was going to see Maggie Starr before her appointment. She typed one last name in the search engine. Larry Ray Johnson. "I'm

141

researching the corrections officers at Riverbend."

"So you do believe Jimmy Shelton?"

"One minute I do and the next I'm not sure."

She glanced up from the computer. Treece pinned Andi with the spit-it-out look she got when she thought Andi was evading a question. She took a deep breath and released it. "It's that confession he made. I'm having trouble getting past it. That said, I do have enough doubt about it to investigate."

"Good. If it'd involved anyone but your sister, I think you would have come to that conclusion earlier. It's going to be hard opening up those wounds again."

Treece was right on both counts. "I hate to| think about telling Mom and Dad."

"They'll want to know the truth."

"I know." Andi pushed a sheet of paper toward Treece. "Here's a list of people we'll want to interview for the last segment of the documentary on runaways."

Treece reached for the paper. "That'd be something, you know. Especially if we broke the case—man spends seventeen years on death row for a crime he didn't commit."

Andi clicked on a link. "Should bring a lot of attention to the station . . . and us." She shifted her gaze to Treece and caught her surveying the living room. "What?"

"We have to do something in here, spread a

little of your personality around. What are you doing Saturday? I noticed a big sale at Decorate & More."

"Maybe." She surveyed the room, warming to the idea. There wasn't much that said "This is Andi Hollister." At least she hoped she wasn't as bland as the apartment. "How would you decorate this room to reflect me?"

Treece laughed. "Lots of red. Maybe a picture of a bull charging a matador."

"No. Seriously."

"I'd still stick with reds, maybe some other bold colors." She walked to the mantel and picked up an unfired sculpture of a prancing horse that had darkened with age. "Maybe odd-shaped pottery to replace this."

"That stays," Andi said. She fought a sudden rush of emotion. The horse sculpture held a special place in her heart. "Stephanie was working on it when . . ."

Her computer dinged, and she turned to the screen, blinking back tears. She didn't know why she'd gotten so emotional lately. A prescription bottle with two pills in it sat on the table beside the computer. She shook them out and downed them with a gulp of water. They helped with all kinds of pain. She looked up into Treece's disapproving eyes. "Don't say anything. You don't know what it's like to hurt all the time."

"I thought you'd changed to ibuprofen."

"The pain is worse this morning."

"Really?" Treece raised her eyebrows. "On a scale of one to ten, what's your pain level?"

Andi hesitated. "Sixish."

"Less than where mine is, and I haven't taken anything that strong," Treece said. "You need to get off of those things."

Andi squared her shoulders. "I know what I'm doing. Without them, I couldn't stand on my feet all day. So give it a rest."

She squirmed under her friend's stare.

"I'll trust you on that. For now. Have you heard from the hospital about how Chloe is?"

"I called earlier, and they said she was awake and talking to them. I plan to go by there sometime today." Andi frowned at her screen and clicked on a link and scanned the article. "Come look at this."

Treece leaned over her shoulder as Andi read the headline from a Nashville online newspaper. "Riverbend prison corrections officer involved in near-fatal I-40 accident."

She picked up her cell phone and dialed Will's number. When he answered, she asked, "Did you see where one of the guards from Riverbend almost died last night in a car wreck?"

"No. Who was it and when did it happen?"

"Larry Ray Johnson." She scanned the article again. "Happened about eleven last night. If you go back to Nashville, I want to go with you."

"We'll see."

She knew what that meant. "We'll see, my foot," she muttered after he thanked her and hung up. Will Kincade better take her along if he wanted to continue receiving information from her.

"Do you think the accident is significant to Jimmy's case?" Treece asked.

"I don't know, but I think it's worth checking out—someone at the prison stole Lacey Wilson's letter."

Andi noticed the time again and caught her breath. If she didn't leave in ten minutes, she wouldn't have time to stop and see Maggie.

She raced to her bedroom, throwing on clothes. A new prescription bottle sat on her dresser beside an ibuprofen bottle, and she quickly counted out sixteen pink tablets and dropped them in the ibuprofen bottle, leaving fourteen. She figured four a day would get her through to Monday morning.

"By the way," she said from the bedroom, "I'm going to talk to our producer about a story on Laura Delaney's political race. If she wins, and I believe she will, Laura will be the first woman to serve in Congress from this district."

"And?" Treece asked as Andi came out of the bedroom. Then, she did a double take. "How do you get dressed so fast? Oh, never mind. You do everything fast."

"No need to waste time."

Treece laughed. "No one will ever accuse you of that. I don't remember you being interested in covering a political campaign before. What's the real reason you want to do a story on Laura Delaney?"

"If Jimmy didn't kill Stephanie, that means someone else did. Laura lived in the house with Stephanie eighteen years ago, and anyone who lived there falls in suspect territory, even Laura Delaney. I thought if I hung around her, I might learn something."

"That sounds more like you."

Andi gave her friend a grim smile.

"Just don't let the case become an obsession," Treece said. "And leave revenge out of it."

"I'm not looking for revenge," Andi said, thinking of the years she'd spent hating Jimmy Shelton. "But I do want justice."

"Thanks for letting me know," Will said as Andi hung up. He wished he'd had the information about the wreck when he'd been talking to Brad. Not that it would make any difference. He turned back to the files on Stephanie's murder case.

There hadn't been as many as he'd hoped, and he shuffled through them again, searching for the investigating officer's reports. He picked out the folder and opened it, looking for a name.

George Barnes.

Explained the slim case file. George Barnes had retired from the force not long after Will made detective. What he remembered most about him was his attitude of getting by with a minimum of work as he marked time until his retirement.

On one case he worked with Barnes, Will suspected the detective planted evidence to "help" the case, but he'd never been able to prove it. The career criminal that Barnes may have framed denied having the cocaine that was found in his car. Even so, a jury found him guilty and put him away for ten years.

Barnes probably never looked any further than Jimmy's confession. Pain radiated from Will's neck, and he massaged the knotted muscles in his shoulder. His cell phone rang, and he answered, barking his name.

"Uh, Detective Kincade, this is Walter Simmons."

He winced. "Mr. Simmons, I'm sorry, didn't mean to sound so abrupt. How can I help you?"

"Did you hear about one of the COs at Riverbend being in an accident last night? Larry Ray Johnson."

"I heard," Will said. "Do you know anything about it?"

"No, just that he had a bad wreck on I-40 about twenty miles this side of Lexington, Tennessee. He's the one I suspected of taking Jimmy's letter, and—"

"Just a minute, Mr. Simmons. I have someone

I'd like to hear our conversation. Sergeant Hollister is working on another case that might be tied to this one, and I want to put you on speaker, if you don't mind." Just maybe this would be enough to change Brad's opinion.

"Fine with me."

Will hurried back to his friend's office and put the phone on his desk. "Andi called and said one of the Riverbend COs almost died in a car wreck last night. This call is from the corrections officer we talked to yesterday about Jimmy's letter. I'd like you to listen in."

"What does this have to do with anything?"

"He thinks this officer took Lacey's letter."

"Okay, I'll listen, but I'm not sure it'll change anything."

Will punched the speaker button. "Can you hear me, Mr. Simmons?"

"Hear you just fine."

"Sergeant Hollister is here with me," Will said. "Why do you think this Johnson took the letter?"

"I've suspected him of taking things from the prisoners before. Wasn't anything I could prove, just a hunch. I talked to a few of the other guards today after we found out about the accident, and they all said he'd asked questions about Jimmy almost every day. Things like if he got any unusual mail or phone calls. And one of—"

"Mr. Simmons, this is Sergeant Hollister. Didn't the other officers think that was strange?"

"Since he didn't ask the same person every time, nobody thought much about it. Lots of times, we talk about the prisoners. Helps to know what's going on with them and if we need to be on the alert. If a prisoner gets bad news from home, he's liable to do most anything." Simmons hesitated. "But Johnson seemed more interested in Jimmy than anyone else."

"Did you mention the letter after Jimmy received it?" Will asked.

"Ah . . ." Simmons cleared his throat. "I mentioned it to the other COs when I went off duty, and they told Johnson—he works the day shift. Another guard said he saw him near Jimmy's cell right after the shift changed. Jimmy was working in the kitchen."

The question now was, who was Johnson working for? "Do you know why he was so far from Nashville?"

"That's what I was about to say a minute ago. You have to understand that Johnson is always talking about all these things he's gonna do, and it wasn't always easy to tell when he was lying or just bragging. Yesterday at lunch, he told one of the other officers that he was taking off for Vegas next week, that he was coming in to a big sum of money."

"Did he say where it was coming from?"

"No. Sometimes he said he had this rich dude in his back pocket, but he never mentioned a name."

Brad leaned toward the phone. "Do you know what caused the accident?"

"No, but I'd be surprised if it had anything to do with his truck since that Silverado was his pride and joy. It could have passed a Marine inspection, inside and out," the CO said. "Did hear one of the other officers say his brother investigated the wreck and that something went wrong just before the bridge across the Tennessee River. Johnson was thrown out before the truck went into a ravine. They say he's critical, maybe paralyzed."

Will picked up his phone. "I appreciate that you called me. I'll check this out."

"I didn't particularly like Larry Ray," Simmons said, "but if someone tried to kill him, I wouldn't want to see them get away with it."

"I'll let you know what I find out. You be careful yourself." Will's thumb hovered over the disconnect button. "Oh, wait. Was Johnson married?"

"Getting a divorce."

After Will disconnected, he shifted his gaze to Brad. "One more piece of circumstantial evidence to add to the pile."

"It could mean nothing," Brad said. "Wrecks happen every day."

"You think it's another coincidence?" Will chewed his thumbnail as scenarios swirled in his mind. "But let's just say someone messed with the truck. Maybe tampered with the brakes—it'd be hard to tell. And let's take it to the extreme—say Jimmy didn't kill Steph, and whoever did was paying the corrections officer to spy on Jimmy. When he discovered that my cousin received the letter from Lacey, the guard stole it, thinking he could cash in."

Brad tented his fingers. "But even if what you say is true and someone wanted Johnson dead, why would they tamper with his vehicle and take a chance on what happened—him not dying? Why not just kill him outright?"

"An outright murder would bring a lot more investigation into his activities, where an accident would hardly cause a ripple."

Brad shook his head. "You're grasping at straws. There's no way to prove any of that."

"And you don't want to see the possibility that someone other than Jimmy killed your sister."

"How many times do I have to tell you—your cousin confessed and the investigating officer found his prints on the gun and that he'd struck her before. I don't want my family put through another investigation when it's unnecessary. It was bad enough the first time."

"That investigating officer was George Barnes."

Brad's eyes narrowed. "Barnes?"

His friend knew the cop's reputation as well as Will did. "Yes. And that's where I'm starting as soon as I get back from Nashville."

"You'll find him at the cemetery."

Will's heart sank. "Then I'll have to prove it some other way. Maybe Johnson's bank account will give some answers. Could be something at his house."

"You don't have enough probable cause to get a warrant to search his house or his bank records."

Will tucked the case file under his arm. "Thanks, Mr. Sunshine. Maybe the wife will help me out."

∽ 12 ∽

David listened as Will laid out the facts, his antenna going up when he learned George Barnes had investigated the original case. If ever there was a cop who didn't belong on the force, it was Barnes. Rumors of him being on the take had floated around the precinct for years before he retired.

"You say this corrections officer saw the actual letter?"

"He delivered it to Jimmy." Will took out his phone. "Here's the photo he took of it. Unfortunately, he's a terrible photographer."

The letter was no more than a blue blur. "And the letter is gone?"

"Yes sir, and one of the other COs at the prison is in a coma after an accident last night. Simmons indicated the CO had been overly interested in

Jimmy's visitors and mail. As soon as I take care of a couple of things around here, I'm driving to the site."

David tented his fingers. "There's nothing concrete, but in the right hands, it might be enough to get a stay. At least I hope it is—I'd hate to see an innocent man executed."

"That's what I was hoping you'd say."

"Who is Jimmy's attorney? He needs this information."

"Jimmy hasn't heard from his public defender in some time; besides, he retired a couple of years ago. My cousin asked me to talk with Madeline Starr on his behalf. See if she'll take on his case."

"You only have three days. That's not enough time to bring in a new attorney."

"I know, but he insisted. He doesn't believe the attorney he had would be any help, even if he came out of retirement."

"Do you know Ms. Starr?"

"I knew her when she was a college student, and judging by the way she cross-examined me in court on a case, I don't think she remembers me," he said.

"Sounds like she might have raked you over the coals." David twirled his pencil. "Let me broach this with her. I've been in the courtroom with her, and while she's tough, I've found her to be fair."

Will stood. "That would be great. I wasn't looking forward to approaching her. And this frees up my time so I can go to the accident site and get back here by midafternoon. I want to go over to Lacey Wilson's house again."

He stopped at the door. "By the way, Andi Hollister is friends with Ms. Starr, and she indicated she'd go with me when I talked to her. You might want to give her a call."

Will walked back to the desk and wrote Andi's number down. After he left, David called Andi. "This is Lieutenant David Raines," he said after she answered.

"How can I help you, Lieutenant?"

"Will Kincade was just in my office and indicated you might accompany me to see Madeline Starr. I need all the reinforcement I can get."

She chuckled. "I bet Will told you I know her softer side."

"Something like that. Any chance you can go now?"

"Can you wait? I haven't left the house yet, and it'll be at least forty-five minutes before I can be downtown."

"Tell you what. I'll go ahead to her office," he said. "Why don't you come straight there? That way if I've made a mess of it, you can vouch for me. And you can give her firsthand information about Jimmy."

"See you there."

David hung up and glanced out the window at the sunshine. Walking the few blocks from the CJC to Madeline Starr's office on Front Street would give him time to get his thoughts in order. Not to mention, at forty-one, he needed all the exercise he could get. He closed the folder he'd been working on.

To say Madeline had little use for cops was an understatement. The story was, her brother had gone to prison before DNA became accepted evidence. And while it'd been DNA that eventually cleared him, it was after his death at the hands of another prisoner. Now Madeline Starr was on a crusade to make sure no one else suffered that fate. Unfortunately, that usually put him on the opposite side of the fence from the beautiful attorney.

His stomach rumbled at the aroma of something yeasty as he passed the bakery on the corner. It took every ounce of his willpower to walk past it without going in. Mentally, he marked three hundred calories saved and then laughed at the game he played with his weight. But he caught a glimpse of his trim reflection in a mirrored building. Watching his calories and hitting the gym four times a week paid off.

When he reached the law office building, he checked the directory in the lobby. Twelfth floor. Probably a good view of the Mississippi River.

A few minutes later, he opened the door with Madeline Starr's name etched in the glass, and his feet sank into the carpet as he approached the lawyer's receptionist. The nameplate on her desk read Shawna Patterson. Her dark-chocolate eyes zeroed in on the gun on his belt as he showed his badge and said, "I'm Lieutenant Raines. Is Ms. Starr in?"

"Um, she's with a client, but please wait. I'm sure she'll make time to see you." Murmuring something about providence, she punched the intercom just as angry words blasted down the hallway.

"You'll pay for this!"

Shawna gasped. "Oh no! I was afraid of that. I tried to get Ms. Starr to let me call the police."

"What's going—"

A crash jerked his head around, and he ran down the hall with his gun pulled. Madeline's door was partially open, and a man stood with his back to David. Was that a gun in his hand? A glass vase lay next to the wall in a puddle of water.

"You missed, honey," the man said.

"You better leave." Madeline's voice was calm. "I'm sure my secretary has already called the police."

The man raised his hand. "For—"

David slammed the door open and dove toward the man, knocking him off balance. He reached for the gun, but the assailant reacted faster than David expected, backhanding him with the gun.

His head snapped back as black dots blurred his vision and pain shot through his cheek. The assailant wheeled toward Madeline, and David tackled him again, and they crashed to the floor. The gun skidded across the room.

The man outweighed him by at least fifty pounds, and David struggled for leverage, finally wrestling one of his arms behind him. David straddled his back and clamped a cuff on his wrist, then yanked.

"You're breaking my arm."

Panting, David said, "Not yet, but I will if you don't put your other hand behind your back."

When he was slow to move, David yanked the handcuffs again.

"Okay, okay. I'm doing it."

David snapped the cuff in place. For the first time, he heard sirens outside the building. "Next time, don't attack someone six blocks from the CJC," he said as he stood. Three uniformed officers rushed the room. He flashed his badge and said, "Lieutenant Raines. I'm not the bad guy."

Madeline stepped beside him. "Don't arrest him. I think he just saved my life."

David turned to her. "You think?" He didn't mean to raise his voice, but the woman should have let her secretary call the police earlier.

Her face paled, then she lifted her chin. "I could have talked my way out of it."

He clamped his mouth shut. If he answered with what was on his mind, he'd blow any chance of her listening to him about Jimmy Shelton. Pain shot through his cheek, and he reached to touch it.

"Don't. You'll get germs on it," she said, snatching his hand away. She pulled a tissue from the box on her desk. "It's bleeding. Here." She gently pressed the cut on his face. "It doesn't look like it'll need stitches."

Her light fragrance enveloped him.

Suddenly, she jerked her fingers back and held out the tissue. "I'm sorry. I didn't mean to invade your space."

"You didn't. Thank you." Her perfume lingered, nudging emotions David thought long dead. Nothing but adrenaline rush. He took the tissue and stepped out of the way so the uniformed officer could take the assailant out while she explained to the other officers what had happened.

Madeline, dressed in jeans and a blue sweater, recounted that she'd been working on briefs when the man showed up, angry over a case. Someone she represented had escaped jail time for a hit-and-run accident that involved the assailant's daughter.

An image of Alexis popped into David's mind, and he steeled his face to not react. He'd seen more than one criminal get an acquittal because of a slick defense attorney, and in truth, he didn't blame the man for being upset. If someone had hurt his daughter . . .

After the officers left, she turned to him. "There were extenuating circumstances."

"I didn't—"

"Yes, you did. I'm very good at reading people. You probably need to remember that."

"I will." He uncrossed his arms.

"The boy who hit her suffered a blackout caused by a heart arrhythmia he didn't know he had. When he came to himself, he was a mile from the accident. It was dark, and he didn't even know he'd hit anything until the next day when his father asked what happened to the front light.

"He came forward once he read about the hit-and-run and figured out he might have been responsible. He was relieved that the girl's injuries were minor. His family hired me because Thompson wanted him hung, and he carries political clout."

"Political clout?" David hadn't paid much attention to the man. "Did you say his name was Thompson?" When she nodded, he winced. "Tell me that wasn't H. G. Thompson, the mayor's bodyguard?"

"Afraid so."

Relations between the police department and

the mayor's office hadn't been the best with this mayor. "He shouldn't have pulled his gun."

"Agreed." She tucked the cuffs of her sweater in her hands and pulled the sleeves tight as she hugged her body. "What brought you to my office, Lieutenant Raines?" she asked as she walked to her desk and sat down.

Madeline Starr wasn't fooling him. He was pretty good at reading body language himself. She was much too pale, and he figured it'd been sit down or end up on the floor. "You don't have to be strong all the time," he said. "It's okay to be shook up."

"Excuse me?"

Uh-oh. She thought he'd been condescending. Maybe now would be a good time to mention Andi. "I mean, given what just happened here, anyone would be upset."

She continued to take his measure.

"Ah . . . and Andi Hollister said to tell you hello—she's meeting us here. She should be here soon."

She gave him a curt nod. "And by the way, you're wrong—I do have to be strong. You didn't say what you wanted."

For the first time since he entered her office, he heard faint strains of music. "You like Michael Bublé?"

Once again, surprise registered on Madeline's face and then a smile. She glanced toward the

160

phone on her desk, and he realized that was where the music came from.

"I came in early this morning and put on my Bublé playlist. His music helps me to stay focused while I work," she said, her voice warming. "You?"

He was glad to know they shared at least one thing in common. "Just the opposite. It's what I listen to when I get home and try to relax."

"I can see that." She planted her hands on the desk and rose. "I don't know about you, but I could use a little fresh air. Could we walk while you tell me what you came to see me about?"

After Will left David's office, he took the elevator down to the third floor to see the district attorney. He had a good working relationship with Laura Delaney and had been surprised when Andi told him she'd been Stephanie's roommate. He wasn't certain how she'd take being questioned about a murder that happened eighteen years ago.

It could prove to be sticky, with her election bid for the US Congress. She was running on her tough law-and-order record, and helping Jimmy get a stay of execution with no more evidence than Will had . . .

"Jace, is the district attorney in?" he asked her secretary.

"She is, Sergeant. Can I tell her what you want to see her about?"

"It's about a case I'm working on." He hated being evasive, but he wanted to see Laura Delaney's reaction when he brought up the subject of the murder. Not that he thought she had anything to do with it, but often if people were prepared, they filtered their answers.

Jace picked up the receiver and dialed. "Will Kincade is here to see you about a case he's working on."

As he waited for the DA's response, the entry door opened, and from the corner of his eye, he recognized Adam Matthews, Lacey Wilson's ex. Questioning him again was on Will's long to-do list. "Surprised to see you here," he said.

Matthews stood a little straighter. "Yeah, well, I wanted to talk to Laura about Lacey's funeral."

"When is it?"

"Tomorrow at five."

"I'll let Andi know."

"Andi?" He furrowed his brow.

"Andi Hollister. She was friends with Lacey. Your ex-wife had asked Andi to meet her at the airport Tuesday night."

"Why?"

"Maybe because she was Stephanie Hollister's sister? You knew her, didn't you?"

The pilot pinched the bridge of his nose. "The name rang a bell the other night, but I still hadn't put it together until just now."

Connections clicked in Will's mind. "By the

way, did any of the women who lived at the Hollister house work your flights?"

Matthews rubbed his nose. "Not that I remember. I was just a copilot back then."

"Sergeant Kincade, Mrs. Delaney will see you now."

"Are you flying today?" he asked Matthews.

"Got called in for a commuter run—on my way to the airport now."

"When will you be back?"

"Late this afternoon. Then I have another short flight."

"I may want to ask you more questions later today." Will turned to the secretary. "Thanks."

"You know the way," she said.

Will walked down to the end of the hall.

Seated at her desk, Laura looked over her reading glasses and motioned him to a chair. "What can I do for you, Sergeant? Have we discussed this case before?"

He liked the way the DA always cut to the chase. Laura had been the first female district attorney ever elected to the office in Memphis. And she had proven she could do the job.

He chose the leather side chair closest to her desk. "No. I've been moved to the Cold Case Unit. It's my first case."

She nodded. "Congratulations. I understand that's a coveted job."

"Yes, ma'am. I'm working on the Stephanie

Hollister murder from eighteen years ago. I understand you lived in the house with her."

The only indication of surprise was a widening of the DA's eyes. "When did that become a cold case? Jimmy Shelton confessed."

"I know, but certain evidence has surfaced that bears investigating."

"What evidence? It better be ironclad. Shelton's execution has been delayed long enough. People want to see justice served."

Will couldn't keep from mentally changing "people" to "voters." "Justice won't be served if an innocent man is executed."

She took off her reading glasses and hooked a strand of dark brown hair behind her ear. "Has his lawyer filed an appeal for a stay?"

"He doesn't have one right now. The public defender who had his case retired."

She frowned. "I see. And this evidence you mentioned?"

"It's a letter stating he didn't kill Stephanie, and that the author has evidence to back up the claim."

She absorbed the news with little expression. "Do you have the letter with you?"

"No. It was stolen from Jimmy."

"Okay. Then is this person willing to come forward?"

He leaned forward in the chair. "Unfortunately, she's dead."

"Will, you're not talking about Lacey Wilson, are you?"

He nodded.

She slipped her reading glasses back on. "I thought for a minute you had real evidence. No jury would ever seriously consider anything that poor woman had to say. She was my friend, but she was also depressed and paranoid."

"How long have you known Lacey?" he said.

"Since we all lived in the house with Stephanie and flew together . . . I guess eighteen or nineteen years. She had a tendency to depression even then."

"Let's suppose what she wrote is true," Will said. "That someone other than Jimmy killed Stephanie. Can you think of anyone in her circle of friends or acquaintances who might have wanted her dead?"

She gave him a look that reminded him of detention.

"Let it go."

"I can't."

"I suppose any number of women who lost their boyfriends to her," she said with a laugh that was devoid of mirth.

"How about you? Where were you the night she was killed?"

Laura Delaney's face flamed. "Are you insinuating that I had something to do with her death?"

165

"No. I just asked where you were."

"I don't remember. Probably in the house studying. That was when I was working full-time and trying to go to law school at night." She pressed her fingertips together. "Stephanie had a restraining order against your cousin, not that it did any good."

"Do you know why?"

She tapped her chest. "Because of me, after Jimmy hurt her. I'd been begging her for weeks to do something about him, but she didn't want to get him into trouble with the law. One day I needed her car keys to run to the store, and I walked in on one of their fights. I heard them yelling when I came out of the house, but then it went quiet. When I entered the studio, I understood why.

"Stephanie lay on the floor and Jimmy stood over her, his body weaving back and forth. Maggie was there and she was rooted to the floor. I thought Stephanie was dead. I shoved Jimmy out of the way and felt her pulse." Laura looked up at Will. "She was alive, so I yelled for Maggie to call 911. That's when Stephanie groaned and tried to sit up. She insisted that we cancel the call, but it was too late. She refused to press charges. She did get a restraining order later that day."

Laura shook her head as if to clear it. "It wasn't the first time he'd hurt her. When he wasn't drinking, Jimmy was the sweetest guy you'd ever meet. But he was a different person when he was drunk. He had no filters."

As much as Will hated to admit it, she was right about his cousin. And if Stephanie had been killed from a blow to the head, he wouldn't argue that Jimmy was innocent of her murder. But his cousin hated guns. He would never have shot her.

Will noted Laura's answer in his notes. "My aunt said she thinks Stephanie was into something illegal. Do you know what it might have been?"

She stared at him. "You're kidding." When he didn't answer, she pressed her mouth in a thin line and leaned back. "No, I guess you're not. Look, I realize Jimmy is your cousin, but I hope you won't try to paint the victim in this case as a criminal."

"Of course not. I just thought you might know what my aunt was referring to."

"I don't, and if the only evidence you have to clear your cousin is something Lacey Wilson wrote . . . well, let me put it this way. If I took this *evidence* to a judge, he'd laugh me out of his courtroom. If you have nothing else to add to this, I need to get back to work." She returned to her file.

"Before I go, you seem to know Adam Matthews pretty well. Did any of you fly with him eighteen years ago?"

She looked up from the file, a slight frown lowering her brows. "Uh, yes. We all worked for the same airline. Now, if you're through . . ." She glanced toward the door.

"Actually, I'm not. I have a couple more questions I'd like to ask you." Will looked down at his notepad then back up at the DA. "Your husband, Spencer. You met him when you both worked for the airlines?"

Laura scowled. "That's correct, but I fail to see what that has to do with anything."

"I'm always looking at connections. Four flight attendants, living in the same house, your husband also was a flight attendant, and he married you, but did he ever date Stephanie? Or the other two women?"

"You'll have to ask him that."

"You don't know?"

She shrugged. "Who my husband dated before we married is of no consequence to me. I landed him." She smiled at her own joke, then shrugged. "Actually, he dated both of them, Jillian first. She never knew about Spencer and Stephanie. According to Spencer, there wasn't much to their relationship. After they broke up, they remained friends. Most of the men Stephanie dated remained friends with her after she moved on to another conquest."

Will didn't know if Laura was purposefully showing Stephanie in an unfavorable light or if she wasn't aware of it. "Do you know where I can find your husband? I'd like to ask him a few questions."

She checked her watch. "He left here to go to Donovan Jewelers to pick up my diamond bracelet. Jared is an old friend, so they probably went to the coffee shop around the corner."

Donovan and Delaney. Old money and nouveau riche. Or more aptly, old power and new power, as the Donovans were connected to the old political machine that ran Memphis for years and now Laura was the face of new politics. "Can you give me his cell phone number?"

She hesitated, and then rattled it off. "He doesn't know any more than I do about Stephanie's case."

"I still would like to talk to him."

"You're fighting a lost cause," she said. "And I'm getting behind on my schedule."

Dismissed, Will stood. "I'm convinced Jimmy didn't kill Stephanie. I'll get the evidence and be back."

"When you do, I'll take it to the judge. But you don't have much time."

He tipped his head.

No one had to tell him he was running out of time. That fact was with him day and night.

Madeline Starr wanted him to walk with her? David tilted his head, and for the first time he noticed faint laughter lines around her eyes. So her smile did sometimes go all the way to her deep blue eyes. Maybe this would go better than he expected.

"Walk? Sure."

He followed her to the reception area, where she told Shawna she'd be back in thirty minutes.

"I like your receptionist. She has good instincts," he said on the elevator.

"She's my assistant . . . and much more. I should have listened to her this morning. How about the Riverwalk?"

"Good idea." The walking trail that wound along the Mississippi River would offer a more relaxed atmosphere than the foot traffic on Front Street.

"Lieutenant Raines, I—"

"Call me David." He glanced down at her. She didn't look at all like the last time they'd met, with her blonde hair pulled back in a ponytail. A couple of strands had slipped out of the band, softening the tough lawyer image he remembered from the courtroom. Then, her hair had been in a tight bun on her neck. She'd represented the man he'd arrested, and she'd been relentless in her questioning.

Today she didn't seem nearly as tall and formidable, although she probably stood five-eight or nine. And she had a nice build. He'd noticed when he followed her down the hallway.

"David." She said his name as if trying it out.

"If you'll call me Maggie. It's what my friends call me, and since you saved me from bodily harm this morning, you move from possible adversary into the friendship category."

She did remember their last meeting. He'd have to see what he could do to stay out of her enemy camp. "Do you always talk like a lawyer?"

"What?"

"Bodily harm, adversary, friendship category . . ."

Maggie laughed softly. "I suppose I do."

The timbre of her voice when she laughed quickened his heart. There was something soothing about it.

"Maggie?" he said. "How do you get Maggie from Madeline?"

She gave him a wicked grin. "That information is reserved for really good friends."

"Okay. I'll have to see how to get moved to that category." A brisk south wind blew blossoms from the Bradford pear trees across their path as they walked in silence. It'd probably rain later. He caught a glimpse of the Memphis Queen chugging up the Mississippi, well out of the wake of a barge floating south. He loved the river and the way it energized him. Should come here more often. David's cell phone rang. "Excuse me," he said before answering. "Raines."

"Laura Delaney is not going to be any help with getting a stay for Jimmy."

He recognized Will's voice. "How do you know?"

"I just left her office, and she almost laughed me out of it."

"I'll pass that on. I'd like to meet with you and Brad this afternoon. Why don't I join you at the Wilson house?" When Will agreed, David hung up and slipped his phone in his back pocket, rejoining the lawyer. "Sorry about that," he said.

"That's fine. It gave me a minute to think."

"About?" They started walking again.

Maggie cleared her throat and said, "Umm."

Now she had his curiosity up. "Yeah?"

"I need to apologize for . . ."

She bit her bottom lip, and he liked the way she seemed flummoxed.

"The way I acted this morning." The words came out in a rush. "While I don't think Thompson would have actually harmed me, you probably kept both of us from doing and saying things we'd regret."

"Probably?"

"Yes, probably. Thompson isn't a complete

idiot." She turned to him. "You still haven't told me why you were in my office."

That was more than likely all the thanks he would get from Maggie Starr. He'd take it. "I'm here on behalf of Jimmy Shelton."

Her blue eyes widened. "Jimmy Shelton. That's a blast from the past."

David laughed. "I believe those are the first words you've said that don't sound like a lawyer."

"Ha-ha. What about him, other than he's sitting on death row for the murder of Stephanie Hollister?"

"You have a good memory."

"I suppose. Hard to forget the details of a friend's murder."

"How many details do you remember?"

"It's been so long, I don't know. Ask me some questions, and we'll see."

A jogger approached, and David moved to one side to let him by. "Had Stephanie been acting unusual or nervous?" he asked when they were alone again.

Maggie's walk slowed. "We hadn't been friends that long, and I actually knew Andi better. She was such a cute kid." She glanced up at him. "Now that she's grown, we've become friends on a different level."

He laughed. "Yeah, she said she knew your softer side. What else can you tell me?"

"I lived in the house because of Laura

Delaney—it was Laura Cole then. We were in a couple of classes together, and I was driving back and forth from Senatobia, Mississippi, and looking for a place to live closer to the university when she told me about Stephanie."

"That's about an hour away, with traffic."

"It is. I lived with my parents. Laura introduced me to Stephanie, and my parents came up and met the Hollisters and approved the arrangement." She glanced up at him. "Can you see that happening today?"

David tried to picture life with his daughter, Alexis, in a few years. "No, but I wish it did."

They walked on. "Thinking back," he said, "what was your impression of Stephanie?"

Maggie looked toward the river, a view she never tired of. "Stephanie was beautiful, but I don't think she knew it." At first, she had been intimidated by Stephanie's poise, but after they formed a bond working with the clay, Maggie had discovered a warm heart. "From what I observed, she was looking for something, and she broke a lot of hearts. Jillian said that Stephanie didn't date any one man very long."

"How about her relationship with Jimmy Shelton?" David asked.

"It was an on-again-off-again relationship, but in between beaus, she always went back to him. I think she loved him, but he had a lot of problems. Toward the end, she just wanted him gone. We rarely talked about him. In fact, I probably talked to Stephanie more about pottery than anything else.

"She was a very good sculptor, and actually gave me a discount on the rent for helping her in the studio. I remember a day right before she was killed. It was one of the few times we discussed Jimmy. We'd been working a couple of hours, and I asked her to show me how to make the dancing horses . . ."

Stephanie rolled a small piece of clay between her palms. "First I wrap clay around the wire form, then roll out small pieces and build to it," she said.

"You make it sound easy." Maggie picked up a coil of wire that Stephanie used to form the armatures. "How do you make them look like they're prancing?"

Stephanie paused with the piece of clay in her hand, puzzlement on her face. "I never thought about it. I just twist the wires together until it looks like a horse, then I twist them more to get their legs just right."

"I would hate to see any horse I built."

"You can do it." Stephanie tossed her a small pair of needle-nose pliers. "Try it."

"I don't want to waste your wire."

"Don't worry, I can always reuse it if you mess up." She continued to smooth clay over the armature.

Maggie cut several lengths of wire. "I haven't seen Jimmy around lately."

Stephanie shaped the withers with her thumb. "You won't. I broke it off with him again."

"Because of JD?" Maggie asked.

She jerked her gaze to Maggie. "What made you say that?"

"I don't know . . . I saw you and JD the other day. He seemed very interested in you."

"No, not because of JD. There's nothing going on between us." She leaned closer to Maggie. "At least not after he got back with Jillian. It's Jimmy's drinking, which is all the time lately. When he's drunk, he's crazy jealous." Stephanie pinched off another piece of clay and pressed it into the rump. "I've actually started seeing someone new. Jared Donovan. He even asked me to marry him."

Maggie widened her eyes. "That fast? You couldn't have had more than a date or two."

"I know. But that's the way he works—he sees something, or someone, he likes and goes after it. But don't worry, I didn't say yes."

"I'm glad."

Stephanie smoothed more clay on the horse and turned the sculpture for Maggie to see. "This one is my diamond in the rough. I think it'll be the best one yet."

The studio door opened before Maggie could answer, and Jimmy sauntered in.

"Don't you ever knock?" Stephanie sniffed the air as he walked closer. *"You smell like a brewery."*

Maggie got a whiff of alcohol when he walked by her. *"I think I'll go to the house."*

Stephanie shook her head. *"No! Please stay."*

Maggie would much rather be somewhere else, but she did as Stephanie asked and focused on the armature.

Jimmy planted his feet, but that didn't keep him from swaying. *"Ah, you know you're glad to see me."*

Stephanie's fingers stilled. *"You're drunk, and you're not supposed to be here. If my parents come by, they'll call the police. Now, leave."*

"No. We gotta talk. I wanna marry you." He fumbled in his pocket and pulled out a small ring box. *"I just picked this up."*

Maggie saw that tears rimmed Stephanie's eyes as she focused on the horse's leg.

"Well, I don't want to marry you."

"Why?"

"Because you don't keep your promises. Here it is, two in the afternoon, and you're already soused. You can't control yourself or your temper when you're drinking."

"I'm not drunk. Had a couple shots, that's all. I'd never hurt you, Steph."

She touched her cheek. *"You already did."*

He dropped to his knees beside the table where

she was working. "I didn't mean to. I . . . I just saw you with that guy, and something snapped. I love you. You have to know that."

He turned to Maggie, his gray eyes pleading for her help.

"Tell Steph I won't hurt her."

Goose bumps raised on Maggie's arms. She didn't like being a party to this. "Why don't you go home and sober up? Then she might talk to you."

"No. I want to talk now!"

Both women flinched as his voice boomed in the room.

"And I told you I don't want to talk to you. We're over with." She splayed her hands. "Done. Finished. Understand?"

He reached for her, almost knocking the sculpture off the table. She shoved him away. "Get out of here until you get sober."

"I'll quit. I promise."

"Yeah, right. I've heard that before. There's no future with you. I told you I'm not spending my life wondering where you are, if you're drunk and maybe driving." She looked at the ring box in his hand. "How did you get to the jewelry store?"

He shrugged and looked toward the ceiling. "Not gonna tell you."

"You drove. You could have killed somebody. Now go home, or I'll call the police myself."

He grabbed her wrist. "No. I'm not leaving. Not until you say you'll marry me and take this ring."

She jerked away from him and marched to the phone on the wall. "I'm giving you one last chance to leave."

He lunged toward her. Maggie screamed as Stephanie stumbled, hitting her head on a worktable. Maggie froze, and then somehow Laura was in the room, shoving Jimmy away.

"Call 911," Laura shouted.

The words galvanized Maggie, and she grabbed the phone. When the operator answered, she gave the house address and described what had happened.

"I didn't mean to hurt her." Tears ran down Jimmy's face. "I promise, I didn't . . ."

"Well you did." Maggie wet a cloth and knelt beside Laura. Stephanie was so pale. "I called 911, and an ambulance is on the way."

"Good. She hit her head. Can you get some ice from the fridge?"

Stephanie's eyes fluttered open. "No. Call them back and tell them not to come. I'm all right." She tried to sit up and grabbed her head. "Where's Jimmy?"

Laura sat back on her feet. "Sitting on the sofa, mumbling something about not meaning to hurt you. Now, lay still. And we're not calling them back. I'm sure the police will come too."

"I wish you hadn't done that. He didn't do it. I fell."

Maggie stared at Stephanie. Why was she lying for him? "You didn't fall. He shoved you down."

To this day, Maggie didn't understand why Stephanie kept insisting that she had stumbled over a block of clay. She turned to David. "When the police arrived, she held to that story. At that time I hadn't dealt with anything like that and couldn't make sense out of it. Later I realized she felt bad about breaking up with him and didn't want to see him go to jail."

‒ 14 ‒

On the steps of the CJC, Will checked to see if he had a message from the highway patrolman who had investigated Larry Ray Johnson's accident, and he did. The patrolman could meet with him at one. He thought about calling David again but decided to wait until he knew more.

It was ten thirty, and the site of the accident was an hour and a half away. He'd be pushing it to stop and question Spencer Delaney, but with only three days until Jimmy's execution, every minute counted right now. He dialed the number Laura had given him for her husband.

"Hello?"

"Mr. Delaney, this is Sergeant Will Kincade with the MPD. I spoke with your wife and she gave me your number."

"Okay," he said. "What do you want?"

Background noises indicated he was likely still at the coffee shop with Jared Donovan. "I'd like a few minutes of your time. Do you mind if I drop by the coffee shop? My questions won't take long."

Silence stretched over the line. "What's this in reference to?"

"A case I'm working on."

"I can tell you anything you want to know over the phone."

"I see. Is Mr. Donovan with you? I really wanted to speak with him as well."

Silence again, then Delaney cleared his throat. "We're at Java Junkies on Union."

"That's where your wife said you probably were. Thanks. I'll be there in ten minutes."

When Will entered the shop, the two men were sitting at a round table near the back. Neither saw him, and they seemed to be in deep conversation. He ordered a cup of coffee and observed them while he waited.

Delaney, the taller and more muscular of the two, looked as though he might work out every day. Donovan had a softer, refined air. After the barista handed Will his coffee, he walked to the table.

"Good morning," he said, showing his badge. "Thank you for seeing me."

"This won't take long, will it?" Delaney said. "I have an appointment in a few minutes."

"No." Will took out his notepad. "Just wanted to ask a couple questions about Stephanie Hollister."

"Stephanie?" Donovan echoed her name.

"Why are you asking questions about her?" Delaney said. "She was murdered twenty years ago."

"Eighteen, and I'm looking into her murder," Will said. "According to my information, you both dated her."

Irritation crossed Donovan's face. "I don't understand why you're looking into the case. Her ex-boyfriend confessed, and he has a date with the . . ."

His words trailed off when Will speared him with a sharp gaze. "I have proof he didn't do it."

Delaney snorted. "If you're talking about the letter from Lacey Wilson, you don't have any evidence."

"How did you know about the letter?"

His face reddened. "Same way you knew we were here."

Laura. Figured. "Where were you two the night Stephanie was killed?"

"You surely don't suspect either of us in her

death," Donovan said. "I loved her. I was planning to marry her."

"Did she return your love?"

"Of course she did. It was just a matter of time before she said yes."

His tone indicated no woman in her right mind would turn him down.

Donovan stood. "I don't have time to sit here and be accused of something I didn't do and don't have any knowledge of."

"Before you go, can you tell me where you were the night she was murdered?"

The jeweler rubbed his jaw. "That was eighteen years ago. I don't have a clue where I was that night. And if you have any other questions, take them up with my lawyer."

He tossed a five on the table and walked away. Will turned to Delaney. "Seems like if he was in love with Stephanie, he'd remember where he was when he learned she'd been murdered. How about you, do you know where you were?"

"In a restaurant, eating a sandwich with Jillian, who I was dating at the time. We'd pried Laura away from her studies long enough to come with us. Cops were all over the place when I dropped them off at the house."

Will wrote his answer in the notepad along with Donovan's. Spencer Delaney remembered right away where he was, but his wife and Donovan did not.

David slowed his steps and Maggie followed suit. It sounded as though an intoxicated Jimmy Shelton had been capable of shooting Stephanie. The question was, had he done it? "How about the other roommate. Jillian Bennett. Did you know her?"

"So-so. She and Spencer Delaney were practically inseparable until Stephanie's murder, and then they broke up, and a few months later, Spencer started dating Laura."

"So Spencer Delaney had a relationship with both Jillian and Stephanie before he ended up married to Laura?"

"Yes." Maggie shook her head and laughed. "I know, it sounds like a soap opera. But he and Laura seem very happy together."

"What happened to Jillian?"

"She disappeared from the scene not long after Stephanie's death."

"What was she like?"

"She was very independent and wanted to go to law school after she received her bachelor's degree. That was about our only connection, and I've often wondered if she followed through. If you find her, I'd like to have her address."

He nodded. "Was Jillian good friends with the others?"

"She and Stephanie were good friends, went to high school together, but the others—no. Their connection was their jobs—they were all flight attendants—but I don't think any of them liked it. I was the only one going to school full-time." Maggie stopped. "I do remember that Jillian seemed very close to Stephanie's mother. And we better turn around so I can get back to the office."

"Mind if I ask a few more questions while we walk back?"

She tilted her head toward him. "If you ever decide not to be a cop, I'd gladly hire you to question my clients."

He wasn't sure that was a compliment. "I'm just trying to get a picture of what was going on when Stephanie was murdered, but I'll just make it one more question."

"Why don't you ask Laura? Don't you work with her?"

"I do, but I have another reason for coming to you first that I'll get to in a minute. Do you remember if she was hanging around new friends? Or does anything unusual stand out in your memory?"

"I think that was two questions," she said, looking up at him. She smiled before answering. "I remember she was focused on Andi's surgery . . . I probably would have attributed any tenseness to that."

"How about Lacey Wilson? What do you remember about her?"

"That's now three."

"So it is." He was surprised by how much he enjoyed her sense of humor. He raised his eyebrows, signaling he wanted an answer, and she obliged.

"Not much from that time frame. I got to know her better after Stephanie died and the Hollisters needed their house back. For a year I rented an apartment with Laura and Lacey." She slipped her hands in her jacket. "Lacey had made an appointment with me for the day she died."

He noted that on his pad. "Do you know why she wanted to see you?"

"No. I was so busy that day I didn't realize she'd missed the appointment until Laura called yesterday with the news about her death. I certainly would not have pegged Lacey for suicide, though."

"I'm not certain she committed suicide."

Maggie stopped. "What do you mean?"

"There are a lot of unanswered questions about her death." He turned to face her. "Since you knew her, and you're good at reading people, let me ask you something."

"Okay, but I hadn't talked to her in years. I was surprised when I learned she'd made an appointment."

Too bad Maggie hadn't kept up with Lacey. It would have been nice to have inside information on the victim. "Do you think someone who kept detailed records on everything would kill themselves and omit a suicide note?"

"Over half the people who commit suicide don't leave a note." She tilted her head. "Give me more."

"She'd booked a flight to Hawaii for Tuesday night, and her bags were by the back door."

"Is that all?"

"She was meeting Andi Hollister at the airport before the flight with information of some sort about her sister. And she planned to go to Riverbend."

"Add her appointment with me that afternoon, and that does put a different spin on it." She walked in silence for a few minutes. "If Lacey didn't commit suicide, then someone murdered her, like Stephanie."

"That's what I'm thinking."

Maggie stared toward the river again. "I've always wondered about Jimmy's conviction. He was so in love with her, and I never saw him with a gun. But then there was his alcohol problem, and when the detective said he'd confessed . . ."

"I know. People don't usually confess to crimes they didn't commit, except George Barnes was the investigating officer, and he wasn't above coercing a confession."

She frowned. "That's why you were in my office. You don't think Jimmy killed her, and you want me to take his case. But what does Lacey have to do with Jimmy?"

He glanced around. "Why don't we sit?" he said, pointing to a wrought iron bench.

The wind had picked up, blowing a loose strand of hair across her face. It was strange seeing Maggie dressed so casually, and for the first time, he noticed her eyes were the color of her sweater, and both were the color of the forget-me-nots his mother grew when he was a child. Probably the only flowers other than roses that he knew by name.

She brushed the hair from her eyes. "Exactly what is your interest in this?"

"Jimmy's execution date is Sunday night at eleven fifty-nine. Tuesday he received a letter stating the author had evidence that he didn't kill Stephanie Hollister."

She leaned toward him. "What's the evidence?"

"I don't know—the letter disappeared."

"Then get in touch with whoever sent it."

"Lacey Wilson wrote it."

"Oh." Maggie sank back on the bench. "How do you know there even was a letter?"

"A corrections officer saw it and photographed it, but unfortunately he wasn't a great photographer. He wasn't even good. The photo was too blurry to read. The letter is the only evidence we have. That and the possibility that Lacey Wilson was murdered." He didn't want to mention the guard suspected of stealing the letter until he had more information. "I don't know that we have enough time to pull a case together."

She gave him a wry grin. "And that's where I come in."

He acknowledged her guess with a matching grin. "Jimmy asked Will to talk to you, and I offered to come in his place to see if you'd be willing to take his case."

She didn't bat an eyelash. "I'll get started today. First thing we have to do is get a stay of execution and then get to work finding that evidence."

He stood and offered his hand to pull her up. "Come on, I'll walk you back to your office."

A few minutes later, they walked inside Maggie's building just as Andi stepped off the elevator.

"Oh, good!" she said. "Your secretary said you had gone for a walk. I'm glad I caught you two. Did David tell you I planned to come with him?"

"Yes." Maggie hugged Andi. "I've missed our lunches."

"Me too, but I've been so busy with these documentaries, I haven't had time for lunch."

David believed that. Andi was thinner than she appeared on TV.

"So that means you want something other than asking my help for Jimmy Shelton," Maggie said.

"You know me so well," Andi said with a laugh. "I want to find Jillian and thought you might know where to find her."

"I'm afraid not. Like I just told David—I don't know where she is."

The TV reporter's shoulders drooped. "It looks like I'll have to ask my mom. She mentioned at Christmas that Jillian had sent a card, and then she got all sad about Stephanie." Andi made a face. "That's why I was trying to find the address without asking her. But if I get it, do you want to ride along with me Saturday when I check it out?"

Maggie tilted her head. "Count me in. I'd like to see Jillian again."

— 15 —

At the TV station, Andi laid out her proposal for the story to her producer, and once he was on board, she went to her office and called Laura Delaney. The DA's secretary gave her an appointment for eleven the next day. Then she called Will. He was on I-40 not far from the site of the accident.

"I thought you were going to let me go with you."

"I believe the conversation went more like you told me I *better* take you if I went to Nashville. That's hardly the way to get an invite. Besides, that's not where I'm going."

Andi cringed. If only she could curb her sharp

tongue. "You aren't going on to Nashville to talk to the corrections officer in the hospital?"

"No, he's in an induced coma. Walter Simmons sent me contact information for the estranged wife, but she's out of town until Saturday. She agreed to talk with me then, so I'll go whether I can see Johnson or not."

"I'd like to go with you this time. Please."

"Figured that."

"Oh, wait, Saturday? Can't go. Maggie and I are going to find Jillian." Pain shot down her leg. How long had it been since her last pill? After another jolt, she didn't care how long it'd been and fished the bottle from her purse.

Once she swallowed two pills, she said, "If you're still going to Lacey Wilson's house today, I'd like to tag along."

"We'll see," he said.

She was pretty certain she could get approval to work on the case from the police director. "What time will you be back?"

"Shooting for three thirty. Like I said, we'll see."

Yes, they would. She ended the call, then dialed the police director, securing an appointment with him at one. Good. Time enough to go by and check on Chloe. As she drove away from the TV station, she checked her rearview mirror for any suspicious cars. Ever since the man attacked her, she had the odd sensation someone was watching her.

●●●

On the third floor of the hospital, Andi signed in to the ICU and stuck the temporary pass on her jacket. For a second, her head swam. Maybe she should have left off the pills. No, the pain had eased. In fact, she felt as though she could leap over tall buildings. Tamping down a giggle, she hurried into the ICU.

A US Marshal had replaced the policeman outside Chloe's room who had been there the last time. The curtain was pulled back from the window, and while the marshal examined her ID, she observed the sleeping teenager. It was hard to believe this sweet-faced girl had been put on the streets for prostitution.

Chloe's eyes remained shut when Andi stepped inside the room. A heart monitor beeped a soft, steady rhythm, and she stood for a minute watching Chloe's chest rise and fall evenly.

Someone had shampooed Chloe's platinum hair. From the roots, it looked as though her original color may have been chestnut. Two bags dripped solution into her IV. Probably antibiotics.

A cuff on her arm inflated, and the teen's eyes flew open. "What—"

"It's just your blood pressure cuff," Andi said. When Chloe continued to frown at her, she said, "Do you remember me? I'm—"

"I remember. What do you want?"

"Just to visit."

Wariness replaced fear. "I never should have called you, but after I watched your story on the news, I thought maybe you could help me get off the streets. And I really did want to warn other girls about running away."

"You would have died if you'd stayed in that situation." Either from a drug overdose or a beating. "How are you feeling?"

"Like a two-ton truck fell on me. How do you think I feel?"

At least she was still fighting. "Like a two-ton truck fell on you."

Chloe pressed her lips together, but not before Andi saw a hint of a grin.

"I knew there was something I liked about you," Chloe said. "I guess you know a US Marshal has been to see me."

"Yeah. There's one outside your door too. What's going on?" If the US Marshals were involved, Chloe's pimp was big.

"They want me to testify about what I know. If I do, I'll have to go into something he called WitSec."

"Witness Security Program," Andi said. "How do you feel about that?"

Chloe's blue eyes narrowed. "What's with you and this feeling stuff?"

"Nothing. I just want to know how you feel—your health, about going into hiding."

The girl lifted her shoulders in a quick shrug.

"At least I'll get to go to school again." She snorted. "None of my old friends back in Oh—I mean, people I know wouldn't believe I just said that."

Sounded like she was about to say Ohio. "Is it possible some parts of your old life wherever you're from weren't that bad?" She couldn't imagine what Chloe's life had been like to make her run away from home.

"It was bad enough that disappearing into that program actually looks good. Besides, I can't go home."

Evidently, she'd had a hard life. Her heart broke for Chloe. *Chloe.* It was a beautiful name, one that wasn't stuck on a baby girl at the last minute. Her mother had put time into finding just the right one. "What happened to your mom?"

The girl startled. "How did you know something happened to her?"

"She took pains to find a pretty name for you. Stands to reason if she were alive, you would never have run away."

Chloe's chin quivered, and she blinked her eyes rapidly. "She died last year from cancer, and my stepdad married the next month. When he . . ." She glanced toward the cup of water on her tray. "I'd give anything for a soda."

Pieces of Chloe's puzzle fell into place. Even though the teenager spoke with the cadence of the street, Andi never felt the street was her natural language. At one time, she'd probably had a normal life. Someone, her mom more than likely, had taught her compassion or Chloe wouldn't have wanted to warn other girls about the dangers of running away from home. "Is your dad still living?"

"Who knows. He checked out when I was three—I hardly remember him. Then Mom married—" She took a shuddering breath and wrapped her arms across her chest. "Oh, that hurts so bad."

"Do I need to get a nurse?"

Chloe shook her head. "I'll be okay."

And she probably would. The teenager was a survivor, and that, Andi understood. While her own life hadn't been easy with her sister's murder and then heart surgery four days later, she couldn't imagine being in the teenager's place. "Do you still want to send a message to those teenagers out there thinking about running away?"

The steady beep of the heart monitor jumped to over a hundred.

"We'll do it in shadows and alter your voice. No one will ever find out it's you."

The teenager's face went from gray to white, and her heart rate jumped again. "But *he* might," she whispered.

"Who is he? Is he your—"

"No! That's Jason. I'll tell you anything you want to know about him, just like I will the marshals, but the other man . . . I don't know what his name is . . ." She raked her hand through her hair. "He's like a ghost. No one knows what he looks like, but I've heard some of the other girls talk about him. He knows everything, and even Jason is afraid of him."

Andi checked the monitor again, surprised a nurse hadn't come rushing in. "I won't ask you about him. Just tell me about Jason."

"I think I want to rest now."

"May I come visit again?" She didn't want to push Chloe too hard until she was recovered.

"Maybe next week."

Andi nodded and took a card from her purse. She'd come back Sunday. "Call me if you feel like talking before then. And I promise if you agree to the interview, no one will know who you are. Between the marshals and me, you'll be safe."

"Like I was last night?"

Andi stiffened. The girl's words burned in her chest. She should have contacted Will or Brad when Chloe first called her. If she had, the teenager would not be lying here in the ICU. And Treece wouldn't be recovering from an injury. Once again, she'd been reckless not only with her life but two others, as well.

"I've been thinking about it since I've been in here," Chloe said softly. "I think maybe I shouldn't talk to you."

"I don't blame you for being afraid, and if you don't want to talk to me, I'm okay with that. I would like to come see you again to see how you're doing."

Chloe held Andi's gaze and finally nodded. "That'd be okay."

At the door, she paused and looked back. "I'll see if they'll let you have a soda."

"Thanks."

Andi pulled the sliding door back.

"I will tell you this . . ." Chloe said. "Wednesday night was going to be my last night with Jason. I heard him arguing with someone on the phone about me being shipped out. I was scared. I'd heard about some of the other girls they'd shipped out . . ."

Andi walked back to the bed. "I don't understand something. We tried to get you to leave with us. Why did you refuse to get in the car?"

Chloe chewed her thumbnail. "You don't know what it's like. My mind was so messed up with the drugs Jason gave me, I didn't know what I was doing. I was scared—I saw what happened when another girl ran away from him, and he found her . . ." Tears spilled down the teen's cheeks.

Andi gathered the girl in her arms. "Oh, Chloe, I'm so sorry."

The girl's thin shoulders shook as she sobbed on Andi's shoulder.

"It's going to be okay," she murmured, gently stroking Chloe's back.

Andi just hoped that was true.

Memphis Police Director Marcus Kennedy extended his hand to Andi. She stretched to her full five feet four inches, but Kennedy dwarfed her at six-four.

"Thank you for seeing me on such short notice," she said as they shook hands.

"Always glad to talk to the media about getting good publicity. I like the story you're doing on runaways. When will we see the documentary on cold cases?"

Good. He remembered giving the go-ahead on letting her have access to the cold case files. "That's what I'm working on now. The case I ended up choosing to profile may be related to a current case, and the detective isn't too happy about my involvement. Nothing solid there yet, but I don't want to get booted and lose what work I've done."

A grin stretched across his dark face. "Wouldn't happen to be a case a certain Sergeant Brad Hollister is working on, would it?"

Kennedy read her well, and even though she tried to will her body not to react, heat flushed her face. "Yes, sir. It hasn't been determined if the current case is a suicide or homicide."

He rubbed his jaw. "We haven't had a problem

yet with you tagging along on cases, and you've attended the citizen police academy, right?"

"Yes, sir." She waited, trying not to hold her breath. "I believe the positive publicity our stories generate will be great for public relations, given there's been so many negative stories out there lately."

Kennedy sat on the corner of his desk and propped his hand on his knee. "Great point."

He reached behind him for a memo pad. "I'll send an email to Brad's boss that I'd like you to be a consultant on the case, and that should take care of it."

Andi was glad she'd learned long ago it paid to go straight to the top. Just wait until Brad said something this time.

"Thank you." She beamed at him. "I'll make sure you don't regret this."

─ 16 ─

Wind from passing eighteen-wheelers buffeted Will as he stood at the edge of the interstate. Larry Ray Johnson's pickup had left the right lane without a skid mark and rolled into a ravine. Will turned to Richard Lee, the state trooper standing beside him, and shouted over the traffic, "You say the truck is at a body repair shop at the next exit?"

"Yeah. King's body shop. Take a right at the

exit and it's about a mile. You can't miss it," Lee said. "But if you'd like, I'll lead the way."

"Good deal." Will wrote down the patrolman's cell number, then climbed into his car with the accident report he'd given him. Cause of accident was mechanical. Bolt in the tie rod had worked loose. A note by Lee stated there appeared to be no alcohol involved.

He followed the patrolman to the body shop that was as easy to find as he'd said. They drove around the back to where the Silverado sat on a trailer. Some time in the past Johnson had raised the suspension on the pickup about four inches and replaced the original tires with mudders.

Judging from the flattened cab, the truck had rolled more than once. If Johnson hadn't been thrown out, he probably would have died instantly. Will examined the raised suspension and the right front wheel that flopped out at a right angle.

"When that bolt came out, wasn't no way the driver could keep it on the road," the trooper said. "Not traveling seventy miles an hour on the interstate. Driver is mighty lucky to still be alive."

Will agreed. He'd called an hour ago, and, according to the nurse he talked with, Johnson was still in critical condition and could not be interviewed. Will pointed to the end of the tie rod where it had separated from the steering knuckle. "Do you think raising the suspension caused this?"

"If it did, there would be wrecks happening around here all the time. Got a lot of the jacked-up trucks on the road. This one isn't as bad as some."

"How long will the truck be here?" Will asked.

"Till the TBI gets through with their investigation."

"Why did you call in the Tennessee Bureau of Investigation?"

Lee nodded to the tie rod. "There was no reason for that nut to come loose, and I just felt better asking them to take a look."

"You have my card," Will said. "Would you give me a call when the investigator is coming? I'd like to either be here or speak to him."

Lee pocketed the card. "Sure thing."

Will thanked the trooper and headed back to Memphis, calling David and updating him on the way. His cell phone rang as he exited I-40 to fill up his car. Andi. "Hello, Ms. Hollister."

"Where are you, Sergeant Kincade?"

Her tone indicated he was late, and he checked his watch. "It's barely two forty-five. I've stopped just outside of Memphis to refuel. Where are you?"

"At Mom and Dad's. Did you discover anything interesting?"

"I'll tell you about it when I see you—at three thirty. I'll pick you up."

After seeing Larry Ray Johnson's pickup,

201

somehow he had to talk Andi out of getting involved in Lacey Wilson's case. If his hunch was right, and Lacey had been murdered, and if that same person had tried to kill the corrections officer by sabotaging his truck, this guy played for keeps.

Of course, he could be all wrong, but he rarely was. For Will, solving a crime was like putting a five-hundred-piece puzzle together. His brain seemed to know how the pieces came together.

Andi was waiting for him in her parents' driveway when he pulled up. "I'll follow you."

He got out of his car. "About that. I don't think this is a good idea. Reporters don't belong at a crime scene."

"Will Kincade, you promised."

His heart sank. He had promised. But only if she got permission from Director Kennedy, and maybe that hadn't happened. Before he could ask, she put her hand on his arm, her fingers sending electricity through his body.

"If Lacey's case can shed light on my sister's murder, you're not going to lock me out of this. I promise, I won't report it on the news, at least not until we catch the real murderer."

"There is no we." He didn't blame Andi. If the roles were reversed, he'd want to be in on the investigation.

She stepped back. "Suit yourself. But it's a free country, and I can go wherever I please. Director

Kennedy has given me carte blanche with this case. See you on the nightly news." She turned to walk away.

With Kennedy's backing, she could do just what she said. She had him over a barrel. "Wait."

If he let her work alongside him, he could at least keep her out of trouble.

She turned around, victory in her eyes. He was in a no-win situation, and she knew it. His mistake had been in taking her to Nashville in the first place. In more ways than one, judging by the way he wanted to pull her into his arms and kiss her. "Come on, if you're going with me."

She ducked her head, but not before he saw the grin spread across her face.

"I better not hear one word about this investigation on the news."

"I promise I won't report anything until it's over," she said as she slid into the front seat.

"Your brother's not going to like this," he muttered.

"I can handle Brad."

He didn't know about that. "How's your arm?"

"Still sore, thank you for asking," she said. "What did you learn at the accident scene?"

"Part of the steering mechanism failed, and Johnson lost control of the truck."

"So it was an accident?"

"Didn't say that," Will said, making a right turn onto the street where Lacey Wilson had lived.

"The trooper has asked the TBI to take a look at the truck."

When Will approached Lacey's house, Brad's car wasn't in the driveway. Instead, a black Cadillac sat in the middle of the concrete drive like it owned the place. He called in the tag number to Emily.

"Whose car is it?" Andi asked when he hung up.

"It belongs to Laura Delaney."

"I have an appointment with her tomorrow. Wonder what she's doing here?"

"I don't know." Delaney couldn't have missed the crime scene tape. "But I think I'll find out."

The front door was partially open, and voices floated down from the second floor. At least two people. "You stay here until I see what's going on," Will said.

Will slipped inside. Drawing his gun—just in case—he eased up the stairs. He wanted to see what they were doing before they realized they weren't alone.

"I don't see anything."

"Keep looking. There has to be something."

The district attorney was here with a man, and it sounded like her husband. He frowned at the snatches of conversation coming from the room. What were they looking for? From where he stood, a mirror reflected clothes strewn over the bed, and he holstered his gun.

"Police," he said, rounding the corner into the bedroom and holding up his badge.

"Oh!" Laura Delaney clasped her chest.

Spencer jerked upright from the closet with a pair of shoes in his hands.

"Sergeant Kincade, you scared two years off my life!" Laura glared at him.

Will planted his feet. "This is a crime scene, Ms. Delaney. What are you doing here, and when did you arrive?"

"Crime scene?" she said. "We talked about this earlier. Lacey committed suicide. We just arrived and were getting clothes for her funeral."

"Homicide hasn't been ruled out."

Laura dismissed his words with a wave of her hand. "It's not a homicide. She's been depressed for years." She turned to her husband. "Isn't that right?"

"Yep," Spencer said, and then slid his hands in his pockets.

He was about as talkative now as earlier. Will motioned them out. "For now it's a crime scene, so you need to leave."

She pointed to a gray crepe dress on the bed and the shoes. "May we take these clothes?"

He glanced over the simple dress and nodded, then followed them downstairs.

At the front door, Laura turned to him. "Keep me informed about this case, if you don't mind. Lacey was a good friend, and if it is murder, which I doubt, I want the person responsible caught."

"So do I, Counselor."

He walked outside with them, and the skin on the back of his neck prickled when he didn't see Andi. Where was she? It was unlike her to miss out on anything. As Laura and Spencer pulled away, Brad turned into the drive.

"Who was that?" he asked as he stepped out of his white Suburban.

"Laura Delaney." Will scanned the yard. "She was picking up clothes for Wilson's funeral. Evidently had a key. Have you talked to Andi? She was in the car when I went in the house, and now she's gone."

Brad's face flushed as red as a match head, and for a second, Will thought his friend's head might explode.

"You brought Andi here? Why? This is police work; she doesn't belong here. And if Wilson was murdered, Andi might get hurt."

He'd known Brad wouldn't like her being at the house, but his reaction went beyond what he expected. "The director approved—" He stopped when Andi came around the corner of the house. "Where have you been?"

Andi ignored his question and planted herself in front of her brother. "I heard that. Just what's wrong with me being here? Stephanie was my sister too. Besides, I'm a volunteer sheriff's deputy, *and* I completed the MPD Citizen Police Academy. And if that's not enough, your director gave me permission to document this investigation for my cold case series." She stopped long enough to take a breath and then added, "You should have the email in your inbox."

Will tried not to laugh. Some sisters cajoled, but not Andi. She got her ducks in a row and laid out her case.

"This case has nothing to do with Stephanie's, which isn't even a cold case," Brad said, shooting a dark look at Will, "but evidently I can't do anything about you being here." He palmed his hands up. "Just don't get in the way. And nothing leaves this site. No photos, no conversations. Nothing."

She saluted him. "Yes, sir."

"And try to think before you rush into something," he added.

That was a low blow, and Will gave her an encouraging smile as he handed her a pair of latex gloves. "Wear these when we go inside," he said to her, "and if you find anything, let me know." Then he turned to Brad. "You were telling me about the investigation . . ."

His friend took out a notebook. "The woman two doors down went to church with Lacey and confirmed the ex-husband's statement that she was there every time the doors opened. A couple of the neighbors believe if it is suicide, the husband drove her to it, and if it's murder, he did it."

"I don't believe she committed suicide," Andi said.

Neither did Will. "Did any of them mention the mechanic that Lacey was having problems with?"

"Yeah, the neighbor who called Adam Matthews. And the neighbor across the street saw a man lurking in the neighborhood this week. But the description she gave would fit about any white male over six feet tall. The one thing all of them mentioned was Lacey's depression." He put the notebook away. "How about you. Did you discover anything at the scene of the wreck?"

"The right tie rod came loose from the steering mechanism, causing Johnson to lose control."

"An accident?"

"Evidently the state trooper doesn't feel that way. He called in the TBI to look at it."

"You're still trying to pull a rabbit out of the hat, Will. Let's go in and see if we can find any real evidence."

Will followed his friend into the house.

"Exactly what are we looking for?" Andi asked.

"A suicide note would be nice. Barring that, anything that gives a clue as to why she died, and evidence she might have been murdered," Brad said over his shoulder.

"So you *do* think she was murdered." Andi's voice rose in triumph.

He turned around. "No, just covering all the bases until the medical examiner makes a ruling. While he confirmed she was intoxicated with a blood alcohol level of .15, that wasn't enough to kill a woman of her size. I figure she drank to give herself courage to commit suicide. She even rinsed her wine glass when she finished."

"Why didn't she throw the wine bottle away?" Will asked. His gut feeling said it wasn't suicide.

"That and no suicide note are why we're looking for more evidence."

Andi pulled on the gloves. "She may have been drinking when she called me Tuesday morning. She didn't make a lot of sense, other than insisting that I meet her at the airport."

Brad gaped at her. "Why haven't you told me this before?"

"Because when I asked if she was drinking, she said no, that she hadn't slept in days. Sleep deprivation does that, you know."

"Do you remember exactly what she said?" her brother asked.

"Not really. Something about a journal she had. I assumed it was things she'd written about Steph."

"If anything comes to you, write it down. Anything that might give us a clue to her frame of mind."

Will slipped his hands into a pair of gloves as he crossed the living room floor. It didn't make sense that a woman who was flying to Hawaii later that day would commit suicide. He stopped to ask Andi a question, and she crashed into him, losing her balance.

Will grabbed her by the arms to keep her from falling. Their gazes collided, and for a second, it seemed everything stopped as heat rushed through his chest.

She rubbed her nose. "What'd you do that for?"

"What?" Was she talking about the way he'd held her longer than necessary?

"Stop like that." Her brown eyes softened as she stared up at him.

"Oh." He swallowed the grin that wanted to spread across his face of its own volition as her lips parted. For a second, he forgot everything except how much he wanted to pull her into his arms and kiss her. Brad's footsteps on the stairs brought him to his senses.

"You never said where you were when I came out of the house."

~ 17 ~

Jimmy paced the small room where he waited for Jillian Bennett. In seventeen years, she'd never come to see him. Why now? The door opened, and she stepped inside the narrow cubicle and sat on the other side of the glass window.

"Jillian?" He tried to find some resemblance to the woman he remembered, but everything about her had changed. Her curly blonde hair was now mousy gray and secured with a band. Nondescript gray clothes covered what had been a shapely body but was now gaunt and straight. She reminded him of photos he'd seen of women during the Depression.

"Yes. Sorry I didn't come sooner," she said, her voice low, hesitant.

He asked the question that had been on his mind ever since the warden told him she wanted to see him. "Why now?"

She blanched. "Believe me, I didn't want to."

His hope that she would help him evaporated. From the looks of her, Jillian couldn't seem to help herself, much less him. When she continued to sit and say nothing, he said, "Are you all right?"

She gave a shrug. "Haven't eaten hardly anything in two weeks, not since I read that your . . . execution date had been set."

That made two of them. "Did you know Lacey Wilson wrote me a letter saying that I didn't kill Stephanie?"

He didn't think it was possible for Jillian's face to get any whiter, but it turned a ghostly shade of pale.

"I shouldn't have come." She tried to stand, but her knees buckled, and she sat down hard.

"What's going on? What do you know?"

"I'm so sorry," she said and struggled to her feet. "I thought if I saw you, I could . . ."

She closed her eyes and took a deep breath. "Don't you see, he may have followed me here . . . or . . ." She looked over her shoulder. "How could I be so stupid? He'll have people working here, watching you. They'll follow me home."

She rushed to the door and opened it. "God forgive me, but I can't help you."

The door slammed shut behind Jillian, and the tiny ray of hope he'd had that she might know something and help him dimmed. She knew something, all right.

But she wasn't going to tell.

Andi's stomach did the flipping thing she hated as she caught herself staring into Will's eyes again. Even when she was a sappy thirteen-year-old following him and Brad around, she'd noticed those blue eyes.

"Where were you earlier?" he repeated.

She gave herself a mental shake. Getting lost in his eyes was not on her agenda. "Next door. The neighbor was working in her yard, and I thought I'd ask her a few questions. Did Laura Delaney tell you what she was doing for over an hour in the house?"

"What? She told me they'd just gotten there."

"So she wasn't alone."

"No, her husband was with her. They came after clothes for Lacey's funeral."

"I checked out Lacey's Facebook page last night, and she was friends with Laura. She left comments sometimes."

"Good thinking."

Facebook was usually the first place she went to get information on people. She glanced around the house. The area they were standing in was similar to hers with an open concept design—living room, dining room, and kitchen all together —except Lacey's was on a grander scale. "Brad went upstairs. What room do you want me to take?"

"How about the kitchen, and I'll take her bedroom."

After Will disappeared down the hallway, Andi turned in a slow circle, deciding where to start first. It was hard not to compare this house to the one she'd been in yesterday. Walter Simmons's house had exuded warmth, comfort, even . . . *hominess.* That was the word she was looking for. It wasn't a word she'd use to describe Lacey's place.

Andi flicked her gaze over the combination kitchen and living room. The person she'd talked to occasionally over the years had more personality than this house reflected, and it was hard to bring the two together.

If Lacey was the decorator, she must have been going for sterile with the modern black sofa and glass and steel tables. Reminded Andi of her own apartment, except . . . She examined a grouping of Grant Wood numbered lithographs on the wall. Lacey Wilson had a much larger budget, and the minimal look was on purpose. There was a difference.

She walked to the kitchen island and pulled out a drawer. Utensils neatly arranged. She moved on until she found the drawer that was in every kitchen, even this one. The junk drawer. Except this one was neat. She took everything out and piece by piece returned it to the drawer. Halfway through, Brad came back downstairs.

"Find anything?"

Her brother shook his head. "I got to thinking about the fireplace."

Andi followed his gaze to the living room, where charred logs reminded her someone had lived . . . and died in this house. "What about it?"

"I remembered while I was upstairs that someone had started a fire recently. Coals were still hot the night she was found—that was the reason I didn't check it out then."

She nodded and turned back to her task. She finished the drawer without finding anything—although she wasn't sure exactly what she was looking for. She figured she'd know it when she found it.

Andi took a step back when she opened a pantry door. She'd never seen anything so neat and orderly in her life. Lacey was definitely OCD. Not one can or box was out of place. And in order from large to small. And every can faced out with the name brand showing. A woman this compulsive would not kill herself and not leave a note behind.

"Look what we have here," Brad said from the living room.

She hurried to the fireplace, and Will joined them. "What is it?" she asked.

Brad held up a three-inch fragment of paper. "Nice stationery. This piece was against the brick at the back of the fireplace. Can you make out the letters on it?"

Andi looked closer at the paper. It was a corner piece, and there was a down stroke of the pen. "Could be half of a capital A . . . and it's blue, like Jimmy said his letter was."

"I think you're right," Will said. His cell phone rang, and he stepped away to answer it while Brad took a paper sack from his satchel and bagged it.

"Find anything in the kitchen?" Brad asked.

"Not yet. Lacey was a neat freak. I still have the cabinets to go through."

Will returned. "That was Lieutenant Raines. He's on his way."

"Why?" Brad asked.

Will hesitated. "He agrees with me that this case is possibly connected to your sister's death."

Uh-oh. When Brad clamped his jaw like he just did, someone was in for an argument, and this time it was Will.

"So do I," she said before her brother could jump down his friend's throat.

"Him, I understand. Jimmy is his cousin," Brad said, jerking his head toward Will. "But you? How can you be taken in by someone who confessed?"

"If you'd just go see Jimmy and then look at the facts, you—"

"No! Lacey Wilson's case has nothing to do with our sister's death." He sliced the air with his hand. "I looked at the reports from eighteen years ago again today, and I didn't see anything in them that contradicted the evidence. But you— you let your emotions get in the way. You always fight for the underdog, and right now, Jimmy Shelton is the underdog." He turned to Will. "And I blame you for it."

She clamped her jaw to keep from saying something she'd regret. When Brad believed he was right, she didn't think even God could change his mind. She wheeled toward the kitchen. Pain stabbed her in the back.

"Ahh!" She grabbed for the counter.

Both men jumped to help her into a chair by the desk.

"What's wrong?" Will said.

She pressed her lips together to keep from crying as sweat popped out on her face. "It's my back," she said through clenched teeth.

Andi fumbled in her pocket for the small pillbox she'd stashed there, then stilled her hand. If Will saw them, he'd bug her. "Give me a minute. I'll be okay. Can one of you get me a glass of water?"

Will obliged. "You really need to get that fixed," he said.

"Get what fixed?" Brad asked.

"My back." Reluctantly, she explained how she'd hurt it and waited for the sermon.

"You should have called me instead of climbing the fence. I would have taken care of it. Besides, what you did was trespassing."

Leave it to Brad to stick to the letter of the law.

"Well, I'm fine now." And she was, or would be as soon as she could take the pills. When she had time, she'd have the operation, but right now she had to rely on the pills. "Go back to what you were doing—but not the arguing. Let's save that for later."

The corner of Brad's mouth twitched. She didn't think he was going for it, and then he shook his head. "I'm not wrong about Jimmy."

He was never wrong. She didn't know how Will put up with him. She let his remark pass. There'd be time later to argue. Right now all she wanted was for them to leave the kitchen so she could take the Lortab before the pain hit again.

Why not take them now?

How did Treece get in her head? Because that's what her friend would say if she were here. Andi shoved the thought away. She needed the medication, and she didn't want to defend herself or explain her actions, something she shouldn't have to do anyway. Besides, she'd been taking the Lortab for three months now, and she wasn't addicted. If a doctor thought she needed them, that should be enough.

As soon as they went back to their tasks, she took out the pillbox and took out two, quickly downing them. Gingerly she put one foot on the floor and breathed a sigh of relief. Very little pain.

Since she was already seated at the desk and going through it wouldn't require her to stand, Andi started with the drawers. *When did one tablet become two?* The question came out of nowhere, and she paused in her search. When had she increased them? She'd only taken one Lortab earlier this morning. Hadn't she? Or was it two? Not that it really mattered—the prescription said one to two as needed for pain, so there shouldn't be any problem.

Andi refocused on the top drawer, where she found a sheet of paper with a list of items and serial numbers, and she scanned it. Laptop, tablet, printer, cell phone, TV. In the margins were notes where Lacey had contacted technical support for the printer. Andi needed to make herself a similar list—she always had to look up a serial number whenever she called for technical support.

Twenty minutes later, energy surged through her as endorphins released in her brain. That's what she'd been waiting for. She reached for the square wicker basket on the corner of the desk. Her heart kicked up a beat as she realized the basket was where Lacey kept her writing supplies.

She picked up a pale blue box with a ribbon around it. Inside was light blue stationery, just like what was in the fireplace . . . and maybe Jimmy's letter. She imagined Lacey sitting at the desk writing letters. Would she take out several sheets or one at a time?

Several, she decided, and examined the top sheet. Sometimes people pressed hard enough that impressions were left on the underlying paper, but this sheet looked clean.

She'd read about the technique of shining light across stationery at a low angle. Supposedly, it created shadows on the paper. There had been a flashlight in one of the drawers. Andi found it, then looked for a spot in the room with low lighting. She tried it, and her shoulders slumped. The stationery was smooth as satin. Maybe Lacey was like Andi and didn't like to use the first sheet of a tablet. She tried the second sheet.

A minute later, Andi caught her breath when letters appeared under the light. Her heart leaped into her throat as she made out a name. *Jimmy.*

"Will! Brad! You better come here. I think I found something."

As she moved the light over the paper, more words appeared, but many were unreadable— as words seemed to be superimposed on other words. Still, Jimmy's name was plain. He'd been telling the truth about Lacey writing him.

"What'd you find?" Will asked as he came from the office.

"This." Andi pointed to the stationery. "It's blue, like the paper Brad found in the fireplace. And watch this."

She shined the light across the sheet again, and Will leaned forward. She couldn't keep from grinning when he caught his breath.

He straightened up and grabbed her in a bear hug. "There *was* a letter!"

"What are you talking about?" Brad asked as he joined them.

Will pointed to the stationery as the doorbell rang. "Proof that Lacey wrote to Jimmy. Show him," he said over his shoulder as he walked to the front door. "Or wait. David's here, and you won't have to go over it twice."

— 18 —

The men shook hands, and then David cocked his head toward Andi. "Doing a story on this case for tonight's news?" he asked, sliding a questioning gaze at Brad.

"No, she's not," Will said quickly.

"Actually," Andi said, "Director Kennedy approved me being here. I'm putting together a documentary for WLTZ on cold cases, and I believe this case may be linked to my sister's death. I found something that I was about to show Brad."

"Then by all means, continue," the lieutenant said.

Once again Andi shined the flashlight so the letters appeared. All three men bent over to look.

"I took a photo of it, and if we had a printer, we could print it out."

"I have a better idea," Will said. "We have equipment downtown that will take care of deciphering what's on the paper."

"But the long and short of it is," David said, "it looks like Lacey Wilson wrote your cousin a letter."

"That was stolen," Andi said.

"And the person who may have stolen it is lying in an ICU bed fighting for his life," Will added. One look at Brad's face told him he didn't agree with the direction they were headed.

"Where are your facts?" Brad said. "The guard probably just had an accident, and Wilson's death may be a suicide. And even if she wrote Jimmy a letter saying he didn't kill Stephanie, with her problems, she may have been lying."

"Believe what you want," Will said. "But I think Lacey Wilson was killed to shut her up. Same thing with the guard, only he hasn't died yet."

"Can I make a suggestion?" David said.

Brad and Will turned to him.

"Can we go over what we do know?"

"Here?" Brad asked.

"I don't see why not," Will said. "Why don't we sit at the kitchen island?"

Brad rubbed his jaw. "Andi's not a cop, and I don't like her being involved. It's too easy for civilians to get hurt in an investigation."

"Get over it," Andi said.

David handed Brad his phone. "I just checked my email, and this is from the director. You'll have to take it up with him."

As they gathered around the island, Will swallowed a grin that Brad wouldn't appreciate. He was certain Andi was hiding one as well when she bent over her purse.

Andi pulled several sheets of paper out. "I talked to Maggie again, and she'd gotten the

222

name of the psychologist Lacey was seeing. I added it to this list I compiled with the names and addresses of people Lacey and Stephanie were involved with," she said. "I'm sure the psychologist won't talk to me, but I plan to interview the others for the documentary. You're welcome to come along. Saturday Maggie and I are going to look up Jillian."

She handed her brother a copy, and Brad pushed it away. "Steph's case isn't a cold case yet, and the Wilson case is still a possible suicide. I'm not even sure why the three of you are here," he said as his cell phone rang. He glanced at the ID. "I need to take this. Excuse me."

Will drummed his fingers on the granite. They were here because if it turned out Lacey Wilson was murdered, that case could very well be tied to Stephanie's. After Brad stepped out of the room, Will scanned Andi's sheet. "You don't have an address for Jillian."

"I know. She corresponds with Mom, and I plan to ask her for it later."

Will turned to David. "Did Madeline Starr say whether she'd take Jimmy's case?"

"She started on the paperwork late this morning and plans to Skype with him this afternoon."

Tension eased in Will's shoulders. If anyone could get a stay, it was the defense attorney. He wrote that on his notepad. "She didn't take your head off?"

David laughed. "Nah, she owes me one after this morning."

Before Will could ask the details, Brad stepped back into the room, much more subdued than when he left. He took his seat and folded his hands on the table. "Where's that list Andi had?"

"What made you change your mind?" Will asked.

A flush crept up Brad's neck. "That was the medical examiner, and it looks like I owe you an apology."

"What do you mean?" Will said.

"Scrapings from Lacey Wilson's fingernails revealed particles of skin beneath them, and it wasn't hers. But the clincher is, she had no carbon monoxide in her blood stream."

"What?" Will said.

"The tox screen showed three times the normal dose of amitriptyline in her blood. The anti-depressant coupled with a glass of wine is what killed her. By the time she realized what was happening, she could only put up a token fight. He'll be releasing a ruling of homicide later today." Brad shook his head. "Not what I expected."

Will did a mental fist pump that his hunch had been right. "I wondered why she was drinking when she planned to drive to Riverbend that day. Whoever killed her must have slipped her the drug in her wine and then washed the glass."

"But what's the motive?" David said.

"That's easy," Andi said as she massaged her back. "She knew who killed Stephanie and she was going to tell."

Brad held up his hand. "If she knew all these years, why did she suddenly decide to reveal it now? And if Jimmy didn't kill Steph in a drunken rage, who had a motive to kill her?"

Will drew a cross on his notepad. "Where Lacey is concerned, I think she'd lived with this knowledge as long as she could."

"Surely she wouldn't be stupid enough to tell the murderer what she was going to do."

Brad was right. But maybe she told someone else, and they passed the information on. "Have you gotten her phone records?" Will asked him.

"She only had the cell number, and I should get the phone records before five today."

"How about recent calls?" David asked.

"Erased . . . except for two Andi made to her Tuesday evening."

"So," Andi said, "whoever killed her deleted the calls?"

"According to the neighbor, Lacey was OCD—erasing phone calls might have been automatic." Brad rubbed his chin. "There's one more scenario I think we should consider. Jimmy could have had her killed from prison. It's happened before, and your cousin has nothing to lose."

Will pressed his lips together, mostly to keep from taking his friend's head off. He couldn't understand why he was so resistant to Jimmy being innocent. "But she wrote to him. The impressions left on her notepaper prove that."

Brad rocked back in his chair. "The impressions don't show what she wrote yet. Only his name. We'll have to wait until it's examined by the electrostatic machine, and until then, Jimmy is still my primary suspect for Stephanie's murder."

"How about the corrections officers?" Will asked. "One saw the note, and the other one is in a coma in a Nashville hospital. How did Jimmy get that done?"

"We still have to look at the possibility that Johnson's wreck could have been an accident," Brad said. "And maybe Jimmy paid off the other corrections officer."

"No." Andi shifted in her chair. "That man wouldn't take a payoff. I'm in Will's camp."

David raised his hand. "Let's look at everything calmly and compare the two scenarios."

Brad checked his watch. "Adam Matthews's flight is due in thirty minutes." He stood. "I want to be there to question Lacey's ex-husband again."

"Do you mind if I go with you?" Will asked. He turned to Andi. "I'll drop you off at your parents' house first."

"I'm not sure which gate," Brad said, "but it's flight 651 if you want to meet me there."

After he left, Andi said, "I'm sorry he's being such a pain."

"Why is he so dead set on Jimmy being guilty?" David asked.

"No clue," Will said. He gathered the notes and slid them in his briefcase.

Andi poured a glass of water from the pitcher on the table and fumbled in her purse. "I think I know. Besides being stubborn, he's spent so many years believing Jimmy did it, he's going to need facts, not suppositions."

"That's Brad," Will said. His friend had ticked him off more than once by accusing Will of going off on wild-goose chases. "He's like that with all his cases, not just this one. But when he closes a case, it's closed."

"Then perhaps we better let him work on the Wilson case by himself until he has his proof," David said.

Suddenly the contents of Andi's purse spilled out on the table, and Will's eyes widened as the top on an ibuprofen bottle popped off and pink tablets scattered. Instantly, he recognized them from his work at the mission. *Lortab?* She'd said yesterday she was taking ibuprofen. No, she'd said what she was taking was a little stronger than ibuprofen. Lortab was a *lot* stronger. Andi scooped up the pills and dumped them back in the bottle. Her lips tightened when she caught him watching her.

"Are you ready?" she said.

"Yeah."

He held his tongue until they were in the car. "How—"

"Don't start on me. My back has been killing me, and besides, I'm only taking what my doctor prescribed."

"Does he know how many you're taking?"

"I only take one when the pain gets bad."

"Don't you think it's time to get your back fixed?"

"Do you know how long I'll be out of commission? At least six weeks. I don't have time for that right now. So let it rest."

He thought of so many things he'd like to say. Like how easy it was to get hooked on the pink pill. But he'd learned working at the mission to wait. Anything he said right now would be met with total resistance. Instead, he started the car and pulled out of the driveway.

The drive to the Hollisters' was quiet. When he stopped in front of the house, Andi cleared her throat.

"Mom's making spaghetti tomorrow night. That's when we're telling my parents that Stephanie's case has been reopened."

"Brad told me." He'd forgotten that Barbara Hollister always made spaghetti on Friday nights. "Why haven't you told them yet?"

She glanced toward the house. "Dad's been

having problems with his heart, but we're afraid they'll accidentally find out, and that would be worse."

Learning the case had been reopened would be hard for the Hollisters.

Andi touched his arm. "You're almost family. Would you be there too?"

Her hand sent an electric jolt up his arm. "Are you sure? They might not want me there."

"They never blamed you, Will. I'm not saying that reopening the case won't upset them, but it would be horrible if the truth doesn't come out and Jimmy . . ." She hugged her arms. "That can't happen."

No, it couldn't. He rubbed his jaw, then moved his hand to massage the tight knots in his neck. Family. In his memories, the Hollisters were more family to him than his own mother. *"You need to forgive her, and not just for her sake, but your own."* He shook off his aunt's words and squeezed Andi's shoulder. "I'll be there."

"Good. I'll tell Mom she'll have an extra person around the table."

Just as Will turned into the airport terminal, his cell rang. "Kincade."

"It's Walter Simmons. I'm working an early shift today, and when I came on, Jimmy asked me to call you. Someone named Jillian came to see him, and he's real upset."

Jillian went to see Jimmy? "Thanks, Walter." If they could find Jillian, they might break this case wide open. "Tell him I'll be at the prison in the morning."

"Good. 'Cause I think he's lost all hope."

"Let him know I'm working on it. We're going to solve this." Will just hoped that was true. He parked in short-term parking and quickly walked inside the building. A quick check of incoming flights showed 651 was landing at B-27.

Brad was standing with his legs planted wide at the arrival door when Will arrived at gate B-27. It was hard to know what to say to his friend that wouldn't make things worse.

"The plane just landed," Brad said. "He'll probably be one of the last off."

Will had passed a Starbucks on the way to the concourse. "Want me to grab us a coffee while we wait?" When Brad nodded, Will walked the short distance to the kiosk and ordered two black coffees.

"Hazelnut okay?" he asked when he returned. The frown on Brad's face was worth the joke.

"You're kidding."

"Yeah." He wanted it to always be like this with Brad.

"Sorry for the way I acted back at the Wilson house."

"Apology accepted."

"Maybe we can get facts to go with your suppositions."

That was a step in the right direction. He and Brad moved back as the door opened and passengers flowed out of the jet bridge. They finished their coffees and dumped the cups in a receptacle just as the crew walked through the door.

"Captain Matthews," Will called as Adam Matthews walked past them.

He turned around, his eyebrows raising in recognition. "So soon, Sergeant Kincade? What can I do for you?"

"We have a few questions," Brad said.

"Can we walk as we talk? I have to check in to another flight in twenty minutes."

They fell in beside him. "You never sent me that list of names," Brad said.

"I didn't have any time to kill. How about I send it later tonight?"

"I would appreciate it." Brad nodded to Will.

"Originally you said you didn't know Stephanie Hollister," Will said.

"What can I say?" Matthews shrugged. "Tuesday night I was sweating bullets that you'd arrest me for Lacey's murder. I forgot, plain and simple." He stopped and turned to face them. "Gentlemen, I didn't kill my ex-wife. I don't have an alibi, but an innocent man shouldn't have to have one."

"Tell us about your relationship with Stephanie," Brad said.

"There wasn't one. She was just one of many

flight attendants I knew." He folded his arms across his chest. "If you have any more questions, I'd like to have my attorney present."

Which effectively shut them down.

At six, David finished writing his notes on the Stephanie Hollister case and closed the folder. Outside the small window in his office, sparse white clouds contrasted with the blue sky. Mare's tails. That's what his grandmother called the wispy clouds.

He unhooked his phone from his belt and dialed her number.

"Hello," she said, her voice strong for a ninety-plus-year-old woman.

"Hey, Grams, what are you doing for supper?"

"Hey, Davy-boy," she said. "I'm going out to eat with one of my favorite men."

Grams was the only person in the world who could get away with calling him Davy-boy, and since he hadn't called and asked her to dinner, she must be referring to his brother, Eric.

"Rats. I wanted to take you out."

"You can always join us. I'm sure Eric wouldn't mind."

"Maybe another time." David did not want to spend the evening listening to his brother's exploits in the FBI. Not that his brother meant to be obnoxious, but the conversation always turned to his job.

"How's my girl?" Grams asked.

"Alexis is fine. It's spring break, and she's with Lia's parents." They were taking her to Disney World. The trip was bittersweet for David—Disney was something his wife had always wanted to do with their daughter. The house had been especially empty with Alexis gone.

After he spent a few minutes asking about the happenings at Rosewood Manor, he hung up and grabbed his jacket. The whole evening stretched before him like an endless corridor. March Madness was still going on even though it was April. The University of Memphis had made the play-offs, so maybe he could watch the basketball game.

His cell phone rang just as he closed his office door, and he checked the ID. Madeline Starr. With a lighter mood, he answered. "Raines."

"I know you have caller ID. I thought we were going by first names."

"Sorry. Would you like to hang up so we can try it again?"

A hollow laugh followed. "No, now that I have you on the line, guess I'll keep you, especially since I need to talk to you about Jimmy Shelton."

He winced at the tension in her voice. "Have you eaten?" He didn't know where that came from other than he really didn't want to go home and eat by himself.

"Lunch or dinner?"

"That kind of day, huh?"

"Yeah," she said, "and you were part of the reason. I think you owe me dinner. Do you have any place in mind?"

He searched his memory for a place downtown. "How about the Spaghetti Warehouse?"

"It's great and near my apartment. I can run home and feed Suzy."

"Let me guess," he said. He tried to picture Maggie Starr with a dog—poodle maybe? No. "What kind of cat do you have?"

"How do you know it's a cat?"

"You look like a cat person."

"Why thank you, and Suzy is a kitty I adopted from the shelter two years ago."

He didn't know why it pleased him that he'd guessed she had a cat. "See you there in twenty minutes."

The Spaghetti Warehouse was only a few blocks away, and downtown traffic had long since cleared out, but David wanted to give her plenty of time.

"Sounds good."

"Text me when you arrive, and I'll tell you where I'm sitting."

He loved eating at the restaurant that had been renovated from a warehouse, and he usually ordered whatever was the special of the day. When he arrived, he asked the hostess for a quiet spot, since the restaurant was a favorite hangout for locals and was already filling up. Maybe he should rethink eating herc.

Get a grip. This wasn't a date. It was work. Nevertheless, he was pleased when the hostess seated him at a quiet corner table.

When his phone dinged a text, he relayed the location of their table to Maggie and enjoyed the view when she came into sight. She'd changed the jeans and sweater from earlier for a blue dress that, for lack of a better word, flowed. And the ponytail was gone. Her blonde hair curved under, barely skimming her shoulders. He stood and pulled her chair out.

"Why, thank you," she said, sounding surprised. "Sorry I took so long."

"You didn't. I only just got here. And helping a lady with her chair is rule number twelve in my grandmother's Rules of a Gentleman."

"I like your grandmother. She evidently had a lot to do with your raising."

"My dad died when I was eleven, and we went to live with my mother's parents."

"We?"

"My mom and brother, Eric."

"Eric . . . Eric Raines, the FBI agent?"

So Maggie knew his brother, which shouldn't be a surprise. He masked a stab of jealousy with a smile. "The one and only."

"Do I detect a hint of the green—"

"No, you don't. Eric is great at his job, and he's

a good brother." There was no green-eyed monster. "Then . . . you're close?"

He cocked his head. "Why the third degree?"

"Probably because I'm a defense attorney, and I'm used to digging into people's lives to find out what makes them tick." The corner of her mouth twitched. "I especially like to grill cops."

He'd been on the other end of her grilling, and it wasn't pleasant. "Why did you become a defense attorney?"

She'd been leaning toward him, but now she sat up straighter, putting distance between them. "It's a long story, and I see our waitress coming."

Maggie Starr didn't like having the tables turned. They probably should stick to work-related conversation, anyway. At least for a while. Besides, he knew the answer to the question he asked. Evidently, her brother with his wrongful conviction and then death was a sensitive subject.

The waitress set their water down and took out her pad and said, "Are you ready to order?"

David raised his gaze to Maggie. "Do you have a favorite here?"

She tilted her head toward the waitress. "Do you have the fifteen-layer lasagna today?"

The waitress, who was barely old enough to serve alcoholic drinks, smiled. "Yes, ma'am. And it is very good."

"Then that's what I'd like, with a house salad and a glass of unsweetened tea."

The waitress looked at David, and he shrugged. "Sounds good to me, only sweet tea."

After the waitress left, he asked, "Did you talk with Jimmy Shelton?"

"Yes. The warden allowed us to Skype, and we had a good first meeting—I recognized him from when I lived in the house with Stephanie and he lived next door, even though his appearance has changed quite a bit." Maggie blinked and looked past him.

David turned to see where she was looking. A man who seemed vaguely familiar walked toward them, wearing a sport coat and a smile that could only be for her. David glanced at her face and found it unreadable.

The man stopped at their table. "Maggie! I'm surprised to see you here after you told me you'd be working this evening."

"Hello, Jared. I am working." She palmed her hand and said, "Jared Donovan, Lieutenant David Raines."

Donovan held out his hand to David, and he half rose to shake it. "Good to meet you."

"Raines?" Donovan said, puzzling. "I've seen that name recently in the newspaper."

"Probably my brother, Eric," David replied. "He usually gets all the publicity."

"No, I believe it has something to do with a cold case."

"Then, it was me. I'm the head of the Cold Case

237

Unit." He didn't recall the article Donovan referenced. He wished he could place where he'd seen the man. Not around his usual haunts, for sure. Judging by the coat and the diamond ring on his left hand, they didn't travel in the same circles.

While David rarely noticed clothes, he recognized cashmere when he saw it. The jacket fit the man like it'd been custom made for him, and he wore it with the ease of a man used to expensive clothes.

Donovan glanced at the empty chair beside Maggie. "Do you mind? Only until your food arrives, of course."

"I was just about to invite you," Maggie said. "Maybe you can help us with a case we're working on."

David masked his surprise as Donovan sat in the chair. He waited for her to lead the way in this conversation.

Donovan leaned toward her, clasping her hand. "I'd rather talk about you letting me walk you home." Suddenly he glanced toward David. "Don't mean to intrude, but she did say it was work, so this isn't a date, right?"

Maggie answered for him, slipping her hand from Donovan's. "No, it isn't a date, but how did you know I walked here?"

"You always walk, and by the time you finish eating, it'll be getting dark. Maybe *you* feel safe downtown, but you don't need to walk home alone after the sun goes down."

So the man knew her pretty well. He probably even knew how Madeline got changed to Maggie rather than Maddie.

"If I feel I need an escort, David is here. And he has a gun," she said with a polite smile.

Donovan pressed his hand to his chest. "You wound me."

While he appeared to be joking, David detected a slight reddening of his neck. Donovan wasn't used to being turned down. Was Maggie playing hard to get?

Donovan leaned back in the chair. "So, what are you working on, then?"

"The Stephanie Hollister case."

"Stephanie's case? But I thought Jimmy—I mean, isn't he about to be . . ." He let his words trail off.

"Executed?" Maggie said. "Not if I can help it."

She turned to David. "Jared also knew Stephanie and Jimmy. Jared actually dated Stephanie for a while. Didn't you ask her to marry you?"

Red crept into his face. "But then she was murdered and you came along."

Evidently Stephanie Hollister was quite the social butterfly.

Maggie flashed Donovan a quick smile. "You mean until she turned you and your diamond ring down. And you don't like being turned down."

"No one likes that, but I have lots of patience. Like with you. You'll finally come around," he said, winking. "Has new evidence been uncovered?" he asked, shifting his gaze to David.

"Something like that," he replied. "Do you remember where you were the night Stephanie was murdered?"

— 19 —

"You're the second person to ask me that today, and I'll tell you what I told him—Stephanie Hollister died eighteen years ago," Jared Donovan said, his expression never changing. "Why would I remember where I was that night?"

"Who asked you earlier?"

Donovan took a card from his pocket and glanced at it. "Sergeant Will Kincade."

David didn't recall Will mentioning Donovan. "Have you remembered anything since then?"

"I did think about it." He scratched his chin. "I was probably in Brussels or maybe Paris. Eighteen years ago, I was just starting in my mother's company and regularly accompanied her on her gem-buying trips."

Donovan Jewelers. TV ads. That's why he seemed so familiar. His family owned *the* premier jewelry store in Memphis, and Donovan made the perfect spokesman.

The waitress approached with their meal, and Maggic smiled. "Jared, it was good seeing you."

He acknowledged her hint with a smile. "You too. There's a fundraiser for Le Bonheur next Friday evening. I'd love to have you accompany me."

She tilted her head. "Call me tomorrow. If I'm free, I would enjoy that."

He stood and bowed slightly. "I will. Nineish?"

"Yes."

David made a mental note to never use the term *ninish*. It sounded downright silly coming from a man.

After the waitress served their plates, he took a bite of the lasagna and said, "I'd forgotten how good this is."

"It's my favorite." She hesitated. "Sorry about the intrusion."

He waved her off. "Nothing to apologize for. But you don't like him much, do you?"

"I like him fine, but a couple of years ago, he got a little too serious, so I try to keep him at arm's length now."

"You mean serious, like marriage?"

She sipped her tea. "Yes. And I wasn't ready for that. And I'm still not."

He'd wondered why a woman as beautiful and accomplished as Madeline Starr wasn't married. Wasn't sure he wanted to ask now. "So, earlier I sensed that everything didn't go well with your meeting with Jimmy."

Her mouth twitched. "Our meeting went well. It was the meeting with the DA that didn't."

"Laura Delaney? I thought you two were friends."

"We are, but it stops at her office." She forked through her salad. "And thank you for not asking why I'm not married."

"I figure you have your reasons."

"I do, and it's nothing dark and mysterious. I simply haven't found the person I want to spend the rest of my life with."

"Good enough." She seemed perplexed, and he laughed. "I actually understand what you mean. I had that kind of love once—you'll know when you find it."

Memories blindsided David. Lia, beautiful and exotic with her long black hair softly framing her face as she walked down the aisle the day they married. In the hospital the day their daughter was born, love flushing her face and shining from her dark eyes. In the morgue, her lifeless body on a table. A band tightened across his chest, choking off his breath.

He laid his fork on the table and took a deep breath. David had no choice in when the memories hit, but he was usually able to keep his emotions at bay. He focused on the wedding band on his left hand, waiting until he could speak without his voice cracking.

"I'm sorry. I didn't mean to—"

"Not your fault." He picked his fork up again. "What did the DA say, and why did you go to her?"

Maggie shrugged. "I'm petitioning the Tennessee Court of Criminal Appeals tomorrow in Jackson, but unless new evidence surfaces right away, they'll turn us down. I went to Laura because the DA can cut through the red tape. She could have bought us time."

"Why wouldn't she help?"

"For the same reason the first DA pushed for the death penalty—politics. He had *big* political ambitions, and she's running for Congress. Neither want to be viewed as soft on crime." Maggie shrugged. "Her words, not mine. Besides, she believes he's guilty."

"Who was the DA eighteen years ago?"

"Frank Olsen, our present governor. I stopped by the courthouse and found the transcript of the trial."

"That means we need ironclad proof." Even Eric couldn't help him without it.

"If you definitely tie Lacey's death to Stephanie's murder, it would help. Where do you stand there?"

"It's moving. The medical examiner ruled it homicide late today after scrapings under her fingernails revealed traces of skin."

"We have such a short time frame that unless you come up with new evidence, I'm afraid it

243

will come down to executive clemency, and we have two strikes against us there."

"Two? What besides the governor being the DA on the case?"

"He's not fond of me. Do you know anyone who could influence him?"

"Olsen and my brother went to college together. I did call him when the issue of the letter came up. He said basically the same thing the DA said—the letter wasn't enough evidence of his innocence. If we get something solid, he'll call the governor."

"If we get something solid, we won't need him or Laura."

Surely there was someone else they could go to. They ate in silence until he said, "Have you remembered anything new from this morning?"

Maggie placed her knife and fork on the empty plate. "While I was writing the brief, I thought about the men who came around. Jared came by every day if he was in town. And Jimmy, of course—he was always hanging around." Her eyebrows lowered. "There was this older man . . . he was probably only in his thirties, but I was nineteen then, so he seemed ancient. He came around a couple of times, looking for Stephanie. Gerald Caldwell. He was a private investigator."

David put the name in his smartphone. "Do you know where he is now?"

"Yes. Office building down the street from me. Laura can tell you more about him. I think he's on retainer with the city."

His cell phone rang, and he glanced at the ID. "Excuse me a minute." When she nodded, he stood and walked near the door to talk. "Raines."

"I have the preliminary report on the impressions on the stationery."

"What does it say?"

"Bottom line, Lacey Wilson wrote the letter saying Jimmy didn't kill Stephanie," Will said. "She claimed to have evidence to prove it and planned to explain everything if he'd allow her to visit him. It was too late when he received the letter. She was dead."

"Do you have any idea what this evidence might be?"

"Not a clue, but there were other impressions on the stationery. One of them was a letter to Andi, again with a reference to her having evidence that will exonerate Jimmy."

David pressed the phone closer to his ear. "Does Andi know what it is?"

"No, but I wonder if that's what the intruder wanted Tuesday night. Andi thought she was being followed when she went to meet Lacey. If Lacey's attacker found the letter to Andi, he may have followed her home."

"Keep an eye on her."

"Oh, I will, sir. And I plan to take a look

around Stephanie Hollister's studio where she was murdered."

"You think you might find something there?"

"It's possible. No one has been in the studio since right after the murder. I doubt that George Barnes went to much trouble searching it after Jimmy confessed."

"Keep me updated," David said.

"There's one more thing," Will said. "Walter Simmons called. Jillian went to see Jimmy today, and she had to give an address. He's supposed to call me back with it. At any rate, I'm driving to Nashville first thing in the morning to talk with the warden about Larry Ray Johnson. I'd like to know his history and if anything else has ever come up missing where he's suspect."

"Good idea. Let me know what you find out." He hung up and hurried back to his table. "Sorry about that, but it was about the letter Jimmy received. We now have proof Lacey Wilson wrote it and that it said basically what he indicated—that she had proof of his innocence."

"And she's dead, and no one has a clue what proof she was talking about."

The anguish in her voice echoed what David felt. Somehow, somewhere, there was evidence of Jimmy's innocence. But time was running out.

She rubbed the back of her neck. "Do you know anyone on the parole board?"

"I did once, but his appointment ended. Another

thing Will said—Jillian went to see Jimmy today. Will is driving to Nashville tomorrow to talk to his cousin."

She looked thoughtful. "I wonder if he'd mind if I rode to the prison with him. I could meet him in Jackson."

"I'm sure he'd be glad for you to. I'll give you his cell number, and you can call him." He glanced at her empty plate. "Dessert?"

She hesitated. "I'd love to have one of their brownies with ice cream and caramel, but I better pass."

He motioned to the waitress. "We'd like your brownie to split. That way," he said, turning to Maggie, "it won't be so many calories."

"You are a man after my own heart, but you get the bigger half."

A subdued quiet had fallen on their conversation, and when the dessert was delivered, he really had no appetite for it. A man's life hung in the balance and he was eating dessert? He took a couple of bites. Evidently, Maggie had the same thoughts as she pushed her half-eaten brownie away. "Are you ready to leave?" he asked.

"Yes."

As they walked out of the restaurant, the sun hung low in the western sky, creating a breathtaking sunset. "Do you mind if I walk you home?"

"You don't know where I live."

"Has to be close if you walked."

She ducked her head. "I would be honored. It's this way."

David inhaled. "I love the way it smells in the spring. Do you smell that honeysuckle?"

"Right now all I can smell is garlic," she said with a laugh. "But, yes, I do smell it. Reminds me of home."

"Senatobia, Mississippi."

"Yep."

They walked north, past warehouses. "You really should take Donovan's advice and not walk here after dark."

"I'll take that under consideration," she said with a straight face.

He glanced at her. Maggie Starr's head came to about his chin, and even in the silky blue dress, she exuded a competent, don't-mess-with-me aura. Her comment probably had been tongue-in-cheek.

Suddenly her left arm shot out, stopping just at his Adam's apple, and he reacted instinctively, grabbing her arm. She slipped out of his hold and twisted his arm behind his back.

"I forgot to tell you. I have a blue belt in tae kwon do. If this had been a real situation, I could've flipped you on your head."

"Thank you for restraining yourself," he said, rubbing his arm. "But there are guns out here, you know."

"Which is why I rarely walk from my place to

the Spaghetti Warehouse. But tonight, I figured I'd get a ride home . . . or at the least, someone with a gun to accompany me on my walk."

Andi checked the rearview mirror, and when the street was clear, she pulled into the drive and behind her apartment. Once there, she sat in her car, processing the afternoon. It was almost six. She wasn't sure where the last couple hours went.

The euphoria from discovering the imprints on the stationery was fading. Andi took a shivering breath. She'd promised the station producer the third video on runaways by morning, and hours of work stretched ahead. For once, she wished she'd let someone else edit their film, and just as quickly discarded the idea.

She reached in her bag for the ibuprofen bottle. The documentary was her and Treece's baby, and no one else was touching it. But she needed a little boost to get the work done, and it would be better to take the pills now before she went upstairs to Treece's prying eyes. Something nagged at the back of her mind as she swallowed them, but she couldn't pin it down.

Andi climbed the back stairs, marveling at the red-gold sunset. Living on the second floor had its perks. And that reminded her of Mrs. Casey. She always missed their landlord when she went to visit her daughter. Brad had called the older woman and talked with her after the break-in, and she'd been stunned someone had broken into Andi's apartment.

At the top of the steps, she knocked on Treece's back door instead of going into her apartment. Maybe she'd had a chance to work on the segment that would air tomorrow. When there was no answer, she knocked louder.

"Hold on a minute," her friend called through the door. "Let me turn off the alarm."

Alarm? That's what had pinged Andi's brain. Had she set hers this morning? While she waited for Treece, she unlocked her door and pushed it open. When the alarm didn't sound, her stomach tightened. She'd forgotten. Again. The thing wouldn't do any good if she didn't arm it.

Andi scanned the room, and everything seemed okay. She returned to Treece's side just as she opened her door. "Did I wake you?"

Treece stretched and winced. "Not really."

"How's your shoulder?"

"Hurts. I've been icing it. But I'm getting pretty good at using my left hand."

Andi wanted to ask if she'd worked on the documentary, but Treece seemed about to burst. "Did you get out today?"

"No, but Reggie came over."

"I imagine he had plenty to say about me." Andi twisted her hands. What if Reggie had talked Treece into quitting the team? She did not want to lose Treece, not as her working buddy or her friend. "I probably deserve whatever he said."

"Yes, you do. But we didn't spend much time talking about you."

A smile played at the corner of Treece's mouth, so it couldn't be too bad. "Give."

A full-blown grin lit up her face. "He asked me to marry him."

"What! Get outta here!" She snatched a quick look at Treece's left hand. "You didn't say yes?"

"I said I'd think about it."

"Why did you do that? Reggie is a great guy and he loves you."

"He smothers me."

"Oh." There was that. "But only because he worries about you . . . because of me." Her heart sank at the truth of her own words. How many times had she put Treece in danger to get a story? Besides last night, at least three other times came to mind.

Treece squeezed her arm. "Who's to say I couldn't get in trouble on my own?"

Andi pressed her lips together to hold back the tears that burned her eyes. "Thanks for trying to make me feel better," she said once she swallowed the lump in her throat.

"Enough," Treece said, waving her good hand. "You will be happy to know I've been looking at tomorrow night's segment. There's still work that needs to be done. A couple of segues need to be smoothed out, and there's one scene that needs to be cut—I don't think we should use the shot of the establishments on Beale. They would not appreciate it, and anyway, prostitutes don't hang around there because of so much security."

She was right. "I'll take care of that tonight."

"I hate to leave all the work for you as late as it is, but . . ." Treece rubbed her shoulder.

"Don't worry about it. I'm good for another six hours." Actually, the way she felt, she could go all night.

"Are you okay?"

She looked up, and their gazes collided. "Yeah, why?"

"I don't know. You just have this . . ." She formed a ball with her hand. "Energy. How many of those pills have you taken today?"

Andi shrugged. "Not many. Did I tell you we found the stationery that Lacey wrote the letter to Jimmy on?"

"You're kidding? So there really was a letter?"

"Yeah." She filled her in on what had happened at Lacey's, and then she said, "You won't believe that house. I wish you could see it. It belongs in that magazine that's all about minimalist design. She has five Grant Wood lithographs in a grouping on one wall and nothing else. It looks great."

Interest flickered in Treece's brown eyes. "Let's do something like that with your apartment."

"Works for me. Speaking of my apartment, I

better get to work on the film." She grabbed her bag. "You didn't change anything, right? I can use the copy I have on my computer?"

"Yes. Want me to keep you company?"

"Let me work on it awhile first, and if it isn't too late, I'll call you to see what I've done."

Andi crossed the hall and unlocked her door. She'd forgotten to mention the alarm. Just as well. Treece would only worry and blame it on the Lortabs. She slipped inside and scanned the room again.

Wait a minute. She didn't remember leaving the shade up on the kitchen window. Maybe she should call Brad, or Will. She took out her phone to dial Will while checking to see if anything had been disturbed. Remote was still where she left it by the recliner. The papers on her table looked the same. And the apartment had that empty feeling, like she was the only one in it. She must have left the shade up too.

She jumped when someone knocked on her back door. Will stood on the deck, and she hurried to let him in. "You scared me. What are you doing here?"

"Sorry. Just wanted to tell you what the electrostatic image report said. Did you turn the alarm off?"

"Ah." She glanced toward the panel. "You don't hear it going off, do you?"

"You forgot to arm it, didn't you?"

She flushed under the steady gaze of his blue eyes. "Okay! I forgot. I was actually about to call you until I figured out no one's lurking about." Then she pointed to the decals on the back door and the window. "If the intruder had come back, he would have seen that red sign on the door and windows. He wouldn't have known it wasn't armed."

"Lucky you. Have you checked your bedroom?"

She dropped her gaze. One day maybe he wouldn't look at her like she was a complete idiot. "Not yet," she mumbled. "And I guess it wouldn't make me mad if you checked."

When he moved past her, pulling his gun, relief spread over her like a comforting quilt. She might actually get used to someone looking out for her.

Treece stuck her head in the open doorway. "I heard voices."

"It's just Will, checking out the apartment."

"Did you forget to set the alarm?"

"What is this? Pick on Andi day? Why does everyone automatically think I forgot to set it?"

"Maybe because you did?"

She made a face just as Will returned to the living room, holstering his gun.

"See, I told you no one was here," she said.

"Don't forget again," he said sternly.

"Yes, sir. Why did you come over? You could have called and given me the report. And how did you know I was home, anyway?"

"Brad."

She jerked her phone out. That stupid app he put on her phone. She moved her thumb to delete it but hesitated. Her brother would just put a tracking device on her car if she did.

"I figured you forgot to arm the alarm, and I came to help you check out the apartment."

She turned and raised her eyebrows at Treece, who held up her cell phone.

"And I wanted to take photos of your apartment. I thought as long as I can't work, I could pick up a few things to decorate."

"Oh. Thanks." Andi wrinkled her nose. "Could one of you maybe send me a text in the morning and remind me to set the alarm?"

"Yes," they said in unison, then burst into laughter.

"Don't know what we're going to do with you, girlfriend," Treece said, shaking her head. She handed her the cell phone. "Would you do the honors?"

Andi obliged and took shots from every angle, then handed the phone back. "You can change everything except this," she said, picking up the clay sculpture. Over the years it had turned almost black.

"Could we at least move it to the bedroom?" Treece asked.

"Let me think about it." She rubbed her thumb over the horse's head and down the mane. A small piece of clay broke loose from the rump. *No. It can't crumble.*

She tried to smooth the dry clay, snagging her thumb on a piece of wire. She stuck her thumb in her mouth, tasting her own blood.

Treece cleared her throat. "Okay, you're in good hands. I think I'll retire to my apartment."

"You don't have to go," Andi said.

"Yes, I do. I'm tired."

After Treece closed the door behind her, Andi turned to Will. "Now will you tell me what was on the stationery?"

"Basically everything Jimmy said was there— that she had evidence that he didn't kill Stephanie. She planned to explain everything if he allowed her to visit him. Unfortunately, he didn't get the letter until after she was dead."

"What do you think this evidence is?"

"I don't know." He hesitated and wouldn't meet her gaze.

"What?"

"There were other letters imprinted on the stationery. One was to you and mentioned that she had written Jimmy, but he hadn't responded. She wanted to tell you before she left the area that he hadn't killed your sister."

"Was there anything else?"

"She said that you have diamonds in your possession. Then she scribbled lines through what she'd written."

"You're kidding. Why would she say that?" She wrapped her arms around her waist.

"I don't know, but I wonder if that's why someone broke into your apartment Tuesday night."

"He was looking for diamonds, all right." She glanced around the room. "But there's certainly none here. Do you think Lacey told the person who killed her that I have these diamonds?"

"That or he saw the letter."

The hair on the back of her neck rose. What if the intruder had known she'd forgotten to set the alarm? What if he'd entered the apartment and had been waiting for her when she returned?

She stared at the figurine in her hands. Suddenly, she didn't want to be alone. "You don't have to go just yet, do you? Have you eaten?"

"Picked up a couple of burgers on the way over. They're in the car. Want one?"

She wasn't hungry, but if it kept him here for a while longer, she'd eat. She set the horse back on the mantel. "Let me get some plates."

When she turned around, he had the horse in his hands, studying it. "Stephanie was quite ood. Why don't you have this fired?"

She quelled the impulse to tell him to be careful with it. "It's so old, I'm afraid it might explode in the kiln. I think I'd die if I lost it." He set it back on the mantel, and she breathed again.

"I still don't understand why it's so special. Don't you have other things that your sister made?"

257

"Yeah, but . . ." Most of the time, Andi was able to block that night from her mind. "I'll tell you about it while we eat."

She had cleared off her table and pulled up the stool from the bar by the time he returned from his car. She really needed to get more furniture. When Andi took the top off her burger, she said, "You remembered."

Will smiled. "Mustard, pickle, no onion."

Andi ducked her head, pleased that he'd gone to the trouble. After they finished the burgers, Andi made a pot of coffee. "Danish or lemon cookies?"

"Cookies."

When the coffee was done brewing, she poured each of them a cup and arranged the cookies on a plate. "The sofa?"

He nodded and sat down. "You were going to tell me about the statue."

"Yes, I was." She hadn't thought about how close Will would be on the sofa, or maybe she had. She took a deep breath and closed her eyes, going back to that night. "For the first time in months, we were celebrating . . ."

Andi could barely wait to tell Stephanie the good news.

"Do you think she'll be surprised?" she asked. Her sister had been so worried.

Mom grinned. "I think she will."

Just today, they'd been told the doctor would donate his services, and with Le Bonheur accepting whatever they could pay, the surgery had been scheduled.

"I'm sorry I got sick," Andi said. She hated being a burden and wished she were grown instead of just thirteen. Then she could take care of the bill herself, 'cause she knew her dad. He'd work and pay every penny of the hospital bill even if it took him forever.

"Honey, you can't help it. Just like Dad can't help losing his job."

And insurance, Andi wanted to add. If she was going to get sick, why didn't God let it happen two months ago when they had insurance? She cringed. What if lightning struck her for thinking something like that?

Mom parked in the driveway behind Steph's '68 Miata, and Andi rushed inside the studio.

"Guess what, Stephanie! The doctor—"

Stephanie lay sprawled on the floor with red paint on her chest.

The screams echoed through Andi's head, first her mother's then her own. She fell to her knees beside her sister. "Please, Steph," she sobbed. "Don't die."

Her sister's eyes fluttered open. "The horse . . . yours . . ."

Andi looked up, and Will's eyes were shiny, just like she knew hers were. "She gave me the horse. Then she was gone."

• • •

Will wanted to take Andi in his arms and kiss away the pain in those brown eyes. He was pretty sure she would not rebuff him. But if he ever kissed her, he wanted it to be at her invitation and not because he'd taken advantage of her vulnerability. Instead he said, "I'm sorry."

She hugged her arms to her body and continued like she hadn't heard him. "When I turned around, I saw Jimmy on the sofa with a gun in his hand. He was so drunk I don't think he even knew we were there."

Will had never heard the details of how Andi and her mom found Stephanie and then discovered Jimmy with the gun that killed her. "What happened next?"

"Everything else about that night is a blur. By then Mom had called 911 and the police arrived . . ." She brushed her hair back with her fingers. "I think Maggie was there, and Laura." She looked up and shook her head. "The others probably were too, but I just don't remember."

Could he be wrong? Was it possible that Jimmy had killed Stephanie? He chewed his thumbnail. No. He didn't believe that. He needed to look at the file again, and it was in the car.

But not now, and not here with Andi. She needed rest, and if she got involved with the file, that wouldn't happen.

He took her hand and wanted to hold so much

more when their gazes locked. "I hate to leave you, but you look done in." She started to protest, and he put his finger on her lips. "For once, listen to me. Lock the door behind me and set the alarm, then go to bed."

She gave him a tiny smile. "Yes, sir," she said softly.

He kissed her lightly on the forehead. "I wish I could believe you'd do that."

"I have film to edit."

"Aren't there people at the station who can do that?"

She looked up at him under raised eyebrows. "You know me better than that. It's mine and Treece's project, and *nobody* works on it but us."

"At least take a nap before you get started," he said and stood.

She walked to the door with him. "That I may do."

At the door, he said, "Do you think you could let me into Stephanie's studio tomorrow? I hate to bother your parents."

She froze. "I haven't been in there since that night. No one has, really. Dad locked it up as soon as the police were finished."

The pain in her eyes sent a dagger to his heart. "Forget it," he said softly. "I'll get Brad to help me."

She took a shaky breath. "Thanks."

Once he was in his car, he debated whether to

go home or study the file right there in the car so he could keep an eye on Andi's apartment. From his vantage point, he could see the whole driveway and street.

He'd stay at least until she went to bed. He reached in the backseat for the file and used the light on his phone to sort through it. It was obvious from reading Barnes's notes that he believed from the outset it was a cut-and-dried case. Jimmy killed Stephanie, and once he had Jimmy's confession, coerced or not, he wasn't about to look any further.

Will sorted through the papers, looking for the report on gunshot residue that should have been conducted on Jimmy's hands and clothes. Frowning, he repeated his search. It wasn't there. Evidently, Barnes didn't conduct one. Why hadn't the public defender picked up on that?

If there ever was a no-good, lazy cop, it was Barnes. Will snapped a photo of the report and emailed it to David with a note of what it was and where it came from, adding that Jimmy had not been tested for gunshot residue.

Then he sent the same report to Brad. It would take showing his friend how badly Barnes botched the investigation to get him fully on board. His cell phone rang, and he turned the flashlight off before he answered. "Kincade."

"Will. This is Madeline Starr. I understand you're driving up to see Jimmy in the morning.

Could you pick me up in Jackson and let me ride along with you? I hate that drive alone."

"I'd be honored, ma'am."

"Great. And it's Maggie, not ma'am."

"See you in Jackson, say nine?" A red glow on the street caught his eye. A man was standing at the entrance to the drive with a cigarette in his hand.

"Nine should be about right. I'll be at the courthouse."

"Great. See you then."

Will hung up and sat still. The moon was covered with clouds and there was no overhead light on the side of the house, so he couldn't see the man's features, only shadows from the streetlights. He was only assuming it was a man by the size. Six-one at least.

The red glow bounced on the drive as the man threw the cigarette down then walked to the back of the house. Will scooted down in the seat and unstrapped his gun. He bunched his muscles, waiting.

With stealth, the stranger eased under the faint light from the porch. He was dressed in a dark hoodie and dark pants. As soon as he reached the steps, Will sprang from the car, his gun raised. "Police! Put your hands where I can see them."

The man whirled around and broke for the street. Will chased him, tackling him at the corner of the house. Air whooshed from the man's lungs.

"Wait! I'm a private investigator!" He reached toward his jacket.

"Keep your hands where I can see them."

He halted halfway to his pocket and held his hands up. "Okay."

Will climbed to his feet. "Stand up and tell me who you are and what you're doing here."

Grunting, the man pushed up from the ground. "Gerald Caldwell. Caldwell Investigations. I have my credentials in my front pocket."

Will patted him down and pulled a .38 caliber Smith & Wesson from a shoulder holster.

"I have a permit to carry."

"I don't doubt that, and this is a good way to lose it. Let me see your credentials."

Caldwell fished his wallet out and flipped it open. "Can we sit down somewhere? When you knocked me down, I hurt my knee."

"How about at the CJC?" The credentials looked legit.

"There's a Waffle House around the corner. How about there?"

Will might get more out of him at the fast food place, and he wasn't worried about the detective running off, since Will knew where to find him. "I'll follow you."

After they arrived, Will followed Caldwell into the Waffle House. Two truckers sat on stools, leaving them their pick of booths. Will ordered coffee, but Caldwell ordered a full breakfast with waffles. In the lighted restaurant, Will remembered seeing the private investigator around the courthouse, and understood why some of the cops called him the Hawk with his hooked nose and dark eyes.

"Haven't eaten since noon," he said.

"So, tell me why you were snooping around Andi Hollister's apartment."

"A client asked me to contact her."

Will waited.

"That's privileged information."

"I can always take you downtown and ask."

"All right," Caldwell grumbled. "I can give you maybe a little more. After her segment on runaways on Tuesday night, I got this call from a parent. She wanted me to contact Andi about her daughter."

"So why were you lurking around the back of the house? Why not just call her?"

"I tried calling the station and was told they would give her my number. When I didn't hear anything, I thought I'd stop by and see her. I tried the front door and no one answered," he said. "When I saw there was a light on, I figured she was still up. It's only ten, so I was going to knock on her back door."

"How did you get her address?"

Caldwell eyed Will. "Uh, phone book?"

Andi was listed in the phone book? Was she nuts? That was an invitation to all the crazies in

Memphis. He wondered if Brad knew. Something else occurred to him—he'd just seen Caldwell's name in the list of people Barnes had interviewed. "Your name was in the case file on Stephanie Hollister's death. Why?"

The private investigator shrugged. "Wasn't that in the report?"

"I thought you might have remembered something since then." Whatever was said between Caldwell and Barnes wasn't in the report.

"Nothing has changed."

"Then you won't mind going over it again. Why did Barnes interview you?"

The waitress approached with his breakfast, and Caldwell leaned back. "Looks good, young lady."

She set Will's coffee in front of him. "Cream?"

He shook his head, and as soon as she left, he repeated his question.

"Give me a minute to remember." He cut into the sausage and popped half a link into his mouth. "Okay, it was like this. I had a client who wanted the Hollister woman checked out. Seems her son was interested in her and she wasn't happy about that."

Will hadn't expected that. "So, did you discover anything?"

"Should be in that report you have."

"That wasn't the question I asked."

"Let me pull it together while I finish eating."

Evidently, Caldwell suspected there was no

report on his conversation with Barnes, maybe even knew there wasn't. Will nursed his coffee until Caldwell finished his meal. His gaunt frame indicated he didn't eat like this all the time, or he had an extra fast metabolism.

"That was good." The investigator blotted his mouth with a napkin. "I don't understand why you're looking into the Hollister case. The woman is dead, and her killer is scheduled to be executed in three days."

Will restrained himself from reaching across the table and grabbing the thin man by the shirt collar. If he knew that much about the case, he also knew Will was Jimmy's cousin. Why was he baiting him? "I just joined the Cold Case Unit, and I'm looking into it," he said evenly.

"It's not a cold case. Jimmy Shelton was convicted."

"Why do you know so much about this case?"

"How about I trade information? I'd like to know Jillian Bennett's whereabouts. You give me that and I'll tell you what I discovered when I investigated Stephanie Hollister."

"Why do you want to know where Jillian is?"

"That's confidential. How about it?"

When Will didn't answer, Caldwell said, "It's worth the trade."

"I don't have to trade, I can subpoena your files."

"But then it'd be too late to save your cousin."

— 20 —

At nine o'clock Friday morning, Andi viewed the changes she'd made to the video for the evening news. *"Do you think you could let me into Stephanie's studio?"* Will's question wouldn't go away. She refocused on the video, and a few minutes later saved it to an online site for the producer.

Now if she could get an interview with Chloe. She dialed the hospital room, and Chloe answered. "Good morning, this is Andi Hollister."

"Morning."

"How are you?"

"Okay."

One-word answers weren't good. Maybe this wasn't the right time to do an interview. She didn't want the girl to think interviewing her was the only reason for Andi's interest. "I'm coming downtown in a bit. Is there anything I can bring you?"

"No."

"Are you upset with me, Chloe?"

There was silence on the other end. "No. I . . . I just don't feel good."

"How about a milk shake? That always perks me up."

"No, really, I'm not hungry. But thank you."

Chloe's voice had that I-want-to-hang-up tone. "Okay, just call me if you need anything."

"Andi . . ."

"Yes?"

"Never mind. Good-bye."

The line went dead, and Andi stared at the phone. Something was bothering Chloe. She thought about her schedule, wishing she had time to stop by the hospital.

Her thoughts returned to Will's request. Andi pushed away from the computer and paced her apartment. She'd like to help him. Really, she would.

She rubbed the front of her legs. Maybe it was time to face whatever it was that sent her into panic mode just thinking about entering Stephanie's studio. Before she could change her mind, she texted Will to meet her at the studio at three thirty. Her parents had just resumed their Friday afternoon golf game with another couple, so they'd be away from the house all afternoon. He texted back a thumbs-up emoji.

When had she taken the last dose of Lortab? Had to be at least eight hours ago. *What's your pain level?* Andi blocked Treece's warning. Her friend didn't understand. And as soon as Andi had time, she'd get off the pain pills. But right now, she needed them, not just for pain but also to curb the anxiety that dogged her.

An hour later, euphoria rode with Andi on the

elevator to the district attorney's floor at the Criminal Justice Center. A moment later, she was ushered into Laura Delaney's private office. A side door opened, and Laura stepped into the room.

Andi had interviewed her a few times for the station, and each time she'd been impressed that the forty-year-old attorney could walk in four-inch stilettos. She swallowed a laugh at the image of herself in those shoes.

Gold bracelets clinked on Laura's arm as she moved toward Andi in a white blouse and gray skirt that matched the gray heels. A matching gray jacket hung on a rack by the door, ready to be slipped on when needed. The district attorney was the picture of success.

"How can I help you today?" Laura took her place behind the desk and motioned Andi to a leather side chair.

"I'd like to make a documentary on your congressional race," Andi said. She perched on the edge of the chair and put her feet flat on the floor to keep her legs from jiggling up and down. Suddenly her head swam, and she gripped the chair arms for balance.

"Really?" Interest lit Laura's eyes, and she held up her index finger. "Let me get Spencer in here."

Andi took a deep breath to clear her head while Laura texted her husband. A few minutes later, Spencer Delaney entered the office. He embodied the tall, dark, and handsome cliché, and if ever a couple were a perfect match, at least outwardly, it was the Delaneys. Andi could easily see them in a glossy brochure for a luxury car.

She laid out her idea for the documentary. "One last thing," she said, wrapping up. "The documentary won't air until after the election, four months from now, but it will air whether you win or lose."

Andi was banking that Laura would win, though. The DA was well liked while her opponent was relatively unknown.

Laura's shoulders straightened. "You are looking at the next representative from this district."

"That's what I'm counting on," Andi said.

Laura stood and walked to the window that overlooked downtown Memphis. After a minute, she turned, and after a quick glance at her husband, extended her hand. "I look forward to working with you on this."

"Good!" Spencer Delaney clapped, his brown eyes dancing.

Andi rose and shook her hand. Laura had perfected the political handshake. Not too tight, but firm. She'd perfected the smile as well with teeth showing and eyes focused totally on Andi as though she were the only person in the room.

Laura winked at her husband, then refocused on Andi. "Do you think you can keep up with me?"

"I'll try."

"I believe you. When you were a teenager, you were very determined even then to become a reporter . . . until you became ill."

That was a time Andi didn't like to remember. "Stephanie was a rock for me back then."

A gentle smile curved the DA's lips. "Stephanie was a jewel, and she was very concerned about the operation. She worried that you might not have it because of insurance issues."

Nice way to say money problems. "I don't know why she thought that. Le Bonheur takes what the family can pay, and the doctor donated his services." But she had known that Steph worried about the money situation her family was in. And it was Steph's life insurance policy that eventually paid the medical bills. A fact that made Andi determined to live up to Stephanie's expectations of her.

Laura worried a tiny Band-Aid on her hand. "Your sister was very proud of you. Whatever happened to those movies you made when you interviewed the four of us about our overseas flights?"

"You remember the movies?"

An indulgent smile followed. "It was kind of hard to forget when you were always there with your camera."

Her trusty 8mm Kodak. She'd pestered the other flight attendants living with Stephanie until each of them allowed her to video them and answer her questions. She wondered where those films were.

"I really wanted to be a flight attendant," Andi said. "But Steph wanted me to get my journalism degree and become a reporter. Wouldn't hear of me following in her footsteps."

Laura nodded in agreement. "She wasn't happy flying. I think she would have liked being an artist, you know, with the clay, but there wasn't a lot of money in that back then."

Stephanie had loved creating her figurines. If only she'd had more time . . . "Money isn't always the most important thing in life."

"I don't know about that," Spencer said. "I think it ranks right up there at the top."

Both women laughed, and Andi tilted her head toward Laura. "I didn't know my sister the way you did. You know, as an adult. Can you tell me what she was like?"

"She was beautiful, inside and out."

At times Andi couldn't remember what her sister looked like, but today a clear picture of Stephanie surfaced with her long dark hair framing nearly perfect features. She had their dad's hazel eyes that were more green than brown. But it was her vibrancy that brought it all together.

Laura returned to her desk and sat on the corner. "Stephanie was one of those rare people who could fit into any situation, and with her looks, she should have been in Hollywood."

"I don't believe that Jimmy killed her." What possessed her to say that?

"Are you kidding?" Spencer said. "He was insanely jealous. Jimmy Shelton had motive, means, and opportunity."

Laura agreed, nodding her head. "You never saw the bad side of their relationship, especially after she broke up with him. With him living next door, he could still walk into the studio anytime he wanted to. I remember one time in particular. We were working the same flight later in the day, and I had gone to see what time she was leaving for the airport.

"When I stepped inside the studio, Jimmy lay sprawled on the sofa, drunk as usual, and Stephanie was crying. The wet cloth Stephanie pressed against her cheek didn't hide the bruise."

"Jimmy hit my sister?" She didn't remember any of this.

Laura bit her bottom lip and stared at a point on the wall over Andi's head. "Stephanie said he didn't mean to, and she even defended him. I tried to get her to call the police, but she was afraid he would go to jail because of the barroom fight he'd gotten into. I told her then he was going to kill her if she didn't do something, but she didn't believe Jimmy would seriously hurt her."

She shifted her gaze to Andi. "Your sister was trying to help him, but she wasn't qualified to deal with his problems."

Andi had no idea of any of this. Was she wrong about Jimmy? Was it possible he really had killed Stephanie?

"Since yesterday when Sergeant Kincade questioned me about Stephanie's . . . her death, I've thought a lot about that night." Laura stared at a spot on the floor. "I remembered how I kept after her to get a restraining order against him until finally she did. The night he killed her, I was home studying, and I called her. I begged her to call the police when I learned he was with her in the studio. But she assured me she would be all right, that he'd passed out on the sofa."

Spencer jingled the change in his pocket. "And then Jillian and I made you go with us to get something to eat," he said and turned to Andi. "We were at a barbecue place when we found out what happened."

Laura raised her head. "I just regret that I didn't call them myself after I hung up from talking with her. I don't know if you're aware of it, but Madeline Starr is trying to get a reprieve for Jimmy, but she'll never get my help."

"Yes, I'm aware." Judging by the hard tone in her voice, there'd be no changing Laura Delaney's mind about Jimmy's innocence. Andi had felt the same way until Wednesday, and after hearing

Laura's story, it was hard to remember why she'd changed her opinion. *The letter from Lacey.*

She turned to Spencer. "You mentioned motive a few minutes ago. Did anyone else have a grudge against my sister?"

He crossed his arms over his chest. "Only the men she dated and discarded. Men like Jimmy."

His words triggered a memory she'd long forgotten. "Did you ever date my sister? Seems like I remember seeing you two together in a red Mustang convertible."

"We went out maybe a time or two." He crooked a smile. "You have a good memory. I wish I still had that car." He smiled lovingly at his wife. "You made me get rid of it because Stephanie liked it so well, remember?"

"Spencer Delaney, I did no such thing. I was never jealous of Stephanie."

In spite of Laura's words, her voice went up an octave. A nerve had been struck.

"Losing Steph was so hard, but I remember you being very kind to me at the funeral," Andi said, directing her words to Laura. "In fact, all of the roommates were. I always felt bad that you had to find other places to live right after that."

"We all understood. I'm sure it was hard for you and your family to move back."

It was beyond hard. "I haven't told my mom about Lacey yet. She was very fond of her."

"She hasn't seen it in the paper?"

"They only get the weekend edition, and it never aired on TV—a carjacking and kidnapping had priority."

"Poor Lacey." Laura cast her gaze toward the floor and shook her head. "I feel so bad that I let her down. I keep asking myself what I could have done to prevent this."

"Honey, you begged her to get help," Spencer said. "What else could you do?"

"Why do you think Lacey's death is a suicide?" Andi asked.

"What else could it be?" Spencer said. "She was in her car with the motor running."

"Did you know she'd written Jimmy Shelton a letter?"

Laura glanced at her husband, then back to Andi. "Will Kincade mentioned it, but any letter from Lacey Wilson will not be helpful to Shelton. She was unstable."

Andi had wandered into territory she hadn't intended to. "Did you let Jillian know about Lacey?"

Laura's eyes widened. "I forgot all about her."

"Mom has her address, but if you have it or her phone number, I'd like to get it now. To let her know."

"You're still in touch with Jillian?" Laura asked.

"Mom occasionally receives Christmas cards from her."

"Really? Why would she stay in touch with your mom?"

And not me, Laura's tone implied. "Jillian went to high school with Steph. She was in our house all the time as a teenager."

"Just ask your mom for Jillian's address," Spencer said.

She shrugged. "I hate to bother her."

Her mother would want to know why Andi wanted the information, and then she'd have to tell her Brad and Will were investigating Stephanie's death before Andi was prepared to tell her.

Laura walked to her desk and picked up the telephone. "Jace, would you check my contacts for a Jillian Bennett?"

"Knight," Andi said. "That's her married name."

"She's married?" Spencer asked.

"Apparently so. The University of Memphis gave me that information."

While they waited, Andi said, "I don't remember what happened to Jillian after everyone moved out. You and Maggie and Lacey moved into an apartment together, but Jillian seemed to just disappear."

"She wanted to go to college, but I didn't know she went to the U of M." Laura exchanged glances with her husband. "Do you remember?"

"She dropped out of sight. I haven't thought about her in years," he replied.

A few minutes later, the secretary brought the

information to Laura, and she glanced at it before handing it to Andi. "I don't have a phone number for her."

The address was one that she'd already found. Jillian hadn't lived there in years.

Laura flashed her politician smile. "When do you want to get started on this documentary? I assume you'll be hanging around the office and that you'll be at any political rallies I'm scheduled for."

"That's my plan. If you'll make a schedule, it will help." Andi took a video camera from the bag she'd brought. She would bring a cameraman for the actual interviews. "I'd like to film you working in your office today."

"If you two ladies will excuse me, I have work to do," Spencer said.

"You don't want to get in on the filming?" Andi said.

He waved. "Oh no. Laura is the photogenic one. The camera doesn't like me."

She wanted to laugh. With his chiseled jaw and muscled arms, Spencer Delaney would look good digging ditches. An image of him straining those biceps with a shovel popped into her mind.

Biceps strong enough to put an unconscious woman behind the wheel of a car.

When Will arrived early at the truck stop just outside Jackson, Tennessee, Madeline Starr was already there.

"The petition for a reprieve is filed," she said as she fastened her seat belt.

"Do you think we have any chance of getting it?" He didn't want to get his hopes up.

"There's always a chance, though harder without Laura Delaney's help. If it weren't for her upcoming election, I believe she would have helped us," Maggie said. "But she has a strong segment of voters in her district who are very high on law and order and low on coddling prisoners. A few of them are big contributors to her campaign."

"And if she supported the stay and whatever evidence we uncover is thrown out, it would hurt her at the polls," Will said.

"You got it. We should hear something from the petition today or tomorrow. And a few prayers would certainly help."

If quantity of prayers counted, they should get the reprieve. "Thank you, ma'am."

"I told you, it's Maggie."

An hour and a half later he forgot and called her ma'am at least three times. The last time, she called him on it.

"I'm sorry," he said. "But my aunt was a stickler about Jimmy and me calling anyone in authority ma'am or sir."

"But I'm probably not even five years older than you."

Will's neck burned. "If it's any consolation,

I'm having the same problem with David."

She laughed. "Yesterday was the first time I've really had a conversation with David other than cross-examining him in the courtroom. Tell me a little about him."

Will reviewed what he knew about his boss and how much of it he could relay. He liked Maggie, but the lieutenant was . . . "He's very private," he finally said. "Widowed, with a daughter around ten, plus he's a great boss."

"I didn't know he was widowed. What happened to his wife? Or is that part of the privacy?"

"No, it's public knowledge, but he never talks about it. She was murdered, and the killer hasn't been caught."

"Is that why he lobbied for a Cold Case Unit?"

He glanced at her and then just as quickly returned his eyes to the interstate. "So you do know something about him?"

"I always research the background of witnesses in my cases but somehow blocked the part about his wife. Now that you mention it, I remember my information indicated she went by her maiden name."

"She did. Lia Morgan was a well-known photographer before they married, and most of the time she used that name rather than Raines."

A text alerted, and Maggie checked her phone. "Laura reminding me that Lacey's funeral is at five. Do you think we'll be back in time to attend?"

"I plan to be. I told Brad I'd be back by three thirty to check over the studio where Stephanie was murdered, and the cemetery is only ten minutes away from the Hollister house."

"You think you'll find something the original investigator missed?"

"I hope so."

"Is there a report on what the crime scene techs found eighteen years ago?"

"No report. I don't know if crime scene techs even went over the room after Jimmy confessed. George Barnes was the investigating officer, and he didn't even conduct a gunpowder residue test on Jimmy."

"You're kidding," she said.

"No. Can you use that?"

"Yes. I've successfully defended three people he arrested. If the court in Jackson turns us down, I'll definitely use that in my appeal."

Will flipped on the turn signal and took the exit to 155 North. "We're five minutes from the prison."

Maggie became increasingly quieter as they entered Riverbend. He knew how she felt, especially when the doors clanged shut behind them. He didn't know how Jimmy had stood being locked up here seventeen years.

As before, Jimmy was sitting at the table when they entered the small conference room. Walter

Simmons had warned Will that Jillian's visit had left his cousin shaken, but he hadn't expected total defeat. Everything about Jimmy said he'd given up. He hadn't shaved and his clothes looked as though he'd slept in them. "Are you all right?"

Jimmy raised his head and looked at him. "Sure. Fine and dandy. I don't suppose you have a reprieve or a stay order in that briefcase, Ms. Starr?"

"Afraid not, Jimmy. But we're not finished. We have two days."

He dropped his head again and stared at the table.

Will sat across from him. "Look at me."

He continued to stare at the table.

"I said look at me."

Jimmy lifted his gaze.

"I promise you, I'll do everything in my power to get the evidence to set you free."

"I know that, Will." He turned to look out the tiny window. "When Jillian showed up, I thought she had come to help me get out of here. But when she walked through that door to leave, I knew it was over." He pressed his fingers against his temples. "I'll almost be glad when Sunday night gets here. I . . . I can't take much more."

"Don't talk like that!" Will wanted to shake him. "Let's go over everything again, starting with Jillian's visit. What did she say?"

Jimmy slumped in the chair, then he shook himself and with a fortifying breath, sat up straighter. "She was scared. Said she shouldn't have come. That 'he' had someone here at the prison watching me. That's when she practically ran out the door." He balled his hands. "The last thing she said was God forgive her, but she couldn't help me."

So Jillian did know something. Something that sent her into hiding. "Did you tell her Lacey was dead?" Will asked.

"Didn't get a chance."

"I talked with your mother yesterday," Maggie said. "She thinks Stephanie was into something illegal. She had to get that impression from you. What do you think she was doing?"

"I don't know." He palmed his hands. "I can't think anymore."

"You have to!" Will almost shouted.

Maggie restrained Will with her hand and then turned to Jimmy. "Do you think she could have been smuggling drugs into the country?"

"No! Stephanie wouldn't touch drugs."

At least that got a rise out of him.

Maggie leaned toward Jimmy. "If she was involved in illegal activities, do you think she was the only one in her circle of friends involved?"

When he didn't respond, Will said, "You have to help us here. We can't do it by ourselves, but if she was involved in something, Jillian and Lacey and maybe Laura were in on it." He turned to Maggie. "Were they ever secretive, maybe quit talking when you came into the room?"

"I wasn't there long, and if that had happened, I probably would have brushed it off as being the new person. About the only thing I remember is that Stephanie was really worried about Andi's operation."

"She was," Jimmy agreed. He ran his hand over his gray hair. "I just thought of something. I heard her and Jillian talking once, and Jillian told her not to mess everything up. When I asked about it, Stephanie said it was something about work. I never could get any more out of her."

"Do you know anyone else who might have had a motive to kill her?"

"I have lain awake so many nights trying to come up with someone who might have had something against her. And I always come up blank. Everyone liked her."

"None of the women in the house were jealous?" Maggie asked.

He looked toward the ceiling, then at her. "Maybe Laura. She envied Stephanie's looks, and she always wanted Spencer, and I hear she got him. Steph and Spencer dated, you know."

Maggie tilted her head. "Stephanie dated Spencer? But she told me there was nothing between them." She frowned. "Stephanie was quite upset that Spencer had dumped Jillian. That happened before I went to live there, but she and I discussed it once."

"Jillian never knew he broke up with her because of Stephanie. I'm the only one who did, and only because I happened to see them together when they thought no one was around. But it didn't last long. I think Steph felt guilty about it. Didn't bother Spencer—he moved on to someone else. But it wasn't Laura. I think she was much later."

"How about Adam Matthews?" Will asked. "Did you know him?"

Jimmy repeated the name. "Was he a pilot?"

Will nodded.

His cousin's eyes widened. "Oh yeah. He hung around some. Seems like he was interested in Lacey."

"They married, but it didn't last long," Will said.

"I never liked him. He was too slick, even more than Spencer."

— 21 —

After Spencer left, Andi videoed Laura at her desk, then on the phone. The last shot was a silhouette of her standing at the window looking at downtown Memphis. "Next time I'll bring someone to video, and I'll interview you."

286

"Send me a copy of the questions you plan to ask," Laura said.

"Sure thing." Andi put the camera away. "Thanks for talking about Stephanie with me today. Do you mind if I ask you another question?"

"I won't know until you ask."

"You were closer to my sister than anyone, except maybe Jillian. Do—"

"Jillian was not your sister's friend," Laura said.

"But they were, had been since grade school."

Laura shook her head. "Honey, Jillian is no one's friend, and she was very jealous of your sister."

That couldn't be true.

"Ask around," Laura said.

Andi took out a notepad. "I'd like to do that. Can you give me a list of people to ask?"

"Lacey would have been the first person I'd put on the list—oh, her funeral is at five today, if you want to come. Back side of the cemetery."

Andi mentally ran through the rest of her day. She could take a change of clothes when she met Will and Brad at three thirty and get dressed there. "I'll be there. That list?"

Laura looked toward the ceiling. "Talk to Gerald Caldwell, or Madeline Starr, or even Jared Donovan—he was absolutely smitten with Stephanie and asked her to marry him."

"I know Maggie, but who are the other two? Oh, wait. Are you talking about Jared Donovan, the guy who owns Donovan Jewelers?"

"That's the one, and Gerald is a private investigator. Both of them were part of the circle."

"Circle?"

"Stephanie's castoffs." Laura's lip twitched, then she smiled. "Not intentionally. Your sister didn't know the effect she had on men. Every man she dated fell in love with her, and why not? She was beautiful and kind, but Stephanie was looking for the perfect man."

"We both know that man doesn't exist," Andi said with a laugh.

"Absolutely. And when flaws showed up as they eventually do, Stephanie lost interest and moved on."

Andi stared at the two names she'd written down. "Where can I find them?"

"Gerald's office is a few blocks from here on Front Street, and you'll find Jared at Donovan Jewelers on Union."

Andi stood and shouldered her camera bag. "Thanks. I'll give you a call tomorrow or the next day about filming an interview."

"Thank *you*. And I'll get my speaking schedule to you."

In the elevator, she reached in her bag for the ibuprofen bottle and hesitated, trying to remember if she'd already taken some this morning.

No, she was certain she hadn't taken anything.

After she stepped off the elevator, she downed two with a swig of water, and then peered in the bottle. Only six tablets? There should be more. She distinctly remembered dropping sixteen Lortabs in the ibuprofen bottle yesterday morning. Enough to do until Monday morning. It was only Friday.

She'd taken ten tablets since then. That had to be wrong. Ten high-powered Lortabs, and she wouldn't be able to walk.

"Stronger people than you have become addicted to pain pills. You start out taking only one and then you're taking two and pretty soon two doesn't do it . . . It happens before you realize it."

Andi squeezed her eyes shut as if that would block out Treece's voice in her head. She was not addicted to the pills and only took them because of the pain. But could her body be building up a tolerance for them? Maybe it was time to think seriously about surgery.

Straightening her shoulders, she hurried out the door of the CJC into bright sunlight and decided to walk to the private investigator's office. The sun was warm on her back, but nothing like July and August would be. When she reached Front Street, she walked south, enjoying a view of the river.

Maggie's office was on Front Street. She could

stop by after she talked with the PI. No—Maggie was with Will. Andi admired the office building as she entered. The man must be successful—offices at this location were not cheap.

After checking the directory in the lobby, Andi took the elevator to the third floor and found his office. A pleasant-looking older woman looked up when she approached her desk.

"May I help you?"

"I'd like to see Mr. Caldwell."

"Do you have an appointment?"

"Uh, no, but it's really important." She hadn't considered she might need an appointment.

"That's what everyone says. Give me your name and I'll check with him for what day next week he can see you."

Next week? "Andi Hollister, but I *must* see him today."

Her eyes widened. "The news reporter? I love those documentaries you and Treece Rogers do." Her brows lowered. "Well, not love—they're so sad, but I'm glad someone is bringing attention to all those poor girls."

"Thank you." The words warmed Andi's heart.

"I guess I can check with him to see if he can fit you in today." She picked up her phone and spoke briefly with Mr. Caldwell. She gave Andi an odd look when she hung up. "He'll see you now. Just go through that door, and his office is the second door on the right."

Yes! Andi hurried through the door and into the hallway.

Gerald Caldwell's door was open, and he looked up from his computer screen. "Come in, Ms. Hollister."

Andi faltered as his almost-black eyes burned a hole in her. She didn't know what she expected, but not this somber man with a sharp nose over his thin lips. A hawk—that's what he reminded her of. She held out her hand. "Mr. Caldwell, thank you for seeing me."

After the briefest hesitation, he smiled, and it was like flipping a light switch as he shook her hand and a smile softened his face. "Forgive me for staring, but you look so much like your sister."

"I don't believe I've ever been told that," she said.

"Your features are the same. You are quite lovely in your own right. Have a seat. And then tell me how I can help you."

The man's office was Spartan, and she sat in the only other chair in the room. "I want to talk to you about my sister. I didn't realize you would remember her so well, since she died eighteen years ago."

"Most people who met Stephanie Hollister would remember her, even that long. What do you want to know?"

He'd thrown her off balance, and she gathered

291

her thoughts. Laura had said Steph dated him, but she couldn't wrap her mind around this fiftysomething man being one of her sister's beaus, even though he would only have been in his mid to late thirties then. Still, it was evident Gerald Caldwell could turn on the charm when he wanted to, and most men had wanted to around Steph. "Why were you investigating her?"

"You're asking me to break confidentiality." He closed the laptop and leaned back in the chair. "However, you may have information I need on another case, one I planned to see you about last night until I was detained. Perhaps we can trade information."

He was also cunning, and as he moistened his bottom lip, she realized it wasn't a hawk he reminded her of, but a wolf licking its chops. "If it's confidential, would that be ethical?"

He shrugged. "It's been eighteen years. Whatever reason they had for hiring me is well in the past."

"What information could I have that you would want?"

"I've been hired to locate Jillian Bennett."

"Jillian? Why?"

"It's a legal matter. An inheritance, actually."

Right. Andi was wasting time here, and she had no confidence that if he told her anything it'd be the truth. She stood. "I'd like to help you, but I don't know where she is."

292

"No problem." He stood as well and pursed his lips. "You know, it's been so long, I suppose there'd be no harm in telling you that my client had a son who asked for his grandmother's diamond ring. He planned to give it to your sister if she accepted his proposal."

Andi managed to keep her mouth from dropping open. Some guy's *mother* hired Caldwell to investigate Stephanie? "What did you report back to her?"

A shadow crossed his face. "That she had no worries. Unfortunately for the son, your sister said no." He paused, an expectant expression on his face.

Quid pro quo. "You might find Jillian if you look under her married name."

He chuckled. "Unfortunately, that's a red herring. As far as I can ascertain, she never married."

Will called Andi and Brad on the way home from Nashville to make sure they knew Lacey's graveside funeral was at five. With the cemetery close to the Hollister house, they would have thirty or forty minutes to look over the studio. He checked his watch. Three forty-five. He was fifteen minutes late, so where was everyone?

He walked behind the detached garage and checked to see if the studio was unlocked and he could get a head start. No, still padlocked. The building was actually a small two-room house that Tom Hollister's grandfather had built, and that was probably the only reason Tom hadn't torn it down after the murder. He'd padlocked it instead.

The padlock looked as though it hadn't been touched in years, and he saw that the keyhole lock had been replaced with a newer lock that could be opened from the inside, something Andi couldn't do when Brad and Will had locked her inside and gone to play ball. He felt bad about that now, actually had felt bad when they did it, but she'd been such a pesky little kid, always wanting to tag along.

Will wasn't sure what he expected to find inside or even what he was looking for, only that he had a sense there might be something in the studio to help break the case.

While he waited for Brad and Andi, he surveyed the backyard, remembering the good times they'd shared here. Will had spent more time in this yard than in his aunt and uncle's. He glanced toward the two-story house where they'd lived. He'd hated leaving that house, but after Jimmy's arrest for Stephanie's murder, his aunt couldn't bear to stay.

He returned to his car as Andi pulled into the drive. His mood lightened as she climbed out of her Corolla. He'd thought about her all day, and when this case was closed, he planned to ask her out. "Good afternoon," he said as she approached. She seemed a little unsteady.

"You too."

Suddenly she stumbled, and he reacted, catching her in his arms. "Whoa," he said and reluctantly released her.

"Ow!" She grabbed his arm again. "I think I sprained my ankle."

"Let me carry you to the back porch." He swept her up in his arms, amazed at how light she was. "This is getting to be a habit. Not that I mind."

"Sorry." She looked back at the ground and then gazed into his eyes. "What'd I stumble over?"

She hadn't stumbled over anything but her own feet, and her pupils were the size of pinpoints. His mouth dried, remembering the pills he'd seen her take. "Are you still taking something for pain?"

"Put me down," she said sharply. "I can walk."

Once she was standing, she glared at him. "Have you been talking to Treece?"

"No." But maybe he should. "Are you all right?"

"Of course I am. Just need a drink of water, maybe something to eat, that's all."

"You haven't eaten lunch?"

She shook her head. "Haven't had time."

"Did you eat breakfast?"

"Don't remember."

He'd bet she hadn't. They didn't have time for this. The funeral was in an hour, but he was afraid she'd collapse if he didn't get food in her.

"I'm sure there's something in the house to eat. Peanut butter, maybe. Why don't I make you a sandwich?"

"I'm not hungry, that's why." She rubbed her nose with the back of her hand and then swayed as she stared at him. "I want to get this deal with the studio over with, and then I'll eat."

He hadn't realized how difficult this might be for her. "You don't have to go into the studio. Brad will be here soon."

"That might be a good idea." She took a step and hopped. "Oh!"

"That does it," Will said and swept her back up in his arms. This time she didn't protest. "Do you think the back door is open?"

"Probably not, but I have a key in my pocket." She rested her head on his chest and sighed. "Thank you, Sir Galahad. For everything."

She was definitely not normal. He carried her to the back of the house and set her on a chest freezer in the garage. "Can you sit there a second?" he asked as he took the key she held out.

Andi nodded. "Sorry I'm so much trouble."

"You're not trouble. But I do want to talk to you about the pain medication you're taking." He unlocked the door and handed her key back. "Let me see your ankle."

Will slipped off her shoe. Her ankle didn't seem swollen, but he massaged it anyway.

"That feels good," she said.

If she only knew. "Can you put weight on it now?"

Gingerly she put her foot on the floor, then she smiled. "It doesn't hurt. You must have magic fingers."

"Yeah, right. How about that sandwich now? Maybe a glass of milk?" One way or another, she would eat.

"Sure." She carried her shoe to the kitchen chair and sat down. "Peanut butter is in the pantry, bread is in the bread box, and milk is in the fridge."

After he washed his hands, he made two sandwiches. "I haven't eaten, either," he said as he sat across from her. He curbed the impulse to ask about the pain meds again. She'd just get defensive and probably wouldn't eat. But they weren't done with the subject.

They ate in silence. Andi stopped at half a sandwich and pushed the plate away.

"You're not finished."

"Later. I'll get the key for the studio."

"I told you, you don't have to do this. Brad should be here any minute."

She clasped her hands together and worried a hangnail on her thumb. The kitchen clock ticked in the background. "You don't understand. I need to do it."

Maybe she did need to face whatever it was in the studio that held her in its grip. "Well, hurry. I'll clean up the table while you get the key."

— 22 —

Andi escaped to the washroom before Will could question her about the pills again. Her head was beginning to clear, but it scared her to think how she'd felt just ten minutes ago. Almost like she was floating and everything was sparkly and bright. And Will . . . he'd looked good enough to kiss.

She sucked in a deep breath. Maybe Treece and Will were right to be concerned. What if she'd had a wreck on the drive over and hurt someone? She had to be more careful about taking the pills that close together. It definitely could never happen again.

In the washroom, she scanned the three rows of keys. Each tag was labeled with what they unlocked in alphabetical order, and she took the studio key from the hook on the third row.

Did she really want to do this? Maybe it'd be better to give the key to Will and stay out of the studio. *No.* Eighteen years was long enough to run away. She turned and marched back to the kitchen.

Andi stopped short when she saw her brother. "Where's Will?"

"Went to his car." He held up a paper. "Got the physical report back on the stationery from Lacey

Wilson's house. She wrote a letter to Jimmy, all right, but she also wrote one to you." He nodded to the key in her hand. "Is that to the studio?"

"Can I read it?" Andi said, ignoring his question. She hated it when he only gave her partial information.

"That's why I brought it. Figured you'd want to see it." Her brother chuckled and handed her two sheets of paper. "Ran into Commander Kennedy. He's singing your praises. How did you get in with him, anyway?"

She made a face at him. "My winning personality, I guess." She scanned the photographs. It was amazing what technology could do. The indented impressions on the letter dated in March appeared in black. Other letters appeared in white.

"The letter in white was written the day Lacey died. It was to you. The other one is the letter Jimmy received," Brad said.

While Will had told Andi what the report said, seeing it in black and white helped her grasp it better. She scanned the opening of the letter to Jimmy, then homed in on what was important . . .

First, I want to apologize for not coming forward sooner. I have no excuse except I was afraid to. Even after I became a Christian three months ago, I couldn't make myself take responsibility for what I did, really for what I didn't do. But I want you to know there hasn't been a night that I haven't thought about you and your circumstances.

I have decided to leave Memphis and go where no one can find me. That's why I'm writing to ask if I can visit you before I leave. I'll explain everything when I come, if you'll allow it. Most of all, I need your forgiveness for not telling you sooner that I have proof you didn't kill Stephanie.

"What proof do you think she had?"

"She doesn't say in either of the letters. The last two pages have the letters she started to you."

She shuffled the papers and pulled them out.

Dear Andi,
Jimmy Shelton didn't kill Stephanie, and I can tell you who did. Actually, you have diamonds in your possession—

Lacey had marked through the words and started over.

Dear Andi,
I have information that will exonerate Jimmy Shelton in the death of your sister. I contacted him, but he never responded.

Once again she'd marked through the words. Andi read the next page.

> Dear Andi,
> I am so sorry I didn't come forward earlier. Stephanie was my good friend, and I let fear and greed overcome what I knew was right.

That was all she'd written? Why hadn't she finished the letters? Unless she'd decided to tell her in person. And what diamonds could she be talking about? And what did they have to do with Stephanie's murder?

Andi raked her fingers through her hair. All this time there'd been evidence within reach about Steph's murder? She took a shaky breath as Will opened the back door. "What evidence do you think she was talking about?"

"I don't know," Brad said. "But maybe Stephanie hid something in the studio."

Andi followed her brother to the studio but held back as he unlocked the door. "Do we even have time to do this? And what are we looking for, anyway?"

Will checked his watch. "It's four ten and the cemetery is ten minutes away. That gives us thirty minutes."

"I have to change my clothes," Andi said.

"Maybe this would be a good time to do that," Will said.

The gentleness in his voice brought tears to her eyes, and she looked away to keep him from seeing.

"No. I told you I need to do this." She followed them into the studio but kept her eyes averted from the spot where she and her mom had found Stephanie.

She could do it. It was only a room. If she could go into Steph's bedroom in the house, she could do this. "What exactly are we looking for?" she asked again.

Brad surveyed the room. "Anything that looks like it doesn't belong. Or a place Steph might have hidden something."

"I'll search the glaze room," she said. Anything to get out of the room where her sister was killed. She walked to the smaller room. Glaze buckets on runners lined one wall. A table with pieces ready to go into the kiln, a shelf with greenware . . . She really ought to fire those pieces. Next week, maybe, if the kiln still worked.

Stephanie always kept a journal, and Andi didn't remember seeing it after her death. "Brad," she said, going back to the main room. She couldn't believe she hadn't already thought about the journal. "Stephanie kept a journal. Do you know if Mom still has it?"

"I've never heard her mention it, but you know Steph would *not* have left it where Mom could find it, anyway. Do you remember what it looked like?"

"She always had to have this special notebook. It wasn't very big, maybe five by eight, and it was black and had an elastic band on the top."

"Then that's the size hiding place we're looking for."

Andi returned to the glaze room and searched every nook and cranny in the room. Nothing. She wished she'd been closer in age to her sister. If she had been, Steph might have shared more of what was going on in her life. Andi couldn't think of anything her sister could have been involved in that resulted in someone wanting to kill her.

Steph always said she had to set an example for Brad and Andi. Steph was Andi's hero, and she would not have been involved in anything illegal.

Will stuck his head in the doorway. "You need to get dressed. We're leaving in five minutes."

"Five minutes? I'll have to be late."

"I'll wait for you."

"Go ahead. There's no need for you to wait," she said, then hurried from the studio to her car for her clothes, then went inside the house to change. Eight minutes later she walked out the back door, dabbing on her lipstick. "You're still here?" she asked when she saw Will.

"Yeah. Brad went on, but you can ride with me."

What was he talking about, ride with him? "I'll drive myself."

"I'd rather you ride with me. I'll drop you off and you'll already be here for supper."

He'd asked about the pills, and now he didn't want her to drive. She must have done something totally stupid when she wasn't herself. But her head was clear now. Andi planted her feet. "There's no reason I can't drive myself. I feel perfectly fine, and my ankle is perfectly fine."

He shook his head. "I'm sorry, but you'll either go with me or stay here. You're not driving."

She held his gaze until she realized he wasn't budging. "Okay," she said with a curt nod.

It wasn't long before they turned in to the cemetery and drove the winding road around to the back. He hopped out and hurried around to open her door.

"Thank you for making sure I arrived in one piece," she said stiffly.

He bowed. "Sir Galahad is always at your service."

Heat infused her cheeks as she faintly remembered calling him that. What else had she said? She shook her embarrassment off and walked to the group of people under the tent.

"I'm so glad you made it," Laura said, taking her hand. "I wish there were more people here."

Andi looked around. "I felt like I should be. I see Maggie's here," she said.

"Yes. And a few people Lacey went to church with."

A man in a black suit approached Laura, and Andi squeezed her hand. "I better get a seat."

She joined Maggie in the back row. "I'm glad you're here."

"I was afraid no one would come."

A black Cadillac pulled behind Will's car, and Jared Donovan climbed out of the driver's side.

"Why do you think he's here?" Maggie asked.

"I don't know." She glanced at Will to see if he took note of Donovan's arrival. He had. She turned her attention to the front when the pastor stepped to the small podium.

Lacey Wilson's graveside service was a simple one with no flowers other than a casket spray of red roses. Fifteen minutes after the pastor began, he concluded with a prayer. Andi sighed. A handful of mourners, none who seemed very sad, a few minutes' recap of a life, and it was over. She pressed her lips together. She wanted her life to count for more than that.

She stood when Maggie did. "See you in the morning at my place around nine? We'll go in my car."

Maggie gave a low chuckle. "You mean you don't want to go in my VW Bug?"

"That's exactly what I mean," she said with a grin. "See you in the morning."

The hair on the back of her neck rose as she walked to Will's car. She turned and scanned the small crowd. Had one of the men standing by the grave broken into her apartment? And maybe killed Lacey? And Stephanie? Which one? The ex-husband, Matthews? Or Spencer Delaney? Was Spencer the real reason Laura wouldn't help free Jimmy? And Jared Donovan—why was he even here? Everyone present had been in the circle of friends eighteen years ago. They were all suspects, except Maggie.

Will couldn't get Andi off his mind as he dressed for dinner with the Hollisters. By the time he dropped her off at her parents', whatever she'd taken seemed to have worn off. But she had obviously been high when she'd driven there. What if . . . He took out his cell and quickly dialed Andi's number.

"Are you still at your parents'?" he said when she answered.

"Yes. Why?"

"I just wanted to make sure you didn't need a ride."

"I can drive myself, Will." She sounded annoyed. "Why are you asking me this?"

"Andi, there was something going on this afternoon. Was it the pain pills?"

"No! I just hadn't eaten. I was fine as soon as I got food in me. Probably my blood sugar dropped."

How he wanted to believe that.

"I haven't had a pain tablet since early after-noon. There. Satisfied?"

"I just don't want you to get hurt . . . or hurt someone else."

"I won't. I promise."

He'd have to trust her. "Okay. See you soon."

"Will . . ."

"Yes?"

"Nothing. Thanks for caring."

If she only knew. But what if they started dating and messed up their friendship? None of his relationships worked—why would this one be different? And it wasn't true, like he let everyone else believe, that the women always broke up with him.

Truth was, once the initial chase was over, he lost interest and the relationship died a natural death. Nobody's fault, except his for thinking he could keep doing the same thing with different results. And he'd rather have Andi as a friend than not at all, because once he kissed her, he would cross a line that couldn't be uncrossed.

Kiss her? Where did that come from? The doorbell rang, and he hurried to answer it, hopping on one foot until he slipped his loafer on. He didn't remember Brad saying he'd stop by. It rang insistently once more before he got the door opened to his mother's brittle smile. His stomach sank. "What do you want?"

"I know Mae told you I wanted to see you, so why didn't you call?" she said as she walked past him into the apartment.

He pushed the door shut, rattling the windows. "Let me see," he said, taking out his cell phone. "Hmm, looking under Mother, I don't see a number . . . Let me look under Cass. Nope. It must have gotten deleted, maybe in one of those updates."

She patted his cheek. "You always were a funny kid."

"How would you know?" He ignored the voice whispering forgiveness in his ear. "You were never around unless one of your husbands kicked you out. But then, you never were good at relationships."

Cass flinched. He'd scored one that time, but for a second, he wished he hadn't. His mother brought out the very worst in him.

She lifted her chin. "I understand you don't do much better on that front."

Touché. Vindication spurred him on. "What do you want? Or, should it be, how much? Although I'm surprised that you're already out of money. That last husband was loaded."

"Yeah, well, I signed a prenup, and a quarter of a mill doesn't go as far as it used to. But I don't want any money from you this time." She fumbled in her purse and drew out a pack of cigarettes, her fingers shaking as she extracted one. "Do you mind if I sit?"

"As long as you don't smoke or plan to stay long. I have dinner plans." His phone dinged an incoming text, and he glanced at it. His aunt. It was a little late to warn him that Cass was on her way over. "Excuse me a minute while I respond to this."

Will was glad for an excuse to leave the room. If his mother wanted a new relationship with him like his aunt said, she sure went about it in a funny way. In his bedroom he read the message and closed his eyes, wishing Aunt Mae had never learned to text.

Please reconsider seeing your mother. She has cancer. Inoperable. She really does love you, Will. She just doesn't know how to show it.

And she wouldn't come begging, either. He dropped his head. He didn't know what his aunt expected of him. Obviously more than he could give.

In the hallway, he stopped short of the living room and observed his mother. All bluster was gone. Cass's shoulders drooped as she leaned against the sofa, one hand pressed to her mouth. The unlit cigarette dangled between the fingers of her other hand.

She was so frail. *Inoperable cancer.* A lump formed in his throat.

Cass hadn't come for a handout, but he didn't think he had it in him to give her what she wanted. Will swallowed the lump down. He could at least try to be civil.

He coughed and she jerked upright, squaring her shoulders. His apartment had the kitchen and living room combined, and he walked to the refrigerator and took out a bottle of water. "Like something to drink?"

"No, thank you. Get your business taken care of?"

"What? Oh, the text. Yeah."

Inoperable cancer. The words chased themselves. "How long do you plan to be in Memphis?"

She gave him a curious glance. "I don't know."

"No new boyfriend on the horizon?" He had to keep up the pretense, at least until she told him about the cancer herself. Maybe she didn't notice the softer edge to his voice.

"No, not presently. How about yourself—girlfriend?"

"No, you were right before. Can't seem to keep one."

"Relationships are the pits and highly overrated." She stared at the unlit cigarette, then looked up at him and took a deep breath.

Whatever she was going to say was lost in the coughing fit that rocked her body. He grabbed another bottle of water from the refrigerator and uncapped it. "Here, see if this helps," he said, handing it to her.

She sipped deeply, then said, "Sorry, that happens sometimes." Cass handed him the cigarette she'd broken in the coughing spell.

"Really need to give these cancer sticks up."

He hesitated, trying to come up with the expected comeback. "If you do, you'll send the tobacco companies into a recession."

"Yeah." She gave him a crooked grin. "Well, it was good to see you." Cass stopped at the door. "Will . . ."

He waited. Now that he was really looking at her, he saw what a shell of a woman she was.

"Thanks for letting me come in," she said and opened the door and slipped out.

The door closed with a soft click, and his feet, rooted to the floor, refused to move. Judging from how much weight she'd lost since the last time he saw her, death wasn't far off, and then there'd never be an opportunity to make things right.

Still, he didn't open the door and call her back. He couldn't be the first one to make a move. It had to come from Cass.

— 23 —

Andi sat on the porch of her parents' house in east Memphis. She loved this neighborhood, and most of the neighbors had lived here when she was a child. For as long as she could remember, Friday night meant spaghetti or lasagna or something Italian.

As a child, Friday night was when she could

invite friends over to eat because there'd be so much. Will and Jimmy had been regular guests until her parents moved to the big house in Germantown. Will because he was Brad's best friend, and Jimmy because he was always wherever Stephanie was.

But even after they moved, Will found a way to get to their house on Fridays until his aunt and uncle moved away from Memphis, taking him with them.

Andi inhaled the honeysuckle that filled the air, bringing back memories of breaking off the end of the bloom and licking the sweet liquid from the stamen. Of all the bad things that had happened when she was thirteen—her dad losing his job, her operation, Stephanie's death—moving back home had not been one of them. Her gaze slidto the studio where they'd been earlier.

She was glad now her dad hadn't torn the old house down—something he'd mentioned doing more than once. Odd that a bad thing was now a good thing, with the crime scene basically preserved. But how were her parents going to react to the news that the case was being reopened? The concrete that had lodged in her stomach earlier grew heavier.

Will had arrived a few minutes ago and was saying hello to her parents. She guessed she better join them.

The aroma of garlic and oregano met Andi at the front door, making her mouth water. "Mom," she called.

"We're in the kitchen." Her mother's voice floated from the back.

Her heart stilled when she saw Will. He glanced up, catching her gaze and holding it.

She should have changed into something more appealing, like the pink sweater she'd just bought, instead of the tights and long green shirt that reached halfway to her knees. At least she'd cinched a blingy silver belt at the waist.

"Something smells good," she said, still looking at Will. She gave herself a mental shake. This was just Will. Brad's friend. The same one who watched after her even when she didn't want him to. The same one who almost kissed her Wednesday night. "Can I help with something?"

"Set the table. Your dad should be here soon with the dessert."

"Where's Brad?" Will asked.

"Tied up on some case. He said he'd be here by seven."

Andi checked her watch. Seven fifteen. Her brother was cutting it beyond close. Surely he wasn't going to leave telling their parents about the case to her. The back door swung open, and her dad came into the room, bringing a flat white box with Sally's Bakery written on the side. She grabbed it. "You went all the way to

313

Midtown for a cheesecake! What's the occasion?"

"You'll see."

Andi exchanged glances with Will. The pinched look on his face reflected her feelings. It was bad enough to be the bearer of bad news, but if her parents were celebrating something, she didn't want to bring them down. The back door opened again, and Brad entered the kitchen, wearing his gun and still in the clothes he'd worn earlier. He must have come straight from the CJC.

"Smells like Little Italy around here," he said. "And cheesecake for dessert? We never have store-bought desserts unless there's a special occasion."

"You haven't changed your clothes," her mom said, disapproval in her voice.

"Sorry, Mom. I'm hungry," Brad said, and then he nodded toward the box. "So . . . ?"

She shooed him toward the dining room table. "It will wait."

Midway through the meal, Brad cleared his throat, and Andi kicked him under the table. She wanted him to wait until they knew what her parents' announcement was.

When her dad consumed his last bite of cheesecake, he glanced at his wife. "Ready?"

She nodded, beaming. Andi had never seen her so excited.

Her dad sat a little straighter. "I've been offered an early retirement package, and I'm going to take it. Your mom and I are selling the house and buying a motor home so we can travel."

Traveling around the country had been her dad's dream for as long as Andi could remember. But with the case reopened, it'd make selling the house nearly impossible. Who wanted to buy property where someone had been murdered?

Andi and Brad exchanged looks, then she shifted her gaze to Will, who was sitting next to her father.

Confusion played in her dad's eyes. "Well, don't you have anything to say? Congratulations, maybe?"

"What's the matter with you all?" her mom demanded.

Brad was the first to speak. "I'm sorry. I'm really glad you're going to retire."

"Me too," Andi added. She gave Will a "say something" look.

"Yeah, that's great, Mr. Hollister." Excitement eluded Will's voice, as it had the others.

Barbara Hollister sat back in her chair. "Well, if you get any more excited, you might get arrested for *not* disturbing the peace." She folded her arms. "What's going on? I suspected something when Will popped up—not that I'm not glad to have you, son, but you never come to dinner anymore."

Brad took a breath. "Stephanie's case is going to be reopened."

Dead silence met his statement. Blood drained from her dad's face, and he jumped to his feet. "Why?" He spit the word out. "Sunday it will be over with."

Andi pressed her jaw together until it hurt. *Tell them, Brad.* She didn't want to be the one.

"Mr. Hollister . . . Mrs. Hollister," Will said, looking from one to the other, "my cousin may not have killed your daughter."

Andi leaned forward. "He's right. Jimmy Shelton received a letter saying he wasn't her murderer."

Her mother opened her mouth, but no sound came out. She looked toward her husband, but he was staring at Will.

"This is the way you repay our kindness?" he said. "Spreading lies. Your cousin killed my daughter. He confessed. I knew he'd hurt her one day, just not physically. And now, you."

Will's face was ashen. "I—"

"Don't say a word." Her dad rubbed his arm. "I've seen the way you look at Andi. Same way Jimmy looked at Steph. You hurt Andi and I'll—" He pressed his hand against his chest, then felt in his pocket. "Where's my nitro—"

Andi screamed as he fell.

"Call 911!" Will jumped to catch Tom Hollister, and with Brad's help, eased him onto the dining room floor.

"Tom!" Barbara knelt beside him. She looked up at Will. "Help him."

"Yes, ma'am." The desperation in her voice spurred Will to work faster. He ripped Tom's shirt open. "Do you feel a pulse?"

"Can't find one," Brad said. "Come on, Dad. You can make it."

"I don't think he's breathing, either." Will started compressions. "Do you have a defibrillator?"

Brad shook his head. "Never had a need for one before now. We can change places if the ambulance doesn't get here soon."

"I'm good."

"The ambulance is on the way," Andi said.

They weren't far from a cardiac hospital. Soon a siren reached Will's ears, giving him the energy to keep going. A few minutes later, he gladly released Tom Hollister to the paramedics' care.

He found Andi in the living room, placing a washcloth on her mother's forehead.

"Mom almost fainted," she said. "And I convinced her to lie on the couch."

He couldn't bring himself to look either of them in the eye. He was afraid he'd see blame there.

Barbara Hollister removed the washcloth. "How's Tom?"

"The paramedics are taking care of him." Will turned as Brad came into the room.

"Dad's responding," he said. "And they're getting him ready to transport."

Barbara struggled to sit up. "I'm going with him."

Andi went to get her mother's purse, and Will turned to Brad. "I'm not going to the hospital."

"Nonsense," Barbara said. "You helped save his life."

"This might not have happened if I hadn't been here." *"I've seen the way you look at Andi."* Tom Hollister's words rang in his ears, and he imagined they were probably hearing them again too. "If he knows I'm there, it'll upset him."

"This wasn't your fault, son. We had to be told about the investigation, and I don't know what got into my husband." She squeezed his arm. "If Jimmy Shelton didn't kill my Stephanie, I want you and Brad to find out who did."

He covered her hand with his. "We will, Mrs. Hollister. I promise you that, but I still don't think I should go to the hospital."

"You can keep us company, if nothing else."

"Yeah," Brad said. "You don't have to go back and see Dad. At least not until he figures this thing out."

Will couldn't bring himself to look at Andi.

"Yeah," she said softly. "Come with us."

He looked up, and their gazes collided.

"Besides, we both know Dad was way off base—on everything he said."

He released the breath he'd trapped in his chest. He and Andi could go back to normal.

So why didn't that make him happy?

318

– 24 –

Once they made it to the hospital, it became a waiting game, and Andi hated waiting. As soon as her dad was stabilized, her mom was allowed in the unit to be with him, and Andi paced back and forth in front of the darkened window. Why was God allowing this to happen?

She'd struggled with that question when Steph died. Why did God take the ones she needed? She didn't know how Brad could stand so calmly and talk to Will.

The doors to ICU opened, and her mother hurried toward them.

"They're taking him to the cath lab soon, and Dad sent me out here to tell you both he's going to be all right," she said. She nodded to a beige phone on a nearby table. "They'll call us as things progress."

Relief turned Andi's legs to rubber, and with tears stinging her eyes, she found a chair and sat in it. Her mother joined her and handed her a tissue.

"Are you okay, sweetheart?"

Andi dabbed her eyes and nodded. She didn't trust her voice. Her dad had always been bigger than life, her rock when her sister died. He was the one who told Andi after her heart surgery that she could be anything she wanted to be, that nothing should stop her from conquering the world.

Will handed her a cup of water, and she gratefully sipped it. That he'd seen her distress and wanted to do something about it touched her. She lifted her gaze, and the pain in his eyes almost undid her. *"I've seen the way you look at Andi. Same way Jimmy looked at Steph."* Was it possible? She pushed the thought away.

"He's not going to die," Will said softly. "I'm here if you want to talk."

Not now. She couldn't. "Thanks. But I'm fine."

Will nodded and walked back to where Brad stood looking out the window.

Her mom squeezed her hand. "Our Will has turned out to be a fine young man."

Andi's gaze followed him. Broad shoulders that tapered to a narrow waist . . . he had indeed turned into a fine specimen . . . Wait, that wasn't what her mother meant, and where had that thought come from?

Her own devious heart, that's where. Falling in love with Will was a dead end. Too many complications—like he was her brother's best friend and she knew from Brad that Will never dated anyone for more than a couple of months. She didn't believe for one minute that the breakups were his fault. No woman in her right mind would reject Will. And if there was one thing she didn't want to be, it was one of his rejects.

Refocus. "Do you really think Dad will be okay?"

"Now that he's here, I do. I'm just thankful the doctors discovered he had a blockage before . . ." She shook her head. "The doctor said it's in his main artery. Said he was lucky it happened when he was close to a hospital with people who knew what to do."

Andi jumped when the beige telephone rang. Brad snatched it up and listened intently. "Thank you," he said and hung up. "Someone came in worse off than Dad. There'll be a slight delay before they start, but it shouldn't be long before they take him."

Andi tensed. She didn't like this. Not one bit. Every few minutes she glanced up at the clock on the wall as she paced the room. Fifteen . . . twenty . . . sixty . . . Time ticked off slowly. Finally, her mother motioned for her to sit beside her.

"But what if something happens to Dad while they're waiting?"

"Your pacing won't stop it. Nothing is going to happen to him. God has this," her mom said, "and he's here with us."

Was that supposed to give her comfort? God had Steph too, and look how that turned out. Andi didn't ever remember a time when God was there for her, anyway. Her mother gasped, and Andi realized she'd said the thought out loud.

"Honey, you know better than that."

Andi ducked her head. "I'm sorry, but I don't see God here."

"He's here, honey, and this is one time you can't run ahead of him," her mom said gently.

"What are you talking about?"

"I'm talking about all the times you've gotten tired of waiting for something, so you make it happen. And things don't turn out like you think they will."

Even though the words were spoken gently, Andi sensed the restraint in her mother's voice. She traced her finger over a crack in the vinyl chair. *Chloe.* That hadn't turned out like she thought it would. She stiffened when her mom put her arm around her shoulders, and then forced her body to relax.

Her mom withdrew her arm. "You're too independent and self-sufficient, honey. Always have been, even as a baby."

Andi dug at the crack in the hard plastic, breaking her nail. She couldn't help it that she didn't need anyone.

A chuckle came from her mother. "Stephanie loved to be cuddled, but there was no cuddling you. No, I'd pick you up, and you'd get stiff, like just now. Then off you'd go, out of my lap, running to *do* something. It only got worse after Stephanie's death."

"I'm sorry the wrong daughter died." Andi clapped her hand over her mouth, trying to grab the words that had been trying to escape for years.

"Oh, Andi." Her mom's voice broke. "No . . . I—"

The shrill ring from the telephone grabbed everyone's attention. Andi jumped up, but once again, Brad snatched the receiver and then listened, nodding his head. "Thank you!"

He turned to them. "They were able to take him on to surgery and everything went great! They said we could see him now."

"Yes!" Andi turned and grabbed her mom, who'd also stood. "He's going to be okay!"

"I told you so. But honey, we need to talk—"

"Forget I said that, Mom. I was just stressed. I didn't mean it. Come on, let's go see Dad." Ignoring her protest, Andi tugged her mom toward the door to the recovery room. She glanced over her shoulder. Will wasn't coming.

"Go on," he said. "I'm fine."

"Are you sure?" Her dad had always spent a lot of time with Will. What happened tonight had to be killing him.

"Go," he said, motioning with his hands.

With one last look, she followed her family through the doors. Dread filled her stomach the closer she came to her dad's room. He'd been so gray . . . and lifeless. What if there'd been damage and he couldn't do what he wanted to in his retirement? That'd be a slow death for him.

"Hurry," Brad said from the room.

Pressing her lips together, she rounded the doorway as her mom kissed her dad on the forehead. He turned and saw her.

"Hey, pumpkin. Sorry I scared you."

Her dad lay flat, but his color was awesome. Pink cheeks and his eyes sparkled. Tears sprang to her eyes, and grinning, she wiped them away with the back of her hand. Wires were hooked everywhere, and a monitor beeped a steady rhythm.

"Give me a hug," he said, holding out his arms.

She bent over, careful of the wires and sandbag on his upper leg, and hugged him. "You look great."

"Doc says I'm lucky. Personally, I think it was God looking out for me." He looked past her, and a frown crossed his face. "Where's Will? I owe that young man an apology."

"He's in the waiting room," Brad said.

"Well, get him in here."

"I will." Andi hurried back to the waiting room, but Will was gone.

Will exited the hospital and jogged to his car. What a day. First, he'd learned he was losing a mother he'd never actually had, and now the only man who'd ever treated Will like a son hated him. Mr. Hollister had taught him how to throw a curveball . . . taken him fishing . . . most of all, he'd talked to him like he was worth something.

That was important to a kid who didn't have a father. Not that he'd ever been mistreated by his uncle. But the man had been too busy to notice Will. He didn't know his dad, and the only story he'd ever heard about him was that his mom had called him from the hospital to pick them up after Will was born. She'd waited outside in the cold until darkness convinced her that he wasn't coming. And so they went to live with his Aunt Mae and Uncle James, who lived next door to the Hollisters. Or, at least *he* went to live with them. He was four when he realized his mom wasn't ever around.

He slid behind the steering wheel and slammed the door just as his phone rang. *Andi.* He didn't want to talk to her right now and let it ring as he drove to his apartment. He'd brought a copy of Stephanie's case home, and this would be a good time to go through it again, piece by piece.

Once he was home, he picked up this morning's newspaper he hadn't opened and carried it to his desk, where he checked his email. The state trooper had emailed that a TBI agent would be at the body shop tomorrow. Will shot him an email, saying he'd be there. Then he moved to his sofa and opened Stephanie's files.

He separated Barnes's reports from the others, laying them on his coffee table. Will had gone over everything twice already, and he picked up the toxicology report. He scanned it, stopping halfway down the sheet.

How had he overlooked this? Amitriptyline and more than a trace in Jimmy's blood. It was no wonder that he didn't remember what happened or that it didn't kill him, like Lacey. Amitriptyline combined with alcohol was lethal most of the time. But what was amitriptyline doing in his system in the first place? The way Jimmy drank, no doctor would prescribe the antidepressant for him.

Suddenly it hit him. Both Lacey and Jimmy had the antidepressant in their system. The same MO.

But first he had to make sure Jimmy didn't routinely use the drug. He took out his notepad and wrote a memo to ask Jimmy about it tomorrow. Then he took a picture of the tox report and sent it to Maggie with a request to see if it was in Jimmy's court records.

After another half hour of rereading the reports, he leaned against the sofa and rubbed the muscles in his neck. Tomorrow would be a long day, and he needed to get to bed, but he was wound like a compressed spring. His gaze landed on the morning paper, and he opened it up, scanning the headlines. That wouldn't help him relax, so he turned to the sports page, then remembered the play-off game tonight that would determine who U of M played in the final round. Maybe he could catch the score.

Will turned on the news just in time to catch the sports report. *Yes!* He pumped his fist. The team he thought the Memphis team could beat won and would advance to the play-off. With a sigh, he turned the TV off and scanned the rest of the paper, stopping at a page he loved to read.

Today's "Days Gone By" section featured a front page from the nineties. "Kidnapper Loses Last Bid for Parole" was the headline. He scanned down the page, noting that on that date, Hurricane Floyd was dying out after devastating the coast of North Carolina. Then his gaze caught the word *diamond* in another headline. "African Nations Work Together to Rid Supply Chains of Conflict Diamonds."

A quick scan of the article told of how diamonds were being smuggled into the US through various channels. According to the article, an elaborate network of airline employees was smuggling rough diamonds from Sierra Leone through cities like Paris, Brussels, and London. The diamonds were bringing in millions to fund the civil war.

Was it possible? No, surely Stephanie wasn't

involved in anything like this. Will had read articles on conflict diamonds and the staggering amount of money that could be made by corrupt officials through diamond smuggling.

But how about the couriers? The ones actually bringing the diamonds to the States? How much did they make? Will dialed Brad's number. "How's your dad?" he asked when Brad answered.

"Much better when I left. Where'd you go?"

"Home. I'm going over Stephanie's case files." He hesitated. Brad sometimes reacted the same way as his dad. "Andi's heart operation . . . was it life-threatening?"

"No. Well, Mom and Steph thought it was, but actually, Andi could have waited until she was older to have it. That's what Dad wanted to do— wait until he had a job and the money or insurance to pay for it."

"So why didn't she wait?"

"Le Bonheur accepted her as a patient, and the doctor waived his fee. Dad would have paid every penny of it back, but Stephanie had a hundred-thousand-dollar life insurance policy with the airlines, and when it came in, they applied it to Andi's operation. It didn't cover the whole cost, but the balance was manageable for Dad. Why do you want to know?"

"No particular reason." He couldn't tell Brad what he suspected yet. "I found a blood panel in the file, and Jimmy had amitriptyline in his system."

"You're kidding. Just like Lacey."

"Yeah. I figure the killer thought if it worked once to knock someone out, it'd work again. Once she was out, he could put her behind the steering wheel and start the motor. I bet he didn't figure on the drug killing Lacey outright since it didn't kill Jimmy."

"I wonder if that came out at the trial?"

"I don't know. Maggie has the transcript, and I faxed the report to her." It was good to have Brad fully on board. "I'm going to Nashville tomorrow to ask Jimmy if he ever used GHB recreationally. Want to ride with me?"

"Yeah, depending on how Dad is."

"Good. I had an email from the state trooper too. A TBI agent will be at the body shop examining Larry Ray Johnson's pickup tomorrow and I'll check on that as well." Will started to hang up, but Brad cleared his throat. "Yeah?"

"Look, you know how Dad can be sometimes. He's really sorry about what he said. Do me a favor and talk to him."

"Sure. If he gets to come home tomorrow, I'll do that. See you around nine." Brad might change his mind if he knew that Will thought Stephanie was involved in diamond smuggling. Heaviness settled in his stomach as different scenarios worked through his mind.

Another thought hit him. What if Stephanie had decided to keep a few of the diamonds? And what if Lacey Wilson knew where she hid them? Could that have been the evidence she had? He searched for the electrostatic latent image report and found the letters he was looking for.

Dear Andi,
Jimmy Shelton didn't kill Stephanie, and I can tell you who did. Actually, you have diamonds in your possession—

Evidently she didn't like how she'd started the letter and marked through the words and started over.

Dear Andi,
I have information that will exonerate Jimmy Shelton in the death of your sister. I contacted him, but he never responded.

He skipped down to a line in the letter on the next page.

and I let fear and greed overcome what I knew was right.

What if diamonds were why Lacey Wilson was killed? And maybe even Stephanie?

Andi put a dollar bill in the drink machine and punched the button for a bottle of water. Her brother had left the hospital thirty minutes ago to pick up clothes so he could spend the night with their mom.

Her fingers shook as she took out two more Lortabs. What was this, four today? Or six? Couldn't be six. And when did she exchange the ibuprofen bottle for the prescription bottle? Oh yeah. She'd only had four left and had grabbed the others when she went home to change.

"What are you taking?" Barbara Hollister asked.

She dropped the bottle, and it rolled to her mom's feet. "Something for my back." She bent to retrieve it, but her mom was faster.

"Lortab? How long have you been taking these?"

"Since I hurt my back." Andi reached for the bottle, and her mother reluctantly released it.

"That's strong stuff. What's wrong with your back?"

Andi shrugged. "Something about a disc. Do you still have Jillian Bennett's address?"

"Somewhere . . . in my Christmas list, I think. But changing the subject won't work this time. You don't need to keep taking those pills."

"Mom." Andi stretched the word out to two

syllables. "I know what I'm doing. I won't take these any longer than I absolutely have to, but right now, they're getting me through the day. I can't take time to have the operation the doctor wants to do."

"There are other options, like physical therapy. Have you tried that?"

"Not yet. I just want to get through this thing with Jimmy, then I'll see about it."

Her mother opened her mouth to say something then seemed to think better of it. "I'll look for Jillian's address in the morning, after I get your father home."

"Thanks. Are you sure you don't want me to stay with you?"

"Brad has already insisted, and there's no need for you both to stay. You'll sleep better in your own bed, anyway."

After getting her mother to promise to call if she needed anything, Andi drove home, blinking as lights from oncoming cars blinded her. After every turn, she kept watch in her rearview mirror for anyone turning with her. Had she set the alarm at her apartment before she left today? She couldn't remember.

When she pulled up behind the house, the area was lit up like Christmas. Treece must have turned on all the outside lights. No one could find a shadow back here to lurk in. She climbed out of the car, and the warm night wrapped around her.

She loved April—when it wasn't storming. Andi tilted her head. Was that music? She searched for the source, but it seemed to float on the soft breeze that touched her cheek. Swaying to the beat, she danced up the steps. She felt good.

A minute later, she fumbled with the key. Why wouldn't it fit the lock? There. Finally she had the door open, but now something was beeping.

She sang, mocking the sound. "Beep, beep, beep, beep—"

The alarm. What was the code? Her mind blanked. How long did she have to put the code in? She couldn't remember, but it wasn't long. Her nose itched, and she rubbed it. Oh yeah. Stephanie's birthday.

"Thank you, Mr. Alarm," she said when the beeping ceased. She flipped off the outside lights and plopped on the couch. Her eyes drooped. Maybe she'd just sleep here.

At eleven JD had almost decided Andi wasn't coming home when she pulled into the drive and parked in her usual spot behind the house. He pressed his back against the wall away from the light flooding the yard, his dark clothing blending with the brick. He waited as she took her time getting out of her car.

Is she singing?

Andi climbed the steps to the back door and unlocked it. The steady beep of the alarm alerted him that she was getting better about setting it.

She closed the door, and a few minutes later the outside lights went out, then the apartment went dark. He forced himself to wait a good fifteen minutes before he eased to her car and knelt beside the wheel. Where to put the magnetic transponder so he could track her? The wheel? No. It might accidentally be seen. He placed it under the front fender.

Now, if she went looking for Jillian and found her, he could take care of his last problem. He might even get back the diamonds she stole. Scratch that. Jillian had probably sold them years ago. But he could have his pound of flesh.

He froze when Andi's back door opened and she hurried down the steps. Thank goodness he was on the passenger side. She never saw him. As soon as she pulled out onto the street, he started to leave, then looked back.

Her door stood slightly open.

She hadn't set the alarm.

He sneaked up the steps, his black clothing making him almost invisible, since Andi had killed the outside lights. Inside the apartment, he used his cell phone for a light and quickly and systematically searched the living room for anything the diamonds could be hidden in. And not just the diamonds.

If Andi had the diamonds, she probably had the missing journal pages. Unless one of the others had given her details, the only information on those pages could be the names of who was involved in the smuggling. That was enough to put him in jail, even though Andi probably wouldn't know what she had.

He glanced around the room. What he was looking for could be anywhere. He tapped the fireplace mantel to see if it had a false board, but no, it was solid. He was batting zero for the night. First he hadn't found anything at the studio, and now nothing at Andi's apartment.

He clenched his jaw and flipped open a pocketknife, slashing the cushions and chairs. They had to be here somewhere. He stormed into the bathroom and grabbed a lipstick container. He jerked the shower curtain back and left her a message.

He wanted those diamonds.

See, God, I don't need you to help me. I can do it myself. And just watch me. I'm going to save Chloe.

The blaring of a car horn jerked her out of her thoughts.

Disoriented, Andi looked through the windshield. Red light! She slammed the brakes, skidding the car sideways into the intersection. The other car whizzed past on the wrong side of the road, the driver bearing down on the horn.

The car had almost creamed her. Shaking, Andi

moved her Corolla out of the intersection and pulled into a vacant lot.

Where was she? She shook her head to clear it, and her focus sharpened. The clock on the dashboard read 11:45. She was in her car, gripping the steering wheel. She opened the door and tried to get out, but the seat belt held her tight. She bent over, fumbling with the catch, and sweat dripped off her forehead onto her hand. Finally the seat belt came loose and she stumbled out of the car.

The night air hit her clammy skin, and she shivered. Not because she was cold but because she had no idea where she was or how she got here. Unless it was the Lortabs. How many had she taken? She couldn't remember. Her hands shook, and she wrapped her arms across her\ body, tucking her fingers under her arms. She was so thirsty.

Andi reached back in the car for a bottle of water to wet her dry mouth. The other car had missed her, which was a miracle. She scanned the area. Which way was home?

She felt in her pocket and almost cried when her fingers closed around her phone. Andi climbed back into the car. She pushed the center button on her phone, and a message popped up. *What can I help you with?*

"Directions home." Thank goodness she'd programmed her home address in the phone.

When she pulled into the driveway, she was a

total emotional wreck, and by the time she climbed the stairs to her apartment, she was a physical one. Without turning on a light, she set the alarm and went straight to bed.

She'd deal with this in the morning.

— 26 —

At five the next morning, Will's alarm went off, and he crawled out of bed. He'd fought the bed all night, at times dreaming about diamonds.

Will had a hunch that the four flight attendants were involved in smuggling. Jillian had disappeared, Stephanie and Lacey were dead, and Laura refused to help with the stay of execution. If this were true, it would blow the case wide open. But he had to find evidence linking the diamonds to the deaths.

His first stop of the day was Stephanie's studio. There hadn't been enough time yesterday to really go over it, and it made sense that if there was any evidence still lying around, it would be there.

More than likely no one would be home, but unless things had changed, a key to the house was under a planter on the back porch. He could retrieve the key to the studio from the keys hanging on a peg in the washroom off the kitchen and not bother anyone.

At seven, Will pulled into the Hollister drive. What was Brad's car doing here? Maybe he was staying with his mom. Will wouldn't blame him with everything that was going on. He looked for the Hollisters' sedan. Not here, which meant Mrs. Hollister had already left for the hospital, or it was in the garage. He hoped she wasn't here. Other than Andi, Barbara Hollister was the last person he wanted to see after last night.

He'd always had a close relationship with her, mostly because she was so involved in her children's lives, and he was always with Brad. Will didn't remember her ever missing a ball game or an award ceremony when they were in school. She'd even come to a couple of his games when Brad wasn't playing.

Why hadn't Cass loved him? The question caught him off guard, before he could block it or the pain it brought. He steeled his heart against more pain, but it was too late. The floodgates had opened.

What was wrong with him that his own mother hadn't loved him? And if she couldn't love him, no one else would. Probably not even God. No. He knew that was a lie. Will's problem was with people on earth.

He had to get out of the car and away from these thoughts. But they followed him as he went to get the morning paper in the drive, only now his thoughts were focused on Andi. Before her father's outburst, he'd actually harbored a hope that she might care about him, and not like a brother.

Last night when she walked into her mother's kitchen and smiled at him, she lit up his world. For the first time, he fully realized he wanted her in his life.

His cell dinged a text, and he checked his phone. His mother.

I need to see you today.

He texted her back.

Can't today. Going to Nashville.

She'd be disappointed, but how many times had she disappointed him? Why couldn't she have been more like Barbara Hollister?

Can you give me five minutes on the phone?

I'm sorry, but I'm really busy.

His finger hovered over send. When he was a kid and so angry with Cass, he'd dreamed of this day. Her wanting to spend time with him and him getting even for all the times she'd been too busy for him.

Her gaunt frame flashed in his mind's eye, and

his body stilled. Getting even. Was that what he was doing? He lifted his gaze. Light, hazy clouds streaked the morning sky, and the sun warmed his face. Maybe he could meet her halfway. He deleted the text.

> Can I call you in about an hour when I'm on the road? Shouldn't have any distractions then.

He hit send.

A second later, a smiley face popped up.

He picked up the paper and started to the back door when Barbara rounded the corner from the back of the house.

Her hand flew to her chest. "Oh my goodness!"

"I'm sorry. Here's your paper." Once he handed it to her, his hands seemed to be in the way, and he stuck them in his pockets. "Is Mr. Hollister all right?"

"Yes. We were blessed to discover the blockage. The doctor called it a widow maker. I think Tom'll come home later today. Where did you go last night? Tom wanted to talk to you."

"Home," he said, not looking at her.

"I see. Have you had breakfast?"

"Just coffee, but I'm not hungry." He stared at the tops of his shoes, wanting to ask if Andi was here. "I just stopped by to check out something."

"Here?"

"Yes, ma'am."

"Well, whatever it is, I think you need to have breakfast first. You can eat with Brad, and it'll be like old times."

She didn't leave him much choice, and he followed her.

At the corner of the house, she stopped. "Will, about last night. I—"

"Let's just forget it ever happened," Will said, ducking his head.

"I just wanted to say, I'd be proud if you wanted to date Andi."

He wasn't sure he heard her right and he looked up, catching her smile. "Thank you, but I don't think Andi—"

"Nonsense. I've seen the way she looks at you."

He didn't know what to say and followed her inside through the back door to the kitchen. He nodded to Brad, who sat at the table with a mug in his hand.

"Andi's not here," Barbara said, slipping her hand into a red oven mitt. "She went home last night and Brad stayed here with me, even though I told him he didn't have to. Biscuits are coming out in one minute."

When his mother turned to the stove, Brad shot Will a look he knew well. His friend had something he wanted to talk about but not in front of his mother.

She slid a cookie sheet from the oven and

placed it on a trivet then set plates with scrambled eggs and bacon in front of the men. "You never said what you wanted to check on."

"It's something Brad can help me with." Will buttered a biscuit and bit into it. "Mmm. This is so good. You should open a restaurant, Mrs. Hollister."

"Thank you, but you wouldn't be changing the subject, would you?" she said, lifting her eyebrows.

"No, ma'am." He focused on his plate and noticed Brad did the same.

Barbara disappeared down the hall. A few minutes later, she returned and set her purse on the counter while she hooked an earring in her earlobe. "Have either of you heard from Andi?"

"I haven't," Brad said, and Will echoed him.

"That's strange. She usually calls by now," she said. "I'll phone her from the hospital."

Will swallowed down the dread that rose in his throat.

Brad shook his head. "She's probably just sleeping in. Last night was pretty hard on all of us." He pushed back from the table. "Should I go with you?"

"No, just come by this afternoon. Otherwise . . . well, you know your dad as well as I do. His feelings will be hurt. Set your dirty dishes in the sink."

As soon as the door closed, Brad turned to Will.

"Do you have time to help me search the pottery studio again?"

"That's why I'm here. Yesterday was so rushed we could have overlooked something."

"I still have the key."

Will followed Brad to the studio and almost bumped into him when he stopped abruptly.

"Someone's been here," Brad said, pointing toward the door.

The hinge that held the padlock dangled against the door. Will balled his hands. Whatever they missed yesterday, it was probably gone now. "When do you think this happened?"

"Either when we went to the funeral or while we were at the hospital. I'll call Mom and see if she noticed anything yesterday afternoon."

"I'll get the crime scene unit here." Will took out his phone and put in the call. He'd never noticed how easy it would be to break in to the studio. The building was off to itself, and it would be easy for someone to slip behind the garage and jimmy the hinge off.

"The break-in had to have happened while we were at the hospital," Brad said, hitting the disconnect button. "Mom said she walked past the studio late yesterday afternoon to put out scraps for the feral cats around here, and it was padlocked then."

"You stay here and wait for them," Will said. "I'm going to check on Andi."

• • •

Sunlight filtered through the open blinds, waking Andi. Her insides quivered like Jell-O. She turned over to go back to sleep, and the events of last night slammed her.

The hospital. Her dad. She sat up in bed and looked at the clock. Eight! She never slept that late. She looked down. Why did she still have on the clothes she wore last night?

The image of a red light came crashing back. She'd almost had a wreck.

Andi tried to swallow, but her mouth was so dry she couldn't even wet her lips. She stumbled to the bathroom and swished tepid water in her mouth. Her fingers shook as she reached for the bottle of Lortabs in the cabinet. It was the only place she could keep it where no one would see it.

Empty. When did that happen? Her purse. She had another bottle in her purse. She shut the medicine cabinet and caught sight of herself in the mirror. She leaned closer, her heart slamming against her ribs. Red-rimmed eyes stared back at her, and her hair was a tangled mess. She touched her hollow cheeks. When was the last time she'd eaten?

Andi shifted her gaze back to her eyes. They stared back, dull, unblinking. What had she become?

A junkie.

She blinked, and the reflection blinked.

No. She couldn't be. Other people became addicted. Not her. She was only taking what the doctor prescribed. Andi read the label on the empty bottle. *One to two tablets every six hours as needed for pain.* She did the math in her head. Eight tablets maximum.

She was pretty sure she hadn't taken more than that and turned on the hot water tap, then groped for her hairbrush on the counter, dropping it. Her hands shook as she picked it up and then brushed through her hair.

When the water warmed, she wet a cloth and bathed her face before brushing her teeth. Making herself presentable would make her okay again. Except the quivering inside her begged for a pink tablet.

Andi stumbled to her bed and reached for the ibuprofen bottle in her purse. Just one. To get her through the day. Then no more. Wait, those were gone. She searched for the prescription bottle she'd switched to.

She shook the bottle, and two pills spilled out, scattering on the floor. Her cell phone dinged as she dropped to her hands and knees and corralled the pills. There had to be more than two. The phone dinged again.

Something's happened to Dad. She snatched the phone, and after she read the text, she sagged against the bed. Only her mom texting she'd found Jillian's address. Where in the world was Doskie, Tennessee?

Andi examined the two pills in her hand. How many had she taken yesterday? She'd have to think back to how many pills she'd started with, and her brain couldn't do the math.

Treece's warning about addiction flashed in her mind, and she brushed it aside. She was not addicted. She thought back over the last three months. In the beginning, she'd only taken two a day. So how had she gotten to this point—taking who knew how many a day? And what was she going to do about it?

She wasn't even sure she knew where to start. Or if she could. She needed help. Her phone rang, and she looked at the ID. "Morning, Mom," she croaked.

"You sound terrible. What's wrong?"

"Didn't get a lot of sleep."

"I'm sorry, honey. Did you get my text with Jillian's latest address? I can't believe how that girl moves around."

"I got it. How's Dad?"

"Doing great. I'm here at the hospital with him. But . . ." Hesitation crept into her mother's voice. "They want to run a few tests before they send him home."

"What kind of tests?" Cold chills ran over Andi's body, and she didn't know if it was from her mother's words or the pills her body craved.

"His heart rhythm is a little out of whack."

"Mom, that's not a medical term. What did the doctor call it?"

"A-something. I can't remember the exact name."

"Atrial fibrillation?"

"I think that's what he said."

Andi wiped sweat from her forehead. She needed to check on her dad. She searched her closet for something to change into. "I'll be there as soon as I can get dressed."

"There's no need to come this morning. It's nothing serious. Go see Jillian like you planned. Or stay at home and get some rest. You looked terrible last night. I'm worried about you. You're much too skinny."

"After I get through working on this story, I'll let you fatten me up," she said. So much to do today . . . But she couldn't go anywhere until she showered.

Andi shuffled into the bathroom and pulled back the shower curtain to run the water. And froze. Blood drained from her face, leaving it as cold as the message on the white tile in her shower.

Last warning. Give me what I want.

"I'll call you back, Mom." Black dots swam before Andi's eyes. She grabbed for the shower curtain as her knees buckled.

She came to on the cold tile floor, unsure of

how long she'd been out. Will. She needed Will. With shaking hands, she dialed his number. He answered on the first ring.

"I'm sorry I didn't answer last night."

"I . . ." She swallowed. She hadn't thought this through. If she told him about the message, she'd have to tell him about leaving her apartment last night . . . and that she'd been stoned. "Uh . . . Dad wants to see you."

"I don't think that's a good idea."

"He wants to apologize." She'd never been so thirsty in her life. Andi rose to her knees, then stood. Nothing seemed to be broken, and the dizziness had passed. *Don't look at the message.*

"Are you all right?"

"Yeah, just tired and worried. Go see him. Please."

"Maybe later. Someone broke in to the studio last night," he said.

"What?" Even though Andi heard what he said the first time, she couldn't process it. She believed she'd die if she didn't get a cold glass of water.

"I wanted to go over the studio again before I went to Nashville, so I went by there, and someone had broken the lock. Brad is waiting for the crime scene unit now. Are you and Maggie still going to see Jillian?"

She rounded the corner to the living room and gasped.

"What's wrong?"

"My apartment . . ." Her knees buckled, and she sank to the floor. "It's been trashed."

"I'm on my way."

— 27 —

Will called Brad as he sped across town. "Someone trashed Andi's apartment. How far away are you?"

"I'm still at Mom and Dad's waiting on the crime scene techs."

"Stay with that. I'll take care of Andi." Will took the last corner almost on two wheels. "I'm almost there."

He wheeled into the driveway, slammed on the brakes, and jumped out. Andi sat on the deck, rocking back and forth. It barely registered that she had on the same clothes from last night.

"I couldn't stay in there," she said when he topped the steps. "Steph's horse is gone, and it's my fault."

He knelt beside her. "It's not your fault. I'm so sorry this is happening."

"Yes, it is my fault." She buried her face in her hands.

He turned as Treece opened her back door.

"What's going on?" she asked, tightening the belt on her robe.

He waved her over. "Can you help her? I need to check inside."

"Of course." Treece hurried to Andi's side. "What happened?"

Andi's answer was lost as Will stepped through the open back door and scanned the room. Books lay on the floor where they'd been dumped from the bookcase. Pillows and cushions were shredded. He took out his phone and once again called for crime scene techs.

Will raked his fingers through his hair. How had this happened if Andi was here last night? Unless it happened while she was at the hospital, but if that was the case, why hadn't she seen it when she came home?

He walked back to the deck. Treece had wrapped a comforter around Andi's shoulders.

"What's going on?" Treece asked. "All she'll say is 'it's gone.'"

"Someone broke in and trashed her apartment looking for something. He took the horse sculpture Stephanie made."

"No, I have it," she said.

Andi jerked her head up. She grabbed Treece's arm. "What? You have it?"

"Yes. I took it yesterday afternoon because I wanted to fix the chip for you, but . . ." She shrugged. "Reggie came over and I never got around to it. I'll go get it."

"There's something else you need to know,"

Andi said to Will after Treece left. "Whoever did this left a message in my shower. That's really why I called you."

Will bolted for the door before she finished speaking. Why hadn't she told him already? Something was going on that he didn't understand.

The shower curtain lay crumpled on the floor, and he read the message on the tile. *Last warning. Give me what I want.* It looked like the intruder had written it with a red marker and then turned the shower on so the writing ran and looked like blood.

Resolve settled in Will's stomach. He strode to the deck where Treece had returned with the horse. "Both of you pack a bag," he said. "You can't stay here until we catch whoever is doing this."

"Why are they doing this?" Andi cried. "What do they want?"

Treece shook her head. "What they want doesn't matter. Whoever did it is desperate, and if you'd been home, they would have killed you."

She was right. "You have to leave," Will said.

"Where did you go last night, anyway?" Treece asked. "I heard your back door shut, and when I looked out, you were pulling out of the drive. I texted and called, but you never answered."

Andi's already pale face grew even paler, and

she pressed her hand against her mouth. "I . . . just went out. I must not have set the alarm. Did you hear anything while I was gone?"

Treece shivered and hugged her arms to her body. "No. I took ibuprofen for my shoulder and went back to sleep."

Andi turned to Will. "Do you think someone was watching my apartment and saw me leave?"

Will could kick himself for not watching the house since he caught the private investigator lurking about. He'd checked him out, though, and there wasn't a hint of scandal about him anywhere.

But what if he'd discovered Stephanie had been smuggling diamonds? And she stole some of them? The PI could have been hired to get the diamonds back, and maybe he thought Andi had them?

Or . . . The pieces of the puzzle fell into place. Maybe it wasn't the PI but whoever had killed Lacey. If he found the letters she'd written, the killer believed the diamonds were in Andi's possession. And if he'd killed twice to get them, he wouldn't hesitate to kill again.

The look on Will's face scared Andi.

"How did he know I didn't set the alarm?" She rubbed the horse's back, her fingers seeking the hole where it had chipped.

"What you said—he was watching your apartment. Something alerted him when you left that you hadn't set it."

She knew what that was. He probably could tell she was stoned. At least he hadn't gotten Steph's sculpture. Her fingers ran over something hard, and she glanced down. At first her mind didn't comprehend what she was seeing, then she realized there was a piece of glass or a rock embedded in the clay. "Why would Steph put glass in this horse?"

"Glass? Let me see." Will took the sculpture from her and examined it. "I think I've found what your intruder was looking for. If I'm not mistaken, this is a rough diamond, and there may be more."

"Diamond?" Andi and Treece said in unison, then Andi asked, "How did a diamond get in Stephanie's sculpture?"

Will's whole body stiffened, and he wouldn't meet her eyes.

The hair lifted on the back of her neck. "What are you not telling me?"

"Andi . . ." He stopped to take a deep breath.

The way he said her name . . . suddenly she didn't want to know. A Volkswagen Beetle pulled into the drive, and she'd never been so glad for a diversion, even if she'd totally forgotten that she and Maggie were driving to middle Tennessee to look for Jillian. "It's Maggie."

The attorney climbed out of her car and shaded

her eyes with her hand. "Good morning. Andi, did you get the address for Jillian?"

"Ms. Starr?" Will said.

"Why does everyone look so surprised? Didn't you tell them what we were doing today? And Will, if you call me ma'am or Ms. Starr again, I'll throttle you."

"Yes, ma'am—Maggie," he said.

Maggie held an eight-by-ten photo in her hand as she climbed the steps. "I had a friend age a photo I found of Jillian. It shows how she should look now." She stopped at the top of the steps. "Made you one too, Will."

"Mom texted me the last address she had for Jillian," Andi said, pulling herself together. "It's a PO number in Doskie, Tennessee. It won't take me long to get dressed." She turned to Will. "I can go into my bedroom, right?"

"No, not until the crime scene techs get through. But they should be here any minute."

Andi groaned. "I can't wait, and I can't go looking for Jillian in what I wore last night." Her voice broke. What was wrong with her? Her nerves were as raw as hamburger meat.

Maggie shot Andi and then Will a concerned look. "What's going on here?"

Will started to say something, but Andi cut him off. "I'll tell you in the car."

"Why did you sleep in your clothes?" Treece asked.

Andi couldn't meet her eyes. "I was tired."

"I see."

Her friend's tone of voice said she didn't, but Andi didn't offer any other information.

"They might be a little big, but I have some jeans you can wear," Treece said. "And a sweater, and my boots should fit."

"Thanks." She squeezed her friend's hand.

"But I can't help you in the makeup department," Treece said, smiling.

No, Treece's makeup wouldn't work on her light skin.

The CSU team was in her apartment by the time Andi had showered and dressed. She took the egg sandwich Treece handed her and forced herself to eat it. "You'll go to your parents' until this is over?" Andi asked.

"Definitely. But I think we need to talk."

Andi didn't. Not today. "I'll call you tonight with whatever information we discover."

"That's not what I'm talking about," Treece said gently. "I want to know what's going on with you."

"Nothing." She forced herself to not look away from Treece's probing gaze this time. A muscle spasm in her back made her wince. "Do you have any ibuprofen?"

"Ibuprofen?"

Andi took a shaky breath. "Yeah. I don't think I should keep taking the Lortabs."

Relief showed in Treece's eyes. "I have an extra bottle. Let me get it."

She returned with the bottle and hugged her. "I read somewhere you can't just stop taking the Lortabs cold turkey. You need to get help."

"I will Monday." Andi almost cracked. Kindness undid her every time. "Thanks," she whispered and hurried out the door to where Will and Maggie talked on the deck.

"I'm ready." She wished she felt half as good as she sounded. If only her insides would quit shaking. "Can I go inside and get my purse?" she asked Will.

"I'll get it for you. Is it in the bedroom?"

"No, the sofa."

"Are you certain you feel up to going with me?" Maggie said. "You look a little pale."

"I'm fine. What were you and Will discussing?"

Maggie hesitated. When Will came out of the house carrying Andi's purse, she said, "Andi wants to know what we were talking about."

That look again as resignation settled in his shoulders. He handed Andi the purse.

"I showed Maggie the diamond you found in the horse. It and some of the words that Lacey Wilson used when she wrote to you indicate your sister may have been smuggling diamonds into the country. I'm taking the sculpture downtown to x-ray it."

Stephanie smuggling diamonds? Icy tendrils

356

curled around her body, and she groped for a deck chair to steady herself.

"No!" Andi palmed her hands out. "Steph would never do anything illegal."

He sighed. "I know you don't want to think that, but I'm afraid everything indicates she was—look at the diamond we just found."

She shook her head, trying to clear it. "I never would have believed you'd do something like this."

"Andi, I'm a cop, and when I see evidence like this—"

"If she was smuggling diamonds, why would they be hidden in the horse?"

Will's gaze dropped, and so did his shoulders.

He thinks Steph was stealing them. It was as though she'd been dropped down a rabbit hole. The sculpture. What had he said about it? "What are you going to do with the horse? It's all I have left of my sister."

"I'm only going to scan it. I promise I won't damage it."

Her chest heaved. "I don't care what you find. My sister did not smuggle diamonds into this country." Disappointment lay heavy in her heart, but she pushed it aside. "I'll prove you're wrong. I'll find Jillian, and she'll set the record straight."

She turned to Maggie, who stood frozen, dismay written on her face. "Are you ready to go?"

Maggie threw a look at Will, but Andi didn't wait to see his reaction. She ran down the steps to her car. A minute later, Maggie slid into the passenger side.

"Will is only—"

Andi held up her hand and blinked back the tears stinging the back of her eyes. "Please, don't defend him, and I don't want to talk about this."

"Okay," Maggie said slowly. "We'll stay off the subject of Will Kincade unless you bring it up."

"That's so not happening." She fastened her seat belt and turned the key. "I knew my sister. She wouldn't do anything illegal, and when we find Jillian, she'll confirm that."

"I hope so," Maggie said as she fastened her seat belt. "Would you like me to drive? Or we can go in my Beetle."

"You're joking, right? About the Beetle." She shot a quick glance at Maggie. "You're not."

"Well, you are really upset."

"I'm fine. And I'll be careful."

Maggie settled back in the seat. "See that you are," she said.

— 28 —

Treece laid her hand on Will's arm. "Andi will get over this."

"I don't know. She loved her sister. And I can't ignore evidence because of how I feel about Andi." He wrapped the horse in bubble wrap the crime scene unit had given him. The CJC had a scanner that he could use to look inside the sculpture.

"Give her time to process all of this."

He patted Treece's hand, and his fingers brushed over the ring on her finger. "Hey, Reggie proposed?"

She beamed at him. "And I said yes."

He hugged her. "I'm happy for you. He's a good guy. And now if you're ready, I'll follow you to your folks' house."

Twenty minutes later, Will returned Treece's wave from her parents' front porch. He wished a little of her happiness could rub off on him. He'd thought Andi was the one, but if she couldn't understand that he was a cop and couldn't look the other way when the evidence didn't suit him, then they weren't on the same page.

Before he pulled away from the curb, Will dialed the number he had for Larry Ray Johnson's estranged wife and identified himself. "I had hoped to drive to Nashville today, but the hospital informed me that your husband is still critical and in a coma. I thought I'd see if you're willing to answer a few questions over the phone."

"Soon to be ex-husband. We're getting a divorce," she corrected. "That's what they told me too. I don't know why you want to talk to me. Like I told the state trooper, I don't know anything about the accident."

"Did your husband ever talk about earning extra money?" he asked and heard a slight gasp over the phone.

"How did you know? It took me three years to find out someone was sending him a hundred dollar bill every month."

Will braked for a slow-moving car, then waited for it to make a left turn. "Do you know who sent it?"

"Not their real name. It was somebody he called JD. Larry Ray told me about it one night when he was drinking. Said this JD guy called him up out of the blue and offered him a hundred dollars a month to keep a watch on one of the prisoners. He was to call him if anything unusual happened."

"And you don't think JD was his real name?"

"I don't know. Larry Ray didn't think it was."

He gripped the steering wheel. "Does he have a phone number for this man?"

She hesitated. "Look, I don't want to get him in any trouble . . ."

Larry Ray had gotten himself in his own trouble. "Giving me the number won't make any difference in what happens to your husband. But if I'm right, JD caused the accident that put Larry Ray in ICU."

"Oh no," she said softly. "I could tell he was afraid of this JD. I don't have the number, but it's on his cell phone."

Will thanked her and disconnected. When he pulled into the parking garage across from the CJC, he scanned his contacts for the state trooper's number. Once he answered, Will asked if Johnson's cell phone had been found.

"I'm not at headquarters, but I can check and call you back."

The call came ten minutes later as Will stopped by his desk.

"It wasn't found, but it could be in the pickup. Or with Johnson at the hospital. I'm tied up with another wreck, but I can check the pickup when I finish," he said.

"I'm meeting a TBI agent there at one," Will replied. "Why don't you come then if you're free?"

The memory of Will standing on the deck, his face mirroring the pain in her heart as Andi had spun out of the driveway, lingered. She'd idolized Will since she was a kid, and down deep she'd been stupid enough to think they might have a future together.

Andi straightened her shoulders. She should have known it was too good to be true. That his cousin would come first. A muscle spasmed in her back. What she needed was one of those pills.

"I'm going to top off the gas tank," she said and pulled into the service station at the next corner. "Would you like something to drink?"

"No, but I'll pump the gas while you're inside," Maggie said.

Inside the station, Andi paid for the gas and a drink. She searched her purse for the pill bottle. If Will saw it, he'd probably removed it. Her fingers closed around the bottle, and relief surged through her. She flipped the cap off and shook out the last two pills.

She hesitated, flashing back to the red light last night.

What's your pain level? That's what Treece would say.

Come on, my back hurts, and I feel lousy. She uncapped the water bottle, not believing she was standing in the middle of a convenience store arguing with someone who wasn't even there. Already her skin was crawling, and flu-like symptoms had hit her body. With clarity she hadn't had in a while, she knew it wasn't pain demanding the pills—she was going into withdrawal. If she was going to find Jillian, she needed a Lortab.

Andi stared at the two pills in her hand. Was she going absolutely crazy?

"Can I help you, miss?"

The clerk startled her.

"What?"

"I asked if I could help you."

"Thank you, I'm fine." But she wasn't. She stared at the pills again, and the desire to take one overwhelmed her.

But, what if she gave it an hour? She had the water. She could take them whenever. Grabbing the bottle, Andi hurried back to the car.

"Would you like for me to drive awhile?" Maggie asked.

"Would you?" Andi didn't feel like concentrating on traffic, so she climbed in the passenger seat and put the name of the town from the address her mother had texted into her GPS. "Doskie is two hours from Memphis," she said as the phone instructed them to take the next ramp on I-40.

"How old do you think the address is?"

"Mom says it's the latest one she had." Andi caught her breath. "Dad. I better call and see how he is."

"What do you mean? Is he sick?"

"He went to the ER last night. He had a blockage and they put in a stent." She explained what had happened as she dialed. When her mom answered, Andi asked, "How's Dad?"

"Test shows he has a slight electrical problem. They want to keep him here until Monday when his cardiologist will be back."

Her mom's voice was tight, and Andi gripped the phone. "Is he going to be all right?"

"They say he will be, but he may need a pacemaker."

She'd heard of those. Putting one in wasn't usually dangerous. "Well, keep me informed. I'm on my way to see Jillian."

"Be careful, honey, and tell her hello for me."

"Sure, Mom," she said and disconnected.

"I always liked your folks," Maggie said.

"Me too," she replied, and they both laughed.

"How is your dad?"

Andi sobered. "The doctor says he needs a pacemaker." *God has this.* "Do you think God controls everything that happens to us?" she asked.

Maggie frowned. "I don't think of him as *controlling* everything. More like he allows things in our lives."

"Why does he allow bad things?"

Maggie sighed. "I don't know. And sometimes what looks bad at first turns out to be a blessing in disguise. Like your dad."

"What are you talking about? How could my dad's heart attack be a blessing?"

"You said he had a blockage in his main artery and no symptoms. A lot of men die from that kind of heart condition. But they discovered his and fixed it because he had a heart attack."

She hadn't thought of it that way.

Maggie tapped her fingers on the steering wheel. "You know, God isn't waiting for us to mess up so he can 'get us.' "

"Feels like it to me sometimes," Andi said with a hollow laugh.

"He'd much rather we depend on him and not get in the mess in the first place."

"You sound like Treece. She's always on me about running ahead of God."

"She sounds pretty wise."

"I suppose." She thought about the pills in her purse, how she had come to depend on them but couldn't depend on God. Maybe it was time to change that. She pulled the sun visor down and checked the traffic behind them to see if anyone was following.

"I hope we find Jillian, but with only a town and a post office box, I have my doubts," Maggie said.

Andi flipped the mirror up. She did too. "I've done some checking, and I didn't find any trace of her anywhere except for a Facebook account that had no posts, no photos, nothing—except a city on the other side of the state from where she lives. It's almost like it's a plant."

"I think she's hiding from someone," Maggie said.

"So do I. And I think she holds the key to this whole case," Andi said as her phone rang. *The hospital.* Her mind automatically went to her dad, ratcheting up her heart rate. "Hello?"

"It's me, Chloe."

Andi's heart slowed as her muscles relaxed. "How are you?"

"Better. They're moving me to a safe house today."

"That's great."

"Um . . . I really need to see you before I leave. I . . . I did something really bad."

"Oh, Chloe, I'm sorry, but I'm on I-40 and an hour away from Memphis. But it can't be that bad. Can it wait until I get back?"

"I'll be gone." She sounded close to tears.

"Can you just tell me?"

"I'll try. You see, I . . ." Silence followed, then a deep sigh came through the phone. "I can't do it. Just be careful and I'm sorry." The line went dead.

"That was strange," Andi said.

"Who was that?"

"A runaway I tried to help and ended up getting her shot." Andi dialed Treece's number. When she answered, Andi said, "Can you go to the hospital and talk to Chloe? She just called and wanted to tell me something in person, but I'm too far away from Memphis to turn around and come back, and she's being transferred to a safe house later today."

"I planned to visit her this morning."

"Good. See if you can get her to talk about it."

"Will do. Are you all right now?"

"I'm fine." She was still disappointed in Will.

"I talked with Will. He hates what happened, and he wrapped the sculpture really carefully before he left with it. X-raying won't damage it."

"I don't want to discuss him. He had no right accusing Stephanie of smuggling. She wasn't the only flight attendant living in the house."

"That's just it. He believes they all might have been involved."

"You're kidding." She glanced to her left. "Even Maggie?"

"No, only the flight attendants. Did you know they all flew internationally?"

She did. What if Will had been right? The man who broke into her apartment was looking for diamonds, and in spite of what she'd said to Will, no one but Stephanie could have put the diamonds in the sculpture.

Was it possible her sister really was a smuggler?

David surveyed the ceramic studio. A fireplace took up most of one wall, and a sofa sat near it. A worktable was in the center of the room, under the light. A potter's wheel was positioned near the door, and in a small adjacent room were five-gallon buckets. Glazes, he suspected. Dried up, for sure.

Dust coated everything, and had even before the crime scene unit dusted for fingerprints. He was told they'd gotten good photos of shoe prints, but that was all. The burglar hadn't thought about the dust from years of neglect and hadn't seen the footprints he left behind in the dark, although they would have to be separated from the ones left yesterday.

"This was my great-grandparents' first home," Brad said, standing beside him. "And the only reason my dad didn't tear it down after Stephanie died out here."

That explained why there was a fireplace in such a small building. David tapped the mantel, looking for a hidden compartment, but it sounded solid. He turned around.

"Where do you want to start?" Brad asked.

"File cabinet, I suppose, unless you know of any place your sister might hide something."

"I wasn't into clay—too busy playing sports— but Andi was out here all the time. Let me call and see if she's remembered if Stephanie had any secret hiding places."

David wandered over to the file cabinet and opened a drawer. Nothing but glaze recipes, invoices . . . He closed it and opened another.

"Andi didn't remember any secret places," Brad said, "but she'll call back if she does."

"Any word on whether any evidence was recovered at her apartment this morning?"

"Just like here, no fingerprints. Oh, and by the way, if my mom happens to come out here, she hasn't been told about Andi's break-in. Or any other details of this case."

David gave him a thumbs-up. "Did anyone other than your grandparents live here before it was turned into a ceramic studio?"

"Mom and Dad. They lived in it while our house was being built. Personally, I thought it was a waste of a good apartment for my sister to use it for a pottery studio. But Dad didn't want to go to the expense of putting in heat and air—it's cooled with fans and heated by the fireplace. Not that it bothered Stephanie."

David laughed, then turned and caught Brad staring at the fireplace, an expression of wistfulness on his face.

"She pit-fired her art pieces in it. Sometimes I wonder if she'd lived whether she'd be this famous potter by now." He looked away. "Sometimes I wish Dad had torn down the studio."

David understood why, and he certainly would have understood if Tom Hollister had torn the building down. After his wife's death, David would have moved out of their house if it hadn't been for uprooting his daughter. Still thought about it sometimes, even after five years. "I'll start with the filing cabinet."

Brad nodded as his cell phone rang. "It's Treece." He answered and listened. "Right now?"

he said. "Okay." He pocketed his phone. "She wants me to come to the hospital and talk to the girl who was shot Wednesday night."

"Go ahead. I'll keep working."

"I won't be long."

After Brad left, David started with the file cabinet, going through every piece of paper. An hour later, he dragged a two-step footstool to the cabinet and sat down to go through the bottom drawer.

A shadow crossed the door, and he looked up, recognizing Brad's mother. She was petite like Andi but with lighter hair. She frowned, clearly not remembering him. "Mrs. Hollister, David Raines. We met at a fundraiser once."

"Oh, now I remember, Lieutenant, and call me Barbara," she said. "Have you discovered the reason someone broke in to the studio?"

"Not yet." She seemed reluctant to enter the building. "You can come in, if you'd like. The crime scene unit is finished."

"I'll stand here." She flattened her lips but scanned the room from the doorway. "This is the first time I've looked inside since that night." She took a step back. "If you need anything, I'll be in the house."

He followed her outside. "Do you know of any hiding places in the studio?"

Her mouth relaxed, and a tiny smile tugged at the corners. "Stephanie didn't realize I knew she'd found it, but yes, there is one. Tom's grandfather built this house, and he made a hidden compart-ment in the mantel. It's where he used to keep his cash. Steph kept her diary there. I never read it, of course."

He hated to ask her to come back inside. "Could you tell me how to find it?"

She squared her shoulders. "I'll show you. I just realized how silly I'm being by refusing to enter the studio."

"You don't have to—"

"Yes, I do." She marched through the door to the fireplace. "It's right here." She turned a piece of molding on the mantel, and a thick panel slid back. "What's this?" she said and pulled out a sheaf of papers.

"Here," he said, examining the two-inch board that hid the opening. No wonder it didn't sound hollow when he tapped it. The grandfather was a smart man. "I have on gloves, let me take them."

When she handed the papers to him, he spread them out on the table and scanned the writing. "Is this Stephanie's handwriting?"

Barbara peered over his shoulder and caught her breath. "Yes. Those are the cities she used to talk about flying into." Suddenly she straightened up. "Do I need to leave since this is police business?"

"You don't have to leave, but maybe you shouldn't read this."

"I understand," she said and backed away.

David returned to the papers. There were four pages with writing on front and back, and they looked like some sort of log. The last page contained a journal entry.

Jillian is upset. But I know she's taking diamonds out of her shipments and replacing them with inferior rough stones. JD will be furious when he finds out when I go to the FBI.

I should never have let him talk me into bringing those diamonds into the country, but at least I only did it once. I should have gone to the FBI then. What if customs had searched my purse yesterday? I can't believe he stashed those diamonds in my purse. He'll come back tomorrow looking for them, but I'm taking them to the FBI. Until I do, they're safe in the horse sculpture. Can't tell Laura.

He looked for another page, but there wasn't one, and he flipped back to the first page and tried to make sense of the log.

Delivered to AJ:
Paris—November 10 - 3 - SH
Paris—November 12 - 5 - JB
Paris—December 3 - 9 - L
Paris—December 10 - 10 - JB
Paris—December 20 - 9 - L

The list went on. As he studied the pages, his heart sank. Will believed the four flight attendants in the house were smuggling diamonds into the States. David had hoped it wasn't true, but what if this was a log of their activities? SH had to be Stephanie, but her initials appeared only the one time. JB must be Jillian Bennett. The two Ls listed—was that Laura or Lacey? And who was AJ?

— 29 —

Will leaned forward to view the image on the scanner. The stone Andi found showed clearly along with two more in the horse's belly.

The tech beside him whistled. "That's a good-sized diamond."

"Looks like it's about the size of a quail egg."

The tech pushed a button, and a scale appeared. "If a quail egg is an inch and a half by three quarters of an inch, yeah. How many carats do you suppose that is?"

He forgot Carl was a total city boy. Will pulled up a website on his tablet that showed photos of uncut diamonds and their cost. After converting the size to millimeters, he said, "According to this, eighteen to twenty carats."

"But you won't know until you weigh it," the tech added.

And that was his problem. He'd promised Andi he wouldn't destroy the horse. He found a comparable rough diamond on the website and scrolled down to the price.

Forty to fifty thousand dollars? That couldn't be right. He rubbed his eyes and looked at the screen again.

Carl looked over his shoulder. "Are you kidding me? The stone we're looking at in that horse might be worth forty-five thousand dollars?"

"I don't know." Will dialed a gemologist he knew and described the rough stone. "I believe it was smuggled into the country."

"The shape sounds like an octahedron, and it's probably high grade, since no one would go to the risk and trouble of smuggling inferior diamonds," his friend said. "You say it's about twenty carats?"

"I can't weigh it, but according to the dimension we're getting from the scanner, it should weigh about that. And there's two more, half that size."

"I really need to see them, but a ball park figure—if the clarity is good and the right shape—it could easily be worth around forty-fifty grand, twenty-five for the smaller ones. Maybe more, depending on their quality."

"What would they have been worth in the late nineties?"

"All three of them . . . Again, this is just a rough

guess, probably in the neighborhood of seventy or eighty thousand."

Will thanked his friend and hung up. Money like that could easily get someone killed. He rewrapped the horse in bubble wrap and locked it in the property room, hoping it wouldn't get broken. Andi was already furious with him, and if anything happened to the sculpture, she'd never forgive him. Might not anyway.

He checked his watch. Eleven. He'd have to hurry to catch the insurance investigator.

He was approaching the I-240 split when his phone rang, and he pressed the answer button on the steering wheel. "Hello."

"Will, it's Treece. I'm at the hospital with Chloe, and she just told me she set us up Wednesday night."

"What? Never mind, I heard you. Did she say who was behind it?"

"She doesn't know. Her pimp had Chloe call and get Andi to meet her that night. Chloe didn't know they were going to attack us."

He flipped on his right signal and took the loop that would take him by the hospital. "I'll stop on my way out of town. Call Brad and get him to meet us there," he said. "But do me a favor. Don't say anything about the diamonds and Stephanie. I want more information before I tell him."

"Brad's on his way, and I won't say anything."

Fifteen minutes later, he pulled into the hospital

parking lot and hurried inside. Brad and the marshal were already in Chloe's room when Will walked through the door. The fifteen-year-old's face was ashen.

"Am I in trouble?" she asked in a small voice.

"Of course not," Brad said. "We just need to ask you a few questions."

"I don't know anything except I heard Jason talking to somebody on the phone, and then he made me call this number and talk to Andi. He told me if I'd do it, he wouldn't sell me to this other guy." She wiped her eyes with the back of her hand. "I didn't know anyone would get hurt."

"It's okay." Treece wrapped her arms around the girl.

"Where can I find this Jason?"

"I don't know," she wailed. "I don't know where anything is in Memphis. I got off the bus somewhere downtown, and Jason kind of protected me when this other guy harassed me."

And the next thing the poor kid knows, she's hustling. Will turned to the marshal. "What time is Chloe supposed to be transferred to the safe house?"

"Late this afternoon."

Brad spoke up. "I'll get Reggie to bring mug shots of local pimps and see if she can identify Jason from any of them."

"Good. One of you call Andi and let her know.

I'm meeting a TBI agent on the other side of Jackson about Larry Ray Johnson's pickup."

Brad gave him a curious glance. "I'll walk out with you."

"Sure."

As they rode the elevator to the lobby, Brad asked, "Do you have time to run by the studio? David is already there, and the crime scene unit should be through by now."

"I don't have time. I'm meeting the TBI agent at one. Besides, Andi is the person you want—she spent a lot of time in the studio, and she might know where Stephanie kept things she didn't want others to see."

"Andi's on her way to Doskie, Tennessee, wherever that is." Out on the sidewalk, Brad stopped him. "What's going on with you and Andi?"

"What do you mean?"

"There could be only one reason you'd ask me to talk to Andi for you—there's a problem between the two of you. What gives?"

"Nothing."

"Come on, I've been watching you two. You're obviously falling for her, and I think she feels the same way. What happened?"

Will tapped his fingers against his leg. He wasn't ready to get into this with Brad, but when he called his sister, she'd probably tell him. "This morning . . ." He didn't want to do this.

"What?"

"Andi found a rough diamond in the horse sculpture, and I found two more with the scanner."

"Diamonds in that ugly sculpture of Andi's?" Brad rubbed his forehead. "How did diamonds get there?"

Will suppressed a groan. Why couldn't this wait? It was enough that he'd probably lost Andi over it. He didn't want to lose his friend today as well. "Look, you'll have to either wait or ask Andi. I don't have time to explain."

Will started to walk away, and Brad grabbed his arm. "Wait a minute." Then his eyes widened, and he sucked in a breath. "Are you—"

"Yes, that's exactly what I'm saying." Will planted his feet. "I told Andi I thought Stephanie was smuggling diamonds."

"Do you have proof?"

"Not yet, but last night I came across an article about diamonds being smuggled into the country by airline employees. And Lacey mentioned diamonds in one of the letters she'd started to Andi."

"I have to think about this." Brad took a step back, and then suddenly he exploded.

Will saw the punch coming and ducked, but he wasn't quick enough. Brad's fist caught the side of his cheek. Will grabbed Brad's wrist and twisted his arm behind his back. "I'm not fighting you."

Brad struggled to break free. "Yes, you are," he said over his shoulder. "You just accused my dead sister of smuggling. She can't even defend herself."

"If she's not involved, then put that energy into finding out who is." Will released him with a shove and walked to his car. He didn't know which hurt more, his cheek or his heart.

"I'll make you eat your words," Brad called after him.

Will kept walking. Anything he said would only make his friend angrier. He hoped Brad did find evidence that pointed to someone else. But Will didn't see that happening. Either Stephanie smuggled the diamonds in and stole the three in the sculpture or she was hiding them for someone else. Either way, Will believed the diamonds got her killed.

— 30 —

"I've never been to Doskie before," Andi said. "But it's beautiful." They were off the interstate and approaching the downtown area. "We're in the foothills of the Appalachians."

"I bet it's pretty in the fall," Maggie said as they parked in front of the small post office. "You know, they may not give us Jillian's address."

"Only one way to find out." Andi climbed out

of her car and followed Maggie into the building. A postal worker was locking the door to the lobby. Andi checked her watch. "Do you close at noon?"

"Yes, ma'am."

"Can we get in?" Maggie asked. "It's really important that we speak to the postmaster."

"Sorry, he's not here."

"Can we speak to the next person in charge?" Maggie asked.

"That'd be the woman at the window, but as you can see, we're closed."

"But it's a matter of life and death."

"Honey, you have no idea how many times I hear that."

"This time it's true," Maggie said. "I'm a lawyer, and the man I represent will die if we don't get the information we need."

The clerk shot them a dubious look, but she didn't reject their request outright.

"Please," Andi said.

"I gotta hear this," she said and unlocked the door.

They followed her inside.

"This attorney and her friend say they have a matter of life and death to discuss with you," the clerk said.

"You don't say," the second in charge said. "They'll have to wait until I'm finished with Mrs. Darby."

Andi rubbed her thumb against her fingers. Why weren't they taking this seriously?

Mrs. Darby finished and moved to the counter, where she took her time putting her money away. Andi wished the two clerks were as interested in hearing what they had to say as the dowdy matron. Andi took a better look. She hadn't seen a floral print dress like that since her grandmother was alive. Or thick hose and sensible black shoes. The woman was dressed for a different century.

"Now, what can I do for you?" the clerk said.

Andi brought her attention back to the clerk as Maggie stepped forward.

"We have a post office box for Jillian Bennett, but we need her physical address, Ms. . . ."— Maggie glanced at the nametag—"Bergman."

The two women exchanged glances. "If you're an attorney, you ought to know we can't give that information out," Ms. Bergman said.

Andi's heart sank. Bergman was going to take a hard line. But sometimes being a TV reporter helped. She fished a card from her bag. "I'm Andi Hollister—"

Mrs. Darby's fit of coughing cut Andi off. When she caught her breath, she said, "Hannah, if you'll unlock the door, I'll be on my way."

"Be right there, Mrs. Darby."

While Hannah was opening the door, Andi handed Ms. Bergman her card. "I'm with WLTZ in Memphis, and I'm working on a story that involves the woman in this photo," she said as Maggie took the photograph from her bag.

"She sent a Christmas card from this post office," Maggie said, "and her box number is 129. Have you seen her?"

Hannah returned to the counter, and the two clerks passed the photo between them, then exchanged looks. A chill filled the post office.

"I'm sorry, but we can't help you," the assistant postmistress said.

"Can't or won't?" Andi said. It was evident the two women knew Jillian.

"Excuse me?" Ms. Bergman looked over her glasses at them.

"You obviously recognize her."

"No, actually, we don't—at least I don't. Do you, Hannah?"

Hannah shook her head. "There's something familiar about her, but she's not one of our patrons."

Ms. Bergman said, "Even if we knew her, people around here value their privacy."

Andi balled her hands. They were so close, but the women seemed to be telling the truth.

The chill deepened as the assistant postmistress folded her arms. Maggie tugged on Andi's arm. "Come on. Maybe we'll have better luck somewhere else." She nodded to the women. "Sorry to have bothered you."

"Yeah, thanks." Andi blew out a breath. Everything seemed to be stacked against them. They stopped outside the door in the lobby.

"Where do we go now?" Maggie asked.

"Local hardware store." It was the first place Andi checked when she was looking for information in a small town. "We'll show the photo around. Unless there's a Walmart nearby, Jillian probably does business there."

They found a hardware store two blocks down, and when they showed the photo, the storekeeper stared at it, then took his cap off and smoothed his hair back. "Why are you looking for her?"

Andi shot a look at Maggie. They hadn't really thought about a cover story.

"I'm an attorney," Maggie said and fished a card from her purse. "I hope the woman in the photo can help me with a case."

"I see," he said and studied the photo again. "Not sure, but this *could* be Mrs. Darby. Can't remember her first name. She's been living here about five years, comes in occasionally for plumbing supplies for that old house of hers."

Mrs. Darby is Jillian? Andi looked down at the photo. It was way off. "Could you tell us how to get to her house?" Andi asked.

He looked them over, and she gave him her most appealing smile. "Guess it won't hurt. But let me write it down—easy to get lost on those roads."

Neither spoke until they were outside the store.

"We were that close," Andi said. "And now she knows we're looking for her."

"It may not be her. He just said it could be her," Maggie said. "But let's go find out."

They got in the car and started driving. After twenty minutes of twists and turns, Andi made yet another turn onto a road barely wide enough for two cars. Two turns later, they were on an even narrower sand road. She wondered what drivers did when they met someone, and then saw a turnout.

"It says here there should be posted signs along the road. Have you seen any?" Maggie asked.

"No. I've been too busy making sure we didn't go off in a ditch."

"I think we're lost."

Will's cheek throbbed as he drove away from the hospital. Dark thunderclouds formed to the west. Maybe he could outrun the thunderstorm. A text dinged on his phone, and he glanced at it while sitting at a stoplight.

Cass. His mother was the last person he wanted to deal with.

Be safe.

The fight went out of him. Hard-nosed Cass he could deal with, but not this softer Cass. He tapped on the details of the text and called her.

"Hello," she said. "I thought you'd forgotten."

"I told you I'd call when I got on the road." That didn't come out like he meant it to. "Sorry, didn't mean to sound so abrupt, but I got a late start."

"You don't have to explain. I'm just glad you called. You sound upset. Are you?"

"You could say that."

"Can't be me 'cause we haven't seen each other. Tell me who, and I'll take care of them," she said with a chuckle. "Or, some people like to spill their guts to strangers. I'm willing to listen."

He never knew when Cass was joking or serious, but this time what she said touched a chord. "I think I lost my best friends today." He couldn't believe he'd just blurted that out.

"Oh Will, I'm sorry. That stinks."

"Yeah." An image of Cass the last time he saw her popped into his mind's eye. She would never make the first move, never say she was sorry for not being there for him . . . except she had, kind of, when she came to see him yesterday. He couldn't believe it'd been less than twenty-four hours.

"I don't know what to say, except if they're really your friends, they'll be back. And if not, they weren't your friends to begin with."

She had a fit of coughing, and he waited for her to catch her breath.

"Thanks." He'd like to believe they'd get over

it, but if it took him looking the other way . . . he couldn't. Just like he couldn't look the other way if he discovered Jimmy actually killed Stephanie. Jimmy. Will had less than forty-eight hours to dig up evidence that he could take to a judge for a stay of execution.

If Laura Delaney had been onboard and presented the evidence they had to the appellate court and requested a stay, it would have been enough to get a stay. But if she was in on the smuggling, he understood why she was fighting him. If the appellate court didn't rule in favor of Jimmy, their last chance would be the governor.

"You still there?"

"I'm sorry, I was thinking about Jimmy."

"Mae's worried sick. Are you closer to getting a reprieve?"

"I hope so." *Didn't David say something about his brother knowing the governor?* Why didn't he already have him working on getting clemency? His heart ramped up. Maybe it was time to push that idea.

"Uh, can I call you back? I just thought of someone I need to call."

"Sure."

He winced at the disappointment in her voice. "How about once this is over, I take you out to eat?"

"Really?"

"Really. You can name the place."

"That would be nice, but you don't have to."

He hesitated. "But I want to."

After he hung up, he realized he really did want to take her out to eat. Something was different about her, and maybe they could have a second chance at a relationship. He pressed a button on his steering wheel and said, "Call David Raines."

For once the machine understood him, and David was soon on the phone. "What can I do for you?" he asked.

"Didn't you say your brother knows the governor?"

Silence met his question, and then David cleared his throat. "I did. I'd hoped that we'd get the evidence to take to a judge before now. I'll call my brother first thing in the morning."

"Thank you, sir."

"Anything new?"

"Yeah, but I'd rather brief you in person. I'm on my way to meet a TBI agent about the guard's pickup." Will checked his watch. He'd barely make it by one.

"How about as soon as you get back? I'm at the Hollister house, searching Stephanie's studio."

"I'll call you on the way back to Memphis."

— 31 —

An hour later, Will turned into the body shop parking area and drove behind the building. A white Ford SUV sat near the back doors, and a man in jeans and a sport shirt stood near the wrecker loaded with Larry Ray Johnson's pickup.

Will approached him. "I'm Will Kincade," he said and showed his badge. "That's quite a mess, isn't it?"

"Yep." He pointed to the badge on his belt loop. "Ross Carter, TBI agent. I'm waiting for someone with tools to cut the cab off."

"Did you look at the undercarriage?"

He nodded. "Saw where the tie rod end came out. That just doesn't happen often, not with a vehicle that's been kept up like this one."

Will's thoughts too. They both turned as a fire engine pulled around the corner of the building and two firemen hopped off, wielding cutting tools. Following the fire engine was a Tennessee patrol car, and Will scanned his memory for the patrolman's name. Lee. Richard Lee.

"Sorry I'm late." Lee carried a briefcase, and he nodded at both men. "But I stopped off at headquarters and picked up the envelope with Johnson's personal effects. Thought I'd take it to the family—he died an hour ago."

The news shook Will, and he balled his hands. Every lead seemed to be slipping away. Whoever caused this accident was ruthless, and Will wanted to nail him. "Any leads on the accident?" Will asked.

Lee took out his notebook. "There's a truck stop five miles west of where it happened. Showed the photo from his driver's license around the establishments, and one waitress remembered seeing him. Said he came in by himself, and then another man joined him. It wasn't long until Johnson left—skedaddled is the way she put it."

Yes! "Did you get a description of the other man?"

Lee nodded. "Big guy with a beard. He ordered a steak sandwich to go." He took a drawing from the briefcase. "I don't normally do this with wrecks, but this one really bothered me, so I had her describe the man to a sketch artist."

Carter looked over Will's shoulder at the sketch. "Mean-looking dude."

Indeed he was. Will examined the photo. The man's neck was much skinnier than his chest. *Does he have on a fat suit?* Will focused on the eyes. It was the one part of the body that was almost impossible to disguise. Color could be changed, but not how the eyes were set in a person's face or the arch of the eyebrows.

He'd seen those eyes before, but where? "Do you have a name for the waitress?"

"Josie Weatherford. She's at the Blue Cafe. It's in the Exxon Service Plaza."

"Got this door off," yelled one of the firemen.

Will turned just as the fireman working on the other door pulled it loose.

"I think we can get in there now," Carter said and then turned to Will. "You want to take the passenger side?"

"You bet." He appreciated the agent letting him examine the wreck. Will wasn't sure what he was looking for, but he pulled on a pair of latex gloves and started with the glove compartment. Nothing evidence-worthy there, then he pried the console open. A fat envelope lay in the bottom with the corner of a hundred-dollar bill showing.

"Looks like money here," Will said. *A payoff.* His fingers shook as he took the envelope out and counted the money. "There's twenty thousand dollars here."

He handed the envelope with the money in it to Carter. "Maybe we can get latent prints from it."

Carter put the money in a white bag. "Think it might have come from gambling?"

"The nearest casino is at Caruthersville, across the Mississippi, but wouldn't they pay that kind of money with a check, not cash?" Will asked. "I think it's payoff money. Johnson's wife said he told her one night after he'd been drinking that someone named JD was paying him a hundred dollars a month to watch one of the prisoners."

"Do you know which prisoner?" Carter asked.

"Jimmy Shelton. He's sitting on death row for killing Stephanie Hollister. I think Johnson stole a letter that possibly could have gotten Shelton a stay of execution." Will nodded at the white bag. "I think he traded the letter for that, and whoever he was dealing with tampered with the steering mechanism on his truck."

"But why?"

"Because Shelton didn't kill Hollister."

"Hey, look at what I found!"

Both men turned toward the highway patrolman who'd continued to search the truck. He held a cell phone.

"See if it works," Will said.

Lee powered the phone up. "Got a little juice. I'll check his calls."

Now if the number was still on there. Will and Carter crowded around the phone as the highway patrolman scrolled down the list. "There're only two calls that aren't identified, the same number, one incoming, the other outgoing."

He punched the top number and put it on speaker.

"I'm sorry, but the voicemail for the person you are calling hasn't been set up. Please try your call later."

"The number probably belongs to a burner phone," Carter said. "And it can't be traced, and there won't be a history of where the incoming call originated. Any idea of the identity of this person, other than the name JD?"

"No, he's like a phantom." Will stared at the drawing again. *Who are you?* "I believe he's killed three people now. Just can't prove it yet."

"What did you find?" Brad asked from the doorway.

David and Barbara looked up. David hadn't heard him drive up. "Your mom knew of a hiding place, and these papers were in it. They look like some sort of journal."

He took another look at Brad. "You look shell-shocked. Anything going on?"

Brad's jaw hardened, but he shook his head. "It's been a long morning. How's Dad?"

"Aggravated," Barbara said. "He wants to come home, but the doctors want him to stay. Every time he walks down the hall, his heart rate jumps to over 150. He'll have tests Monday."

"He needs to stay there," Brad said.

"I know, but you know your dad." She checked her watch. "I better get back to the hospital."

She stopped at the door. "Let me know what those papers are, okay?"

"Will do," David said.

As soon as Barbara was out of hearing range, David said, "What's going on? You look like you lost your best friend."

Brad grunted. "I think I have."

"I don't understand."

Brad folded his arms across his chest. "Will accused Stephanie of smuggling diamonds."

David glanced at the papers Stephanie had hidden and rocked back on his feet. "I'm afraid I may have bad news."

JD parked in front of the Doskie post office as two women walked out the door wearing postal uniforms. He'd hung back too far, and now the car tracker was showing an error message. It couldn't connect to the satellite. At least when he reviewed the data on his tablet, it showed the car had stopped at the post office. "Wish me luck," he said to his companion.

"Excuse me," he said, getting out of his car. His companion remained in the car. "I'm with the FBI, and I need to ask you some questions." He flipped open his wallet, showing a badge.

Their eyes widened, and the older of the two stepped forward. "I'm Karen Bergman, assistant postmaster. How can I help you?"

The badge did it every time. But which way to direct the conversation? Ask about Jillian or Hollister and Starr? Where he found Jillian, he would find the other two. "I'm looking for this woman." He handed her three age-enhanced photos of Jillian. One had aged her on the thin side and one with added weight. The third one had simply aged the photo.

Bergman nodded. "This looks kind of like the same woman those two women were looking for."

The tracker had been right. They had stopped at the post office. "Do you know where I can find her or them?"

"The photo they had looked like this one." She pointed to the version that had been aged without other enhancements. "And it didn't ring any bells, but this skinny person . . ." Bergman glanced at the other woman. "Wouldn't you say this is Mrs. Darby if her hair was cut short and dyed platinum?"

"Yep, could be her," Hannah said. "She lives in a cabin overlooking the river. I can give you directions."

He pulled a notepad from his pocket and handed it to her. Five minutes later, he was back in the car. "Directions to Jillian's house."

The directions looked easy enough, but when he came to a washed-out bridge, JD swore. He'd missed a turn somewhere. "See if you can get a fix on our position."

"There's still no signal. This tracker just says it's locating. Oh, wait. The map's coming up. Looks like they're on some sort of road parallel to where we are. River is about a half mile away."

"Good. We'll hike in and stay south of them."

"Do you think they've found Jillian?"

"I hope so."

"What do you plan to do with the women once we get what we want?"

"Not sure yet. The river is always an option." JD exited the car and opened the trunk, choosing two rifles from the four he had stashed there.

A fire wasn't a bad option, either.

— 32 —

Will nodded to Lee and Carter. "Let me know if you find anything pertaining to this case."

"Are you going on to Nashville?" Carter asked.

"Not with Johnson dead." The only reason he would drive to Nashville would be to see Jimmy, but he didn't have any news to share with him. His time would be better spent finding the person who set his cousin up.

"Thanks for the help," Carter said. "This is a murder investigation now, so any information you get, I'd appreciate it if you'd share it."

"You got it," Will said.

Back in his car, he checked his phone for messages, then debated calling Brad to see if he'd found anything in the studio. Not wanting to risk another confrontation, he chose David's number instead. When he didn't answer, Will left a message for him to call. If David didn't call back by the time Will reached Memphis, he'd reconsider calling Brad.

Once he was on I-40, Will looked for the exit with the Exxon Service Plaza. Ten minutes later, he exited off the interstate and parked in front of the Blue Cafe. Now if Josie was working, he'd be in business. His stomach growled as he walked to the counter. He hadn't eaten since breakfast at the Hollisters' and looked over the menu on the wall behind the counter. Steak sandwich looked pretty good. "Do I order here or take a seat?" he asked the waitress whose name was stitched over her uniform pocket. Ruth.

She looked him up and down. "I can take it. What will you have?"

"Steak sandwich with fries and coffee."

"That'll be eight-fifty."

Will pulled a ten-dollar bill from his wallet. "Is Josie here today?"

Ruth nodded to the corner. "She's taking her lunch break."

"Thanks." Will walked to the corner booth, where an older woman was polishing off a hamburger. "Josie?"

"Who's asking?"

"Will Kincade, Memphis Police Department." He showed his badge.

"You're a far piece from home. What can I help you with?"

"Sergeant Lee with the Tennessee Highway Patrol said you served the man involved in the wreck Wednesday night."

Josie nodded. "I told the patrolman all I could remember."

"How about the man he met here? The one you described to the sketch artist. Have you remembered anything else about him?"

She dipped a fry in ketchup and bit into it. "You want to sit? Kind of hurts my neck looking up at you."

"Thank you." Will sat opposite her in the booth and leaned forward. "A lot of people come in here. Why did you remember him?"

"His hands."

"What about his hands?"

"They didn't match his clothes. He was a big man and looked like most of the men who come in here. But when he paid me, I noticed his hands were soft, and it looked like he had clear polish on his nails. Hunters and farmers around here don't get manicures. Heck, most of them have grease embedded around the nails."

Ruth brought his sandwich, fries, and coffee and set them in front of him. "Cream?" she asked.

"No, thank you."

She kept standing by the booth. "Y'all talking about that guy that had the wreck? That state trooper said the tie rod came loose. My husband is a mechanic, and when I told him that, he said somebody tried to kill that fella. Is that true?"

Will took a sip of his coffee. "That's the way it looks."

Across the table from him, Josie nodded. "One of the men who was here when the trooper was asking questions said if a person knew what he was doing, a minute and a half is all it'd take to loosen the nut and pry the rod loose."

"Really?" Will hadn't realized it would be that easy. He looked up at Ruth. "Did you see either of the men?"

She nodded. "I was on the cash register when the guy that ended up in the hospital came up to pay. He was real nervous. Sweating when he left and muttering something about JD being crazy."

"He said JD? Are you sure?" That was the name Larry Ray's ex had given him.

"What it sounded like. Then he tore out of here like a bat out of Georgia. He gonna make it?"

Will sighed. "I'm afraid not. He died earlier today."

"Cryin' shame," Josie said. "Just a cryin' shame."

"I agree." He took two cards from his pocket and handed each one. "If either of you remember anything or if the other person comes in again, would you call me?"

Both of them agreed to do that, and Will said, "I'll move to another table so you can eat in peace."

"No need." Josie stood. "Time for me to go back to work."

Will dialed Walter Simmons's cell number, and when he answered, Will said, "How's Jimmy?"

"I don't know, but I can call you back after I see him. Got called in to work after one of the COs got sick."

"Great. Would you ask him if the name JD means anything to him?"

"I sure will. Uh, do you know how Larry Ray is?"

"I'm afraid he died earlier today."

"That's bad, man."

"Yeah." He thanked Walter, then washed up and ate his meal. Fifteen minutes later, he was on the road to Memphis and his cell phone rang. Brad's name came up on his dash. He answered, hoping Brad wouldn't ream him out again. "Hello?"

"You were right, and I owe you a big apology." Brad's voice was tight.

"What?"

"David is here with me, and you're on the speaker. He found pages that look like they were torn from Stephanie's journal. She documented trips where diamonds were smuggled into the country, and evidently she was in on it at least once."

"I'm sorry," Will said.

"Yeah, me too," Brad said. "It's going to kill Andi. But Stephanie was going to the FBI with the diamonds she had hidden in the horse sculpture."

"In her notes," David said, "she was really angry with somebody named JD and may have threatened him. Could be why she was killed."

A sour taste filled Will's mouth. "I just talked to a waitress who said Larry Ray Johnson met with someone named JD just before his wreck."

"Where are you?" David asked.

"Thirty miles east of Jackson. Why?" Will heard Brad say something to David, then Brad spoke into the phone again.

"According to Stephanie's notes, Jillian was involved in the smuggling operation."

Will's gut twisted. "Andi and Maggie are on their way to find Jillian."

"I know. I've tried to call them, and neither of them answer," Brad said. "That's why I called you. You're closer to them than we are."

Jimmy paced his small cell. Why hadn't he heard from Maggie or Will? He stopped at the small window and gripped the bars. Why couldn't he remember everything that happened the night Stephanie died instead of bits and pieces?

He turned as Walter Simmons came to his cell. "What are you doing here? You don't work this shift."

"Someone got sick." Walter unlocked his cell door. "Warden said you can work in the kitchen."

"Great." Anything beat sitting in his cell. He walked ahead of Walter. "Can you stay a few minutes? The chaplain hasn't been by this week, and you're about the next best thing."

"Warden said I could visit with you, and there's this Ping-Pong table on the way to the kitchen. Thought we might see how rusty you are."

Gratitude flushed through Jimmy. For the most part, the corrections officers in Unit 2 were decent men. His shoulders sagged as he realized why Walter was trying to lift his spirits. No one held out any hope he'd get a stay of execution.

For years Jimmy had wondered how he'd handle this. Somehow, he'd thought he'd never have to. Which was crazy. He blew out a deep breath, calming his nerves a little. If he could just quell the rolling in his stomach. "What's the weather like outside?"

"Cloudy. Supposed to rain later."

Seemed fitting it was an overcast day. The waiting was the hardest part. He turned to Walter. "How's your family?"

"Good. Praying for you."

"Thanks."

"You want to play a game of Ping-Pong?"

"Sure it won't get you in trouble?"

Walter's eyes were sad as he said, "Nah. Not this weekend."

Jimmy picked up the paddle and bounced the white plastic ball against the table. Good ole Walter. Trying to help him get his mind off his trouble.

"You can go first," Walter said.

Jimmy served the ball, and the guard returned

it. This time Jimmy sliced it and Walter missed.

"Yeah!" Jimmy grinned at him.

"I'll get you."

They batted the ball back and forth until it caught on the net. "My point," Jimmy said. "Have you heard anything on Johnson?"

Walter's face grew serious. "Your cousin Will called an hour ago and said that he died."

"That's sad," Jimmy said. "I didn't like him, but I hate he died. Do you know if he ever woke up?"

"Never did. Will asked me to run something by you." Walter whacked the ball across the net. "Do the initials JD mean anything to you?"

Jimmy's muscles turned to Jell-O, and he dropped his hands, letting the ball sail past him. "What did you say?"

"Are you okay?"

Chaos reigned in his head. He had to sit down, and he stumbled to the chair. *JD*. It'd been so long since he'd heard that nickname, he'd almost forgotten, and it triggered an avalanche of memories.

Jillian and Spencer. Him and Stephanie. Double dating. Then it all changed when Spencer made a play for Steph at a time she was angry with Jimmy and his drinking.

"Leave now, or I'll kill him and make it look like a murder-suicide." He sucked in air. It was the memory that had eluded him for years.

Stephanie cradled in his arms. Spencer putting the gun in his hand. Jillian arguing.

Jimmy looked up at Walter. "Do you know what this means?" Without waiting for an answer, he said, "I really didn't kill Steph."

Walter took out his phone and dialed. "I'm calling your cousin."

"Let me talk to him," Jimmy said, and Walter turned over the phone.

A call beeped in on Will's phone, and he looked at the ID. Walter Simmons.

"Hold on a second. I need to take a call." He switched calls. "Walter?"

"No, it's Jimmy. You wanted to know if I knew anyone who went by the name JD. Well, that made me remember something."

Jimmy paused, and Will heard him take a deep breath. "Go on."

"It's just . . . I can't believe they did this to me."

"Did what?"

"I remember everything now. Spencer telling Jillian if she didn't leave, he'd kill me and say it was a murder-suicide. And get this, Stephanie told me once that Spencer's full name is James Spencer Delaney Jr., and that some people called him JD. When he went to law school, he dropped the nickname, but he started using his middle name, Spencer, so he wouldn't be confused with his father. So JD could refer to him."

Will gripped the steering wheel. Nothing was ever simple. "This will help. Thanks, Jimmy."

"It's me who should be thanking you. And Will . . . if this doesn't turn out the way we want, don't feel bad. You've done all you can do."

"It's going to turn out, okay? Got that?"

"Yeah, cuz. I got it."

Will switched back to Brad. "JD could be Spencer. Have you heard from Andi?"

"No. And neither of them answer their phones. But I put an app on her cell phone, and it works off a satellite. Let me see if I can get her location."

"Do you know what town they were going to?"

"Doskie, Tennessee," Brad said. "I have her location. I'll text it to you."

Will pulled over to the side of the road and googled Doskie on his phone. He'd already passed the exit.

"What time were they supposed to get to this town?" he asked when Brad called him back.

"Should have gotten there around noon. I've sent you the address that pops up on this app. It looks like they might be somewhere beyond it, though."

"I'll find her. You find Spencer."

"Gotcha. And be safe."

Will tapped on the address Brad sent, and relief spread through him. He was only about twenty miles from their location.

— 33 —

A quarter of a mile past a narrow side road, the road turned from gravel to dirt, and the trees seemed to close in on them. Andi eased the Corolla over ruts and potholes. "Do the instructions say anything about a dirt road?"

"No. Maybe we should have turned on that side road."

"That's what I was thinking," Maggie said.

"We should have asked how far the house is." Andi glanced down the steep hillside. "These are not hills, either."

"I'd call them mountains myself," Maggie said. "Do you think Mrs. Darby is really Jillian?"

"I don't know, but she did get nervous when I mentioned my name. And did you notice how thin her hands were? They didn't match her body at all."

"Come to think of it, her face was thin too. Can you think of a better place than this if someone wanted to hide out?"

They drove in silence, going deeper into the forest.

Maggie leaned forward and peered through the windshield. "I think we're lost. Find a place to turn around," she said. "We need to go back and get better directions."

Andi scanned the woods. The trees were so thick, it was impossible for sunlight to break through. Her scalp prickled. What if someone had followed them up the mountain? "There's a fork ahead. I'll turn around there." She glanced toward Maggie. "Do you happen to have a gun on you?"

"Don't carry one, but for once, I wish I did."

She put the car in park. "I need to get out and see how to turn around, but first . . ." She opened the console and searched for the Swiss Army knife she kept there. Once she found it, she slipped it in her right boot.

"Think we'll need that?" Maggie asked as they climbed out.

"I'd rather be prepared than not."

Maggie held her phone up in the air. "And maybe I can get a signal outside of the car. I'd like to call David and let him know where we are."

They both walked to the front of the car. A few yards away, a piece of brush blocked their path. As Andi bent over to move it, something whizzed over her head, then she heard the crack of a rifle.

"Get down, Maggie!" Andi dropped to the ground and crawled to where Maggie was hunkered beside the wheel.

"Who's shooting?" she whispered.

"I don't know." Blood pounded in Andi's head. If she hadn't bent to pick up the brush, she'd be dead. They crawled to the side of the car. It wouldn't offer much protection. "I don't have a good feeling about it. Any chance it might have been a hunter?"

"In April?" Maggie's voice was shaky.

For the first time in her life, Andi was really scared. They were trapped on a mountain with someone firing at them. Brush snapped. "We need to make a run for it in the car. Can you get in the backseat?"

"Yeah! Let's go for it."

Maggie scrambled to open the back passenger door as Andi hopped in the driver's seat and started the car. She threw the car in reverse as a bullet shattered the side window.

The car shot backward and rammed a tree. She yanked it into drive. The wheels spun, burying the back tires in the soft dirt. They were stuck.

"Just get out with your hands where I can see them!"

"What do you want?" Andi yelled. Tremors gripped her stomach. "We're not trespassing."

In her peripheral vision, she saw a man dressed in camos and a ski mask lumbering toward them.

"Let's run for it!" Andi jerked her door open. "You go one way, and I'll go the other. He can't chase us both."

She jumped from the car, and Maggie followed her. The man raised his gun, and Andi ducked behind a huge oak. The bullet thudded into the tree.

"Give up," he yelled. "You can't get away."

She searched for Maggie. She'd dropped to the ground and had almost made it to a thick growth of underbrush. She might have a chance to get away if Andi went in a different direction.

She darted to another tree. The rifle cracked again.

"You want to die in these woods?"

"What do you want?" she yelled.

"Information."

"You have a funny way of asking for it." She ran toward another tree and felt the sting in her leg before she heard the gunshot. She stumbled and pitched toward the tree, crashing into it headfirst.

No! She fought the blackness, but it did no good.

When she came to, she blinked, unable to process two men in camouflage with guns. One of them held Maggie prisoner and threw her down beside Andi.

"Told you not to run."

"You've shot her!" Maggie's tone was indignant as she knelt beside Andi. "Her leg is bleeding."

"It's only a flesh wound," one of the men said. "She'll live."

If Andi weren't in so much pain, she'd kick him with her good leg.

"For now," the other one said. "Let's go."

"I think my leg is broken," Andi said. It

certainly hurt bad enough. The last man's voice was familiar, but she couldn't place it. If only they'd take off the ski masks.

One of the men prodded Maggie. "Get her on her feet."

"Who are you and what do you want?" Maggie asked as she probed Andi's leg.

Andi bit her lip to keep from crying out when Maggie's fingers touched the back of her leg.

"Good. It went all the way through and doesn't seem to have hit an artery." Maggie gave her a reassuring pat on the shoulder.

"Just shut up and get her up."

"She shouldn't walk on it."

"Well, la-di-da, too bad. We can't stay here, and our car is over the ridge."

"Why don't we take our car?" Andi said. She honestly didn't think she could walk twenty steps much less back to civilization.

"I think I can get it out," the taller of the two men said. He handed the rifle to the other man.

She sneaked a better look at him. Tall. Couldn't tell if he was muscular under the camos, but he had piercing black eyes.

The other guy was a little shorter and broad shouldered. "Well, hurry up," he said. "I want to get done with this and get out of here before dark."

The taller man got into the car and rocked it back and forth until it finally pulled forward.

He rolled down the window. "There's a clearing ahead by the river. I'll turn around there."

While they waited, their captor took out a roll of tape. "Secure her hands," he said and reached toward Maggie to hand her the tape.

In a lightning move, Maggie grabbed his shirtsleeve and collar and yanked him forward. Before he could react, she turned and squatted, throwing him over her hip onto the ground. He hit with a thud, and air whooshed out of his lungs.

Andi scrambled for the rifle that he'd dropped. "Good job. Remind me to sign up for one of your classes," she said. "But you better take this. My leg is killing me, and I might shoot him."

"Hold it on him until I tape his wrists." When Maggie finished, she pulled his ski mask off.

Andi had never seen the man before. "Who are you? And why were you shooting at us?"

He glared at them.

"Okay, ladies, you've had your fun. Drop the rifle."

Andi whirled around. Mrs. Darby, minus the white hair and lumpy body, held a gun to Maggie's head. "I said drop it."

Andi hesitated. Surely Jillian wouldn't shoot Maggie.

"Do what I said. It's your fault they're here," Jillian said through gritted teeth. "I don't have anything to lose. Drop. It."

"I have Laura's cell phone number," David said when Brad ended the call to Will.

"Maybe she can tell us where her husband is."

David dialed the number, but it went to her voicemail. "Let me try her home." He quickly dialed it.

"Delaney residence."

"This is Lieutenant David Raines. Is Mrs. Delaney in?"

"No, she isn't."

"Can you tell me where she is?"

"I . . . I'm sorry, but I can't."

He tamped down his impatience. She'd hesitated, so she knew where Laura was. "This is a police matter. Someone may die if I don't talk with Mrs. Delaney. Now, where is she?"

"At her office."

"Thank you." David hung up and speed dialed the DA's office. It went to voicemail. "She's not answering," he said. "We'll have to drive downtown."

Before they reached the studio door, it opened.

"I just remembered this," Barbara said. She held a small mailing envelope.

"Mom, we don't have time," Brad said.

"But, it's from Jillian. She left it with me right after Andi's operation. Asked me to keep it for her. I forgot all about it until just now."

David took the envelope and withdrew a small box. Inside were five rough stones.

Barbara gasped. "Why would she leave those with me?"

"I don't know, but I'll certainly ask if I find her," Brad said.

David put the diamonds back in the envelope. Maggie and Andi had no idea Jillian was dangerous. Maybe if they found her, she wouldn't harm them. "Thanks, Mrs. Hollister."

They hurried out the door to David's car. Twenty minutes later, they got off the elevator on the third floor. The DA's office was open, and Laura's secretary was at the desk, working at her computer. Jace looked up when they came through the door.

"I'm sorry, but we're not officially here, Lieutenant Raines."

"I have to see the district attorney."

"She's not seeing or talking to anyone. We're getting ready for a big case Monday morning."

David planted his hands on her desk. "I want to see Laura Delaney now. Press the buzzer so I can go through. I'll take full responsibility."

The secretary hesitated. "Let me notify her."

"Tell her it's about her husband's involvement in smuggled diamonds."

Jace's eyes widened, and she picked up the phone on her desk and spoke into it. "You can go back."

"Thank you," David snapped.

Laura met them at the door. "What is this preposterous—"

David brushed past her, and Brad followed. "Where's your husband?"

"What?"

"Your husband," David repeated. "Where is he?"

"I . . . I'm not sure. What's this all about?"

"Were you part of the smuggling ring?"

She took a step back. "What *are* you talking about?"

Either Laura could lie really well, or she didn't have a clue what he was talking about. Either way, they were wasting time. "Let's sit down, and I'll explain."

She walked behind the desk to her chair and sat while he and Brad took the two wing chairs. David laid the handwritten sheets on her desk. "These are notes that Stephanie Hollister wrote eighteen years ago. It's a log of smuggling activities."

She scanned the pages, stopping at the last one to read the note. "I don't know what to say."

"Are you L?"

"Of course not. I had no idea about any of this. The L has to stand for Lacey." She leaned back in the chair. "I always wondered how she afforded her lifestyle without a job after she quit flying."

"Do you know who JD could be?" Brad asked.

Hesitation showed in Laura's eyes as she chewed her thumbnail. Then she dropped her hand and took a deep breath. "JD could be Jared Donovan." She shifted her gaze to the window. "And JD is what Spencer's family still calls him," she said, turning back to them.

"Do you know where your husband is?" Brad asked.

"I told you, I don't know exactly. He was meeting Adam."

"Adam Matthews?"

"Yeah. They've been friends since Spencer was a flight attendant and Adam was a copilot. But you're looking in the wrong place for your solution. JD could easily be Jared and not Spencer."

David picked up the journal papers. "Do you know who this AJ is? Once the diamonds were smuggled into the States, it looks like that's who they were delivered to."

Her shoulders slumped. "AJ. Adam Jerome Matthews."

Brad leaned forward. "Do you have a way of tracking your husband? An app, maybe?"

"No. I suggested it once, but Spencer said we didn't need it."

David stood. "We're wasting time here. We need to get to Doskie."

As they hurried to their car, Brad said, "How long will it take to get there?"

"I checked earlier. About two hours. But I have a friend who flies helicopters. He owes me a favor, and if he's free, he'll fly us there in thirty minutes."

— 34 —

The GPS took Will around the town square to a building on the south side. Will stared at the brick US Postal building as he dialed Brad. "Do you have an updated address? The one you gave me is the post office in Doskie."

"That's where they were going for information. We're in a helicopter and will be there in about a half hour."

"I'm going on to see if I can find an address for Jillian. I'll call you, and maybe you can land near wherever they are."

The 911 office. It should have directions to . . . His shoulders slumped. To where? He didn't even know if Jillian lived in this area, and if she did, what name she used. Not her own, for sure.

If she lived around here, who might know her? Probably not the police, since she would avoid them. But she would have to come to town for food and maybe medicine. Will grabbed the photo of Jillian and got out of his car. He scanned the buildings, and an apothecary sign caught his eye.

"Good afternoon," he said to the girl behind the

counter. He showed her his badge. "I'm with the Memphis Police Department, and I'm looking for this woman." He handed her the photo. "I thought she might shop here."

The teenager stared at the photo and shook her head. "My dad's the pharmacist. Maybe he knows her." She turned. "Dad!"

A balding, fortysomething man in a white coat came from the back. "Can I help you?"

"He's with the Memphis police." She handed him the photo. "And he's looking for this woman."

The pharmacist studied the paper. "Do you have some identification?"

Will showed him his badge. "Sergeant Will Kincade, sir."

"You don't mind if I write your badge number down, do you?"

"No, sir." Will tapped his fingers against his leg, wanting to hurry the man. "Do you recognize her?"

"I think so," he said slowly. "It looks a tiny bit like Mrs. Darby, except her hair is white and she's portly."

"Can you tell me how to get to her place?"

"That I can't do. All I have on record is a PO box. Not that I've ever used it. She pays cash every month. You might inquire at the 911 office since everyone has to register their address with the power company in order to get hooked up to electricity."

"Thanks, I'll do that. Where is it?"

"Inside the courthouse, bottom floor. You can't miss it. It'll be the only office open."

Will thanked him again and hurried out the door. The courthouse sat in the middle of the square and was a short walk away. The pharmacist was right. It was the only office open, and Will pushed open the door. After explaining who he was and that he wanted directions to a Mrs. Darby's house, he was given a detailed map.

"It's easy to get lost up there," the 911 clerk said. "So many little side roads. If you get to the river, you've gone too far."

"Can you give me coordinates on her cabin? My friends are in a helicopter."

"You can't land a helicopter there—upper air level is too high, and the trees are too close to the road and too much overhang. Had a kid get lost a couple of years ago and somebody tried to land one. Almost crashed it."

Will thanked him and jogged back to his car. There, he took another look at the map. No wonder the GPS wasn't working. His cell phone rang, and he answered it.

"Where are you?" Brad said.

"Parked in front of the post office. Where are you?" He scanned the square and spied the helicopter swinging in from the west. "Never mind, I see you."

He climbed back out of his car and waited while Brad and David landed on the square.

"What are you doing here?" Brad asked when Will reached him.

"The GPS isn't working, and I backtracked to town. Can you get a location on Andi?"

Brad clicked on the app and waited. "I don't understand. It's not giving me her location."

"We'll have to depend on this map, and use my car—no place to land a chopper."

As they sped away from town, Will asked, "What did you find out from Laura?"

"We tried to call you but only got your voice-mail," David said. His cell phone rang, and he answered it. "What?" After listening for a minute, he said, "Thanks for letting me know."

He hung up and turned to Will and Brad. "The car Spencer is driving is new, and Laura remembered it came with OnStar. She contacted the company and they located the car near Doskie. So Spencer and Adam Matthews are somewhere in the vicinity."

Andi pressed against the bandage on her leg. What she wouldn't give for a Lortab right now, but it was in her purse in the car. Jillian had instructed Maggie on how to bind the wound, but that didn't help the pain.

With the .38 tucked in her waistband, Jillian prodded their would-be captor with his own rifle. "Hug the pine tree," she said. "And you, tie his hands."

Maggie took the rope she tossed her.

"Make sure he can't get loose," Jillian said.

She checked the rope once Maggie finished. "Okay, you two, let's go."

"You can't leave me here!" he yelled.

"Maybe I'll send the game warden to get you."

"What happened to the other man?" Andi said. Jillian hadn't shot him because there'd been no gunfire.

She turned and shrugged. "He won't bother anyone—he's a tree hugger too."

"Who is he?"

"Enough with the questions. Get moving."

"No!" Andi dug in her heels. "I want to know who tried to kill me."

Jillian pinched her lips together. "I see you haven't changed. Spencer Delaney. Satisfied now? And I guarantee you, if he'd been trying to kill you, you'd be dead."

Spencer? "Why?"

"See, that's why I didn't want to tell you in the first place—brings on more questions. Now, move."

Maggie helped her to stand, and with the aid of a crutch Jillian had fashioned out of a branch, she limped down the dirt road.

No one spoke as they trekked toward the cabin, other than Andi's involuntary groans when pain stabbed her leg. Treece's boots were too big and rubbed up and down on her heel. The only comfort came from the Swiss knife pressed against her ankle.

The sun disappeared in a bank of clouds, and quarter-sized drops of rain splattered her face. She hadn't thought she could walk back to the cabin, but a gun to her back made the impossible possible. Once they reached gravel, walking became easier. Andi knew the cabin couldn't be much farther. But what was Jillian going to do with them when they reached it?

Maggie broke the silence. "How did you know they were after us?"

"Saw them when they passed the cabin. I should have kept right on packing."

"What stopped you?" Andi asked.

"Knowing they'd kill you. Couldn't live with that."

The cabin came into sight, and in front of it, a pickup. Jillian's, Andi guessed. The doors were open and boxes were stacked in the seat and the bed of the truck. Jillian motioned with the gun. "In the house."

"Look, can we talk?" Maggie said. "We're trying to stop Jimmy's execution. You have evidence that will clear him or you wouldn't have gone to see him. Tell us what you know. I know you don't want his blood on your hands."

The corner of Jillian's mouth twitched, then she squared her shoulders and lifted her chin. "I'm sorry, but I can't help Jimmy. And I don't want to answer your questions." She waved the rifle again. "Inside."

"Please tell us who killed Stephanie," Andi pleaded, but looking into Jillian's unyielding gray eyes was like looking at death. A band tightened around her chest, constricting her breath. This was not a game. And Jillian was not harmless. And she wasn't going to help.

When Jillian prodded her with the gun again, Andi hobbled up the three steps and through the door and collapsed on the sofa.

"Don't get too comfortable. You have to help Maggie load the truck." Jillian propped the rifle she'd taken from the men against the wall and picked up a double-barreled shotgun.

Andi looked up at her. "What happened to you? You used to be a nice person."

"That was a long time ago, and that person no longer exists. How did you know I was in Doskie, anyway?"

"I believe she does exist. We found you through the Christmas card you mailed Mom last year," Andi said, reaching in her jacket pocket.

"Keep your hands where I can see them," Jillian said.

She stilled her hands. "I was just going to show you."

"I'll get it. And there's no way that my address was on the envelope—I *never* put my return address on anything." She pulled the envelope from Andi's pocket and glanced at it. "That is not my handwriting."

Then she groaned. "I can't believe it. Five years I've been able to live in peace up here, and Helpful Hannah trips me up. She must have added my address after I gave it to her to mail."

"Why have you been hiding out?" Maggie asked.

"Reasons you wouldn't understand. Now, because of you two, I have to find another place. And you're going to finish loading the truck. Grab those." She pointed to six boxes by the door.

"What are you going to do with us?"

"Haven't decided. Now, move."

"I can't carry anything," Andi said.

Jillian stared at the homemade crutch, then sighed. "I can't leave you in here unrestrained." She pulled a rope from her pocket and tossed it to Maggie. "Tie her hands to the wooden arm of the sofa."

Once Jillian checked Maggie's knots, she motioned her toward the boxes. Maggie grabbed two and walked out the door. As soon as they were out of sight, Andi wiggled the rope and tried to slide it off the sofa arm and onto the brace so it would be low enough for her to reach the knife in her boot. It was so close, but she'd never get it this way. She had to get the boot off to get the knife in her hands.

Footsteps hit the porch, and she straightened up.

"Take three this time," Jillian said to Maggie.

Maggie's eyes glanced toward her then darted away. She picked up three boxes.

Buy some time, Maggie. Andi wished telepathy worked. Once they were on the porch, she used her left foot to get the boot almost off, then brought her right foot across her knee. Pain ripped her thigh, and Andi bit her lip to keep from crying out. She jerked her foot back down. She couldn't do it. *God, help me!*

From outside, Jillian yelled, "How can you be so clumsy! Now pick up the boxes and the stuff that fell out. And be quick about it."

The words were music to her ears. Bracing herself for the pain, Andi forced her foot back on her knee. Nausea washed over her. Her head swam. Gritting her teeth, she closed her eyes and inched her foot closer.

Just a little more and her fingers could grab the boot. *Got it.* She blew out a breath, then slid it off, careful not to dump the knife on the floor. Once she had the knife, she opened the largest blade. *Hurry.* Maggie couldn't delay forever.

As soon as her hands were free, she hobbled to the side of the door and waited. Footsteps crossed the porch again. Andi lifted the home-made crutch over her head. Maggie came through the doorway first, then Jillian.

"What!"

Andi brought the crutch down and across

Jillian's shoulder. The shotgun clattered to the floor, and Jillian pitched forward, grabbing for Maggie as she fell.

Maggie flipped her on her back and yanked the .38 from her waistband. "Good job," she said to Andi.

Andi beamed at her. "I think we should tie her up. Then maybe we can get a few answers."

Maggie shook her head. "Tie her up? Yeah. But I think we need to get your wound seen about first. We can question her on the drive down the mountain."

"There's that too," Andi said. "But some of those boxes will have to be moved out of the truck."

The clouds had moved on, and the sun almost blinded her when they stepped out on the porch. Jillian led the way with her hands tied in front of her, and Maggie carried the rifle. She'd hobbled Jillian's feet so that she couldn't easily run.

Andi brought up the rear with Jillian's shotgun. The pain had eased enough that she left the makeshift crutch behind. She hadn't been able to handle both, and the shotgun gave her more security.

Maggie hurried ahead to the truck and started unloading boxes. Andi and Jillian had almost reached the pickup when a crack echoed from the tree line. Jillian screamed and crumpled to the ground.

"Run for the cabin, Maggie!" Andi hit the dirt as another bullet whizzed by. She crawled to where Jillian lay, blood staining the side of her flannel shirt. Her eyes fluttered open.

"Should've killed them up on the ridge," she muttered. "They'll kill us all."

"Not if you have more guns in the cabin," Andi said. When another bullet hit the pickup, she raised up and pulled one of the triggers on the double-barrel. The recoil knocked her backward. Rubbing her shoulder, she said, "That ought to keep them at bay, maybe long enough to get inside."

Maggie crawled to where they were.

"I told you to run," Andi said to her.

She unbuttoned Jillian's shirt. "And leave you? We're in this together," she said. "Doesn't look like the bullet hit an organ. Just need to get the bleeding stopped."

"Do you think if we get her to the front of the pickup, you can crawl around to the back of the house with her? We'd be sitting ducks to try the front door."

"I think so."

Andi nudged Jillian, and her eyes opened again. "Do you have any more shells?"

"In the right front pocket."

Andi unsnapped the pocket and found four shells, then nodded to Maggie. "I'll cover you while you pull Jillian to the house."

Maggie looked down at Jillian. "Can you help?"

She pressed her lips together. "I'll try."

Andi peered around the bed of the truck that partially hid them. Nothing moved. "Go," she whispered.

As Maggie and Jillian inched toward the house, a flash glinted from the woods. Andi fired in the direction she'd seen the flash. This time she was better prepared for the recoil.

Still watching, she crept backward to the front of the truck.

"We made it," Maggie said, her voice low.

Andi glanced to see where they were, then back at the woods. A man in camos crept out of the tree line. She put the shotgun to her shoulder and fired, even though he was beyond the range of the shotgun. He dropped to the ground, and she dashed to the corner of the house.

"Let's get her inside." Holding on to the gun, Andi helped drag Jillian to the back door and into the cabin.

"Where's your phone?" Maggie asked.

"Doesn't work. Limb fell and broke the line two weeks ago, and no one's come to fix it." She shifted, groaning. "There's a .22 rifle under the sofa. And a deer rifle in my bedroom closet."

"That ought to be enough to hold them off until help arrives," Maggie said.

"What help?" Andi said. "Nobody knows where we are."

— 35 —

The minute hand moved slowly as Andi watched the clock over the mantel, her thigh throbbing with each movement of the second hand. It'd been at least fifteen minutes since there'd been any activity from the men. Jillian had recovered somewhat, and under her instructions, Maggie had applied a pressure bandage to her shoulder, and the bleeding had stopped. She'd insisted they prop her against the wall that faced the kitchen. And they'd given her the .38. They each had rifles.

Andi peeked out the window that faced south and scanned the woods, then moved to the one that faced west. Maggie stood sentry at the east window. The blind spot was the north side facing the river. Even if the men realized there was a blind spot, it would be difficult for them to work their way around to the back side of the cabin without being seen. "Do you think anyone has even tried to call us?"

"You know they have," Maggie replied. "I'm sure they're looking for us now. Once they get to Doskie, someone will recognize the photo of Jillian and tell them how to get here."

"I hate to tell you," Jillian said, "but even with directions, they'll probably get lost. It's up to us, ladies." They'd wrapped a blanket around her, and she pulled it tighter. "Why in blue blazes were you so determined to find me?"

"We told you. We're trying to help Jimmy," Andi said, "and I wanted to know what happened the night Stephanie died."

"Why didn't you ask Lacey? Jimmy said she wrote him a letter saying he didn't kill Steph. With what she knew, that should've been enough to get him out of prison, and satisfy you."

She didn't know about Lacey. Andi shifted so she could see her. "Lacey is dead. Murdered."

Jillian gasped. "What?"

"Didn't Jimmy tell you?"

She shook her head. "He killed her," she said softly.

"Who killed her? Jimmy?" Maggie said.

"No." Jillian closed her eyes, and Andi thought she'd passed out. She knelt beside her, feeling her wrist for a pulse.

"I'm still here," Jillian said. She opened her eyes. Andi had never seen such sadness before.

Jillian took a deep breath and released it. "What do you want to know?"

The words dropped like a bomb into the still room.

"Were you there?" Maggie asked.

"I'm afraid so." She shifted on the floor and groaned. "You know, I might not get out of here alive."

"You are not dying here," Andi said. Not when she was so close to knowing the truth. "What happened that night?"

"Are you sure you want to know?" Jillian pinned her gaze on Andi. "Stephanie wasn't perfect."

All Andi's life, Stephanie had been her hero. Maybe she didn't want to hear what Jillian had to say.

"Tell us," Maggie said. "Did Jimmy kill Stephanie?"

"No." Jillian breathed deeply through her nose, and her body shuddered when she exhaled. "JD had called and told me to find out where Stephanie had the diamonds he had slipped in her purse in Paris. When I went to the studio, she refused to hand them over. Claimed she didn't know what I was talking about and she was done with smuggling diamonds into the States."

"No!" Andi planted her feet. "She was not smuggling diamonds!"

"I warned you that you wouldn't like it." Pity filled Jillian eyes. "I went to her studio . . ."

Jillian jerked open the studio door and stormed into the room. Lacey followed on her heels.

"Where are they, Steph?" Jillian balled her hands. If Stephanie didn't give the diamonds back, she didn't know what would happen.

"Would you hold it down?" Stephanie sat on a high stool at her worktable. She bent the leg of

the horse she was working on, then picked up a piece of clay and smoothed it over the wire armature. "Jimmy is dog-drunk and finally went to sleep. You'll have to deal with him if he wakes up."

"Where are they?" Jillian repeated, not quite as loud.

"Where are what?"

"I told you she wouldn't cooperate," Lacey said. "What you're doing is stealing."

"Oh, give me a break," Stephanie said. "Like smuggling isn't. 'Come on, Stephanie, it's easy money. All you have to do is bring a few dirty-looking rocks home,' " she said in a falsetto voice. "That's what you and JD told me, but after that one time, I said no, I'm not doing it again. And then he sneaks those three in my purse." Her gaze hardened. "What is this, anyway? A board meeting? Where're the others? Or did they send you to do their dirty work?"

"I don't know about anyone else—I'm just trying to make you see reason. If you keep those diamonds, we'll all suffer. Give them back to him," Jillian said.

"You mean JD and Adam aren't coming?"

"Leave Adam out of it," Lacey said. She grabbed Stephanie's arm. "You can't just steal those diamonds. They'll kill you, and us too, if you don't turn them over."

"No, they won't." Stephanie shook Lacey's

430

hand away. "Tomorrow morning I'm turning them over to the FBI. Would've today, but the person I need to see was out of town, and if anything happens to me, I've written everything down in my journal, naming names. I've documented everything."

"Where is it?"

"You think I'm stupid?"

When Stephanie cut her eyes toward Lacey, Jillian realized Lacey knew where the journal was. "You didn't name us, did you?"

Stephanie shrugged. "I did, along with dates and how many stones we brought in the time I was involved."

Jillian stepped closer. "Where is this journal?"

"In a safe place. Just like the diamonds." She set the sculpture on a shelf and covered it in plastic. "JD should have left me out of this."

Lacey plopped down on the sofa next to Jimmy and buried her face in her hands.

"Not now, Lacey." Jillian paced the room. She stopped and fisted her hand on her waist. "Where did you hide them?"

"Like I would tell you. They're in a place where you'll never find them."

Jillian closed her eyes and counted to ten, then tried one more time. "Look, if JD promises to never involve you again, will you just hand those over and forget they ever existed?"

The side door opened, and JD burst into the

room. Jillian groaned. He would only make things worse.

"My, my," Stephanie said, "the gang's all here, almost. When does Adam arrive?"

"He's coming. Has she told you where the diamonds are?" he asked Jillian.

She shook her head. "She says she's going to the FBI."

JD took a threatening step toward her.

"Don't come any closer." Stephanie pulled a .38 from her pocket.

Jillian screamed.

"What's going on?" Jimmy said as he raised up with a whiskey bottle gripped in his hand. "Hey! Leave Steph alone."

JD halted. "Give me the diamonds, or I'll take the gun away and use it on you."

"I don't think you can." Stephanie waved the gun.

"Be reasonable," JD said. "Hand over those diamonds I put in your purse, and we can all walk away from this."

"How many times do I have to say this? They are going to stay where they are until I need them."

"Come on, Steph, put the gun down," Jillian said.

Stephanie didn't take her eyes off JD. "No. Not until you all leave."

With Stephanie's attention on JD, Jillian edged closer. She had to get the gun or something terrible would happen.

JD took another step closer to Stephanie, and she raised the gun level with his chest. "Stop right there."

"Come on, honey. You're not going to shoot me. Not after all we've meant to each other."

The gun didn't waver. Stephanie jutted her chin. "You're wrong about that, just like I was wrong about you. You never loved me. You used me, just like you did Jillian. I just hate it took me two months to figure it out."

"I don't know what you're talking about. Come on, give me the gun and then tell me where the diamonds are."

Jillian froze. Six months ago, she thought JD was going to propose. Instead, he broke up with her, saying he only wanted to be friends. She'd clung to the belief he would change his mind. Bits and pieces clicked into place. Stephanie avoiding her until Jared Donovan entered the picture.

Stephanie turned to her. "I'm sorry. I never meant to hurt you, but you're better off without him."

Anger shot through Jillian like a white-hot bullet. "You're the one who stole JD?"

She rushed Stephanie, tackling her and knocking her off the stool.

"Stop!" Stephanie kicked and struggled with her. "He's not worth it."

Jillian wrapped her hand around the gun, and a roar blasted her ears.

Stephanie slumped against her, and the gun clattered to the floor. Jillian pushed her off and climbed to her feet, her chest heaving.

"Steph!" Jimmy staggered to his feet and shoved her aside. "Stephanie," he keened and knelt beside her.

"Why did you shoot her?" JD yelled.

"I didn't. The gun went off." Jillian turned to Lacey. "You saw what happened. She was going to shoot him."

Lacey grabbed Jillian's arm. "It doesn't matter what happened. We have to get out of here!"

"No, we have to call 911," Jillian said.

"Are you crazy? Do you want to go to jail?" JD shook her. "Nothing will bring Stephanie back, and there'll be questions. They'll find out about the diamonds. Go!"

Her mind whirled, thoughts firing faster than she could process. He was right, they had to get out of there.

Jimmy looked up, his glazed eyes staring straight at her. Blood stained his shirt. "Why . . . ?"

"It was an accident, I'm sorry." Jillian's legs trembled and threatened to buckle. She couldn't breathe.

"Steph," Jimmy sobbed. He cradled Stephanie in his arms.

"We have to get out of here." Lacey pulled on Jillian's arm again.

"You two go ahead," JD said and picked up

the Jack Daniel's bottle Jimmy had dropped. "I'll see to him."

Jillian followed Lacey to the door and stopped. She looked back as JD used one of Stephanie's hammers to crush a long blue tablet and pour the powder in Jimmy's glass of whiskey.

"You need something to calm down," he said, holding the alcohol out to him. "Drink this."

She couldn't do it. She couldn't leave Jimmy to take the blame. That's what JD was doing—setting him up. "No," she said. "We can't—"

"Shut up! And get out of here!" Then he turned back to Jimmy. "Come on, drink this and all your problems will go away."

Jimmy swayed, his eyes on JD. "You're my friend, aren't you?"

"Of course I am."

Then, like an obedient child, Jimmy gulped the liquid down, and JD wiped the blood from his right hand with a handkerchief, then used the handkerchief to pick up the gun and place it in Jimmy's hand. "Just hold on to it," he said softly. "I'm going to get help."

Jimmy stared at him. "Yeah," he said, slurring the word. "Get help."

Jillian grabbed JD's arm. "You can't do this."

He looked up at her with eyes as cold as steel. "Leave now, or I'll kill him and make it look like a murder-suicide."

Jillian turned to Andi. "I knew JD would do

it. I'm so sorry. I never meant to hurt Stephanie."

"What happened to Stephanie's journal?" Andi asked.

Jillian sighed. "Lacey found it first. Since she's dead, I assume JD stole it and then killed her."

"Who was this JD?" Andi asked.

"Spencer Delaney."

"You fool. I told you to hold your fire until they were in the truck." Spencer prodded Adam's chest with the rifle. "If you killed Jillian or Andi, you'll pay."

"Are you crazy? Don't point that thing at me. It could go off." Adam shoved the rifle away. "I thought that was the whole purpose of being here—to silence these three."

"You *thought*. That's your problem. Andi knows where those three uncut diamonds are. They're worth over a hundred grand. And Jillian has a handful of others. If they're dead, how do you propose we find those diamonds?" Spencer turned toward the cabin. He wasn't losing them, and once he no longer needed Matthews, he was history, as well. Just like with Jimmy, Adam Matthews would make a good scapegoat.

Spencer surveyed the cabin and surrounding yard. "Do you think you can give me cover while I work my way around to the back of the cabin? Then, when I get inside, I'll call you to come."

"You think you can get in from the back?"

The look he gave Matthews made him squirm. "No, I'm risking my life for the fun of it. If you'd been paying attention when we hiked our way here, you would've seen the north side doesn't have windows."

He pointed to a dead tree at the edge of the woods. "When I get there, I need you to divert their attention while I cross the clearing. Think you can do that without shooting me?"

"Don't give me ideas," Matthews muttered. "I'll take care of it."

Using the brush for cover, Spencer crept toward the dead tree. When he reached it, he looked back to see if his partner was watching. He nodded and Matthews ran forward, shooting at the cabin then ducking back into the brush as the cabin returned fire.

As soon as the shooting started, Spencer ran along the tree line and then made a break for an outcropping of woods twenty feet from the back of the cabin. He was no longer in their line of vision.

They were his now.

"This has to be the road," Will said, looking at the map.

"It looks as though Jillian's cabin is only a quarter of a mile off the main road," David said. "Let's leave the car here and spread out."

"Good plan," Brad said. "And Will, I'm sorry it took me so long to see the truth."

"You just needed concrete proof," Will said and slapped him on the back. "Now let's go save your sister. Again."

They blocked the road with the car and climbed out. Will followed along the drive while the other two slipped through the trees on either side of him. Movement straight ahead stopped him, and he crouched behind a bush.

Gunfire rang out, and his heart nearly jumped out of his chest. Will sprang forward just as a man in a ski mask ran back into the woods toward him.

"Drop your rifle, or you're dead," Will said, leveling his Glock at the man's chest.

The man hesitated.

"Drop it," David said. He stood no more than twenty feet to the left of the man with his service revolver pinned on him.

The man's shoulders sagged, and he dropped the rifle.

"Now, put your hands in the air," David said and picked up the gun.

Will yanked off his mask. "Adam Matthews? Where's Spencer Delaney?"

Matthews glared at him. "I don't have to answer your questions. I want my lawyer."

Gunshots rang out from the cabin.

— 36 —

The back door burst open, and Andi swung around as Jillian fired the .38.

The doorway was empty.

Seconds ticked away.

"Where'd he go?" Jillian whispered.

"Right here, ladies. Drop your guns," Spencer said from the side door. He had his rifle aimed at Andi.

Maggie brought her rifle up, and sweat ran down Andi's back. Spencer would kill her without a moment's hesitation.

"You don't want to do that," Spencer said. "You might shoot me, but not before I kill her."

"Shoot him!" Jillian yelled.

Maggie's gun wobbled.

"Put it on the floor," he said.

She did as he told her, and he kicked it away from her. "Now kick the shotgun out of the way."

After she did, he moved to the window. "It's clear!" he yelled.

He still held the rifle on Andi. "Where are the diamonds?"

"I don't know what you're talking about," Andi said.

Uncertainty crossed his eyes, and he turned to Jillian. "Where are the ones you stole?"

"You think I'm crazy enough to tell you?" she said.

"Let me tell you what's going to happen if you don't. First, I'm going to shoot your kneecap off. Do you know how painful that is? But, if that doesn't loosen your tongue, I'll shoot the other one, before I start with your friends here."

He'd do it too. Andi made eye contact with Maggie. Maybe if they both rushed him, but they'd have to do it before his partner got here. Maggie barely dipped her head.

Suddenly Spencer grabbed Maggie. "You move, and she's dead," he said, looking at Andi. "And there won't be any of that judo stuff, either."

Footsteps stomped on the porch.

"That should be Adam. Open the door," he said, turning the gun toward Andi.

Just as she pulled on the door, Maggie elbowed Spencer in the throat. Grabbing his throat, he bent over, and she cracked his nose with the heel of her palm, sending him backwards while she twisted his rifle out of his hands.

Andi slammed the partially opened door, bringing a loud yelp and a thud. She grabbed the .38 on the floor and swung open the door. The second man lay on the porch. Holding the gun on him, she knelt. Andi's head swam. "Will?"

The paramedic slammed the bay door on the ambulance. A few minutes later, the ambulance eased down the drive, followed by a second ambulance—the one Andi refused to ride in.

"I hope Jillian makes it," Andi said. She still hadn't processed all that Jillian had told them.

"How's your leg?" Will asked.

"Hurts."

"You should have gone with them."

"You know how I feel about ambulances. Besides, that paramedic just got back from Afghanistan. He did a good job of cleaning it up and telling me I need more antibiotics. I'll go to the ER when we get to Memphis."

Will wrapped his arm around her shoulders. "Thanks for helping, but you took too many risks."

"Don't start. It's over."

And it was. Jillian had given David a full statement about what happened eighteen years ago, and he was on his cell phone to his brother in the FBI. Brad had ridden with the county sheriff to take Spencer and Adam to the county jail. They would be extradited to Memphis, probably Monday.

"I'm glad it's over too." Will squeezed her waist. "Do you think Spencer will break first or Adam?"

"Adam." He struck her as the weaker of the two. She turned as Maggie and David made their way to where they stood.

"What did your brother say?" Will asked.

"He put me on hold while he called the governor. Olsen will sign a fifteen day reprieve tonight."

"Why didn't he just release him?" Andi said.

Maggie smiled. "It doesn't work that way. All the legal ends have to be tied up, but Jimmy will be told within the hour that he's getting a reprieve and why."

Andi leaned against Will. They had done it. An innocent man would go free.

"Think it would be okay if I called Jimmy and told him?" Will said.

David slapped him on the back. "If it were me, that's what I'd be doing. We'll wait for you in the car."

The helicopter would pick David and Maggie up at Doskie. Andi stood close by Will as he called Walter Simmons's number.

"Can I talk to Jimmy?" Will said when the CO answered.

"Sure can. He's right here."

Andi slipped her arm around Will's waist while they waited, and he pulled her close for a second, releasing his hold when Jimmy came on the phone.

"Yeah?" Jimmy's voice trembled.

"It's over!" Will said. "Jillian confessed. She shot Stephanie."

Andi had leaned closer or she wouldn't have heard his whispered response.

"Thank you, Jesus."

"Absolutely." Will grinned at her.

"But it was Jillian? How? Why?"

"Andi and I are coming to the prison. We'll explain it all then. I just had to tell you that it was over."

"Thanks, Will. I'll never forget this."

Will disconnected, and they both released deep breaths.

Then his eyes widened. "You can't go to the prison. We have to get your leg seen about."

"I think they have an ER in Nashville. Closer too." She forgot about the wound in her thigh as she looked up at him, and he held her gaze. The tenderness in his blue eyes almost cut off her breath.

"Taking you to the hospital is getting to be a habit. Kindly stop it," he said, his voice husky. "It terrified me when I realized you were in the cabin and Spencer was there with a gun."

"You risked your life for me." No one had ever done that for her before. "Thank you. But I'm sorry I almost knocked you out."

He cupped her face in his hands. "All in the line of duty, ma'am," he said and caressed her jaw with his thumb. "I'd do it again in a heartbeat."

"Shut up and kiss me." His eyes widened as she slid her arms around his neck.

"Yes, ma'am." He planted a light kiss on her lips and then lifted his head.

"Just one?" she teased.

"No." He took her in his arms and captured her lips.

She returned the kiss, holding nothing back. She'd waited half her life for this kiss.

When he released her, he tucked a lock of hair behind her ear. "Does this mean you'll take a chance on me?" he said.

"I think I should be the one asking that question," she said as he took her in his arms again.

Acknowledgments

As always, to God, who gives me the words.

To my family and friends, who believe in me.

To my editors at Revell, Lonnie Hull DuPont and Kristin Kornoelje, thank you for making my stories so much better. To the art, editorial, marketing, and sales team at Revell, thank you for your hard work. You are the best!

To my agent, the late Mary Sue Seymour; you believed in me when no one else did.

To Julie Gwinn, thank you for stepping in and becoming not only my agent but a friend.

To Sgt. Joe Stark, MPD, thank you for always answering my questions, even when I shot them over to you in the middle of the night. And because what you said and what I heard may not always be the same thing, I apologize for not getting it right sometimes.

To my readers, thank you for loving my stories.

About the Author

Patricia Bradley is the author of *Shadows of the Past*, *A Promise to Protect*, *Gone without a Trace*, and *Silence in the Dark*. Bradley has been a winner of the Inspirational Readers' Choice Award, a finalist for the Genesis Award, winner of a Daphne du Maurier Award, and winner of a Touched by Love Award. Bradley is a published short story writer and cofounder of Aiming for Healthy Families, Inc. She is a member of American Christian Fiction Writers and Romance Writers of America, and makes her home in Mississippi. Learn more at www.ptbradley.com.

Center Point Large Print
600 Brooks Road / PO Box 1
Thorndike, ME 04986-0001 USA

(207) 568-3717

US & Canada:
1 800 929-9108
www.centerpointlargeprint.com